P9-BYX-003

HOUSE OF ISRAEL

VOL. 3

A NEW DAWN

OTHER BOOKS AND AUDIO BOOKS
BY ROBERT MARCUM:

House of Israel Vol. 1: The Return

House of Israel Vol. 2: Land Divided

HOUSE OF ISRAEL

VOL. 3

A NEW DAWN

ROBERT MARCUM

Covenant Communications, Inc.

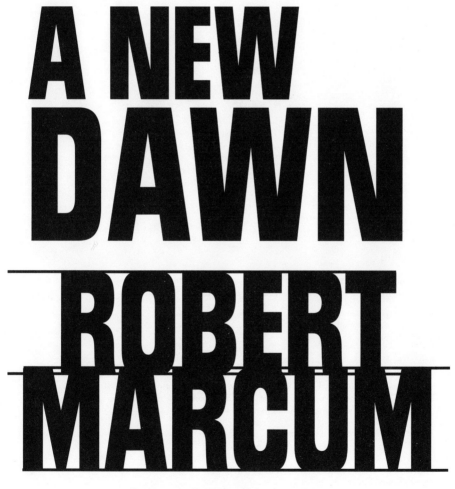

Covenant

Cover image: School Children Salute Jewish State, May 16, 1948 © Bettmann/CORBIS
Cover design copyrighted 2004 by Covenant Communications, Inc.

Published by Covenant Communications, Inc.
American Fork, Utah

Copyright © 2004 by Robert Marcum
All rights reserved. No part of this book may be reproduced in any format or in any medium without the written permission of the publisher, Covenant Communications, Inc., P.O. Box 416, American Fork, UT 84003. The views expressed herein are the responsibility of the author and do not necessarily represent the position of Covenant Communications, Inc.

This is a work of fiction. The characters, names, incidents, places, and dialogue are products of the author's imagination, and are not to be construed as real.

Printed in the United States of America
First Printing: September 2004

10 09 08 07 06 05 04   10 9 8 7 6 5 4 3 2 1

ISBN 1-59156-617-7

List of Characters

Fictional characters

Ephraim Daniels, *American, married to Hannah*
Hannah, *Polish émigré, married to Ephraim*
David Schwartz, *German émigré, adopted*
Elizabeth Schneider, *German émigré, adopted*
Jacob, *Sabra*
Joseph, *Sabra*
Abraham Marshak, *Sabra, rabbi's son, archaeologist, married to Naomi*
Naomi Stavsky Marshak, *Hungarian émigré, married to Abraham*
Aaron Schwartz, *German émigré, David's older brother, missing in action*
Mary Aref, *Christian Arab, married to Aaron Schwartz*
Rachel Steinman, *German émigré, living on a kibbutz in the Negev*
Zohar Mendelsohn, *German émigré, interred on Cyprus*
Wally Bergman, *war buddy of Ephraim Daniels*

Rabbi Mordechai Salomon, *Sabra, Hasidic Jew*
Dr. Yehuda Messerman, *Sabra, friend of Aref family*
Mithra Birkelau, *Hungarian émigré, Danielses' neighbor*
Eliahu Esek, *Israeli intelligence officer*
Benny Berak, *Sabra, fighter with the Jewish underground since a teenager, first with the Hashomer, then with the Haganah*

Rhoui Aref, *Mary's brother*
Ahmed, *bedouin scout*
Saad Shawas, *Islamic resident of Haifa, married to Rifa*
Rifa, *married to Saad*
Emile, *Saad and Rifa's son*

Nonfictional characters to whom reference is made or who play a minor role, interacting with the fictional characters

David Ben-Gurion, *Russian émigré, head of Jewish Agency*
David Sheal'tiel, *German émigré, leader of SHAI*
Eleazar Sukenik, *Sabra, archaeologist, discovered Dead Sea Scrolls*
Abdul Khader Husseini, *commander of Haj Amin's Holy Strugglers*
Haj Amin el Husseini, *Grand Mufti of Jerusalem*
Fawzi el Kaukji, *former Ottoman officer given leadership of ALA*
David Marcus, *American, aid to Eisenhower in World War II, volunteered to help the Jews in their war for independence*

Note: A Sabra is a native-born Israeli.

CHAPTER 1

Zohar was afraid she might be crushed, the crowd of refugees threatening to overturn the ship as they pushed toward the gangway. Desperately clutching her small bag of possessions, her thin body was jostled by others who were just as anxious to touch the ground of Israel. Reaching the railing, she held herself steady, searching the upturned faces of the milling crowd for a glimpse of a familiar face.

Hannah was not coming. Her letter—which Zohar had received while still on Cyprus—said that Ephraim's back injury required immediate attention and they must fly to the States. The letter had promised that Naomi would be at the ship, but Zohar saw nothing of her young friend among the faces that scanned this new crop of refugees from the docks. But if not Naomi, who? With Rachel far south in the Negev and Aaron gone, rest his soul, there wasn't anyone else. Had Naomi gotten the word? Was she even able to come? The country was at war, and Hannah said Naomi was in the Old City. A difficult place, under siege at last word. What if she had been hurt, or worse? If Naomi didn't come—if no one came—she would be on her own, and she knew nothing about her new country except that they were fighting for their country and their lives. But she would find a way. There was no sense getting upset on the first day.

The flow of humanity pushed onto the gangway, and she fused with them. Stepping into the waiting crowd at the bottom, she felt such exhilaration that she considered getting to her knees and kissing the ground. Only the crush of people prevented her from giving thanks for finally arriving after so many years.

She had come out of war-ravished Germany with Hannah, Naomi, Rachel, Aaron, and others, making their way to a refugee camp in southern Italy until their little group had parted ways. She had stayed in Italy until most refugees living there found their way either to Palestine or, by British capture, to Cyprus. With nothing more holding her, she had started for Israel months ago on board the ship *Pan York*. The British had caught them trying to run their idiotic blockade and interred her and seven thousand others on Cyprus, freeing them only days ago after the British finally left Israel.

Pushing her way through the crowds, she heard someone call her name and looked about for a familiar face.

"Miss Mendelsohn?"

Zohar turned to see a man in a khaki shirt and pants. The sleeves of the shirt were rolled up to his elbows, and he wore an American flier's cap, the insignia removed. Of medium height and stocky build, he had wavy blond hair that curled onto his forehead from underneath the slightly tilted cap. He looked vaguely familiar.

"Yes?"

"You probably don't remember me, but I saw you off in Berlin. Wally, Wally Bergman. Ephraim and I were friends and . . ."

"Oh yes!" Zohar said, remembering. "The pilot who flew with Ephraim against the Germans. You . . . you liked Misha, rest her soul."

"Yeah," Wally smiled. "Naomi sent me. She's stuck in the Old City under Arab siege, but she managed to get word to me. I hope my humble services will suffice."

Zohar smiled at Wally's dimpled grin. "Of course."

"Come on, then, let's get you to Tel Aviv. You look exhausted."

He reached for her bag, but she held tight to it; then, embarrassed, she turned it over to him. "Sorry. Force of habit."

Zohar was still the dark-haired, tall woman Wally remembered from Berlin, but she had put on weight, and the dark eyes were no longer dull from post-war trauma. Personally, he found her quite attractive. He managed to make a path for them through the chaos of the dock area and into a spacious building where officials were trying to create some order. "You'll have to show them you're a Jew. Papers if you can, your tattooed camp number if you have nothing else. They aren't being particular nowadays."

She nodded, noticing that many of the men were being directed to a different area. "Where are they going?"

"As soon as they get a gun and a few days' training, they'll be going to the front lines."

"Are we that desperate?"

"Worse. Right now we're fighting on a dozen fronts with little more than small arms—rifles, pistols, that sort of thing. We need artillery, tanks, mortars, and planes, or the new state of Israel will be a thing of the past before it even has a beginning. They say the first shipment of artillery is unloading at Tel Aviv as we speak, and we have four fighter planes from Czechoslovakia, but it's a drop in the bucket to what we need. I'm afraid a lot of these boys will die before they celebrate their first Shabbat here if things don't change."

Once inside the building, Wally took Zohar's arm and pulled her gently toward a young soldier behind a table. He showed his papers, then spoke. "This young woman just got off the boat from Cyprus. I'm taking her to Tel Aviv." Zohar handed the inspector some papers and then showed her camp tattoo.

He waved them on with a tired welcome. A moment later, another man checked their papers a second time before letting them through the gate. He gave Wally a crisp salute. "Captain Bergman."

Once through the gate, Zohar turned to Wally. "He knows you?"

"Nope, just the papers. They're signed by Ben-Gurion and say I am a captain in the new Israeli Air Force, the IAF, which still doesn't exist. Not really. Not yet. Most of our planes are in transit." He smiled. "Right now we fly puddle jumpers and tell ourselves over and over, 'It's a plane. It's a plane.' Fools the Arabs every time."

"Puddle jumpers? I do not understand this term, and calling a plane a plane and fooling the Arabs, I do not understand this either. How could this . . . ?"

"Sorry. My American lingo. Puddle jumpers refers to the Austers and Pipers we fly. Small, without any real guns, and unable to go at speeds and distances that fighter planes, bombers, and transports can go. To fighter jocks . . . uh, pilots . . . like me, you can't really call them planes and . . ." He could see he was only confusing her and smiled. "Forget it. Just a bad joke."

Reaching the street, they crossed to an old, beat-up, two-door sedan. Opening the door, Wally pushed the seat forward, tossing Zohar's bag in the back before putting the seat back again so that she could get in. Closing the door, he went around to the driver's side and got behind the wheel. The engine hardly turned over at first, then roared to life. Wally drove like he flew—with reckless abandon. Zohar, in fear for her life, hung onto both the dashboard and the base of the window as they dodged military and private cars, trucks, donkeys laden with family goods, and hundreds of people, Wally honking the horn at nearly everything.

"Where are all these people going?"

"A lot of 'em are refugees. Some Arab, some Jewish. The Arabs want out, and we aren't discouraging them. The Jews are new and are looking for places to live or headed for other cities like you. The whole country is like this. Civilians mingled with the military, everyone running around like chickens with their heads lopped off. It's chaos."

"Like Germany at the end of the war," Zohar said.

"Yeah, except that the fighting there was mostly over. It's just getting a good start here."

Finally reaching the outskirts of Haifa, they bolted onto the open highway where Wally shifted into high gear. Zohar gripped her safety holds even tighter.

Hannah and the children were in the States with Ephraim. Rachel was somewhere in the south of the country at a place called Neghba in upper Negev. Naomi was under siege in Jerusalem. Zohar had dreamed of seeing them. Now she was disappointed and saddened by how the war had already changed things for all of them.

"Naomi said that I should come to the Jewish Quarter of the Old City and live with her and Abraham in Hannah's home. Is this still possible?"

"No way in or out. The Haganah is trying to relieve them, make it safe again, but it's going to take time. For now we'll have to find you something in Tel Aviv." The Haganah *was* trying, but with no success. The Arab hold was tightening, and the fighters inside the Quarter had suffered heavy casualties. The Israeli Army was asking the few men inside the Quarter to do the impossible—hold on with nothing but knives and their bare hands. They wouldn't last much longer, but Wally figured it was something Zohar didn't need to hear right now. Especially since Wally didn't know if Naomi and her husband would be among the survivors. If there were any.

He reached in his pocket, pulled out an envelope, and handed it to her. "Money Hannah left for you. It will get you by for a while—pay the first month's rent and keep food on the table until you find a job." Hannah had left it with him the morning he helped load Ephraim's stretcher aboard one of the transport planes headed back to Italy. From there they had made arrangements to catch a U.S. military flight back to Washington. His friend had looked pale but determined, ready to do anything needed to get his legs back. The doctors had wanted him to wait a few weeks, get a little stronger, but Ephraim wanted no delays. The sooner he had the surgery, the sooner he could get his family back to Israel.

Zohar nodded a thank-you as she slid the envelope into her purse. Hannah never ceased to amaze her. Even though this money surely must have been needed to get her and the family to the United States, here it was in Zohar's hands, seeing to her needs.

"How does one repay such a friend?" she whispered.

"Sorry?" Wally said.

"Nothing," Zohar said. "Just thanking Hannah for her timely gift. I left Italy with five hundred British pounds. I haven't a shilling left."

"That's a lot of money to spend on an island like Cyprus."

"Most of it was gone by then. A family was a little short of the fare needed to board the ship. The rest was stolen from its hiding place a few days later," Zohar explained.

"Apartments are hard to find right now. More refugees than rooms, but a few open up every day, and I have friends looking out for something for both of us." He glanced at her. "Uh, separate places. I mean two apartments, one for each of us."

She smiled at his embarrassment as her own face turned a brighter hue of red.

"Do that again," he said.

"What?" she asked, unsure of his meaning.

"Smile. You have a beautiful smile."

She blushed even more deeply. "Where have you been staying?"

"At the Hayarkon Hotel in Tel Aviv. It's where all the foreign pilots stay. It's also where the IAF's communications and command offices are, and the war room is set up in the dining hall. There are people coming and going all the time, and it's real noisy. I can't get any sleep, so I figure it's time to find a place of my own."

Zohar looked out the window. The road ran parallel to the seashore, and the blue water breaking on the sand was beautiful. Yet only a few miles away there was a war. "Is it safe to travel this way to Tel Aviv?"

"For now. The Arabs are on the other side of the mountains to my left, up north of Haifa and in the Galilee."

She bent her head to see through the window the mountains he spoke of. "The Carmel range."

Wally nodded. "Transjordan is hitting us from the east, Egypt from the south, and Syria, Iraq, Lebanon, and the rather disorganized but still somewhat effective ALA, from the north. Add to that a rejuvenated bunch of irregulars belonging to Haj Amin el Husseini who seem to have found their third wind in the Holy City, and you have us surrounded by either Arabs or water." He gave her a smile. "They can't win."

She gave a bit of a laugh. "An optimist. Good. I would hate to pay a month's rent from Hannah's hard-earned money only to be driven out in a week."

After an hour's dusty drive, they drove into Tel Aviv. The streets were jammed with people, trucks, animals, cars, and bicycles. It seemed like everyone was carrying a rifle or some other weapon, and all were in a hurry.

"When I came here for the first time a few weeks ago, Ephraim and I had a nice, quiet chat in that hotel over there." He pointed with a nod of his head. "As you can see, things have changed."

He drove through half a dozen streets until they were in a semi-residential area, then pulled the car to the curb. A man sitting at a table sipping a drink saw him, stood, and sauntered to the car.

"'Ow are ye, lad?" the man asked. He was dressed in a British military uniform, but all his emblems were missing. Zohar glared at him and turned her face away.

"Good. Any news?" Wally said.

"There be a place a few blocks down. Another over on Marks Street." He handed Wally a piece of paper. "Is the lady Captain Daniels's friend then?"

Wally nodded, thanked the Brit, and put the car back in gear, driving away from the curb. "His name is William. He deserted the British to fight for us. He and Ephraim were friends because of a Brit by the name of Jack Willis. Along with Aaron, Jack died trying to save Ephraim at Kastel." He paused. "Be careful you don't put all British in the same basket, Zohar. Some of 'em are good guys fighting for Israel."

She nodded, regret evident on her face. "You are right. I'm sorry."

He drove two blocks and pulled over again. "Well, time to hit the pavement. Shall we?"

She looked at him quizzically. "Another of those strange sayings I suppose. Would you explain why we must hit the pavement?"

He laughed lightly. "It means we'll be walking from here. You know, hitting the pavement with our feet."

Zohar liked Wally Bergman and found herself wishing she had applied some makeup, but then shoved the thought aside as foolish. With a face she thought most men would consider plain, and little in the way of a figure that might make up for it, she was not someone this American pilot might like. Though not much taller than her, he was handsome by most standards. Naturally curly blond hair that sometimes poked from beneath his cap set off an angular face with high cheekbones and sparkling blue eyes. Finding ladies would surely not be hard for Wally Bergman. The thought depressed her.

Wally took her by the elbow, directing her down the street. She wondered if the flush in her face and neck at his touch was apparent and, in an effort to hide it, concentrated on the buildings and commotion around them. Turning a corner, they walked along the seafront.

"Beautiful, ain't it? Someday this will be a resort town, you know. A man could do well with a hotel along here somewhere. Make millions."

Zohar gave him a sideways glance. "But this is not our purpose, Mr. Bergman. Homes, apartments—this is what we need. There are millions of Jews yet to come, to find safety in Israel. It is not hotels but homes we must build."

"Plenty of room for those, especially with the Arabs moving out. But there will be lots of rich American Jews that will come to visit, and they will need fancy hotels with swimming pools and fine restaurants."

"Visit? But . . ."

"All Jews aren't going to come to stay, Zohar. They'll keep their mansions and penthouses in the States and make their pilgrimage. You know, come and visit for a while, participate in an arm's length sort of way, give money to salve their consciences. But they won't stay—too inhospitable here when compared to the States."

"That's very cynical, Mr. Bergman."

"Wally, please." He smiled. "Yeah, maybe, but I live in America, remember? I'm also a Jew. I know how they think. Most of 'em will never come. Not to stay."

"I hope you are wrong," she said softly.

Wally stopped to study the address William had given him. "Yep, this is it." He opened a small gate into a bare and sandy yard. They entered and approached the door. The house looked fairly new, and the unplanted yard bore witness of it. Wally's knock on the door brought a quick answer as a rather short, thick woman stood in the opening.

"Yes," she said abruptly in Hebrew, "what is it?"

Wally's tongue was immediately tied, his Hebrew nearly nonexistent.

"Good morning," Zohar said, coming to his rescue. "We understand you might have rooms for rent, and we have come to inquire after them."

She looked at them with a raised eyebrow. "Are you two married?"

"No," Zohar said, turning a bit red. "We are just friends. I have come from Europe. He is from the United States." Then she realized why the woman had asked the question. "No, no, you don't understand. We are not seeing each . . ."

"Nothing available." The woman slammed the door.

"I take it the answer was no," Wally grinned. "I gathered she thought we were seeing each other and doesn't want to be bothered with such a relationship."

"Yes, you are right."

"Better not to rent here then. A beautiful young woman like yourself will have need to entertain, don't you think?"

She blushed, unable to find an answer.

Wally smiled at her discomfort. Zohar was a lot like Misha. Quiet, gentle, unassuming. He liked that. "Come on. My friend said there are new apartment buildings a few blocks from here. Let's give those a try," Wally said.

"Did you see Ephraim and Hannah before they left for the United States?" Zohar asked, hoping to regain her composure.

"Yeah, he looked pretty good, considering," he paused.

"He was flying one of your, uh, puddle jumpers when he was hurt?"

"Yeah. I saw him just a few days before he was shot down at Kastel. He told me he was flying a Piper. I thought he was nuts. Now here I am—doing the same thing. I guess all us flyboys are a bit crazy." His brow wrinkled and his chin hardened. "At least Eph had a good reason. When one of your kids is at risk, you do what you have to. It's just too bad Aaron ended up dead in spite of Ephraim's sacrifice." There was another long silence, both of them sobered by the horrible things Ephraim and Hannah had endured because of the war.

"He asked me to bring him back a Messerschmitt. Things would have been different with a Messerschmitt," Wally finally added.

"Messerschmitt?" Then she remembered. "Ah, yes, the German fighter plane."

"More than just a fighter. It can drop bombs, and it's one of the fastest in the world. Fast enough to keep ground fire from hitting it like that tub Ephraim was forced to fly."

"And you will fly this . . . this Messerschmitt?"

"As soon as enough of them get here."

"Why?"

The questioned shocked him, and he stopped in his tracks. "Why?"

"It is a simple question. Why? Why do you put your life at risk? You say American Jews will not come, and yet you are here. Why?"

They walked for a moment before Wally answered. "I am right about most American Jews, you'll see that. I was flying imports from the States to Europe and doing pretty good. My company had me and some others fly arms in here from Czechoslovakia. That was when I saw Ephraim, visited with him about what he was doing here." He paused. "He wasn't even a Jew, and there he was fighting for Israel in that beat-up Piper Cub. When he went down, I decided I wasn't going to let it be in vain. If he believed enough to fight for this piece of rock and dirt, I owed him. I could pay up by following his example. But that doesn't mean I'm staying, because I'm not. Not any more than most of the foreign fighters coming here. I owe Ephraim, and to a lesser degree I owe my people, but when the debts are paid, I have other things in mind."

They stopped at a coffee shop at the corner. Wally bought them some sweet bread and a Coke. They ate and sipped as they walked. Zohar couldn't remember the last time she tasted anything as good as the sweet roll, but the Coke was warm and bit at her throat.

"What are you going to do?" Wally asked.

"Find work."

"Hannah says you teach school. With both summer and the war going on, I don't think there's much call for teachers."

"I heard there are plenty of jobs in our country's new armament factories, and they need people to help with immigration now that we have a state and have opened our doors to any Jew who wants to come. I have good language skills, and I am sure work will not be difficult to find, but . . ." Her voice trailed off. She was unsure of sharing her real feelings with Wally. They hardly knew each other.

"But you want to do more, get in the fight, make a difference. Is that it?"

She gave him a sheepish smile. "Yes, I suppose it is."

"Bullets make a difference. So do immigrants who can carry guns and fly planes and understand orders because they've been taught Hebrew. Something, as you can see, I'm still struggling with. Working to help guys like me, or getting us enough bullets, is just as important as shooting at Arabs from behind sandbags."

"Yes, you're right."

"Tell you what. The IAF is looking for somebody to teach us Hebrew and needs interpreters and secretaries who can speak multiple languages. I'll put in a good word for you."

"That would be nice, thank you."

They came to the apartment building. It was three stories high, probably the tallest building in Tel Aviv. If they won the war, Wally figured it wouldn't take long before it was one of the shortest. They noticed "Manager" chalked on an apartment door, and Wally knocked. After a moment of shuffling inside, a short, thin man with nearly silver hair and blue eyes answered the door. He gave a smile that made his eyes twinkle.

"You are looking for a place to live?" he asked in accented English.

"Two apartments. One for the lady, and one for myself."

"I have only one but it is very nice with a living room, kitchen, and bedroom, along with a small bath with shower. It has some furniture, but no icebox and nothing but a cot for a bed."

"How much?" Wally asked.

"Twenty-five dollars American money each month."

It was a lot, but at least little furniture would need to be purchased.

"Can we see it?" Zohar asked.

The manager smiled and reached for a key on a hook, closed the door behind him, and led them down the hall to the stairs. They ascended to the second floor and the fourth door down the hall. Unlocking the door, he let them in. A couch, chair, end tables, and lamps were in the living room, a table with four chairs in the kitchen. There was nothing but the cot and a wardrobe in the bedroom. Wally looked at Zohar. "It's yours if you want it."

Zohar smiled, then looked at the manager. "I can pay twenty. I will be a good tenant and work at cleaning to make up the difference."

The man rubbed his stubbled chin in thought. "Twenty-four, and you clean two Saturdays."

"Twenty-one," Zohar said. She sensed a rejection, so she quickly added more. "And I clean three Saturdays, but only when the war is over. Our first duty is to our country, isn't it?" she said with a disarming smile.

He sighed and shook his head. "Very well. But no male guests after ten in the evening." He glanced at Wally which made Zohar blush again.

"Very well," she said. Turning away, she counted twenty-one dollars from Hannah's gift and shoved the rest back in her purse. Handing him the rent, she received a hastily written receipt before the manager headed for the door.

"Can I ask you a question?" Zohar said.

The manager turned back.

"Whose furniture is this?"

"His name was Otto. A German Jew who came here three years ago. He was killed in battle only yesterday. He has no relatives and told me to keep the furniture if something happened. He wanted it to make someone else a good home." His face turned to sadness, and he quickly left the apartment, closing the door behind him.

"A common malady in Israel," Wally said soberly. "Trouble is, it will only get worse."

Zohar felt a bit sick at heart and a bit guilty as she looked at the well-kept furniture. She found herself looking for something personal, a picture or something that might give a face to Otto, but there was nothing.

"Thank you for helping me find this place," she said.

"You're welcome." He started for the door then turned around. "Dinner."

She was confused. "Dinner?"

"Tomorrow night. Would you like to go to dinner?"

She blushed again, her heart pounding. She had never been good with men.

"I'll pick you up at seven." He opened the door and was gone before she could do more than force a slight nod and swipe her sweaty palms on her wrinkled skirt. She must wash and press it. And she must do it before seven tomorrow evening.

SEE CHAPTER NOTES

CHAPTER 2

Mary sat down on a large boulder a few feet from the road to take a welcome rest from the arduous journey. Gazing across the river Litani to the hills and valleys of Palestine, she smiled. Jerusalem was now only a hundred miles away. God willing, she could be there in a few days.

There was a small crowd of refugees fleeing Palestine just across the bridge. They were desperate to escape the war, and all Mary wanted was to go back. For several weeks now it had been her one obsession.

A week after her arrival in Beirut, the Lebanese government had forced her and hundreds of others to relocate to one of the newly created refugee camps for Palestinians. While at the relocation center, a letter sent through the American consulate had found her. It was from Ephraim and Hannah Daniels.

My Dear Mary, I am so sorry to tell you Aaron has been killed at Kastel.

The grief of losing Aaron, in addition to the physical exhaustion of her morning sickness and the horrid conditions of the camp, had made Mary very ill. For several days, she languished in the shade of a shanty with nothing but her shawl for a blanket, late spring rains only making her condition worse. Her brother's family had been moved to the same camp, and they cared for her as best as they could, but it was her faith and determination to raise her child that made her fight off the sickness and despair that meant to destroy them both.

Mary touched her stomach. She had felt the first stirrings of the child only a few days before the letter had come. It had both excited and frightened her. She immediately sat down and wrote Aaron to tell him of their child, to share her excitement while being fearful that those around her might discover her secret. They did not know she and Aaron were married. They did not know her baby's father was a Jew.

Her fear of a reprisal was well-founded. Hatred for the Jews burned like fire over the entire Arab world, but it was especially strong among refugees chased from their homes by the war all Arabs blamed on the Jews. Mary dared not look into many eyes, not even those of her brother's family, for fear they might learn her secret and take her life and the life of her child. As soon as she was well enough to think clearly, she began making plans to get away before her belly started to show and her sisters-in-law saw that the sickness was more than just flu or a bad cold.

It had not been fear alone that had pushed her out of the camps and toward Palestine and Jerusalem. Though the letter had declared Aaron dead, it also mentioned there had been no body found, leaving her with nagging doubt and uncertainty that had turned to determination. He could have survived, and if he did, he would go to Jerusalem.

But determination alone was not enough. There were many obstacles. At first she had thought to use some of her inheritance to take a plane or boat, but those no longer serviced Palestine. She tried to get something to France, where she could catch a plane or a ship to Haifa, but was rudely informed that the Jews were not letting Arabs into the country. In fact, they were imprisoning or turning away those who tried. She thought about flying to Jordan, then going to Jerusalem, but the Jordanian government would not give her the necessary papers, their refugee numbers already more than they could handle. It was either walk or stay where she was and hope that if Aaron had survived he would somehow manage to find her. She had decided the chances of being found were too small to consider.

She knew walking to Jerusalem would not be easy, that the war was spreading, engulfing the entire coastal plain and Galilee through which she would have to go, but it could not be any worse than living with the uncertainty of Aaron's survival. Nor could it match the nightmares of someone discovering her marriage to a Jew and slitting her throat.

She had applied to the authorities the next day and received her papers without argument. The Lebanese government, overwhelmed by the endless stream of refugees moving into their country and afraid it would tip the delicate balance of power between Arabs and Christians, was more than glad to send someone back.

She looked at the growing number of refugees confronting the border guards. How ironic. The Arab armies had entered Palestine sure of victory. This misguided self-assurance had led to defeat after defeat at the hands of a poorly armed but very determined Jewish military. With each loss, more Palestinian Arabs feared for their lives and took flight. Now those very Arab countries that had promised to be saviors for her people were refusing to give them refuge from the conflict they had started. Fools, all of them, and the worst was Haj Amin el Husseini, self-proclaimed leader of her people who cowered in Cairo while telling the Lebanese, Syrians, Egyptians, and Transjordanians to turn his people back to fight for their homes. His stupidity, born of an insatiable lust for power, coupled with the Arab leaders' greed for land and fear of one another, was costing her people everything. How she hated them for it!

Mary looked for Ahmed. Her guide was still conversing with the border guards, but the language was getting more heated. Ahmed waved her papers, jabbing a finger at them, then pointing at her as if the border guard were having a tough time making sense of their wish to go south. She kept her eyes on the ground, her head covered by her scarf. She was the epitome of a modest, humble Arab woman who knew her place. All she was really doing was trying to keep from laughing. The guard acted as if he could read the paper, though he held it upside down and obviously could not make heads or tails of the words.

"You will have to wait," he said, refolding the paper. "I will deliver your papers to Colonel Shukri." He turned on his heel, leaving Ahmed frustrated and angry. It was a simple thing to let them pass, but illiteracy was an epidemic in the Arab world, and they would, as always, have to be patient and let the guard work it through.

Ahmed turned to Mary and shrugged while rolling his eyes. She smiled and nodded her understanding, grateful once more that he was with her.

Mary was no fool. After receiving permission to go south, she began looking for help to make the journey. She was a woman in a world where men cursed any show of independence and refused to deal with women directly. Even in Lebanon, a country that considered itself enlightened with regard to women's rights, Mary's direct approach had not worked, and she had finally used a male proxy to carry out her transactions. To attempt a return through Arab lands she hardly knew, during a time of war, was dangerous. To do it in a country where a male-dominated mentality reigned made it doubly dangerous. She had difficulty finding anyone willing to return except for young fanatics wreaking of machismo and shouting slogans that would mean nothing once they got into a real fight—not the type she was willing to trust with the protection of her virtue or her safety. She kept looking. Finally, an older friend who knew her father in Jerusalem had introduced her to Ahmed, a bedouin tribesman who was paid to bring other refugees from Haifa to Beirut and who was ready to make the return trip. As Mary stood back, the two men argued and dickered until a deal was struck, then Mary was introduced to Ahmed. He would take her, but it would cost her one hundred British pounds.

When she had first seen Ahmed, Mary half suspected her father's friend had been smoking hashish before doing his bargaining or he would not have agreed to such a high price. After all, the bedu scout was old enough to be her grandfather and his slight build, wrinkled muscles, and deeply lined, thin face made her wonder if he would find the grave before he did Haifa. But as she had looked into his eyes, she saw strength and goodness that laid to rest her doubt and gave birth to trust. She agreed with the price, and within the hour, she and Ahmed were on their way out of Beirut.

It did not take long for Mary to discover that she had been right. His quick pace never wavered even though he carried their large, cumbersome bag stuffed with blankets and other necessities. It was she who needed constant stops for rest and water, she who was exhausted at the end of the day, and she who slept too long in the morning. Twice he had talked them past military outposts, and once he had used a strong hand on the arms of some young ruffians, scoundrels who thought to take advantage of Mary by placing their hands inappropriately on her as she and Ahmed passed through the busy, crowded streets of a village south of Beirut. Both young men scrambled away, cursing the old man while rubbing their arms and wondering if they were broken. Yes, Ahmed had been a good choice.

She drank a bit of tepid water from the animal skin as she watched more refugees approach the bridge and join the growing crowd being turned away by the determined Colonel Shukri. The bridge, less than two hundred feet from bank to bank and fifty feet wide, was blocked with several army trucks. A half dozen soldiers blocked the way, their weapons menacingly pointed directly at the first row of refugees.

Mary got up and went to the bank of the river. The sides were steep and brush covered, the deep water swift and black as it rushed west and south toward the sea. No vehicles would cross here, and even the best swimmers would find its current a challenge. It was chillingly obvious why the Lebanese soldiers had set up their check post here rather than further south at the real border with Palestine.

On the far side of the bridge, at least a hundred fifty people gathered, their possessions on their backs, in carts, cars, or other vehicles parked alongside the road. Frustrated, they pushed at one another and screamed at the colonel. Patiently he waited, then raised his hands in the air for silence. When there was no response he ordered the closest soldier to fire his weapon into the air, getting immediate attention.

"I have told you many times," he said firmly. "We are not allowing anyone to cross the border. Your leaders have asked us to stop you and send you home. Go back, fight for your country, for your homes. We have no more room for you."

"No room, you say?" said the burly man nearest the colonel. His face was flushed with anger, and Mary prayed he would not do anything foolish.

"What do you mean, no room?" someone else yelled.

The bearded man stepped forward, then stopped as the soldiers flanking the colonel aimed their guns at his stomach. "Arab military leaders in Haifa and the Galilee sent us," he hissed. "They tell us to get out of the way so that they can get at the Jews! We leave our homes, our land as we are told, and now you tell us you have no room?" His frustration pushed his voice several octaves higher.

"You know the Jews massacre whole villages," shrieked a woman. "They will do the same to us if we go back!"

The colonel raised his hands and tried to quiet them again. "Much of what has been said about these massacres is rumor. We now have it on good authority—"

"It was broadcast over your radio station," said a middle-aged man. "I heard it myself. Your armies have many guns, and yet you cannot protect us! How do you expect us to protect ourselves?"

"Look," the colonel said gruffly, his patience growing dangerously thin. He wagged a finger in the direction of Palestine. "I have told you. Your leaders have ordered us to turn you back. Your Arab Higher Committee and your Mufti command us not to give you visas. They say, send you back, so we send you back. It is not our fault! Now go! Go home and complain to them!"

He was about to turn away when the bearded man took two menacing steps toward him. The colonel felt his men tense and quickly raised his hand for calm while also drawing his own revolver. "Your family needs you. Do not make me kill you when I can do nothing for you."

The bearded man's expression changed, and he stepped back, then turned and pushed through the crowd. There was no more yelling, only dead silence. The colonel shoved his revolver back in its holster, turned, and went to his jeep, his soldiers staying where they were, ready to fire. The crowd cautiously drifted away from them but stayed together, as if doing so would somehow offer protection. Mary breathed easier, then noticed that the guard with her papers approached the colonel and handed them to him.

"He is a soldier who hates what he is doing, but he will do it. This makes him difficult to deal with." Ahmed said it as he stepped to her side, concern in his eyes.

The colonel read the papers, then questioned the border guard, who pointed at Mary and Ahmed. Mary averted her eyes as the two men looked her direction. The colonel nodded to the guard, then came toward them.

"Salaam," he said. Ahmed returned the greeting with a bow. "You and the woman want to return to the south," the colonel said. "Where do you go and why?"

"To Sahalia, it is our home," Ahmed replied.

The colonel looked at Mary. She was dressed in the traditional garb of the Arab bedouin, a request of Ahmed. Her city clothes, as he called them, would raise too many questions. Mary had quarreled with his decision at first. She was raised a Christian Arab in which views of women were much more liberal, and she had not worn the long, black *jilbab* for most of her adult life. She seldom wore a headscarf, and when she did it was wrapped around her neck and did not cover her face. Now, as the colonel studied her up and down, she saw the value of Ahmed's wisdom.

"You are bedouin. Of what tribe?" he asked Ahmed.

"The al Tieb," Ahmed said. Mary knew it was a lie. Ahmed had told her he was of the al Nasariyah. She wondered why the lie, but said nothing, knowing he had his reasons.

"You can go, but not tonight. We close the bridge until morning," the colonel said. "As you see, there is difficulty."

"But, good sir, there is still an hour of daylight, and if your highness would let us cross . . ." Ahmed kept his eyes subservient, toward the ground.

"The bridge is closed," the colonel said adamantly. "You may camp on this side and cross in the morning. By then these people will have been forced to either turn back or camp with the others we refuse visas." He pointed at a large camp west and south of the river. "See there? That camp holds nearly five hundred people already." He shook his head, a concerned look to his brow. "This after only three days! But, it is none of your concern. You go in the morning."

Ahmed bowed slightly. "We thank you for your concern for our safety. We will do as you say," Ahmed said.

"When you cross, be vigilant. There are thieves along the road, and the Jews move troops north, especially along the coast. You would do better to stay in the mountains," the colonel said, handing back their papers.

Ahmed took them and motioned Mary toward a path that ran along the riverbank. As they came close to the river, a man from the other side called to them.

"You! bedouin!" The man's voice was loud, attracting the attention of many others. "Have you come from Beirut? If so, what is happening? Why are they doing this to us?"

Ahmed did not acknowledge the question, and the man had to keep pace with them along the far side of the river.

"Please, tell us. What is happening?" the man repeated in frustration.

Mary could not resist and lowered her scarf so she could speak. "You are not wanted in Beirut," she said.

Shocked by her boldness, he shouted at her. "Stay out of this, woman. You . . ."

"If you want an answer you will listen to her," Ahmed said.

The man pursed his lips tightly, his need to know overpowering tradition, nodding agreement as others joined him across the fifty-foot expanse of the river.

"Beirut is overwhelmed with people just like you," she said loudly. "There is not enough food, and the camps they have made are not fit for pigs. They did not expect so many and were not prepared, and now they cannot take more or sickness and disease may kill their own people. But, if you still wish to go, it is a big border. Go that way," she pointed west, then east, "or that. Find a place to cross this miserable little ditch and walk to Beirut. See for yourself, and watch for your leaders, the ones who now demand that you return and fight while they live in fancy hotels and homes and send their children to Lebanese schools because they can pay the necessary bribes. When you see them, ask why they tell you to go back while they live in luxury, why they were among the first to desert you and the land they want you to fight for."

The crowd grumbled agreement, except for a tall, thin man with a hateful look in his eye. "These are lies! These bedouin know nothing of what is going on in Beirut. They are wanderers with the intelligence of goats."

"If you do not believe us, go and see," Mary said. "I watched them sit at fancy tables and eat roast lamb. They sleep in comfortable beds while denouncing all who flee. Haj Amin expects *you* to go back, but he says nothing to your leaders, his friends, and the families of his friends. He tells you that if you do not return and fight, your homes will be forfeit, given to foreign fighters worthy of them. Go to Beirut. Listen to these words on the radio and read them in the papers. Then you will understand." She started walking again.

"Lies! Haj Amin is a great man, a great fighter. He would never do this to his people. He is in Cairo to make sure the Arabs keep their promises." He shook his finger at Ahmed. "You should control the tongue of your woman, Bedu, or someone might cut it out."

Mary stopped and eyed him across the narrow divide. "If he is such a great leader, why didn't you stay and fight for him? You are a perfectly healthy man who can handle a rifle. Tell us, why did you not stay and die for the great Mufti?"

The man grumbled something and walked adamantly back the way he had come.

"She speaks the truth," Ahmed said. "Anyone who believes otherwise has only to do as she says and they will see."

With that, they left the group grumbling, trying to decide what to believe and what should be done. Mary heard one say, "Some of my relatives have gone to Nazareth. They say that the Arabs control that area and it is safe. Maybe we should go there."

The voices all became a blur of ideas and opinions, and Mary quit listening.

"They are fools. If they do not go back to their homes now, as you are doing, they will never go back," Ahmed said. "The Jews will not let them. Their homes, their possessions, are the spoils of war, and if it were the Jews who left them behind and our people were the victors, we would not give them back. Why should they? Victory always brings advantage. Why else should a person fight? If you win, you take everything. If you lose, you lose everything. There is no reason for war if no one wins and no one loses." They had walked nearly five hundred yards upriver to where the banks were not as steep but the river was wider and deeper. Ahmed dropped the pack of food near some small trees and shrubs and gathered wood.

It was the logic of the bedouin. Warriors for generations, when they defeated an enemey, they took everything and held it until a stronger enemy defeated them. From what Ahmed had told her in their few days together, he had been through many wars. Shrewd, and one of the most well known trackers of the northern bedu tribes, Ahmed had fought with the British since his youth. He served on the tribal council under Sheik Farouk of the Nasariyah, a tribe that had wandered the Galilee and Plain of Sharon for several generations. Over the years, they had become more sedentary, settling in villages north and east of Haifa, but they still had a warring streak in them that made them dangerous to any enemy.

"You lied about your tribe," Mary said.

"The al Tieb fight with the Arabs. The Nasariyah do not. The colonel would make it difficult for us if he knew the truth."

"Why don't the Nasariyah fight with the Arabs?"

"Our tribe fights for advantage. There is no advantage in fighting with the Arabs."

"Don't they promise you Jewish land?"

"It is a promise they cannot keep. The Jews are determined fighters because they have no choice. Where do they go if they lose? The Arabs fight for glory or for loot, and when glory and profit do not come quickly, they will stop fighting. Then they will lose. What will the Jews do with those who oppose them in time of war? They will have no choice but to send them away. It will cost tribes like the al Tieb many lives, their land, their homes, everything. Why fight for someone who will cost you everything?" He looked at the refugees as some settled down at the other side of the bridge while others walked toward the distant camp, resigned. "These people are the same, though they do not know it yet. They support the Arabs and cry for them to come and drive the Jews away. When the Arabs cannot do it, what will the Jews do? Who will lose the most?" He shook his head sadly. "They should not leave. Doing so says they support the Arabs and Haj Amin el Husseini. These are the enemies of the Jews, and to support them is to oppose the Jews. Why should the Jews let them return? To kill them in their beds?" He shrugged.

"But some do not leave because they support the Arabs," Mary said. "You heard them. They are afraid for themselves and their families."

"Their fear is justified but must be controlled if they wish to live in Palestine when this war is over." He paused. "The Jews will trust no one else, and even then it will be difficult. I have a friend, a Jewish muhktar over a village near my own. He was driven out of Europe by the Nazis and swears he will never do it to us, but he is wrong. If we leave him no choice, he will do it. He wants to live without fear just as much as we do."

"No choice? But that makes no sense. Of course they will have a choice."

"The Nazis convinced millions that the Jews were an enemy to humanity. The Nazis made their countrymen deeply fearful of the Jews. After that, it was easy to conduct the deportation and massacre of many men, women, and children while most civilians did nothing to stop it. Fear moves men to do horrible things, things they would never do normally. Is this not so?"

"And you think the Jews are afraid of us," Mary said.

"The Arab world has threatened them with annihilation. They come in force declaring that what the Germans did to the Jews will be a small thing when they are finished. Wouldn't you be afraid?" He sat down, pulled his legs up, and crossed them after the fashion of Buddha.

"We teach the Jews that all Arabs want to drive them into the sea. It is natural for them to believe that all Arabs are their enemies. Like the Germans, the Jews will be unable to sleep at night thinking the enemy is just down the street or living next door, ready to aid other Arabs in butchering them. This fear will help them justify keeping these refugees out of Palestine. It will help them justify taking their homes and their lands. Even those who know it is wrong will turn their heads while others do their dirty work. Through their lies and propaganda, Haj Amin and the Arab leaders think they bring together all Arabs to fight the Jews, but it also convinces the Jews that no Arab can be trusted, that all Arabs wish to kill and butcher them." He paused again, thinking. "A great man once said that when war starts, the first casualty is always truth. In its place will come lies—by both sides—and soon you will have unrest forever."

Mary felt the goose bumps explode across her arms, her heart confirming Ahmed's words. She thought of Aaron. While on their honeymoon in Paris, he had told Mary about his past and how as a teenage Jew living in Berlin with his family, the Nazis had butchered his parents, forcing him to flee with his brother David into the forests. There they fought with the Jewish underground and survived by their wits until much of Germany and nearly all of Berlin had been destroyed. She touched her stomach. Is that what lay in store for her child and thousands of her people? Like Aaron and the Jews of Europe, would they be without homes, enough food, and decent clothing in the aftermath of this war?

"I was told you are married. You should be—you are a handsome woman with many qualities for bearing strong children, beautiful children—but you say little of your husband. Is he the reason you make this difficult journey?" Ahmed removed bread from their bag, tore it in two parts, and handed her the largest piece. Mary took the bread but did not eat, her appetite suddenly gone. She did not answer immediately. Ahmed was a bedu, an Arab, and a Muslim. Though he had shown her only respect, his views on the place of women in Arab society were drastically different from her own. She did not think he would understand her marriage to a Jew. And yet, Ahmed seemed different, a man much like her father who would tell a person where he stood but who would also let others live as they chose. Even then it might be best to answer his question as simply as she could without revealing too much.

"A few weeks ago I received word that my husband was killed at Kastel. His family sent a letter, but it was brief and left many of my questions unanswered. I find his death hard to accept and return to make certain."

"Forgive me, but it seems to me that if he were alive and knew you were in Beirut, he would have come for you," Ahmed said.

"His wounds may be too serious for that," she responded, avoiding the real reason—a Jew in Beirut these days would not live long. "There are other reasons I want to return. My brothers have both disappeared and may have returned to Jerusalem. Though one of them hates me and might wish to do me harm, I need to know about them. I need to know if they are still alive and then let their wives and children know. It is very difficult for them as well."

"This brother who wishes you harm, he has a reason?"

"Yes, in his mind there is a reason." She had said too much. Ahmed was suspicious. There were few reasons an Arab would seek the life of a female family member, and he was guessing at which reason Mary had given her brother.

There was silence between them as Ahmed pulled out cheese, unwrapped it, and cut a piece for each of them. They said nothing until they had finished eating. Ahmed's face gave Mary no clue to what he was thinking, which made her even more nervous. Finally he broke the silence.

"For your husband to have fought and died with Abdul Khader Husseini would have made him a great hero among our people. And yet, unlike any other woman I know, you would choose to speak little of it. Your modesty is admirable."

The battle of Kastel and loss of Abdul Khader had been in every Lebanese newspaper. It had been a great day of mourning among many Palestinian refugees. For Mary, however, it had been a day of celebration. Khader served Haj Amin, and in Mary's opinion, no man had hurt her people more than the Mufti.

Ahmed spoke again. "Kibbutz Allonim is east of my village. It is led by Benny Berak, a good friend to my tribe for many years. For two generations, we have attended one another's celebrations. They danced the debka with us, and we danced the hora with them, but we never married one another's children.

"Then, many years ago, one of our tribe—a man by the name of Ali—had a wife who died, leaving him with a daughter only six months old. He was desperate. He had no one to look after the child while he was at work in the fields. In those days, the children on a Jewish kibbutz were raised communally in a separate house just for the children. The Jews protected the children fanatically, and no one outside the kibbutz was allowed to bring a child to be raised there. Even members of the kibbutz were denied free access to this home. Only the ones carefully picked to raise the children could be with them." He looked at Mary. "The Jews made an exception for Ali. He was allowed to bring his baby to the children's house as long as he wished. She was raised there and learned Jewish ways as well as those of her bedu father. When she was a young and beautiful woman, she was to leave the kibbutz, but Berak, a young man at the time, asked Ali for the hand of his beautiful daughter. Ali was distraught. It went contrary to all he held dear, and yet to deny his daughter marriage to a member of the kibbutz that had done so much for him was also very troubling. Finally he journeyed to the sacred tomb of Abraham at Hebron and prayed and fasted for nearly a week, beseeching Allah with all his heart for an answer. When he returned to Allonim, he gave Berak permission to marry the beautiful Kalifa. They have been married many years now and have four sons. It is a good marriage and binds our peoples together to this day." He sighed. "Unfortunately a holy man of Islam took offense at this action and pressed Ali to destroy his daughter or, at the very least, disown her. If he did not, Allah would have vengeance on him and all his kin for generations to come."

"How horrible," Mary said.

"Fortunately, the attitude of the holy man changed. It seems Ali's brother visited the small mosque to convince the holy man that his interpretation of the Koran was incorrect. Of course, one so learned as an imam is not easily taught, but with the help of a sharp dagger, he became more willing. After that, the holy man left Ali alone." Ahmed smiled. "Though many among the Arab nations do not read and write, Ali's brother was sent to school and learned these skills. He studied your Bible and our Koran, finding that both teach that one should marry in his own faith, but only tradition requires death as a punishment if one chooses otherwise. However, it is hard to change tradition and the false teachings of generations. Sometimes it is best to keep these things to ourselves."

Removing a blanket from their bag, Ahmed handed it to her, then stood. "There is a village nearby. I will go and get us fresh water." He was ten feet away when the sound of distant thunder bounced off the hills around them. There were no clouds anywhere in the graying sky. "Those guns are near the roads we will travel. It will be very dangerous. If you have any doubts, you should consider them carefully before morning."

"There will always be doubts, Ahmed, but my resolve to go to Jerusalem in spite of them is unshakable."

He disappeared in the growing darkness as Mary removed her head scarf and rolled out her blanket. Lying atop it, she stared up at the stars, grateful it was a warm night.

From his story, it was obvious Ahmed had guessed her secret, and yet she did not feel nervous. Ahmed did not seem to be one of those who held to violent traditions, and the more she was with him the more gratitude she had that God had led her to him.

As she turned on her side, Mary winced, then adjusted the small pouch under her clothes until she was comfortable. The pouch held some of the British pounds her father had left her as part of a very good inheritance, most of which was still in the bank in Beirut. Mary thanked her father for his foresighted financial planning nearly every day. She would not have been able to survive without the funds he had provided, and they would give her and her child a future. She carried only enough to pay Ahmed and take care of her needs for a few months if she was careful.

Tears soaked her eyes. It had happened a lot lately. Her father's generosity; fear for her life and the life of her child; uncertainty about Aaron's whereabouts: all were hooked directly to her tear ducts and once more she could not prevent the flow of small rivulets down her cheeks. It took several minutes to get her feelings under control.

Her father had been a doctor in Jerusalem. When he died of a heart attack in November, her eldest brother, Izaat, had discovered papers telling of their inheritance and his responsibility to see that each received his portion. Izaat had come from the Old City to bring her some of those funds so that she could leave the country. It was the last time she had seen him alive.

Izaat was the main reason Mary had gone to Beirut. After she and Aaron married, they lived temporarily in Paris where Aaron worked with the Israeli underground while recuperating from wounds he had received in the bombing of the *Jerusalem Post* building. Though it was the most glorious time of her life, she continued to worry about Izaat, and when Aaron was called home to fight during the desperate weeks of April, she had gone to Beirut. Knowing Izaat had sent his family there earlier, and knowing that if he had, he would either contact them or join them, she had flown into Lebanon. She found his family, but he had not arrived, nor had anyone heard from him. A friend who had supported Izaat in the Old City and had fled himself said that he was told that Izaat had been executed.

Mary had handled the guilt as long as there was hope he had survived. When that was gone, the guilt struck very hard. At nearly the same time, she had received the letter from Hannah about Aaron's death. She had felt like her world had come to an end. For the next month she had wished a thousand times she had gone with Aaron to Tel Aviv, asked hundreds more why Izaat had to die when he was one of the few who had done the right thing. Answers were slow in coming, and it was hard not to be angry at God, to blame Him. Only after many tears and prayers, after immersing herself in the words of the Book of Mormon, had she found any kind of peace. It had come none to soon.

It had been a Saturday night. Things had been particularly horrible that day in the camp. Fights, anger, hatred, the lack of food, water, and a dozen other things had put everyone on edge, and when combined with her own state, she had simply given up.

After long minutes filled with tears, she poured out her feelings to the Lord. She did not know how long she had knelt, how long her desperate cries had poured from her, before she lay down, exhausted.

When she awoke, it was with a start. There had been a dream. She had seen Izaat dressed in white, standing next to their father. They had been discussing something, but she could not hear them. After a moment, both had turned and smiled at her, then her father had come to her. She could still feel the warmth of his embrace as he held her tight, then stepped away and smiled, speaking only a few words.

"Aaron is not here, Mary. Now go. You have much to do before you come here."

Even now, the dream, the words, the warmth of them and his embrace were as real to her as the soil and rock beneath her feet. Yes, there had been moments of doubt, of wondering if it had really happened, but the warmth of his touch and the magic of his words pushed the doubt aside as quickly as it came. Izaat was in the right place, and Aaron was still alive. She finally found peace and a reason to go on.

It was then she had started making her plans to go back to Jerusalem.

She heard Ahmed return in the darkness, take his blanket, and go a short distance away before lying down to sleep.

"Do you hate the Jews, Ahmed?" she asked.

"Hate them? Not yet, but I will hate them if they take my land, my home, or if they drive us away. I think many will hate them if they do this."

"Can we ever live together in peace?"

He laughed lightly. "Can an Arab ever live in peace with anyone? We fight each other as much as we fight outsiders. Unfortunately, to fight is our curse. We seem to believe it is the only way to resolve a dispute. But, maybe there will come a day when even we tire of fighting. Then, maybe then, we will have peace." He paused. "Mary Aref, your secret is safe with me, but you are wise to keep it from others."

She bit her lip, her emotions still at surface level. "Thank you, Ahmed."

They lay in silence for a long time before Mary heard Ahmed's heavy breathing and knew he was asleep. She got to her knees and said her prayers. Ordinarily she would read Aaron's Book of Mormon, now safely stowed in her pocket, but the last few days both fear and the lack of privacy had kept her from it. Tonight, not even the half-full moon in the sky provided enough light, and all she could do was grip it tightly and think of its comforting words and her dream. In spite of the danger, she was doing the right thing.

She could not sleep, her mind racing from subject to subject, finally settling briefly on her brother Rhoui. He had wanted to kill her because of Aaron. Unlike her eldest brother, Rhoui hated Jews beyond all reason, and when she and Izaat had refused to think as he did, he had betrayed them both. She still feared him, still wondered what he would do if they ever saw one another again. He had tried to kill her once. Did he still hate her that much? What was he doing? Was he still alive? How could a man with such hate in his heart live with himself? With others? She pushed the thoughts aside while rubbing the goose bumps from her arms and listening for the sound of the distant guns. Nothing—a lull in the fighting.

She closed her eyes and conjured up a vision of Ephraim and Hannah, Beth and David. Family. Possibly her only family now. Had they reached the United States safely, or would she find them still in Jerusalem? Then the picture of another woman drifted slowly through her memory. Naomi. Aaron thought of her as his sister. She had been at Mary and Aaron's wedding and worked for Israeli intelligence. Could she be found? Would she know about Aaron?

Ahmed shook her. Startled, she reacted with a swing of her arm to fend off an attacker, but Ahmed placed a hand across her mouth and whispered that she must be quiet.

"Come, we have to leave. There will be trouble."

He had their bag ready, shoved her blanket in, and pulled her to her feet. They were nearly half a mile away when several successive explosions shook the ground like a dry rag. Mary gasped while staring back at the bridge, now in a shambles of fire and smoke. Two more explosions blew the remaining stone and wood into balls of flame, dust, and flying projectiles, and the military position erupted in panic. Soldiers ran in every direction, chaos and fear driving them in every direction. Gunfire erupted and screams, shouts, and commands filled the air.

"We cross the river here," Ahmed commanded. "Quickly! The Jews cannot tell us from soldiers in this darkness."

Mary did not argue. She lunged down the bank, fear tying her stomach in knots. In seconds, she was sliding into the cold mountain water, then pushing through it, then swimming for the far bank. Her muscles stiffened, and the swift current threatened to carry her back to the bridge. She swam harder, reached the far side, and grabbed for shrub branches in an attempt to keep her balance, but the swirl of the water caught her dress and pulled her from the shore. Realizing she could not fight the current, she turned into it and swam with all her strength toward an outcropping of trees and stones. She felt the current pulling her away. With the last of her energy, she reached for a branch and pulled herself free of the current. She finally collapsed facedown on the shore, exhausted, her feet still dangling in the cold water.

There was no time to rest. She could hear voices, the sound of guns much closer. She must find cover. Struggling to her knees, she was about to get up when the cold steel of a weapon nuzzled against her neck.

"Hey, Judah! Look what I found." The voice spoke Hebrew with a strong European accent and came from directly above her head. Though too dark to see his eyes, the tone of his voice was enough to give Mary a chill.

"Get up, Arab," he commanded. Mary got up slowly, her hands above her head, fingers extended in surrender, her body shaking from the chill of her wet dress.

"I am a refugee, nothing more," she said in Hebrew. "I have no weapon." She faced her captor.

"Shut up," said the man, jabbing his gun at her midsection. The barrel dug into her growing stomach, and she backed away, afraid for the baby she carried.

"Afraid, little woman?" asked the dark figure ominously while poking the rifle at her midsection again, forcing her toward the water. "Well, I can cure you of that real quick." He stepped closer, raising the rifle toward her heart. Mary saw only the shadow move behind him, then heard the smash of something solid against the soldier's skull and watched him melt to the ground. Ahmed stood over him, rifle butt ready to strike again. When he saw nothing further was needed, he picked up the soldier's gun and threw it in the river.

"Come, we must go," Ahmed said calmly. "They will kill us if they find us here."

To their left, the bridge and Lebanese encampment were both burning brightly, but the sounds of gunfire were gone. Was it over, or just a lull in the fighting? She could see shadowy figures running from the river to the camp, their shouts of anguish and panic giving a distinct chill to the night air. Hunters and the hunted? The uncertainty of what was happening, of what might happen next, drove them quickly away.

"The soldier would have killed me," Mary said breathlessly.

"This is war. No one is safe in war. Only when it is finished will there be regrets for such things, nightmares, a wish to do things differently by those who still have any soul left," Ahmed replied.

She felt her stomach churn and was forced to bend over and purge her body of what little food she had eaten. Feeling more pregnant than ever, weak and frightened, she needed a hand from Ahmed to get moving again.

SEE CHAPTER NOTES

CHAPTER 3

They stayed well away from the road until the stars began to disappear in the growing dark blues of the hour before sunrise. Ahmed stopped, and Mary collapsed to the ground to get off her aching legs and feet, her still-damp clothes chafing her from shoulder to leg.

"Where are we?" she asked softly.

Ahmed pointed to a small village across the valley in front of them. "That is Malkiya. The Jewish Palmach captured it more than a month ago and are probably the ones who blew up the bridge so that the Lebanese cannot come here. I think it is better if we avoid them. We must go higher, go around them." He began climbing, and Mary forced herself to her feet and stumbled after him. Reaching the top of the hill, they rested a moment, and Ahmed pointed out several campfires along the road in the valley below. "Refugees," he said. "It is better to stay away from them. They ask too many questions, and the roads are dangerous. We will stay in the hills," Ahmed said. "You are very tired. Soon we will make camp, build a fire of our own. Come, I know a place where we will be safe."

Mary longed to be warmed by the flames beckoning to her in the valley below, but said nothing, trusting once more in his bedouin intuition. They traveled along the rim of the hill until they reached an outcropping of rocks that would hide them from the road. Ahmed told Mary to rest and he would gather what was needed for a fire. Soon she was warming herself by the flames of a fire nurtured from scraps of wood and dried animal dung.

"Are you still very wet?" he asked.

She shook her head. "Only damp. The fire will dry the rest."

"I will be back soon. Keep the fire small but hot. The dung is best for such things." With that, he disappeared in the darkness.

Mary warmed herself luxuriantly as steam lifted from her clothes, leaving them dry and her flesh warmed. Ahmed returned just as the sun breached the eastern hills and gave a golden hue to the brown grass of a Palestine summer. He tossed her a blanket, sat down, and took bread, cheese, and fresh oranges from a bag Mary had never seen.

"We will sleep here for a few hours, then we walk to Sahalia, the village of my family. My brother will give us horses and tell us the best route to take to Haifa. We should be in Sahalia in a day and a half, maybe less."

"And the blankets, where did you get them?" she asked.

He smiled coyly. "Let us just say that the owner will not miss them until he tries to sleep in his bed."

"You mean he wasn't in his bed?"

"The whole village was at the muhktar's home. I found the house empty and took the blankets." He shrugged. "It is the least they can do for a Palestinian refugee, don't you think?" He grinned, his decaying teeth showing even in the moonlight. She felt warm, but guilty, and it showed in her face.

"If you wish I will take them money," he said.

She removed a few pounds from her pocket and handed it to him. "If you will," she said.

He nodded, handing her back half the money. "It is enough for such blankets and a bit of food."

"I suppose a meeting this early in the day must have been important."

"I got close enough to hear what they were discussing. They try to decide whether or not to leave their village. They worry about the attack we saw tonight at the Latani bridge. They also worry about rumors that elements of the Arab Liberation Army and soldiers of Iraq are coming here to retake Malkiya." He poked at the fire. "The ALA and the Iraqis have little food. They live off the people and take what they want. The villagers fear them as much as they do the Jews, especially since they have been forcing village men to fight with them. These people do not wish to fight, so they talk of how they can stay out of it."

They ate the remaining bread in quiet, the hardships and exhaustion of the day leaving them little strength but for eating. Mary lay down and went to sleep just as the sun began heating the dusty hills around her.

She awoke to the sound of distant battle, her weary body crying out for more sleep, but when she saw that Ahmed's blanket was still folded and unused, she sat straight, then got to her feet, searching for some sign of him.

There were refugees on the road in the valley below. They were moving quickly north, obviously anxious to get away from the sound of gunfire coming from the south where thick smoke hung over the hills.

She looked west and was greeted by peaceful blue skies and a glimpse of the Mediterranean in between two hills.

"Salaam."

Mary turned to see Ahmed working his way up a path toward her, carrying their water skin and several green apples. He handed her one.

"The villagers have decided to leave. I told them Lebanon was closed." He shrugged. "They say it is only closed to those who do not know the roads. They are probably right."

Though the apple was unripe and a bit sour, she was hungry and quickly devoured it while watching young children herding both sheep and goats on a distant hillside.

"They belong to the same village. They gather everything to take with them," Ahmed said.

Even from here, she could see a lot of activity as they prepared to leave. She felt remorse for the fact they might never return, that these hills might never see them again.

Her eyes were diverted by the sudden appearance of several military trucks at the far end of the valley. Traffic pulled over, and people scurried out of the way as if Moses had parted the Red Sea, but the trucks did not stop. Instead, they turned east at an intersection and climbed a dusty road until they cleared the top of a far hill and disappeared over its rim.

"The Haganah does not seem to care about refugees," Mary said.

"There are battles both south and east of us. You can hear the guns," he shrugged. "The Arabs wish to come here, take this road if they can. The Jews must stop them. All traffic from both north and south must travel along this road, and whoever controls it will have great advantage. We must go. We will be in the way of their armies in only hours." He stood and put the bag over his shoulder.

Upon reaching the road, they turned south, the heat of midday mingling with the choking dust stirred up by hundreds of refugees moving north. By midafternoon she had seen abandoned cars and broken-down carts, dead animals, and weak, tired, and ill refugees in makeshift shelters or tents alongside the road. As she looked into their eyes, Mary saw an array of emotions. But the one emotion common to all was fear. Snippets of conversation from anxious men trying to get any information they could were on every lip. The Jews had overrun Haifa and Jaffa, but the Arabs were attacking on every front and would soon have it all back. There was fighting at Nazareth, Degania, Acre, and Tel Aviv. Some thought the Egyptians had taken most of the Negev, while others said they had been stopped at Gaza. Mary's ears pricked up when she heard news of Jerusalem. The city was a war zone. Abdullah's Legion was pummeling the Jews with artillery while the remnants of Haj Amin's Holy Strugglers fought valiantly for the Old City and would take it any hour. Others said that the Jews stopped Abdullah's Legion in their tracks and were pushing them back. Contradictions were everywhere, worsening the uncertainty and fear. Mary was beginning to understand why people were running. How could one live with battles raging all around?

Traffic lessened as the day progressed until it was only a trickle. It was nearly five in the evening when they stopped to drink from their water skin. They sat on a patch of grass just off the road that ran through the middle of a large valley running north and south. Refugees were already stopping for the night, and the sweet odor of fresh-cooked bread drifted on the air, making Mary salivate. After ten minutes' rest, they got up and kept moving south. A hundred yards down the road, a man worked under the raised hood of his car. Two children played next to him while the mother sat on a nearby rock nursing a baby, her face shaded by a stylish, wide-brimmed hat. As Mary and Ahmed approached, the woman pulled away from the baby and covered herself while the children stopped their play, their eyes riveted on Ahmed, his rifle and curved dagger hanging from his belt. The older of the two children, a boy, finally worked up the courage to go to his mechanic father, still unaware he had company.

"You're going the wrong way, aren't you?" the woman asked with a smile as she lifted the brim of her hat slightly. Mary recognized her as the wife of one of the notable citizens of Arab Jerusalem, a secretary to one of the members of the Arab Higher Committee, Haj Amin's puppet governing counsel in Palestine. She looked at the man with his upper torso still under the hood of the car. Yes, it was Yunis, Yunis Mujeeb.

"Hello, Mrs. Mujeeb," Mary said, forcing a smile.

The woman looked at her curiously. "I'm sorry, do I know you?"

"My father is Amos Aref," Mary said. "Your husband came to our house quite often for business, and you and I met at an informal luncheon six months ago."

The woman's smile turned to a sad frown. "Mary Aref. Yes, I remember. I was sorry to hear about your father."

"Mary, Mary Aref. Is that you?"

Mary turned to see Yunis Mujeeb, his hands quickly cleaning themselves on a rag, an apprehensive smile on his face as his eyes darted from Ahmed to Mary, then back to Ahmed again, obviously unsure of why she would be traveling with a bedu. He cleared his throat. "How . . . how are you?"

"I am tired and ready for a hot bath," Mary said, forcing a smile of her own. "This is a friend, Ahmed. He is of the Nasariyah tribe and has been kind enough to help me return to Jerusalem."

Mujeeb nodded at Ahmed but did not offer to shake his hand.

"Come, sit down, rest. It is a long walk to the city of God," Yunis Mujeeb said. He pulled Mary away from Ahmed. As he did, he leaned close and spoke his mind. "It surprises me that you travel with a bedouin, Mary. They are . . . well, dangerous, and for a woman to travel with such a man . . ."

Mary suddenly realized she had never really liked Yunis Mujeeb, and she liked him even less now. Coupled with the ache in her tired bones and frayed nerves, she gave an abrupt answer. "I am surprised that you are traveling at all," Mary said.

He gave her a curious look. "I am not sure I understand."

"The war is not in Beirut, Mr. Mujeeb. It is in Jerusalem. It seems a bit strange to me that all our leaders seem to think they can drive the Jews into the sea from the comfort of hotel lobbies in Lebanon and Cairo."

"Leaders of the AHC have asked that I report to them. I—"

"You don't have to make excuses to this . . . this woman," Mrs. Mujeeb said. "Her father has opposed Haj Amin for years, and obviously his ridiculous stance has her heart as well. It is a viewpoint that will cost us our country if such people have their way."

"We had a country given to us, Mrs. Mujeeb. For the first time in history, we had a chance to make a beginning as a people, but the Mufti's greed, and the greed of the Arab nations, make that impossible now. Now, if you will excuse me, I must go."

"No one here would think of stopping you," Mrs. Mujeeb said coldly.

Mary walked away, then turned back. "By the way, the border to Lebanon is closed. It seems Haj Amin insists on a war, whether the people want to fight it or not. And he forces the Lebanese to turn our people back to fight it for him. Of course, he makes exceptions for men like you, men who are just like him—cowards, one and all."

"You do not understand. The leaders, if they are killed—"

"Heaven forbid. We wouldn't want that, would we? No one to lead. Never mind that hiding in such places as Beirut, Damascus, and Cairo makes it difficult to follow our leaders. Never mind that our leaders have no idea of what it is really like, what their horrid words and impossible policies do to the lives of innocent people while our leaders live like kings." She started to walk away, but her anger got the best of her and she turned back. "If we find peace, if we still have our homes and our lives when this is over, I will shoot the first one of you I see in Jerusalem. I swear it." She hastened down the road, leaving them red-faced and angry, feeling no remorse for her stinging words. Such people did not deserve Palestine, and they most certainly did not deserve to lead. It would be better to live under Jewish rule than under such men.

Ahmed caught up to her quickly, a smirk on his face. "You talk like a man."

"I will take that as a compliment," she said.

"You do not like them," he added.

"An understatement, but let's not think about them. I will only get more angry and spoil this wonderful hike which the stupidity of such people created for us."

He chuckled but said nothing.

Her temper did not cool as mile after mile they passed more refugees, more misery, and more suffering of those forced from their homes. Finally, late in the day, tired and hungry, they slipped from the road and into a nearby field of dry grain stalks to glean a few handfuls of wheat. Several others joined them, and soon the field was covered with refugees looking for a few kernels of wheat missed during the recent harvest.

"We are nearly out of water again," Ahmed said. "I will find a village." Without another word, he strode away.

Mary trudged partway up a rocky hill to sit in the shade of an ancient olive tree. Traffic along the road was picking up again, but Mary noticed that there were fewer cars. Instead, most refugees carried everything in carts pulled by themselves or some ragged animal urged on by a firm stick against its backside or a rope attached to a harness. Both man and beast looked too exhausted to go much further, but most struggled on, their fear and anxiety driving them further north, despite the blistered and bleeding feet of small children. It made her heart ache to think that this was just the beginning of their suffering.

She heard the sudden sound of heavy artillery just over the hill to the east. With each explosive concussion, the ground shook, and fear gripped those around her. Everyone stood still, waiting, hoping it would go away. Then another shell struck. And another. Horses, donkeys, cows, sheep, and children all bolted at the same time but in a hundred different directions. Screams filled the air. Animals ran away with carts; fathers and mothers grabbed children out of the way and ran for cover. A single car burst onto the scene, its horn blaring. It darted left, scattering already frightened refugees, its driver seemingly overcome with panic. Mary held her breath when it struck a cart, knocking off a wheel and shattering its side boards. Goods were thrown helter-skelter, and its owners jumped out of the way just before it reached them. Others dodged its fender as it clipped another cart, then another. It went off the road into the field, driving people out of its path, then banged back onto the road. She grimaced as a man froze and was hit, his body thrown to one side where he lay still as the car slammed into a rock and came to a dead stop.

The shelling stopped, and the only sound Mary heard was that of steam hissing from the car's radiator a dozen feet away. The people slowly gathered themselves together, their eyes riveted on the vehicle, waiting, watching. Finally a woman screamed, running to the aid of the injured man. Others quickly joined her as angry words burst over the crowd. A dozen men walked menacingly toward the offending car, then a rock was thrown, then another and another, breaking windows and denting the metal skin. The first man reached the vehicle and jerked open the door. Grabbing the driver by his clothes, the mob pulled him angrily and thrashed at him with their fists. Frozen by the drama, Mary remained paralyzed for several seconds during which a woman and boy jumped out of the vehicle screaming at the assailants to leave the man alone.

"It wasn't his fault," yelled the woman. A man shoved her aside, and she fell to the ground. The boy, a stout teenager, threw himself into the man but was pushed away.

"Try that again, boy, and I will kill you," one of the assailants screamed.

Mary launched herself down the hillside shouting for them to stop. Shoving aside those who blocked her way, she found herself near the man, only to be grabbed and pushed away. She struck out at her attacker, bloodying his nose while pulling her arm away. Another blocked her path, and she kicked his shins, then shoved another to the side.

"Leave him be," she screamed. "Stop it," she yelled. "You are animals! All of you!" She pushed another, and another, facing them defiantly.

"He is the animal! Look what he did to my brother." The man she had just shoved took a threatening step in her direction. "Now, get out of the way. He will pay for this."

Mary stood her ground. "You heard his wife. It was not his fault."

The man grabbed her arm, tossing her toward the crowd where heavy hands grasped at her while the man aimed his heavy boot at the driver's ribs. A gunshot rang out, and everyone screamed and scattered at the same time. Mary wrenched free as Ahmed stepped forward and pointed his rifle at the midsection of the man about to deliver the rib-crushing kick.

"I will kill you if you so much as touch him," Ahmed said.

Fear crossed the assailant's face, and he stepped away, his hand slowly moving to a revolver stuck in his belt until Ahmed pushed the gun into his ribs. "You would have to be a fool to believe your hand is quicker than my bullet."

The man glanced down at the rifle barrel, then at the stern face of the bedouin who carried it, before lifting his hand away from his gun.

"If my brother dies . . ." He left the sentence unfinished.

"Your time would be better spent in taking care of him than in trying to kill another. Go. And if you come close to this man again, I will not give you a second chance," Ahmed answered.

The attacker wiped his mouth with the back of his hand, deciding whether his pride was worth dying for.

"Mohmar," a voice cried from behind the circling crowd. The man hit by the car pushed through the crowd, a bloodied cloth held to his forehead. "I am all right. Leave it alone."

Mohmar looked hatefully at Ahmed, then joined his brother and walked away, the crowd dispersing with them.

Mary knelt beside the battered driver. As she rolled him over he moaned, his hands covering his face as if to protect himself from further blows. Touching him gently, she spoke calming words that put him at ease. He had jagged cuts in his cheeks and forehead, and his ruddy, mustached face was already beginning to swell. His wife moved quickly to Mary's side, dabbing a handkerchief at the wounds. Tears of fear and relief rolled down her cheeks as her son stood over them, his face pale but angry.

"The car . . . It . . . it . . . Something broke. Father could not control it," he said. He seemed tall for his age, his face growing only fuzz instead of whiskers, but his anger spoke of having lived more years than showed.

Another concussion made the earth jump, even though it hit high on the hill above them.

"Come," Ahmed said forcefully. "The battle is not over, and we are exposed here." A second shell whistled overhead and struck in the field, followed by a third.

"Not again," the woman moaned. Though slight of build, she tugged on her husband, urging him to get up as Mary grabbed one arm and Ahmed the other. When they had him on his feet, they stumbled toward the cover of rocks and bushes as other shells ripped up the valley floor and people once more ran screaming for cover. They dove under carts, cars, and behind small boulders. Others, too afraid to move, were pulled or pushed to the ground.

Mary and Ahmed lowered the injured man to the ground and lay flat on their stomachs and covered their heads. Mary grimaced with each reverberation, praying they wouldn't get a direct hit. Falling debris splattered against her back. Over the next five minutes, the shelling crept farther north along the valley as if searching for victims. Then it stopped as quickly as it had started. Even then, Mary had to work hard to keep from panicking. Never had she experienced anything so horrible, and for the first time, she questioned her sanity for trying to return.

"Now you see why they run to Lebanon," Ahmed said.

As Ahmed got to his feet, Mary lifted her head and stared across the field where the explosions had dug deep holes. A car had been hit directly, and as she was about to get up, its gas tank exploded, sending her to her stomach again.

Finally, she took a deep breath and crawled to the wounded man, his wife and son huddled next to him, their faces pale with fear. His face was covered with blood, and Mary pulled a cloth from her bag and asked Ahmed for the water skin. Dousing the rag, she began tending to his wounds while the woman and her son regained their composure.

"I . . . I can do that," his wife finally said. "I am all right now. Really, I can do it."

Mary handed her the cloth, then stood with Ahmed and the boy and viewed the chaos along the road. The wind carried dust across the valley floor where refugees tried to shake their fear and get to their feet. There were several direct hits on carts, and the exploded car continued to send flames and black smoke heavenward.

"Many are dead," Ahmed said.

Babies and children cried, people moaned and screamed for help while others tried to locate missing friends and family.

Less than fifty feet away, Mary saw a woman, her head bleeding. A man lay very still next to her. Further on, several more sat, moaning, holding wounds or crying for loved ones. There were dead, badly wounded, and panicking people from one end of the small valley to the other.

"We must help," Mary said. She and Ahmed ran to the closest casualties, and Mary knelt by the stunned, wounded woman while Ahmed checked the man for life.

"He is dead," Ahmed said.

Mary ripped a piece of cloth from the bottom of her *jilbab,* and Ahmed tossed her the water skin. Dousing the cloth in water, she began tending to the wounds, when the woman toppled onto her left side. Mary rolled her onto her back only to stare into a pair of glazed-over eyes. She was dead as well.

They spent the next hour helping others. Five had been killed, and Ahmed organized a group of men to bury the dead in two of the craters near the hill, while Mary helped more of the wounded, providing them with quick slings for broken arms and cloth bandages for small cuts.

The sun was touching the top of the hill on the west when Mary saw trucks come into the far end of the valley. They were Jewish, and they were military. Soldiers unloaded from the trucks and fanned out across the valley. The wounded, exhausted, and frightened refugees gasped in unison but did not move. They huddled together, preparing for the end they were sure was about to come.

Ahmed suddenly appeared at her elbow and pulled her back to the rocks where the injured man, his wife, and his son were still sitting. Ahmed told them all to get down and stay quiet, then dropped to the ground, his rifle ready.

Mary's fear returned as she watched the soldiers move across the valley, some refugees finally working up enough courage to flee north while others stayed put, too hurt or afraid to move. Mary was relieved to see that the soldiers ignored the wounded, but she grimaced when a man shook his fist at a soldier, crying, "Look what you have done to us," and received a pummeling for his effort. The pitiful cry for mercy that followed made her skin crawl.

"All of you," shouted one of the soldiers. "Do not resist. We are not here to harm you. If you have weapons, show them to us now, and we will let all of you go. But if we discover any soldier, any armed fighter among you, it will be bad for everyone. If such are here, reveal them now."

"If they find me with this weapon, they will hurt you and the others. I must go," Ahmed said. Reaching in a deep pocket he removed a small dagger and gave it to her. "If they try anything with you . . ."

"I understand. Thank you, Ahmed." She stuck the dagger in her *jilbab*.

"I will return when it is safe." He left the bag of food and blankets and disappeared in the trees behind them.

The soldiers found Mary and the family ten minutes later, searched them only briefly, and were about to move on when Mary spoke. "Why do you shell civilians? None of them can do you harm."

One of the soldiers turned back. "We did not fire on you. We have only a few trucks and our rifles, no artillery. It is the Iraqis or the ALA who fired. They knew we were coming through the narrow pass that leads into the valley and tried to hit us from too great a distance. As you see, their shells fell short."

"You are a liar," the injured man's son yelled. "You are butchers, all of you."

One soldier lifted his rifle to pummel the boy, but another stopped him, then spoke to Mary. "You should keep a tight collar on your dog before we have to shoot him. Our army is moving north to secure our border. Do not go there, or this could happen again. You should go home. It is safer there, and our new state will welcome any who stay and refuse to fight with our enemies." With that he walked away.

The boy was about to speak his mind when Mary grabbed his arm with a firm grip and warned him with her eyes and harshly spoken words. "If you speak, you endanger all of us."

The boy bit off his words, but anger turned his face crimson. "You are a coward," he said through clenched teeth.

Once the soldiers had walked away, he jerked his arm free of her grip.

"What is your name?" Mary asked.

"Emile," he said harshly.

"Emile, you are at least fifteen but of slight build and you have no weapon. I am a woman, as is your mother, and your father is wounded. Should only two of those soldiers take offense at something you say, they could come back here and beat one of us or drag us off to make an example of. We could do nothing about it, nor could you. Call it cowardice if you like, but if you wish to remain free and protect your parents, you should keep your mouth shut."

"Emile," his father said, "she is right. You will keep a civil tongue in your head."

Emile sat down with a thud, his eyes glaring at the soldiers as they walked north. Mary wondered if they could feel the hate scorching them between the shoulder blades.

She knelt down beside the man and his wife and looked at his wounds. The swelling was causing some separation of the cuts, and she knew she would have to sew them shut. "Do you have any first-aid medicine? Bandages, iodine, possibly a needle and surgical thread?"

The woman, still pale, looked at her blankly. It was the man who mumbled a response. "In the car. Emile can show you."

Mary nodded and was about to stand when the woman grabbed her arm. "Thank . . . thank you." Tears filled the bottom of her eyes. "My husband . . . thank you for saving . . ." She bit her lip and got control. "He . . . I don't know why . . . the car . . ."

"Never mind. I'll be back in a few minutes." She forced a smile, then looked toward the car. The soldiers had passed, but several others were staring through the windows as if looking for something. One attempted to open the door, and Mary shouted at him as she ran from the ravine, Emile right behind her. Mary was grateful the looters scattered and quickly retrieved the keys to the car and opened the trunk. She handed the kit, a couple of blankets, and two small pillows to Emile, then retrieved a cloth bag full of food and a suitcase full of clothes before closing the trunk and locking it.

Setting the bag and case down, she got on her knees and looked under the car. Some sort of rod hung down near the left wheel, and though she didn't know what it was, she knew it was probably the reason the car had gone out of control.

"What is wrong?" Emile asked.

"Your father was right. Something is broken." Mary picked up the food and suitcase and followed Emile back to his parents.

She told Emile's father what she had seen.

"A broken tie rod. Without it, I had no control." He looked at his wife. "I am sorry, my dear, but we will probably have to walk from here unless we can find a mechanic among the refugees and convince him to take the time to try and fix it."

She nodded, color finally returning to her face. "Never mind. We'll get there somehow." She forced a smile. "I will make you a bed." She took blankets and started unfolding them. Mary grabbed one and helped.

"He said we should stay in our home. I was frightened and begged him to take us to Beirut. Everyone was leaving. Our leaders told us to leave. They insisted that no one stay, even though the Jewish leaders of the city said we should. Once we started to leave, the Jews changed. They began looting our stores and beating our people. I couldn't stand it anymore. Finally my husband gave in. Now here we are, stuck in this place with the armies of both sides shooting at us. I have made a mess of it, haven't I? A real mess."

"Never mind, Rifa. I am all right."

"Now we go back," Emile said. "We go back and fight them. It is our duty, Father. We can both fight, both defend our home. We must do it."

"Quiet down, Emile. We will discuss it. For now, start a fire. We must eat and rest before we decide," the man said.

Emile mumbled but did as he was told.

Mary laid her back against a tree and closed her eyes, the rush now gone. Her pregnancy once more caused her stomach to churn, and she found herself grateful such feelings did not come often. "What city are you talking about?" she asked.

"Haifa. The Jews have taken most of it now. There are maybe five thousand Arabs still there. Out of fifty thousand! It is an outrage," Emile said angrily.

"Never mind, Emile. Just build the fire," the man said angrily. He gave Mary the best smile he could through puffed and cut lips. “My name is Saad Shawas, and this is my wife Rifa. You have met our son, Emile.”

“I am Mary, uh . . . Aref.” She remembered Ahmed’s warning about her identity. “I am from Jerusalem, but I have been in Beirut locating my family. Now I go back.”

“But . . . but you were safe in Beirut,” Rifa said.

She told them about what was happening in Lebanon. “You cannot cross the border. Emile is right, you should go back, especially if you want to keep your home. The Jews will not harm you if they know you are not fighting them. But if you run—if everyone runs—they will take what you leave behind as spoils of war, and you will never see it again.”

“So the Jews become the Nazis,” Emile said angrily. “Better that the Germans killed them all.”

Rifa was shocked by her son’s words, but it was Saad who reacted. “Emile! Hush! You don’t know what you’re talking about.”

“Don’t I? I am not a child, Father. I see them steal our homes, our cities, and I know that if we don’t fight, it will not be them who will be driven into the sea. And yet you run like a coward. Worse, you make me a coward with you.” He threw aside the few dried sticks he had gathered and stomped away.

“I apologize for my son. He is young and does not understand.”

“He is not alone, Saad,” Mary said. “I tell you only that going north is foolish. Not only will the Lebanese refuse you, but as you can see, the war goes there now as well. When he returns, Ahmed will take me to Haifa. For a few pounds more I am sure he will take you as well. His village is not far, and he has horses. That will speed our journey and make it easier.”

“Thank you, we will decide before morning,” Saad said.

“Good. I saw a water bottle in your car. We will need it.” She stood and went back to the car. Retrieving the water, she was on her way back when Emile joined her, his hands shoved in the pockets of his pants and his jaw showing a determined set.

"I will go with you back to Haifa," he said.

"Do your parents agree with this decision?" Mary asked.

"I am finished following them. I am fifteen and old enough to make my own decisions. The Jews are my enemy, and I will fight them."

Mary thought of her brother Rhoui. Emile had the same defiant hate, the same uncontrolled and misguided determination. It had turned Rhoui against both her and Izaat, and to see it in this young boy saddened her.

"Your mother will need you," Mary said. "With your father hurt—"

"My father is a coward. He refuses to fight the Jews or support Haj Amin. Haj Amin is a great leader and loves our people. I will join his Holy Strugglers and help him take our land from the infidel."

She stopped and faced him. "Emile, where is Haj Amin? Where are the other leaders who ask you to die for them?"

"They are in Jerusalem. They organize . . . they lead our people in holy war."

"Haj Amin is in Cairo. Most of his council are either with him or in Beirut and Damascus. I saw some of them myself a few days ago. They do not fight, but hide, waiting for boys like you to shed your blood to make it easy for them to come back and live as kings. Why would you follow such men?"

"Haj Amin is the Grand Mufti. Allah blesses him with wisdom, and he knows that he must goad the Arab leaders into helping us. Without this, we would have to fight alone."

"And what will be the price we pay for their help? Will Egypt take the Negev, Transjordan the West Bank? Possibly Syria and Iraq will split Galilee. What will we have then, Emile? What will your Mufti give up to butcher the Jews?"

"They . . . they honor the Mufti. They fight for him because he is their spiritual leader, just as he is ours. They will help him set up a great government under Islam. All Arabs will honor him, and soon he will unite the entire Arab world under the banner of Mohammed, blessed be his name. This is why they fight for him, and why I will fight for him," he said firmly.

"You are a fool if you believe this, Emile. Abdullah and Haj Amin fight each other and will until one or the other is dead and buried. The other Arab leaders fear him for the very reason you speak of. They are afraid he will take away what they have gained and will do everything in their power to prevent him from coming to power. Further, you assume that all of us who live in Palestine will accept your Mufti. Haj Amin butchered many Arab Christians in the rebellion of 1936 to 39. Why would any Arab Christian accept a man who would do this to us?"

"You will become Muslim. All men must follow Mohammed. It is Allah's will, and the Mufti has called for jihad to see it done. If you do not convert to God's one religion . . ."

"I will not, and millions of others will not." She took a deep breath, getting her anger under control. One could not argue with such fanaticism. "I will make a deal with you, Emile. If the Mufti comes to power, if the Arab world accepts him as their spiritual leader and lets him rule their kingdoms, I will convert to Islam. But if they refuse, if the Mufti never reaches Jerusalem, you must stop believing in this fanatic and find a better path."

Emile's eyes narrowed. "You will see. The Mufti will come. It is Allah's will."

"Then you have nothing to worry about, but I tell you that your Mufti is nothing more than a bully and a coward who uses Islam to bludgeon everyone, and he will never rule even a small portion of Palestine."

"This is a lie," the boy said. "You cannot speak of Allah's holy man that way, nor of his holy religion. You should be . . ." His voice trailed off.

"I should be what, Emile? Struck down? Flogged? Butchered? Possibly you think I should be imprisoned. Already you speak like your Mufti. Our people do not need tyranny, Emile, they need freedom. Don't you realize that your Mufti has stirred up the Arab world just so that he can deny us this? He wants power, Emile, and he will spill as much blood as he can to get it."

"You speak blasphemy," Emile said stiffly. "He is the Mufti, a great and holy man. I will not listen to this anymore." He started away, and Mary let him go. Talking would do no good, just as it did no good with Rhoui. It frustrated her to no end, but she knew it would never change. Men like the Mufti would exist as long as the world stood, and their fanaticism would continue to cause untold pain to others. How could one possibly fight such men? She remembered something she had read in the Book of Mormon recently. "And he was learned, that he had a perfect knowledge of the language of the people; wherefore, he could use much flattery, and much power of speech." It seemed to describe Haj Amin el Husseini perfectly.

When she reached the trees, she saw Emile, his cold eyes staring at her with a mixture of hate, confusion, and anger. She ignored the stare, and as he looked away, his visage gave her a chill. It was the same expression as Rhoui's when he told her he would rather see her dead than in the presence of a Jew. She must not turn her back on Emile. Though young, the boy's hate was maturing quickly.

Rifa put on a pot of water. Saad rested with his back against a large tree and his eyes closed, a blanket over him. Over the next hour, the two women prepared boiled meat, cooked vegetables, and bread from Mary's bag and the sack of food the family had brought with them. As they talked, Mary learned that Saad had been a worker for the British government and that he had Jewish friends they did not wish to harm. Saad did not believe war was the solution, and though he revered the Mufti because of his office, he did not support his efforts to enslave or butcher the Jews, nor did he feel that such a position gave him any special right to lead Palestine's Arabs. It was then that Emile got to his feet and walked away abruptly.

"Your son does not agree with you," Mary said.

Saad forced a sad smile. "In Haifa, there are many who preach the rhetoric of the Mufti. Unfortunately Emile has listened to their angry words far too often." He adjusted his position to take a plate of food from his wife. "I heard you speaking with him earlier. I said what I said to let him know you are right. The Mufti weakens us internationally, and even if the Arabs win against the Jews, the world will never let him come to power. Someone on the Arab Higher Committee possibly, but not Haj Amin el Husseini." He opened swollen lips to take a small bite of meat, chewing it carefully before speaking again. "Please, do not get me wrong. I feel a great injustice has been done to us, but war will never solve it. When our people discover this, we will find peace again, but it will be through a leader who loves peace more than war." He shrugged in a resigned fashion.

Saad glanced at his wife, and their eyes met. "My wife told you it was her fault we left, that she was afraid. This is only partially true. It is mostly because of Emile that I decided we must leave. You witness the reason."

Rifa handed Mary a plate of food, and the two women joined Saad. While Mary did the dishes, Rifa left the camp with bread and meat for Emile, returning a few minutes later without it.

"At least he is not too angry to eat," Saad said.

Rifa helped Saad to his feet, took his prayer rug, and helped him go a short distance where she left him to do his ritual and returned to prepare a bed for them and another for Emile. By the time Saad returned, Mary had already made her own bed in a stand of shrubs that offered some privacy. When finished, she returned to the fire to warm herself, her mind on Ahmed. There was still no sign of him, and she was beginning to worry.

"He will return," Saad said from beneath the covers of his own bed, seeming to read her mind. "When the bedu make a bargain, for good or ill, they keep it."

Mary nodded, stood, and stepped to her blankets. It was dark, and she knelt to say her prayers. The day had given her much to be thankful for, and the prayer took some time. Then she asked for the ability to stay strong and keep going. When finished, she lay down and stared up at the growing number of stars.

"Can I get to Jerusalem?" she said loud enough for Saad to hear.

"I do not know. Transjordan has laid siege to much of the Jewish portion of the city, and the war is very bad there now."

Turning on her side, Mary closed her eyes, her hand gripping Aaron's Book of Mormon. No matter, she must go back. She must. Somehow she would get through. After that she would decide what to do, but for now she must go. Aaron had survived, and she must find him. With that, her exhausted body drifted into a deep sleep.

CHAPTER 4

"So, what do you think?" Wally asked.

"It is a nice place," Zohar said while looking around the two adjoining rooms. His apartment was much smaller than hers, and it had no kitchen, though a hot plate sat on a table against the wall, an old-fashioned icebox beside it. In the living room, there was a rumpled, overstuffed couch with two wooden orange crates as end tables. With no bed in the room, Zohar assumed Wally planned to sleep on the couch. A larger crate served as a coffee table, and a large oil painting of a landscape hung on one wall. It was beautifully done, and Zohar stepped closer to see the name in the lower right hand corner. French.

"A very nice painting. The colors are wonderful, and the people working in the fields look as if they could step right into the room. This . . ." she squinted at the name again, "Duvier is very good."

"I wouldn't know. I liked the picture, so I bought it. Some guy on the street near the Eiffel Tower. He looked hungry, so I gave him more than it's probably worth. It reminds me of the countryside of New York State." He busied himself at the hot plate.

"You were raised in country like this?"

"Nope, but we vacationed there. My parents are some of those rich Jews I told you about." He smiled. "We lived in New York City and had a summer home a couple hundred miles northwest."

Zohar smiled. “My parents also had such a place, but it was along a river in very many trees. I loved it there. It felt safe until . . . until the Nazis came.”

“Was that when you were sent to the camps?” Wally asked as he unwrapped a package of Gouda cheese.

“Yes. What did your father do for a living?” she asked.

“Dad was in the diamond business until he died a few years ago. My brothers run it now, even though the will named me as a partner and I get a paycheck on profits now and again. Yours?”

“He had his own clothing factory. Men’s shoes, umbrellas, woolen overcoats, and other things. It was another reason we were targeted. The Nazis needed such places to fill their endless need for military uniforms.” A sad sort of bitterness in her voice prompted Wally to change the subject.

“I talked to Ezer Weizman about putting you to work. He says you have to join the Haganah. Maybe you should look at other options,” he said as he sliced the cheese.

“Too late.” She gave a nervous smile.

Wally looked up, his knife stopping in midair. He finished cutting through the cheese. “You joined up today?”

“Yes, it is what I want to do.”

“Do all of Hannah’s adopted sisters come with a . . . a tough stubborn streak?” he asked.

“Yes, I suppose we do. Does it bother you?”

He wiped his hands on a cloth. “Nah, but I don’t like the idea of you packing a rifle while some Arab draws a bead on you.”

She chuckled. “I’m flattered. Actually, they told me I’d have to be in the army to apply with the IAF, and when I told them that I’d like to be assigned with your outfit, they gave me immediate orders. I start in the morning.”

Wally grinned. He could not be more pleased. “Maybe you can straighten out the mess in Weizman’s office.”

"I wish to take training in weapons as well. If some Arab draws a bead on me, as you say, I wish to know how to shoot back," she said. "I'll set the table. Dishes, where are they?"

He pointed to a small cupboard as he set the cheese plate in the middle of the coffee-table crate. "Sorry I don't have a table and chairs yet."

"This is quite comfortable," she said, removing the plates and cups. A few moments later they were ready to eat.

"It isn't much, but it beats the Hayarkon Hotel hands down. Tonight I'll get some sleep," Wally smiled. "Sorry I can't cook you a steak or something, but that kind of food is rare around here right now."

"This is better than I have seen for some time. Thank you." They sat side by side on the couch, and Wally handed her a fruit plate with slices of oranges and apples. They each added cheese, bread, and butter, then Wally poured their cups half full of a cheap red wine he had purchased from one of the other pilots.

"So tell me about your experience in Italy," Wally said. He took a sip of wine.

"There isn't much to tell. I taught at one of the DP camps. The children who had survived the Nazis needed education very badly, and I seem to have a knack for it. I taught ages six through ten basic Jewish and world history, Hebrew language, and writing. We also spent a lot of time on current events, especially those dealing with Hitler's regime and what was happening here."

"And when you weren't teaching?"

"I helped the underground smuggle our people aboard ships along the Italian coast. It was very hard to put them aboard knowing most would end up interred on Cyprus, but we had to keep trying. There were so many." She took a bite of an apple section and chewed before speaking again. "At first, it was very difficult for me. I was rather timid until I met Hannah, and even then I lacked a good deal of self-confidence, but they needed help, and I just made up my mind I was going to do it. I became a good smuggler actually, and I am not so timid as I once was. If I were, we wouldn't be eating this meal together right now."

"Then I am grateful for smuggling." He sipped his wine.

"I went by the Hayarkon. You were right. It is chaos there. All the foreigners gather there to drink and smoke very large cigars or awful-smelling cigarettes, and I have never seen so many women just hanging around as if waiting for something. I told one of them she ought to join the army if she had nothing better to do."

Wally laughed. "I'll bet that went over well."

"She swore at me in Hebrew. What are they waiting for?"

"A date. A night with an American pilot or GI. They're call girls, Zohar. They make their living hanging around such places."

Zohar was visibly shocked. "Here, in Israel? Why, that can't be. Jews selling themselves? I don't believe you."

He smiled softly. "No, I don't suppose you do. What else did you see today?" he asked, changing the subject.

"I went down to the docks. Refugee ships were coming in just like in Haifa. The one I saw carried refugees from Egypt. It seems they are being driven from their homes too."

"Unless we lose the war, there will be more of them," Wally said. "Many more."

"They are very different from Europeans. The differences frustrated the Europeans Jews checking them through."

"One of the challenges of gathering," Wally said. "Arab Jews, European Jews, Jewish Zionists, Jewish secularists, Jewish communists, all with their own grand ideas of how this new state ought to look and how it ought to be run. Throw together a hundred or so different cultures, and you have what Ephraim liked to call 'the gathering.' It will be a miracle to bring the millions who may want to come, but an even greater miracle to keep them from killing each other once they're here."

"Do you know much of Ephraim's religion?"

"Enough to know that if I wouldn't be banished by my own family, I would probably join. Their doctrines about life and death are very intriguing and comforting. I like the idea of having living prophets around as well. Why do you ask?"

"Have you read his book?"

"Yeah, more than once. I just can't bring myself to believe that an angel delivered it to a fourteen-year-old kid living in New York State."

"God should have picked a Jewish rabbi then? Is that it?"

"Nah. The rabbis I know are too steeped in tradition and the belief that the Mishnah and the Talmud are the way God talks to men. If God showed up in person, they'd die of fright."

Zohar laughed. "Yes, I think you are right. I know a few of them myself." About to take a sip, she heard the thud of a nearby bomb, then another and another. The room shuddered, and she gripped her cup with both hands. "That felt very close," she said, a bit nervous.

"Umm." Wally's brow wrinkled as he listened. "South far enough you shouldn't worry." He ate a piece of cheese slowly, the wrinkle to his brow remaining. He had gone to the airport to check on the flying schedule for tomorrow and was told that SHAI was reporting that the Egyptians would be sending bombers to hit Tel Aviv. Because he had heard that the Egyptian air force only had a few useable bombers and fighters—and even fewer qualified pilots—he hadn't taken the report seriously. Maybe he should have.

"Your face tells me you do not believe your own words," she said.

"That easy to read, huh?"

Zohar smiled until another bomb exploded, this time close enough to rumble the ground and shake the room. Wally stood and offered his hand. "Time to get to the basement."

Setting her cup on the table, she got to her feet just as another bomb struck, knocking them both off balance, plaster dropping from the ceiling.

"Get down, flat on the floor," Wally yelled. He grabbed the couch and quickly turned it upside down, telling her to slide under. Getting on the floor, he pushed up the edge and pushed himself next to her just as several more bombs struck around their building, blowing out the windows and collapsing part of the ceiling. He heard the roar, the sound of things shattering and falling all around them. Then it was over.

Wally felt the warmth of her pressed against him, felt her breath against his neck and cheek, felt the fear in the way she clung to him. Though reluctant to move, he shoved the couch aside and scrambled to his feet in the dust-filled room. The few dishes from the cupboard lay shattered on the floor, next to the hot plate that was burning a hole in the rug. He unplugged it and turned it over, then reached down and gave Zohar a hand up. Both of them stared out the space that used to be a window at the fire- and smoke-filled darkness where chaos ensued.

"Come on. Let's see if we can help," Zohar said.

Other tenants were scrambling down the hall into the debris-strewn street. Zohar gasped when she looked back to see that the corner of the building opposite Wally's apartment was missing, smoke and flames filling the night air. Several other buildings around them were in the same condition, and the anguished cries of people needing help filled the choking air.

An unconscious woman lay on her back next to the building. Picking her up at both ends, they carried her away from the precarious ruins.

"You're stronger than you look." Wally said as they laid the woman down to check her wounds.

Zohar gave him a wry smile. "I will take that as a compliment. She has a bad cut on her leg and one on her stomach. The leg wound is bleeding badly. Hold your finger here to slow the bleeding while I find something to use as a tourniquet."

Wally applied pressure on the artery at the top of the woman's leg. "If she wakes up, she'll slap me good."

"As she should," Zohar said. "But it is necessary." She ran back toward the apartment building, and Wally watched with some apprehension as she went inside. But the woman was a warrior. Hardly the timid girl he remembered from their meeting in Berlin. Things had changed and he was glad. Israel would need warriors. The Egyptians were coming.

* * *

Zohar was glad to see that her apartment building had not been badly damaged.

"Some people have all the luck," Wally said in a tired voice but with a slight smile. As they reached the steps to the main door, Wally sat down, and she joined him.

"You look very good in streaks of soot and dust," he said with a grin.

"And you."

"Sorry, Zoe. That was a lousy first date."

She looked at him. "What did you call me?" she said softly.

"Uh, Zoe. You know, short for Zohar. If you don't . . ."

She touched his hand lightly. "No, no, it's just that I haven't heard it for a long time. Only my father used that name. I had nearly forgotten." She smiled. "As for the date, next time you should keep the entertainment less exciting." She wiped dust from her cheek.

He chuckled. "Milder entertainment. I'll remember that."

"Is your apartment safe enough to live in?" she asked.

"You forget, my place is in the fairly stable portion of the building. As such, it is inhabitable," he answered.

Zoe stood. "I begin my new job tomorrow and must rest."

Wally got up as well. "Yeah, me too. Good night, Zoe."

She started up the steps.

"Zoe."

"Yes." She turned back.

"I want to see you again."

"Then it is unanimous. Tomorrow night I cook the dinner. See you at seven."

He smiled and turned away.

"And Wally, remember what I said about the entertainment. Don't bring the Egyptians." With that, she disappeared inside.

SEE CHAPTER NOTES

CHAPTER 5

Naomi felt the reverberation of the explosion and cringed. Renewed in their lust for Jewish blood by the coming of the Arabs, Haj Amin's Holy Strugglers were launching new ground attacks from positions in the Arab, Christian, and Armenian Quarters. Naomi had watched from the walls that morning as elements of the Legion of Transjordan marched down the Mount of Olives, past Gethsemane, across the valley of Kidron, and up the slope to Stephen's Gate, giving additional support to Haj Amin's irregulars. Now their artillery was sitting atop the same mountain, blasting the entire city without mercy.

It had happened so fast. Ben-Gurion had declared the new state of Israel on May 14. The few British forces that had remained deserted the city that night and the next morning, and Jerusalem had become a free-for-all as Arab irregulars and Jewish soldiers of the Etzioni Brigade had taken various important positions in the city center and tried to hold them. Naomi's people had done well in the first two days, taking almost all the area outside the Old City walls except for villages to the east through which the Arab Legion had now come. Unfortunately, the Haganah had not been able to open a lifeline to the Jewish Quarter, nor had they been able to drive the Arabs off the road to Tel Aviv. Both the Quarter and Jewish West Jerusalem, though under Haganah control, were also under siege, and with the Legion now in the city, she and most other Jews wondered if they could hold on.

The Legion was the best trained army of the Arab countries. Led and trained by British officers, they were disciplined and well prepared to use their greatest advantage—artillery. The Haganah had no such weapons, and the punishment the Legion was inflicting could not be answered, breaking Jewish spirits as it demolished buildings and ended the lives of hundreds of valiant soldiers and innocent civilians, leaving them no choice but to hunker down, pray to God their own artillery would soon arrive by ship, and fight harder to make up for fallen comrades.

Another shell hit the Old City and shook the ground beneath Naomi, this one much too close. She finished pulling on her khaki pants and shirt on her thin body, wrapped a scarf around her short, dark hair, grabbed her rifle, and flew down the steps to the tunnels. She must rejoin Abraham.

After their marriage in Ephraim's hospital room, she had returned to work at SHAI headquarters in Tel Aviv while Abraham had come back to the Jewish Quarter to help in its defense. They had been able to meet only twice over the last few weeks, but on the second visit, she had been trapped in the Old City. The British had suddenly left, and the Arabs closed off the final and last exit at Zion Gate. Now there was no way out of the Quarter for anyone but those who surrendered, and after hearing about the massacre of more than a hundred of those who had turned over their weapons to Holy Strugglers and Jordanian troops at the Etzion Block, few in the Haganah considered that any kind of option, at least for now.

Her marriage to Abraham had been controversial at best. She was not Hasidic while Abraham was, and the Hasidic community disdained marriage outside their numbers. Worse, Abraham was also to become a rabbi, and for a future rabbi to wed a Jew who was not Hasidic was tantamount to betrayal. Only a week ago, the elders had met with Rabbi Marshak and stated that they would not accept his son as their next rabbi. It had been very disappointing for Rabbi Marshak and for Abraham, but not unexpected. The Hasids of the Quarter were controlled by Rabbi Salomon, chief rabbi of Jerusalem, a man who had been at odds with Rabbi Marshak and Abraham ever since they had openly supported the creation of a Jewish state contrary to his wishes. Rabbi Salomon did not like change and did not believe that the Arabs would turn against them if they just kept to themselves and did not cause trouble. It seemed to Naomi that Rabbi Salomon was now getting his revenge on her husband and father-in-law, and it did not sit well with her. She had threatened to give Rabbi Salomon a piece of her mind, but Abraham pleaded with her to let it be. Unfortunately, word had come to her that Rabbi Salomon intended to excommunicate Abraham from the Hasidic community. When she heard the news, she went immediately to Rabbi Salomon's home, burst in, and gave him a tongue thrashing before turning on her heel and leaving. Since then, she had not seen the arrogant fool, but her tirade had not helped. The Rabbi would proceed with excommunication before the week's end. She had made a very bad mess of her husband's life.

Abraham had been angry, but the war kept them from speaking of it, their only concern survival. But today they would talk. They must. It was eating her heart away not to make it right with him.

She loved Abraham more than she had thought possible. He was a romantic filled with passion that both his religious front and Hasidic exterior gave no hint of. She could not sleep well when they were apart, and to have him angry at her only made things worse.

Increasing her pace, Naomi quickly found Abraham on the rooftops near the southern wall. They had just driven off another attack when he saw her slipping along sandbags, rifle in hand. He forgot his exhaustion and gave her a smile.

"Shalom," she said as she threw herself down next to him, her eyes on the distant buildings just outside the Quarter's southern wall.

"Shalom. I thought you were resting."

"It is you who needs rest. You've had none for almost forty-eight hours." She remembered her scarf and wiped the sweat-caked dust from his round face and graying hair. Though premature, the gray hair gave him a dignified look she loved. She tweaked his aquiline nose. "Time for sleep."

"Soon," he replied.

"What is happening?"

"The Legion was firing at the Notre Dame Hospice, but now they fire at us. They systematically try to open the way for their ground troops. Only by the grace of God and the determination he has given our men do we keep them from gaining ground, but we can only take it so long before even God cannot give us enough strength."

"They think it will break the spirit of the civilians who remain here and frighten them into leaving. They think that driving us out of the Quarter where we have been for thousands of years will break the spirits of the entire Yishuv," she said.

"They may be right," Abraham responded.

"No, we will never give up. Never."

"You think we are comic strip supermen, but our skin does not stop bullets. If Jerusalem command does not send reinforcements, we can last only a few days. Then the Arabs will come and we will have slaughter." His comment ended abruptly as an Arab artillery shell whistled over his head and exploded behind them, making the building shudder.

Abraham shook his head in frustration, smoke and dust erupting near the Hurva, the oldest synagogue in the Quarter. "That is the fourth shell to hit near the Hurva. It is a warning. They will destroy the synagogues if we continue to fight, I am sure of it. Even now some of the rabbis plead with Russnak to surrender."

"Then they are cowards," she said.

Abraham bit his tongue lightly as he shook his head. "You do not understand them, Naomi. You should not make such judgments."

Naomi grimaced. "Yes, you are right. I'm sorry."

"They are survivors. They and their ancestors have lived and worshiped in these holy places for generations. Can you blame them for trying to save it?"

"No, of course not, but Russnak will not give in. He knows the catastrophe it would be to lose the Quarter, and for them to work against us this way . . . Well, I am sorry, but it just makes it hard to think of them as you do. Especially when they ostracize you the way they do and refuse to let you serve as rabbi."

"They do what they think best. They must. I knew what might happen when I asked you to be my wife. I accept their decision. Not just because they are men I honor, but because it doesn't matter anymore. I am happy, and I have learned that I can serve God without being a rabbi, that my life must go a different direction. It is only my father I feel bad for. He wanted me to take his place. But even if the rabbis changed their minds, I would not follow Father. I believe differently now, and I could not be a good rabbi."

She bit her lip. "I thought you were angry with me."

He smiled. "I was, but not because I couldn't be a rabbi. I was angry because you did not keep your word to me and it upset everything. You do things without talking to me, that is what makes me angry. If we had talked," he smiled, "both of us could have given Rabbi Salomon a verbal thrashing."

Naomi grinned, then kissed him firmly on the lips, causing the men all around to chuckle or clear their throats. "From now on, I will be less impetuous. No decisions without my husband."

"This I must see," murmured the man nearest them.

Naomi hit him playfully. "Quiet, Eli, or I will break your head."

"I expect you will confer with Abraham before you do," Eli said.

"On those things she can do as she pleases, especially since it is your head, Eli. Now watch the Arabs and close your ears." He smiled. "Have you seen my father and mother? And what of Mithra? Are they well?"

Hannah had asked Abraham to look after her neighbor Mithra, and Abraham's father had not been in good health for several months now. Doctor Messerman, the only doctor still in the Quarter, had examined him. He needed more hospital testing to make a diagnosis, but Rabbi Marshak refused to leave his flock, especially now when they needed him most. Abraham's parents lived only a few doors away from Hannah's apartment, but Naomi had not seen them.

"We will go and check on them now, Abraham," Naomi said. "No arguments. You need rest much worse than I do. You must come with me now."

He looked at her with admiration. His wife. Was it a dream? No, they had stood under the canopy, even though a makeshift one, said their vows, and she had become his. How he longed for peace so that he might love her more intently, more completely.

"She is right," Eli said. "They shell us now and will not attack again until night. I can handle this while you get some rest." Eliahu Esek had fought in World War II with the French underground. Eli actually had more battle-line experience than Abraham and understood this kind of warfare better than most, but having only recently arrived from the continent and knowing little of the Quarter, he was only a platoon leader.

Abraham nodded. "See to it then, Eli, but remember, withdrawal from this position would be disastrous for us. If they get past us, they can get to the very heart of the Quarter. We must keep them out, even if they turn everything around us to rubble."

Eli was obviously humored by Abraham's stating the obvious but nodded anyway.

"For this, I will not break your head," Naomi said to Eli.

"My life is complete then." Eli grinned. "Now go, both of you."

Naomi led the way, and they scrambled to the edge of the roof and down a wooden ladder to the street. Keeping to the growing afternoon shadows, they hurried to an apartment that gave them access to the tunnels. From there they found their way to the basement of one of the synagogues where many people were beginning to congregate, their homes under attack or destroyed. Abraham was immediately confronted and begged to get Russnak to surrender before everything was lost. The fear could be cut with a knife as they told of deaths, Arab gains, and the destruction by artillery. One distraught man grabbed Abraham by the shirt and spun him around.

"You Haganah must leave. We all want you to leave. None of this would have happened if you had not come. Go, before you get us all killed and the Quarter destroyed!"

Abraham gripped the man's hand and slowly but forcefully pried it loose, pushed him gently aside, then spoke to the entire room.

"The Arabs have had their hearts set on driving us out since the rebellion of Haj Amin in 1936. They see their chance now, and they will take it. You can fight for your homes, or you can sit idle and let the rest of us do it for you. The least you can do is thank those who bleed for you and pray for their souls when they give their last drop of blood." With that he turned and walked back toward the basement steps and the tunnels. Naomi quickly caught up while admiring her husband's patience.

Going into the tunnels, they looked for Mithra among those who had come there for safety. They found her sitting among a few children, playing games to distract them from the sound of the shells landing in the Quarter. She was just finishing with a round of an old children's song when Naomi and Abraham walked up.

"Are you all right, Mithra? Do you need food? Anything?"

"No, no, I am fine," Mithra said in their general direction. "I brought my blankets and some food, and I will be fine," she smiled.

Naomi had never met anyone quite like Mithra. Hardened and yet tender, blind and yet able to accomplish more in a moment than most could in an hour. The old woman had memorized the path from her apartment to this spot and could cover the distance of several blocks more quickly than most people with perfect vision.

"Very well. We'll talk to you later."

Mithra only nodded, a child crying for another song. Naomi and Abraham had one more stop before they could get some rest.

At the far end of the old Roman Cardo that had been discovered in December, they found several men carrying debris from a tunnel, hoping to soon reach Zedekiah's Cave. The cave, also known as Solomon's Quarries because some rock used to build the first temple had been taken from the cave, was under a large portion of the Old City and was purported to have openings that might be used to reinforce or escape the Quarter. Unfortunately there had been no breakthroughs in long weeks of digging.

The workers greeted her and Abraham with a simple nod of their dust-covered heads.

"Anything?" Abraham asked.

"Nothing," answered the nearest man, his voice tired and discouraged.

"The cave must not come this far west, Abraham. Either that or we are not deep enough," said another.

Abraham nodded. He stroked his side curls as he pondered what must be done. These men were needed for fighting, and to detain them with work that might lead to nothing was difficult. On the other hand, if they found the cave, it might mean salvation.

After a moment of silent waiting, he finally spoke. "Stop and get some rest. Begin again in five hours unless the battle gets much worse."

One of the men called down the tunnel and others slowly appeared. Abraham explained his decision, and the men set their tools to the side and trudged away, their shoulders slumped with exhaustion and defeat.

"Wait for me here, Naomi. I must check something." With that he took one of the lanterns and crawled into the tunnel.

"I wish to look as well," she said, following him.

He looked back for only a moment, then went forward. Next to Hannah Daniels, Naomi was the most stubborn woman he knew. If he were honest, he would admit that it was one of the things that had drawn him to her. But it was also one of the things that frustrated him at times. He expected a woman to be obedient and ask no questions. Naomi expected reasons, and when she set her heels, there was no budging her. This time he was too tired to argue.

They crawled through the dust-filled tunnel for a hundred feet before Abraham stopped. "Does it seem to you that we have turned left?" Abraham asked.

"I hadn't noticed."

Abraham nodded, then moved forward until reaching the end of the tunnel. Pulling an intricate compass from his pocket, Abraham held it in his hand and watched until the needle stood still. As usual, it pointed about halfway between north and east, but this time it seemed to be more north than it had been. "Yes, we have turned. I am sure of it. We must dig to the right."

"As we came over the last fifty feet the slope seemed to ease. Possibly you should go deeper as well," Naomi said.

He nodded while shoving his compass back in his pocket. He motioned to go back when Naomi grabbed his arm.

"Listen!" she said.

He stopped breathing and forced himself to concentrate. Nothing. "What is it?"

"Silence." She smiled. "Isn't it wonderful? No bombs, no clatter of gunfire, no screams for help and of misery. Nothing."

He smiled in the dim light of the lantern. "It has been a long time, hasn't it?"

"A good place to sleep. Nothing to shake you out of it, to keep you from really resting. Oh, how I long for such a sleep."

Another smile from Abraham. "This is not exactly a safe place to sleep, dearest wife. A shell from the Arab artillery could make this our grave."

She lay down and put her head on her arm. “So be it. I am too tired to care. Come, get some sleep.” She patted the narrow piece of ground next to her.

Abraham worked his way into the place next to her. He blew out both lanterns and snuggled in close.

“I love you, Abraham,” Naomi said.

“And I love you.” He kissed her softly on the forehead and was about to move to her lips when he sensed that she was already asleep. With a tinge of disappointment, he closed his eyes. Less than a minute later, he too was asleep.

* * *

Naomi awoke to the sound of a pick axe against stone and looked up to see Abraham at the end of the tunnel, marking the wall in the light of his lantern.

“What are you doing?” she asked, stretching.

“Leaving the men a mark to follow.”

“How long did we sleep?”

“Nearly four hours.” He lay down the pick, joining her as she sat up.

“It seems like twenty. I feel very rested.”

“A few hours of deep sleep without noise is better than twenty hours where your mind is constantly bombarded by sounds. It was a good idea to sleep here, but now we must go.” The taint of disappointment in his voice matched her feelings.

She got to her knees and blocked his way. “First we pray, then we kiss, then we go. Your rules, remember?”

He laughed lightly. “Very well.” He started the prayer as she closed her eyes and bowed her head. She had never thought she would be comfortable with prayer again, but with Abraham it had come easy. His words were backed up with a feeling that came from his heart, and in them she found his faith and leaned on it. Always she came away from his prayers stronger. As he finished, she wrapped her arms around his neck, kissing him with all the love in her heart. He responded in kind, and it was a long, tender moment before she put her head on his shoulder and held him close.

"My heart wants badly to stay here with you. I . . ."

She placed a finger on his lips. "Shh. I know." She kissed him lightly again, then turned and started out of the tunnel. Upon reaching the entrance into the Cardo, both scrambled to their feet, slapped at the dust on their clothes, and hurried toward the exit that would take them back to the streets. Dim light revealed many sleeping bodies, and the absence of bombing told them it must be morning.

Leaving the tunnels, they made a left turn and were soon at the door of his father's apartment. As they opened the door, both sensed that something was wrong and glanced furtively at one another. Turning the corner from the short hall into the bedroom, Abraham saw his father lying on the bed, Doctor Messerman and his mother sitting on either side.

"Oh!" His mother got immediately to her feet and grabbed for Abraham. "I sent for you an hour ago. Didn't they find you?" She hugged him tightly again.

"What is it, Mother?" he asked. His father was breathing evenly, but his face was very pale.

"He . . . he had a heart attack," his mother said.

"Oh no," Naomi said as she put an arm around her mother-in-law's shoulders and pulled her close.

"Doctor Messerman?" Abraham said in a soft, fearful voice. The doctor seemed to have aged ten years over the past few weeks, but his slight, angular frame continued to defy death. Abraham could only wonder how much longer a man of more than sixty years could hold on, how long any of them could.

"That is what I think, Abraham, but I told you, he must go to a hospital, and very soon. If he does not . . . well, another attack will kill him, I am afraid. You must find a way, Abraham. Today if possible."

Abraham gave a slight nod as he sat down next to his father and took his hand. There was no way out of the Quarter without surrender.

The old rabbi's eyes opened slightly, and he tried to smile. "My son," he said, squeezing Abraham's hand. "You must not believe this old son of a camel." His eyes motioned toward the doctor. "I will be all right. I . . . I just need to sleep, that is all. You have . . . more important things to do than worry about an old rabbi with indigestion. A cup of comfrey tea, Mother, that is what I need. Just a little tea." His eyes closed and his head slipped ever so slightly to one side, then he forced it back, his eyes open again. He reached up and grabbed Abraham's arm. "Rabbi Salomon was here this morning. They have decided to seek surrender. Don't you think it is time, my son? The synagogues. We must save the synagogues. They are all we have." He paused to catch his breath, and Doctor Messerman motioned him to quiet down, concern etched in the wrinkles of his face.

Abraham anguished. His father had been one of only a few rabbis who had supported a new government and a new state, and the fight it might take to get them. Now even he was losing heart, and Abraham didn't know what to do. Was this worth destroying the Hurva, one of the world's oldest synagogues? And the Stamboli. Could it ever be replaced? The thought of losing such places made him sick at heart, but if they surrendered, wouldn't it end the same? He didn't know anymore. He just didn't know. But one thing was sure, he could not upset his father again.

"I will talk to Russnak. I will do what I can to save them."

His father forced a slight smile and patted his son's hand. "There is a time for war, my son, but there is also a time for peace. I will let you decide which of these we have come to. If we must fight longer, if there is still hope of winning . . . you decide. I trust you." He grimaced, and Doctor Messerman intervened.

"Enough," he said softly but firmly. He pulled Abraham into the hall, and Naomi followed. "He must rest, and you must go. But I tell you this. If you do not get him to the hospital soon, he will die. Do you hear me?"

"There is no hospital, Doctor, at least none we can get to," Abraham said with some frustration. "The last word we had, the Arabs have cut Hadassah off to us."

Doctor Messerman's face fell as he nodded. "Then I will do what I can, but this is very serious. Comfrey tea will not fix this one."

"Let me know if he gets worse. I must try to be here when . . . if . . ."

The doctor nodded. "You should consider talking to Russnak about surrender, not just because of your father, but because if you don't and the Arabs overrun the Quarter, they will butcher all of us, including the rabbis. Do not forget that as stubborn and mean-spirited as they might be at times, they are as much a part of Jewish life as synagogues or even the Torah. You cannot let them die here."

Abraham nodded, and he and Naomi both left the apartment feeling very tired again.

"He is right," Naomi said. "As much grief as our rabbis have caused you and me, as stubborn and high-minded as they are, they must survive this."

"Yes, and that is why we fight as hard as we do." He paused. "Russnak and I have discussed trying to get them out. Now we will discuss it again." He turned to her. "For now, I must find a way to get Father out, and you will have to go with them. They cannot survive alone."

She started to shake her head, but he grabbed her arms with firm hands. "Naomi, they cannot survive without your help."

Her head went to his chest, and she gripped him tight. He was right, and she hated it. He kissed her on the forehead. "Now go back and take care of them. I will come as soon as I can." With that he left her standing in the street, and she watched him until he disappeared. She would see to her in-laws' safety, but she would not go with them. Her place was with Abraham, and that was where she would stay.

SEE CHAPTER NOTES

CHAPTER 6

Mary awoke with a start, the sun below the eastern hills but turning the heavens quickly to a light blue. Sitting up, she looked for some sign of Ahmed but found none. Where was he? Why hadn't he returned? Fear turned her mouth dry even as she told herself it did not matter. She could get to Jerusalem on her own if she had to.

Mary busied herself folding blankets and had them packed in Ahmed's acquired bag when Saad mumbled at her through his swollen lips.

"What is it, Saad?"

"We wish to go with you." He struggled to his feet, using the tree for support. He glanced over Mary's shoulder at something, and she turned to see Ahmed standing near a large stone a few feet away. She couldn't help grinning even as Ahmed gave Saad the once-over.

"It is a long walk, very hard for you as well as your wife," Ahmed said. He glanced at Rifa who had been rolling up their beds and handing them to Emile for packing. Emile got to his feet and stood by his father.

"I will help him, but we go to Haifa, with or without your help," Emile said.

"A fiery one. Looking for a fight, are you?" Ahmed tossed his rifle at Emile who miscalculated its weight and dropped it to the ground. Red faced with anger, he picked it up and lifted the barrel as if to aim it at Ahmed.

"A bullet. Inject a bullet. You can't shoot anyone without a bullet," Ahmed said. "And the safety. Take the safety off."

Emile eyed the rifle, troubled with the sudden realization that he hadn't any idea what to do with it. He glanced at his father as if to ask for help, then thought better of it and looked harshly at Ahmed, who jerked the rifle from his grip in one quick move, swung it around in an easy motion, injected a shell, and flipped off the safety, then turned the barrel toward Emile.

"Boy, if you want to kill Jews, that's your business. But you had better be ready for it, because all of them I know will fight back, and they will drop you before you can blink. Do you understand?"

Emile gestured with a reluctant nod. As Ahmed lowered the barrel, Mary noted that Rifa, her face pale, started breathing again, while Saad seemed pleased with Ahmed's handling of his son.

Ahmed looked at Saad. "For one hundred pounds I will take you."

"It is a lot, but I agree."

"A lot?" Mary said. "This thief made me pay the same, and I am only one."

"But we traveled much farther." Ahmed smiled.

Rifa handed each of them slices of dried fruit and meat. "I will need time to make packs for our things."

"We have no time. The Arabs are moving this way from Galilee, and more Jews come from Haifa. Take only what you can carry comfortably, blankets, and food for two days."

They hurriedly packed the necessities, leaving the extra with a family of refugees traveling along the road. As they passed the car, Saad took one last, long look before stiffening his back and quickening his limping pace to keep up with Ahmed.

The road was dusty, but traffic moving north was much lighter. Though they saw no soldiers, the surreal sounds of war seemed closer today, most of it coming from south and east of the road, a constant reminder to keep moving. By noon, the noise tapered off, and Mary, her nerves a bit frayed, gave quiet thanks.

They ate a brief lunch of more dried meat and fruit at noon, then climbed to higher ground after Ahmed spied a line of military vehicles heading north. It was late in the afternoon before they arrived at a spot below Ahmed's village a few miles from Mount Meron in the Upper Galilee.

Peaceful, even serene, the village sat on the slopes of a rocky, grass-scattered hill and faced north. Some of its small houses jutted out from the natural fall of the ground, their outer edges suspended on pillars.

"It is too quiet," Ahmed said. He was right—there was no sign of man or animal.

"You will wait here," Ahmed said, a concerned look on his face.

Mary and the others watched him climb the narrow dirt road. He called out several names without receiving answers, not even the bleating of goats or sheep. He disappeared behind the homes, then returned to view a few moments later. He waved for them to join him, and as he disappeared behind the buildings again, Mary led the others up the road. As they entered the single east-west road of the village, Ahmed stepped from one of the homes and joined them.

"There is the stench of treachery here," he said. He motioned for them to stay put while he walked to the far end of the village, his rifle barrel swinging left to right as they passed each hut. Mary saw that the village was a poor one, the small houses and courtyards made of mud brick covered with plaster of the same material and whitewashed. The white had turned various shades of brown from the saturation of dirt from the bricks.

"This place gives me a bad feeling in my stomach," Saad said.

"We must leave here," Rifa added. "Whoever did this may return."

"This is his home, and a brother and his family lived here. When he is ready, we will go," Mary answered.

It was another twenty minutes—even Mary was getting nervous—before Ahmed walked back to them. "They have been taken prisoner. Some blood was shed, but most survived, their tracks leading south. They are under military guard."

"The Jews did this," Emile said stiffly. "They have taken a whole village hostage!"

"We go," Ahmed said.

"Go? Go where?" Rifa asked. "Where can we be safe from such things? If they will do it here, maybe they have done it in Haifa. Oh, have we made another mistake?" Her lip quivered, and Saad tightened his grip around her shoulders.

"It is not the same in Haifa. You will be safe there," Ahmed said. He walked back through the village, the others eagerly following. Haifa could not be more than twenty or thirty miles now. They could travel another five tonight, then the rest in the morning. Along with the depressing spirit of the village, the thought of reaching Haifa gave Mary new incentive.

Within thirty minutes, military vehicles appeared in the distance, prompting them to leave the road and travel cross country through rocky pasture and cut grain fields. Mount Meron stood to the left, the last rays of the sun dancing across its rim.

They stopped to rest, and Ahmed and Mary watched three trucks passing through the valley.

"Jewish or Arab?" she asked.

"Arab. All military movement goes south. A battle is forming and may be the reason my village was forced to evacuate."

"But by which side?"

Ahmed did not answer the question, his demeanor and granite jaw giving Mary the impression of a man determined to avenge some injustice. "We must find a place to stay the night." He was on his way before she could ask further questions, and Mary was so tired all she could do was try to keep up. At dark, Ahmed changed directions and went east until, in the light of a half-moon and bright stars, Mary saw the remains of an ancient ruin.

Too tired to ask what it was, Mary followed Ahmed over stones from a fallen wall and inside the ruins. He led them through the rock-strewn ruins until they were between the half walls of buildings on both sides of what seemed to be an ancient street. From there, they turned left into an open space surrounded by high stone walls.

"We will stay here. No fire. There are both Arab and Jewish troops close by. We do not want their company." He handed each of them food from his bag and told them to eat.

They chewed their food without relishing it.

"I wish I knew what it is really like in Haifa," Rifa said, "how safe it is."

"Haifa is a captured city, under martial law. If there was looting, it is finished now or has been stopped by the Jews. But do not expect it to be the same as it was. It will never be the same. People left. Others will come and take their homes. You are wise to return and make your claim now because later it will be difficult," Ahmed said.

"All our people should be allowed to return," Emile said firmly.

"Would you let the Jews return if they left?" Ahmed asked.

Emile glared at Ahmed. "Anyone who does not fight a Jew who steals his home is a traitor. I will not stop fighting until all Jews are dead and buried."

Ahmed chewed, mulling over an answer. "You are a fool if you think you can conquer the Jews with guns and tanks. They are smart, educated, and know how to get money and make good use of it. Arabs sit around and talk. If you could beat the Jews with words, we would have won a long time ago. But words do not conquer land. They do not buy bullets and weapons. When it comes to education, too many Arabs cannot even read and write, and most listen only to their own tribal leaders. This makes it impossible for them to work together, to organize like the Jews. They each do their own thing, and if they get tired or afraid or if they don't see any profit from looting, they leave and go home. Such rabble can never defeat the Jews." He seemed to be listening to something, then went on. "You say you will fight for Haj Amin. What will it get you? Your home back? Then what? I tell you what. He will take you and put you in his army, and he will march you to Amman or Beirut to fight other Arabs who he considers his enemies. The Mufti will not be happy until he has conquered all Arabs and put them under his heel. He learned from Hitler. Hitler is his idol, and like Hitler, he will butcher anyone who disagrees with him."

"You lie!" Emile said.

"In 1937 my people refused to fight with your Mufti against the British and the Jews. He sent his men to our village and attacked us. We drove him away, but many of our people died." He leaned toward Emile. "Your Mufti butchered my wife. Do not call me a liar. I know the heart of Haj Amin. He is our enemy. I do not love the Jews—I fear what they will do to our people—but I fear Haj Amin even more. He is brutal. And though the Jews might drive us from the land, they do not slaughter us like cattle."

Emile stood, his fists clenched tightly, his face rock hard. "You are wrong. It was not the Mufti who . . . who did those things. Others . . ." He straightened his neck. "The Mufti gathers a great army. They have come to free us, and we will fight with them until the Jews are driven into the sea."

"You speak like a fool," Ahmed said, standing. He left, disappearing among the ruins.

Pulling more bread and cheese from their bag, Mary followed, leaving Emile fuming. She heard Emile begin to denounce his father for not defending the Mufti and had no desire to stay and listen to his ridiculous, unbending words.

Ahmed was watching the valley from the highest part of the ruins, a place where he could see but not be seen. She handed him the largest half of the bread and cheese, then sat on one of the large, square stones below him. It was ten minutes before either of them spoke.

"Islam was meant for a man and his god. Men like the Mufti have turned it into a den of thieves and blood mongers," Ahmed said.

"You did not tell us everything you saw back at your village," Mary said. "You know who drove them out, don't you?"

He did not answer immediately, his eyes and thoughts focused on the distant fires of a large camp. "Do you remember the story I told you about the Kibbutz Allonim?"

"Yes, I remember. Ali and his daughter, Kalifa . . ."

"The kibbutz is just a mile to the east of us, in the next valley. It is a safe place—well defended and hard to conquer. No matter who else may turn against my village, the people of this kibbutz can be trusted. It is a good place to go if trouble should come, whether from Jews or Arabs. Now, go. Sleep. You still have many miles before reaching Haifa."

Though a bit unsettled by the remark, Mary picked her way through the scattered stones of the wall to find her bed. She found Saad and his family already asleep, and she quickly spread her own blankets and climbed between them. Though exhausted, she could not sleep and was soon looking for a place to pray in private. By the dim moonlight, Mary wandered through the ruins until she found a quiet spot near where she had left Ahmed. Kneeling, she once more poured out her heart about Aaron and asked for comfort, and, as usual, her spirit was calmed. When finished, she returned by the same path to find Ahmed still vigilant atop the wall. Returning to her blankets, she snuggled down and listened to the quiet of her fourth night since leaving Beirut. It was warm but calm with no sound of gunfire. This time she quickly succumbed to a heavy sleep. Unfortunately, it lasted only a few hours.

SEE CHAPTER NOTES

CHAPTER 7

Mary was instantly awake at the sound of men's voices. Tossing aside her blanket, she crawled across the dusty ground and shook Saad. He jerked awake and would have shouted had she not clamped a hand over his mouth.

"Wake Rifa. There are others here," she whispered.

He bolted upright and woke Rifa while Mary searched where she thought Emile had made his bed. He was already sitting up, about to speak when she hushed him. They all sat silently, except Rifa who sobbed noisily. Saad hugged her close to comfort her. The voices drew closer.

"They are Arab," Emile whispered. "Surely they will not . . ."

"Quiet! You don't know that just because they speak Arabic," Mary said in the lowest of harsh whispers.

She saw a shadow pass by the entrance to the place where they were hidden and flattened herself against the wall, but Emile jumped to his feet and spoke out before Mary could stop him.

"Hey! We are here," Emile called in clear, loud Arabic.

"No!" Saad jumped to his feet too late. Several armed men appeared both in the entrance and atop the wall, and a flash of a light hit Mary in the eyes. She scrambled for her headscarf and covered her face. Two men shoved Emile against a wall while another commanded the rest of them to get to their feet.

Mary obeyed, averting her eyes even in the darkness, unsure of who was confronting them.

"Who are you, and what are you doing here?" a voice commanded from the doorway.

"We are refugees. We return to Haifa to fight the Jews," Emile said angrily. "Why do you treat us like this? We are not the enemy."

A rifle barrel was shoved into the small of his back, giving him cause to draw closer to the wall. "Do not speak," said the voice.

"Leave the boy alone," Mary said.

A swift slap was her answer. It jerked her head to the right, knocking her off balance, her head spinning. The assailant shoved her against the wall and placed his body against hers, the heat of his breath against her face. The horrible smell made her want to wretch, but she remained still, her hand carefully moving toward the pocket holding the dagger Ahmed had given her.

"Leave the woman alone," the voice from the doorway said. He spoke Hebrew this time. "There will be none of that under my command."

Mary pushed the man back, her fingers tightly grasping the hilt of the dagger in her pocket. If he touched her again she would use it.

"You . . . earlier you spoke Arabic. I do not understand . . . Who are you, and what do you want?" Saad asked.

Several of the men chuckled, but the man at the door silenced them when he stepped into the room. "You heard only the words of our scout. He is a bedouin, but we are Haganah. I need your papers."

Mary wanted to breathe easier but could not. These might be Jews, but there was something about them, something she did not like. She pulled her papers from a pocket and extended them while Saad retrieved those of his family from his jacket. The officer used his light to look over the papers. "These are not in order. You will come with us." He turned and left the room. Mary thought to protest but reconsidered as the foul-breathed rogue eyed her. She grabbed her blankets from the floor and followed the officer, with Saad, Emile, and Rifa behind her.

"Jews. Just as I thought. I spit—"

"Be quiet, Emile. Haven't you done enough damage already?" his father reacted.

Emile's face hardened, but he clamped his jaw shut.

Mary glanced up at the wall where Ahmed had been and wondered where he was, why he hadn't warned them.

"Move," a soldier said, shoving her gently.

They were led to several trucks and a jeep outside the ruins. Told to get into the truck, Mary waited a moment, then darted away to the officer, just climbing into his jeep.

"What is the meaning of this? Those papers are in perfect order, and you know it. You have no right . . ."

"Tonight someone attacked our camp and killed four of my men. You will come with us and answer our questions, and you will do it without argument," he said. One of the soldiers grabbed her arm and pushed her toward the trucks as a young bedu came out of the darkness and hopped into the back of the jeep. The officer signaled for his driver to go as Mary was manhandled into the back of the first truck with the others. She now knew where Ahmed had been—and why. These were the men who had taken his people captive, and Ahmed had gone to help them. From the sound of it, things had not gone well. Obviously Jewish opinion of the bedouin had changed.

As the trucks pulled out, she thought of Ahmed's reminder about the Kibbutz Allonim. Even then he knew it had been Jews who had driven his people out of Sahalia. Only those at Allonim could be trusted.

The army camp they pulled into at sunup was spread out at the foot of the northwest side of the Horn of Hittin. As they drove through a hastily erected gate, the smell of camels, horses, cows, and donkeys crowded together inside a makeshift corral at the northern end of the camp mingled with the scent of burning fires and cool morning air. Mary noticed a bedu Saluki lying in the dirt near the corral. The greyhoundlike hunting dog rose to his paws, his thin, agile body stretching as they passed by. His eyes watched the truck until they were well past, then he settled back again, laying his head on his paws.

As the truck stopped, then honked at several soldiers crossing the road, Mary noted an area where dozens of bedouin tents were pitched behind a second fence and guarded by fully armed soldiers in a variety of uniforms and clothing. Hundreds of people were lying or sitting in makeshift shelters of canvas, blankets, or animal skins, their possessions stacked about them. There were far too many to have come just from Ahmed's small village, but most were bedu.

As they came to a stop, Mary and the others climbed from the truck. She saw the officer who had given orders to bring them here a few feet away and approached him.

"Why have you brought us here?"

He looked her way only briefly, then turned and went into a tent, dropping the flap behind him. The bedu who had jumped into the back of his jeep at the place they were captured approached, eyeing Mary coldly. Like Ahmed, his build was wiry with an aquiline nose and rounded jaw covered with a full beard attached to a moustache. Mary, usually unwilling to bend to such men, listened to her inner voice this time and kept quiet, though she did not avert her eyes.

"I am Mahmoud Dajani, a bedu scout of the Zeidan tribe. I followed tracks to your place of hiding. They are the tracks of a man who killed one of my people and three men of the Haganah. He is bedu, this much I know. You will tell me his name so that I may know my enemy and deal with him."

Mary smiled. "A bedu scout worth his salt would not need help to find an enemy."

His eyes flashed with anger, and he drew his dagger from its scabbard and placed it at her throat before she realized what was happening. "Possibly your life is worth this information."

Mary's own hand crept into her pocket and wrapped around the hilt of her own knife.

"Speak, or I will cut—"

"His name was Ahmed."

Mary glared at Saad, who stood a few feet away. "No, Saad. He won't kill a woman. Not here, in front of his Jewish keepers."

"My Jewish keepers, as you call them, kill Arabs like you every day. They will be glad to have another out of their way," Mahmoud said coldly. The knife dug into her flesh, bringing a few drops of blood. "Speak to me," he said to Saad, "or this woman will die."

"Ahmed is of the Nasariyah. He brought this woman from Lebanon and agreed to return us to Haifa if we paid him. When we arrived at his village, he found it deserted and his people gone. He disappeared during the night. We have no idea where he went," Saad said.

He shoved Mary away and put his knife away as quickly as he had drawn it. "I know him. He is a friend of some of the Jews in these parts, but it will do him no good now. As you see, the Jews have decided his people and many other bedu are their enemies and send them away to Transjordan and Lebanon."

"But you betray our people. You fight for the Jews. You are a traitor to our people and to Allah. For this you should die a most awful death," Emile said angrily.

Mahmoud's hand went to his dagger again. "Close your mouth, boy, or I will cut out your tongue. I am Zeidan. These are Nasariyah and al Heib," he waved toward the captives. "Our enemies. To be rid of them is the will of Allah and will bring much wealth to my people."

"Mahmoud, leave them alone. Guards, take these people to the holding area." Mary looked over her shoulder to see the Jewish officer who had ordered them taken prisoner turn and go back to his tent.

Mahmoud nodded for the guards to take them, and they were nudged at gunpoint toward the holding area while Mahmoud walked away.

"You will find the old muhktar in the center tent." The soldier with the bad breath smiled, revealing his decaying teeth, yellowed with tobacco stains. "Get acquainted. You will be here for a few days before going east to Transjordan."

"Transjordan? But we are from Haifa. We are not bedu and no threat. We must go to Haifa," Rifa said.

"Haifa is Jewish now," he said coldly. "We want no Arabs there. Maybe I will get your home for my work, run your shop, and eat your food, but we will never let you return. Forget you ever lived there." He turned to Mary and reached out as if to pet her head. "Maybe I could make an exception for you. I need a woman with a pretty face to cook my meals and wash my clothes."

Mary stepped away. "Touch me, and I will rip your eyes out."

The soldier's face turned angry, then he grinned and gave a nervous laugh for the benefit of the other guards. "We shall see, little princess. We shall see. After dark . . . though you cannot come and go, we can. We take what we want . . ."

"You may think to come," Saad said, "but if I see you or any of your friends near these women, I swear I will tear you apart with my bare hands." He took Rifa and Mary by the arm and guided them past the guards and into the camp. This time the guard with the decaying teeth did not smile.

"Thank you, Saad," Mary said.

"A little late, Father," Emile said coldly. "If you had stood against—"

"If you had kept quiet, we would not be in this mess," Saad said to Emile. Emile moved ahead of them, anger in his red face.

"Emile, please," Rifa begged. He disappeared between tents as they entered the holding area.

"Let him be," Saad said stiffly.

"We have to get out of here, Saad, and we have to do it soon. If they send us to Transjordan, we will never get back to our homes. Do you understand?" Mary asked.

"But the guards," Rifa said anxiously.

"We will find a way," Mary said. "We must."

"Salaam."

Mary looked up to see a tall man with a gray beard and gray hair, dressed in a tan *aba* held closed at his waist by a fancy gold-buckled belt. The empty scabbard of his short dagger hung loosely from it.

"Salaam," Saad said. Rifa grabbed the scarf from her neck and covered her face, while Mary left hers where it was. She was tired, sick to her stomach, and frustrated with bowing to hopeless traditions. "We look for the muhktar of the Nasariyah. His name is Farouk," Saad said.

The man bowed. "I am Farouk. Though Ahmed hoped you would not be discovered, he said it was possible." He smiled. "Come, my tent is yours."

They walked through the camp, passing other bedu beginning their day as best as they could by starting cooking fires, shaking out their bedding, and hanging it up over rope lines to air out in the sun. Children sat on carpets or in the dirt playing with small stick figures or doing battle with wooden swords.

"When did you see Ahmed?" Mary asked.

"He came here last night. He spoke to me and promised he would see us free again. Unfortunately, he was seen leaving the camp and had to fight. The soldiers say he was wounded. For this reason he may not return."

"Then his village was brought here," Mary said.

"All the Nasariyah are here. Some have been sent to Transjordan already, but most remain. Other tribes have been brought here as well."

"But I do not see many of your young men."

"Most escaped before coming here. Ahmed was going to find them, bring them back. I pray he is still alive and able."

"Ahmed spoke of the friendship between the Nasariyah and the Jews. This seems to have changed," Mary said.

"My people fought with the Jews against Haj Amin and his people during the rebellion. Our position cost us many friends among the bedu who saw us as traitors, but we received promises of lasting friendship from Ben-Gurion and others. Unfortunately, the Zeidan have accused us of massacring a small Jewish village, and the Jews believe them. This commander sent soldiers to our villages. If we had resisted, we would have been butchered."

"Do you know who did attack the Jewish village?" Saad asked.

"Of course. It was the Zeidan." He stopped to let some children kicking a ball pass in front of them. "The Zeidan have always been our enemies. They have wanted our land for generations. Their sheik is the father of Mahmoud and a shrewd man. He plays both sides and takes his advantage where he can. He knows the Jews will send us to Transjordan now, along with many other bedu tribes. If the Zeidan are careful, they will get our villages from the Jews, and the Jews will trust them. Then, if the Arabs start to win, they are in a position to betray the Jews and gain friends among the Arabs." He smiled. "They cannot lose."

They started walking again.

"You do not seem concerned," Mary said.

Farouk shrugged. "In the rebellion, I played a similar game with the Arabs, using the Zeidan as my pawn. The Zeidan escaped to Jordan before they could be captured, returning only a few months ago. They seek revenge, as I would if things were reversed. I cannot blame the Zeidan for what they do. I can only try to change it. If I do, they will lose. If I do not, my people will suffer. It has always been the way of the bedu." Another smile. "I am not so easily beaten."

"They know it was Ahmed who killed their soldiers," Saad said. "I . . . Mahmoud threatened Mary."

"Yes, I saw. They will come for me soon, question me further, but I will return. Even Colonel Yifta and his Zeidan devils will not dare to harm a sheik of my stature." He smiled warmly. "But never mind. Ahmed said that if you were caught, we should accept you under the bond of salt." He bowed slightly. "We will protect you with our very lives." He grasped his scabbard while giving a wry smile. "Though under present conditions it will not be easy."

Mary was honored. Among the bedu, the bond of salt bound an entire tribe to take care of those put under it, even if an enemy.

They reached Farouk's tent and were ushered inside where an older woman waited. Farouk and Saad disappeared through the *sahah* or cloth screen that divided the men's quarters from those of the women. The woman removed a coffee pot from the dirt at the corner of the fire and placed it in the coals, then busied herself with food preparations. She was short but stout, her *jilbab* of traditional black and covered with a *thob* or second dress. The *thob* was embroidered beautifully around the neck and hem, and the designs matched those of the headdress she wore. Unlike bedu of the Arabian desert, she wore no mask—either in private or public—only a headscarf like that of Mary and Rifa that would cover the lower portion of her face when needed. Her wrinkled and sun-darkened face showed years of life among the wandering bedu of the northern Galilee.

Watching their hostess place a thin sheet of dough over the curved iron skillet made Mary's mouth salivate. She had tasted such bread—delicious compared to the stale loaves she and Ahmed had shared.

"Farouk did not say how many of your people were injured in this travesty," Mary said to the woman.

"Two of our young men died in Sahalia, four in the village of Farouk. Half a dozen were injured badly, others with scrapes and bruises from rough treatment." She turned the thin bread over. "Farouk will make them pay for this, especially the Zeidan who tell lies against us and causes our friends to become enemies." She cooked several pieces of bread and took them, the pot of coffee, and a plate of sliced goat's cheese through the *sahah* to the men's quarters. She returned a moment later with the coffee pot. She squatted down and began cooking more bread.

"Your tribe has its own land?" Rifa asked.

"Many tribes are squatters. We are not. Some sit on land they sold to the Jews then refused to leave. The Jews could not push them off the land because the British protected them, but when the British left, the Jews took what belonged to them. Now those tribes want it back and make deals to fight with the Jews who say they will give it to them when their enemies are defeated." She shrugged. "It was all right until this trickery by the Zeidan. They know that if they turn the Jews against us, we will have no friends and must leave the country. But Farouk will find a way. He has always found a way. We still have friends among the Jews, and if Ahmed survived last night's battle, he will bring them here to help us." She handed Mary the first piece of bread. It was warm, soft, and easily torn in two so that Rifa could have half. As Mary expected, it tasted wonderful.

"When did you get ownership of your own land? Few bedu have such wealth."

"Over many years we worked very hard to buy it from our landlords who live in Damascus. We live peacefully with our Jewish neighbors and have unwritten agreements with the local Jews not to fight with or steal from one another and to protect one another from other bedu. Now this has changed." She stood and picked up a large jar after handing them each another piece of bread. "I go to try and find water. Sleep. I promise you will need your strength very soon." With that she left.

Mary found a comfortable spot on the carpets and cushions and lay down. She was about to doze off when Saad came through the *sahah* and sat down near the fire pit. Rifa was already asleep. Mary sat up, anxious to hear what he and Farouk had discussed.

"They have something planned, but he is not willing to share it with me yet. Patience, Mary, we will get out." He paused, thinking before going on. "There are thirty-five, maybe forty thousand bedu in this region. Though the Nazariyah are one of the smallest tribes, Farouk has great influence with others who have their own land or who have not committed to fight because of their feelings about Haj Amin. He was allied with the Jews. To have them turn on him like this may send him into Arab arms. I am not so sure that this is all bad."

Mary sensed his waffling. He was Arab. To have other Arabs, especially the bedu, fight with the Jews could not be good for Arabs.

"Farouk is our way to Haifa, Saad. I remind you again, if we stay here, we will never return to our homes."

Saad sighed. "I am not so sure returning is right anymore," his voice sounded very tired. "For years, Jew and Arab lived side by side in Haifa. We shared many things with one another. Weddings, circumcision ceremonies, business. We were friends. Then the fighting broke out and we could no longer stand one another." There was a piece of bread on a plate near his hand, and he picked it up and absentmindedly nibbled at its edge. "It is hard to understand how it all happened. The Jews quickly defeated the irregulars and elements of the Iraqi and Syrian armies, drove them right out of the city. They gave us fair surrender terms, but our leaders refused them and insisted that we leave even though the Jews begged us otherwise. They said we must stay. We could live in our homes, go to our jobs, everything." He sighed. "And yet our leaders said we must leave. I questioned one of them, a man I know well. He said they could not surrender because they feared Haj Amin and his supporters. To sign their names to a document saying they had given up would mark them as traitors. For this, he would have them killed."

"They were remembering that Haj Amin had butchered such people," Mary said. "You cannot blame them."

"Yes, I know. His reminder helped Rifa and me decide that evacuating would be safer than staying, and there was the promise of the British to safeguard our exit if we wanted to leave. Of course, that was when they were still present in Haifa. Now they are gone. Who will protect us against the Jews if we go back? This is my concern, especially now, when I see what these Jews do to us, even though we are innocent of any wrongdoing. They do not want us around anymore, Mary. Why go back and live among people who feel that way?"

"Ahmed told you, things are different now. The Jews have control of the looting, the people who might harm you," Mary said.

He shrugged. "This may be, but for how long? The Jews have had time to think, to remember. Now some are angry and want vengeance."

Mary knew what he meant. In the past there had been riots in which Jewish sections of cities like Haifa and Jerusalem had been attacked by Arabs. Looting, beatings, and even killings took place. The riot in which she had nearly been killed at Jerusalem back in November, and where she met Aaron for the second time, had been such an event. November. It seemed so long ago.

"Some delayed leaving the city as long as they could. Some of us decided we would stay no matter the danger. We locked ourselves in our houses, hopeful that things would soon settle down." He paused, a dark look on his face. "It was then I began to understand what we had put the Jews through so many times. I knew what Arabs had done to them. I did not want that to happen to us." He sighed. "But even this did not convince me to leave. It wasn't until Emile was beaten that I knew we must go."

"Emile was beaten by the Jews? No wonder he is so angry."

"He was on his way home from a friend's house where he had helped them pack and leave. A group of young hooligans ridiculed, threatened, and then beat him. I could not stay." He ran his hand through his thick hair. "I have thought of this a lot lately and am beginning to think I let my son's ridicule of me push me into a bad decision, especially now when Emile is in so much danger."

Mary could see the fear in Saad's eyes and felt some guilt herself. Perhaps she shouldn't have invited them to return, but he could not blame himself for Emile. "Do you think he would have stayed in Beirut if you had taken him there? Young hotheads like Emile come south everyday, and they do not all ask permission of their fathers. Maybe coming back wasn't right, but it would not have changed anything with Emile."

"But I am his father. I will never forgive myself if something happens to him. He insists he will fight. Emile will not last an hour in a real battle. He talks very tough, but his fight with those hooligans made him cower in his bedroom for days. I am afraid he will not only endanger himself but others if he is sent into a deadly fight." Saad's eyes went to his sleeping wife. "The night we met you, I told Rifa I thought we should go back but that it might be best for me to take her and Emile on to Beirut or Damascus first. She would not hear of it. We are a family, we stay together, she said. I cannot let this decision cost us our son."

Farouk came through the *sahah.* "I am sorry I cannot offer you more coffee, but water is scarce here. You will also find the bathrooms are nothing but open pits around which we have hung what skins we can. The food rations are nonexistent and the main reason they will send us to Transjordan soon."

"I must leave this camp. I cannot go to Transjordan," Mary said.

"Give Ahmed time. At least a full day," Farouk said. "For now, sleep, visit with others in the camp. I will tell you when it is time. Now, excuse me. I have much to do." With that, he went back through the *sahah.*

Saad was already stretching out, and Mary pulled a cushion into place before lying her head on it. She would not wait for Farouk. She could not take that chance. She would leave tonight.

CHAPTER 8

The Arab attack came just after sunrise. Abraham and his men were reassigned to help defend the northern side of the city where it came in direct contact with the Muslim Quarter. Only barricades and an iron gate separated the Jews from the Arabs at this point, and these borders were under heavy attack.

Abraham and his men had been assigned to defend the Warsaw Building—a synagogue and study rooms for Yeshiva students. Three stories high and built around a central courtyard, it was strong and defensible, enabling them to handle the first attacks well enough, even driving the Arab irregulars back. But then several Arabs slipped under their barrage of bullets and were successful in placing homemade bombs against the building, successfully blowing half the northeast corner away. A gaping hole remained, and half a dozen of his men were killed.

They fought as long as they could but were finally forced to retreat, carrying the wounded and dead, half the Arab population of the Muslim Quarter rushing after them. Fighting hand to hand, they were slowly, agonizingly pushed down the street of the Jews toward the Hurva Synagogue, their only consolation being that they were making the Arabs pay heavily for every inch of territory lost. Finally, at the very heart of the Quarter, they stopped the Arab advance and even forced a partial retreat. But they were far from victory. They controlled a small area around the three major synagogues still standing, the civilian population huddled inside them and the tunnels underneath. Another attack like this one and they would be overrun and then butchered.

Abraham lay flat on his back, exhausted, blood dotting his face and arms from several shrapnel cuts as well as the blood of fallen comrades he had carried. Maybe death would be better, he thought.

He thought of his parents. He had asked Russnak to let Naomi take them out under a white flag. Russnak had been reluctant. There were others who would want to leave as well, and that could lead to even more opposition by the rabbis. They had argued, Abraham finally convincing Russnak that letting the civilian population leave would make it easier to fight the Arabs. They had contacted the Arab commander under a white flag. Unfortunately, he had not agreed. There would be total surrender or there would be total annihilation. There would be no more civilians allowed to leave, no matter their condition. Russnak contacted central command by radio and asked for orders. He was told to hang on—they were sending reinforcements right away. Then the battle had broken out and no reinforcements had come. They were at the end of a very short rope.

Getting to his feet, Abraham plodded up the stairs to the second floor of the synagogue, where several men watched the streets below for any sign of a new attack by the Arabs. He found a position overlooking what was left of the Quarter. The Hurva with its great dome still stood watch over the ancient city, but Abraham knew that unless God intervened in some miraculous way, it would soon be gone. Even now he did not understand why it still stood. An easy target for Arab artillery, the big guns simply hadn't been able to hit it. Divine intervention? Abraham did not know. What he did know was that the Arabs would reach its walls with one more concerted attack. Strange, he thought. Here it was May 27, the day they should be celebrating Lag B'Omer, the commemoration of the miraculous halt of the plague that swept Judea at the time of the wars with Rome nearly two thousand years ago, and they were once more fighting a formidable enemy seeking to destroy them and everything they held holy.

He saw Eliahu scramble across the rubble in the street below, then disappear into the building where Abraham stood. A moment later, he heard Eliahu climbing the steps to the second floor and turned to hear what news he brought.

Eliahu wiped his mouth with the sleeve of his dusty shirt. "Word has come from Russnak. The rabbis press even harder for surrender. Two tried to cross the lines under a white flag, and Russnak had his men fire on them. One was wounded, and both returned, but they are adamant now. They have told Russnak that if reinforcements do not come by tomorrow, he will have to kill them all to keep them from surrender."

Abraham's stomach churned. Shooting at the rabbis! Was Russnak crazy? He looked out the broken window again, his gaze on the dome of the Hurva, his jaw set in anger as Eliahu continued.

"In the entire Quarter, we have less than forty men who are not wounded or dead. We have less than ten bullets each for our rifles and no ammunition for the machine guns and no mortars. There is no morphine or blood for the wounded and no place to put the dead." Eliahu bit his lip against the despair that might lead to tears. He had fought in World War II, knew the horror of defeat, of losing friends to battle, and of losing family to the Nazis, but these were nothing to the sense of loss and defeat he was feeling now. He had come to defend the Quarter, the most holy part of Jewish Jerusalem, the place where his father had dreamed of living someday and to which all Jews looked for spiritual strength. And they were about to lose it and the rabbis that made it holy to him. It was more than his exhausted body could take much longer. "Are the rabbis right, Abraham? Is all lost?"

Abraham turned to Eliahu. "I must go and see Russnak. Stay here and hold your ground if you can. If not, retreat to the Hurva, and defend it and our people at all costs. I will return as quickly as I can." He walked past Eliahu.

"Will . . . will we surrender then?" Eliahu asked.

"I don't know, but if we lose these buildings, our homes, it is a small thing compared to losing the rabbis. Do you understand?"

Eliahu nodded as his back stiffened. Abraham patted him on the shoulder and left. He must talk to Russnak, beat understanding into his head if necessary. There must be no more shooting at the rabbis.

* * *

Naomi was returning to Rabbi Marshak's house with what little food she could find. She was reaching for the door handle when a shell reduced the house to a pile of rubble. Moments later, she awoke to find herself buried in debris. Coughing up dust while freeing her arms and upper body, she yelled for Abraham's parents with no reply. Pulling herself from under the heavy boards and beams of the ceiling, she struggled to her feet and toward what remained of the bedroom where she had left her in-laws. Here the entire building had collapsed, completely covering the Marshaks. She screamed for help, her heart in a panic of fearful foreboding. Finding a foot, then a leg, she frantically threw aside stones and timbers, then scraped away the last of the debris to reach Rita Marshak. She felt for a pulse, but there was none. Her eyes flooded with tears, and she sobbed out her despair as neighbors worked their way over, through, and around the dangerous rubble to give her aid, pulling the body from the rubble and carrying it out as others bloodied their hands to reach the rabbi's bed. They found him a few moments later, crushed, his body broken and lifeless. Wailing spread as quickly as the word of his death, and Naomi felt like she would die from the ache in her heart. Someone helped her stumble from the ruins to where the Marshaks were lying in the street, their bodies covered with a blanket brought quickly by a mourner. Naomi fell to her knees beside them, her shoulders slumped, convulsing with sobs of anguish. Once more she had lost those she loved. Once again death by war had come for her family. Would it never end?

* * *

Abraham had made it to within a block of his parents' house when he heard the explosion and knew immediately that it had hit near his home. Fearful for Naomi and his parents, he raced through the shortest route to his parents' street. He blinked at the sight of the destruction, cringed when he saw Naomi kneeling, her chin against her chest, her clothes and hair covered in a thick layer of dust, two bodies covered by a blanket in front of her.

"No!" he cried in anguish. "Nooo!" Stumbling over the last few yards of debris, he fell to his knees next to them, his hand tossing back the blanket to reveal his parents. He cried out, his face turned upward and arms extended. "Dear heaven, no!"

The wailing increased as Naomi put her arms around him and held him tight. He put his own arms around her and sobbed as more and more people came from the tunnels into the street, the word of his father's and mother's deaths spreading like wildfire. In only a few minutes the entire rubble-cluttered street was filled with mourning for their fallen friend.

Abraham felt a touch on his shoulder and looked up to see Rabbi Salomon. He urged them to their feet, then embraced them with tears streaming down his cheeks. He turned to several men and told them to take the bodies to the Stamboli, Rabbi Marshak's synagogue. After the bodies were wrapped in additional blankets and taken from the ground, Naomi pulled Abraham to her. Putting his arm around her shoulder, they plodded after the body bearers, Rabbi Salomon and others falling in behind them, the street filling with their wailing.

The procession walked blindly through the war-torn, tattered, ruined streets, the sounds of war mercifully missing. Reaching the front door of the synagogue, the bearers took the bodies inside and for the next hour all who had known his parents filed up from the tunnels to mourn the loss of one of the Quarter's most knowledgeable and beloved rabbis.

"I feel empty," Naomi said softly as they watched the string of mourners pass by. "And angry. They turned away from him because we married. Now they come here to mourn and say they are sorry. Does God forgive such hypocrisy?"

"God allows penance, Naomi, always. Let them have it."

"Even though tomorrow they will curse your name, even blame you for this because you fight for the Haganah, fight to defend their miserable lives? It is not so easy for me, Abraham. Maybe it is impossible."

A shell struck very close, and the mourners hastened their pace. Rabbi Salomon said a rapid prayer for the dead as the war raged once more. When he finished, those who remained scrambled back to the stairs into the basement and tunnels below, but Rabbi Salomon approached Abraham and Naomi. Naomi stiffened. Abraham felt it and tightened his arm around her shoulders. "Leave it be, Naomi. Leave it be."

"I . . . I don't know what to say," Rabbi Salomon said.

Naomi bit her tongue. *How about you are sorry for the misery and unhappiness you caused the Marshaks? How about, Forgive me, and I was wrong about you?* Her mind raced with what he should say, but she spoke none of it, Abraham's comforting grip on her shoulders helping her keep her mouth shut until he was gone.

"May God give him peace," Abraham said.

"Or a lesson about his prideful nature," Naomi responded.

They helped wrap the bodies in additional blankets.

"They must be taken to where the rest of the bodies—" a soldier said.

"No, I will see to their burial," Abraham said.

"But there is no place," the soldier said. "You know that until the siege is lifted, the bodies cannot be taken from the city to the burial grounds."

"I will take care of it," Abraham said. "Go to your post."

The soldier shrugged, then left the building. Abraham called to several older men, members of his father's synagogue, and instructed them to help him as he ripped a plank from one of the benches, then a second. Placing the bodies on them, they carried them into the basement, then the tunnels, and through the Cardo to where the passage led to the tunnel they had hoped would get them into Zedekiah's Cave. The diggers were gone, all called to the battle, and Abraham and the others carried the bodies deep inside the tunnel. Thanking the others and asking them to wait at the end of the tunnel, Abraham and Naomi stayed a moment while he said a prayer and a final good-bye. Naomi cried.

"Come, we must go," Abraham said after several minutes. They scooted out, and Abraham instructed the others to go back the way they had come. Going to a mound of debris, he pulled several rocks aside and removed three sticks of dynamite before reentering the tunnel. He came out several minutes later and took Naomi by the arm. They were through the passage into the Cardo when the explosions made the tunnel a permanent grave for Rabbi and Rita Marshak.

They met Rabbi Salomon at the top of the stairs of the synagogue. "I will return as soon as I can. Prepare the people for surrender."

"But Russnak will not allow . . ."

"This new attack will change his mind," Abraham said. "Prepare. Bring everyone here and to the other synagogues as quickly but as safely as you can. Keep them in the basements."

Naomi gripped his arm tightly. "I go with you, Abraham." She sniffed. "I will not leave your side again. Do you understand? I . . ."

He put an arm around her and squeezed her in an effort to give her comfort, while still facing Rabbi Salomon. "Do you understand what I am telling you, Rabbi?"

Rabbi Salomon, his face pale and drawn, nodded, and Abraham put a hand on his shoulder. "We will return as soon as we can. See to it." A moment later, they were back in the street, more fearful than ever as the sounds of war grew louder.

"You think we must surrender, don't you? You wouldn't have buried them in the tunnel if you didn't," Naomi said softly.

Abraham could only nod. "We cannot protect the people anymore. The tunnel is a dead end. And if the wrong Arabs break into the Quarter, they will butcher everyone. We are out of choices." Abraham knew now that only surrender would save them from annihilation. He intended to make that point to Russnak, even though he and all other Haganah men would be taken prisoner and probably shot. He held onto Naomi's hand even tighter. Soon, even this blessing would be taken from him, but he could not think of that now. They must leave the Quarter, as prisoners or as free men, but they must leave. Now he must get Russnak to agree.

SEE CHAPTER NOTES

CHAPTER 9

Mary started her last walk around the perimeter of the holding area. It was time to make plans to escape.

Farouk had been taken to the colonel's tent and had returned with deep concern and anger in his eyes. In an immediate meeting of the tribal elders still among them, they had discussed what Farouk had been told and how to respond. Though Mary was not privy to their discussion, word spread quickly that Yifta had told Farouk that his tribe would be moved to Transjordan in the morning and that he should prepare them. Mary suspected Farouk planned some kind of escape, possibly along the way, but she considered it too dangerous to wait. She must find another way out of the camp, and she must find it quickly.

The camp was surrounded by thirty or forty guards spaced fifty feet apart. They were well armed but not especially vigilant, especially in an area directly west of Farouk's tent where a ravine came to an abrupt end just inside the camp. It was here the latrine was located. Mary noticed that the stench kept the guards well away from the ravine's steep slopes. If she could get into the ravine, she would not be seen. It wasn't a pleasant thought, but it had good possibilities.

As she made one full circle of the camp, deciding if her option was the right one, she heard gunfire and yelling that immediately created some chaos in the camp. Most women and children immediately disappeared inside their tents, while men ran in the direction of the commotion. Mary joined them and found Farouk watching some Jews quickly load into several jeeps and dash from the camp to the east.

"What is it?" she asked him.

"An escape," Farouk said as he joined them. "Five of our young men who no longer trust the Jews. They are hotheads, fools, who go to fight with the Arabs."

Mary saw Saad coming quickly toward them, a fearful but angry look in his eyes.

"Farouk, why did you not stop them?"

"I am their sheik, nothing more. They knew my position but have the right to do as they wish." Farouk turned to go. Saad grabbed his arm.

"My son was with them!"

Farouk glared at Saad's hand on his arm, and Saad removed it. "If this is his decision, he is as foolish as the others. Only Allah can protect him now."

Saad paced, his eyes to the east. "The Jews will kill them."

"Maybe, but these sons will be hard to catch." He pointed toward the corral. "They took five of our best horses."

"Then they are not complete fools," Mary said.

Farouk only smiled.

"I must go after them," Saad said.

"If you must go, may Allah be with you," Farouk said. He left them as several men rushed up and said that the council was ready to meet.

"My son is not like his men," Saad said. "Emile has never been in battle, never even fired a rifle. He won't last an hour in a real battle." He glared at the backs of Farouk and his elders. "Now I must go after him."

"After him? But you can't. Look, already the Jews deploy more guards around us, and Rifa could never make such an escape."

"I will find a way. And Rifa cannot go. You must care for her," Saad said as he started to walk away. "I have to tell Rifa I go after our son."

Mary grabbed his arm. "I will not care for Rifa. I have plans of my own."

He turned on her, his nostrils flared with anger. He grabbed her around the throat. "You will stay! I will come for her—for both of you—after I find Emile." He let go of her as if shocked, panic and remorse filling his eyes. "I am sorry. I . . . I don't know what made me do such a thing."

Mary rubbed her throat, unable to respond for a moment, then cleared her throat. "Make your arrangements with Farouk. Rifa remains under the bond of salt, and he will keep her safer than I am able. When you return, she will be waiting."

He nodded and turned away, his shoulders slumped. Mary watched him go for only a second, the chance of escape slipping away as the number of soldiers around the compound doubled. She must go now or there would be no chance at all.

She was in the tent, quickly gathering her things, when Farouk came through the *sahah* and spoke to her, his brow wrinkled with concern. "Saad has told me of your plans. Like his wife, you are under the bond of salt, and your safety is my obligation. I cannot let you take this risk."

"I release you from your bond," Mary said. "I will not stay and go to Transjordan."

"Then wait for the right moment."

She looked up from her task. "Right moment?"

"You will know when it comes." He went back through the *sahah*.

"And you," she said, a curious look on her face. As she stood and put her bag over her shoulder, Farouk's wife and Rifa entered the tent. Rifa was crying. Mary could not blame her.

"I am sorry, Rifa," Mary said.

Stunned, Rifa only nodded, her life coming apart at its seams. For a brief moment, Mary felt overwhelming guilt, but she shoved it aside. She must get to Jerusalem. It was not her fault that Saad could not control Emile and had decided to desert his wife to find his rebellious son. She started for the tent door.

"He is our son," Rifa said softly. "Saad has no choice. Do not judge him harshly."

Mary turned back. "Hopefully my husband waits in Jerusalem. I must go there, and nothing will get in my way. Do you understand? Nothing."

"And if he is not alive?" Rifa asked.

Mary bit her lip against the tears before she could go on. Pointing at her chest with her index finger, she finally spoke. "In here, I know he is alive. This is what drives me, Rifa. It is the reason I live and breathe, and I cannot spend time wasting away in Transjordan where I will never know for sure, and where he can never find me if he is alive. Do you understand?" she begged.

Rifa's eyes searched Mary's. Finally she nodded. "Yes, I understand. May Allah go with you." She stepped forward and hugged Mary, then sat near the fire.

Mary ached for Rifa, wished that she had never let them come. She busied herself with her bag, clumsily removing one of the blankets before shouldering it. There was nothing she could do for Rifa. Rifa was better off here under Farouk's protection.

Farouk's wife handed Mary a small bag of food. "You will see her again," she smiled. "Allah wills it."

Mary gave a smile and a thank-you and then left. Finding a spot where she could sit in the shadows of a tent but still see the guards directly around the latrine, she waited for the right moment Farouk had mentioned. He had been telling her something would happen, something that would increase her chances of escape. She decided she would wait, but only if no other opportunity presented itself first. Her stomach was in knots, goose bumps dancing along her flesh as she thought of what she was about to do. She was a fool, but she could not help herself. She was leaving this camp, and she was leaving before the Jews drove their trucks into the compound to haul them away to endless years of misery in the deserts of Transjordan, where women had fewer rights than they did even in Lebanon. She must go to Jerusalem, and before morning she would either welcome death or be on her way to Haifa. For her there were no other options.

* * *

Ezra Yifta stood in the tent opening watching his men reposition their few armored cars around the perimeter of the holding area. It had been nearly five hours since the escape of a few men, none of whom had been found. Afraid it was only the first volley in a battle for freedom by Farouk and his people, he had redeployed his men. It seemed to have worked. Soon it would be light, and the trucks would arrive from Degania to take the Nasariyah to the border and send them on their way. Then he would be rid of Farouk once and for all. The other tribes could be easily held without Farouk there to cause trouble.

Yifta had spent most of his life in the military and did not especially like his orders, but he was becoming more and more resigned to them each day. The Arabs were making it increasingly obvious they would never stop fighting, and it would be easier to defend Israel if the enemies or potential enemies did not live among them.

Mahmoud approached, leading his horse. The man was archaic but effective, and Yifta admired his tenacity while loathing his lust for the blood of his fellow Arabs.

"We are ready," Mahmoud said.

Yifta nodded, then sipped the very bad coffee he had made earlier. "Make another round of the holding area. I want no one sleeping until after Farouk's people are deported."

Mahmoud mounted his horse and was about to rein it around when Yifta thought of something else. "Did you find the escapees?"

Mahmoud shook his head. "One of them is Farouk's son. He knows how to avoid my scouts. But soon he will run out of places to hide. Soon we will have him and the others." He spurred his gray Arabian and was gone.

Turning toward his makeshift desk, Yifta sensed a stir among the animals in the corral only a hundred yards to the north. He turned back and stepped outside as the animals burst from their corral. He pulled his pistol as the animals came like a flood toward him, realized he would be trampled, and ran for one of the armored cars. The impact of the exploding car lifted him from his feet and slammed him to the ground ten feet away. He lay there, staring up at the heavens, unable to move. Then he passed out.

* * *

The explosion sent fire to the heavens, lighting the entire camp. Yifta's soldiers, most new and inexperienced recruits from Cyprus, dove for cover or ran about in confusion as explosion after explosion destroyed the camp, scattering the animals in every direction.

With the first explosion, Mary stood straight up. She did not know what was happening, but she must move. Fear gripped her heart, cementing her legs to the ground where she stood. She held her bag tight as more explosions rocked the ground and the sound of gunfire erupted all around her.

"Dear God, give me courage," she thought. One of the guards barked a command for his men to stay put, but they were already on the run, diving for cover behind anything that didn't move. There was an opening, to her left, just past the latrine. She forced her legs to move, keeping low and running past the last two tents nearest the perimeter. As she crossed the open area, she saw a guard get to his feet and yell something at her, his rifle going to his shoulder. She ignored him, dodged right, and ran for all she was worth toward the latrine, diving behind its southern edge just as a bullet dug into the wooden wall above her. Slithering under the fence, she got to her feet and ran down the side of the ravine, bullets striking in the dust behind her. Conscious but uncaring of the stench of the black-brown ooze near where she hugged the ravine's wall, she hurried deeper into the shadows, the sound of soldiers' voices coming after her. The stink of human waste quickly behind her, she scrambled into the bottom of the gully and picked up her speed, raising an arm against the sting of wood tearing at her face as she pushed aside the stiff limbs of the underbrush. Suddenly she was through but ran directly into the front of an Arabian horse, knocking her onto her backside with such force that it pummeled the wind out of her. Grimacing, she looked up to see Mahmoud Dajani in the light of the explosion-caused fires of the camp, a wicked smirk on his face.

He was about to dismount when a black shadow flew from the side of the ravine and caught him in midair, driving him over the far side of the horse and slamming him to the ground. The Arabian reared on its hind legs as Mary scrambled backward, then to her feet. She grabbed the animal's reins and held on tightly as he tried to back away, frightened by the fight at his feet. As she got him to move forward, she saw the flash of a slashing blade, and one of the shadowy figures stopped moving. The dark form of the victor turned quickly to her, grabbed her hand, and told her to mount.

"Ahmed!" she said.

He pushed her upward and into the saddle. "Go!"

"No, you are hurt."

"Go, I must stay with my people. There are many more to get out. If I do not find you, another will. That is my promise.

Go!" With that, he slapped the horse on its haunches, and the animal bolted. She looked back while hanging on desperately to the saddle and reins of the fleeing Arabian. Ahmed disappeared in the shadows, and Mary hunched down and urged the horse on to greater speeds until they were at the top of the hill. She brought the horse to a stop and looked down on the scene of chaos and destruction. A dozen fires gave light to shadowed forms darting around in panic. She could see a steady stream of Farouk's people running through a fence at the rear of the camp while fighters protected their retreat, but the Jews were regrouping and would soon find their trail. How could such a large group hope to escape? Where could they go when both Arab and Jew were their enemy?

She did not know, nor could she wait to see or their fate would be hers. Putting her heels to the Arabian's sides, Mary dropped down the other side of the hill, leaving it all behind as quickly as the Arabian could move across the valley of the Jezreel. It was hours later when she finally stopped at a stream where trees would hide her animal and give them both time to rest. Taking a drink, she sat down with her back against the tree. It was nearly half an hour before her exhausted body gave into a listless sleep from which she jerked back to consciousness nearly three hours later, the sun high above her. The horse still stood where she had tied him, his ears straight as if listening. She attuned herself to listen, but heard nothing unusual, and went to the stream to get a drink and wash herself. She lay on her stomach and sucked in the cold, clear water while letting it cool her face.

"Have you never heard the story of Gideon?"

Mary looked up to see a Jew on the other side of the stream, sitting astride a horse of his own. He had no gun in his hand and did not seem a threat, but she still raised up slowly to her knees and dipped her hand in the water, letting it run through her fingers as she spoke. "So he brought down the people unto the water: and the Lord said unto Gideon, Every one that lappeth of the water with his tongue, as a dog lappeth, him shalt thou set by himself; likewise every one that boweth down upon his knees to drink. And the number of them that lapped, putting their hand to their mouth, were three hundred men: but all the rest of the people bowed down upon their knees to drink water. And the Lord said unto Gideon, By the three hundred men that lapped will I save you."

"For a fugitive at least partially responsible for the death of Jewish soldiers, you are not very vigilant," he said dismounting. From one knee, he scooped up some water and sucked it from his hand.

"I don't know what you are talking about," she said, standing. Anxiously Mary searched for others. No one she could see. She gauged the distance between them, wondering if she could get to her horse before he could reach her.

"You wouldn't make it," he said, still sipping water. He stood, his clear blue eyes on her. "Ahmed brought Farouk and a few others to my village. He was unable to keep his promise and asked that I come."

"You are from Allonim," she said, relieved.

He nodded. "I am Benny Berak. Ahmed is sorry he cannot come himself and hopes my meager talents will suffice."

"We'll see. How many died?"

"Twenty. Most of the dead are bedu from the Nasariyah or Zeidan. Ahmed's men were selective about who they killed, knowing our government would make them pay dearly for our losses. The survivors are spread around, hiding or being hidden by friends until I can clear this up with our leaders."

"Tell me, Benny Berak, how many innocent bedu and other Arabs have died in your pogroms?" she asked.

His eyes filled with a mixture of anger and sadness. "War is never pretty, Mary Aref. If it were, mankind wouldn't have lasted a hundred years."

"Is that supposed to justify deporting friends and massacring innocent villagers?"

He gave her a hard look before answering. "I have been fighting Arabs most of my life. I haven't wanted to, but it seems to be the way of things. They come and try to run us out of our homes, rape our wives, steal us blind, and kill any man who tries to stop them. I wish it were different here, but it isn't, and though you won't like it, better them than us. And try not to forget that atrocities are committed by both sides. The only difference is we don't give them as many chances."

"If that's the way you feel, why are you here? Why help Ahmed if he might just turn around and cut your throat? Or why take a chance on me? I might stick a knife in your back just as quick as any other Arab."

He showed a wry smile. "You I'll watch." He started tightening the cinch on his saddle. "Ahmed is family, and I owe the Nasariyah the life of my kibbutz."

"And yet they are treated as an enemy, or worse," she said.

He put a foot in the stirrup and pulled himself into the saddle. "Believe it or not, there is no policy of deportation. At least nothing official. But local commanders have the leeway to push any threat out of the way. When the Zeidan convinced Yifta it was the Nasariyah who attacked one of our villages and killed every living thing in it—and had evidence to back their accusation—Yifta had no choice but to round up Farouk and his people. Now he has even more reason to go after Farouk, so if you don't mind, I'd like to stop arguing who's right and who's wrong and get moving. If I am to stop one of those atrocities you mentioned, I need to get to Haifa as soon as possible."

Mary mounted as Berak started away at a trot, and she put her heels to the Arabian, quickly catching up.

"There was a woman, Rifa Shawas, traveling with me. I assume she is still with Farouk," Mary said.

Berak gave a shrill whistle, and several horsemen came over the edge of a hill. Rifa was with them.

"Thank you," Mary smiled.

Mary had heard of Berak. As a young man he had joined the *Hashomer,* or watchmen, becoming one of its most noted members. The bedouin, always thieves, had learned to respect Berak after he became head of the watchmen in the Galilee and fought them toe to toe, killing a few of their best fighters.

Rifa had her head scarf covering most of her face, but her eyes looked very relieved to see Mary. The other men were bedu and left when Berak and Mary arrived.

"Where are they going?"

"We're getting close to Jewish lines. They'll make themselves scarce until we get into the mountains of Carmel."

"They are friends of Ahmed," she said.

"Yes, Salim, the tall, thin one, is also Farouk's eldest son and next sheik. He has a few words to say to our military leaders in Haifa." They walked their horses, the sound of battle growing louder. Only fifteen miles from Haifa at most, and yet, from the sounds, they might be the toughest miles of all.

SEE CHAPTER NOTES

CHAPTER 10

Wally listened to the briefing with soberness. The Quarter was about to fall, and he wondered whether Naomi and Abraham would make it out alive.

"But they are doing all they can. For us, the concern must be different," the lieutenant giving the briefing said. Wally knew they had tried breaking through the Old City twice but were driven back. Rumor had it that the plan was poorly conceived and poorly carried out. It wouldn't surprise him. The Haganah had good men for the most part—smart, decisive men—but as in all wars, there were a few who had to learn lessons the hard way and at the expense of others' lives.

"The greatest danger to our new state is in the south, from Egypt. Though the Messerschmitts are nearly assembled and ready, we cannot wait. Therefore, you will use your present airplanes to give some support to our troops in the south." The lieutenant pointed to a spot on the map. "The settlements of Yad Mordechai and Nitzanim have fallen into enemy hands. We are losing ground. We must retake those settlements, and we must do it now or the Egyptians will be at the doors of Tel Aviv in two days' time."

Zohar worked in the operations office at the Hayarkon Hotel. She and Wally had had lunch together a couple of times, and he found himself wanting to keep developing the relationship, but last night she had given him little encouragement. He had been slow on his approach, hadn't even kissed her up to this point, and he had tried to remain charming and gentlemanly—and she seemed to like him for it. But when he talked of New York, really talked of the future, a kind of coolness seemed to set in. Perhaps there was another guy. Heaven knew there were plenty of them. More foreign fighters arrived every day, and many were hitting on Zohar for a date. Maybe she had found someone more to her liking.

But he had been too busy to give her the attention she deserved. Called on to constantly fly supplies into the settlements in the path of the Egyptians, haul out the seriously wounded, and, more often than not, drop a few bombs on Egyptian troops before their Spitfires tried to shoot the Israelis down kept him hopping. On one night alone, Commander Ralph Moster had completed thirty-five sorties and Wally had done twenty-seven. No time for any real relationship. Surely she understood that.

He took a deep breath, trying to shove the feeling aside. He could not allow himself to be distracted. Those who did usually ended up burning in the debris of their plane.

"Bergman, you and Goldstein will go out first. You will fly ammunition into Palmach troops trying to retake Mordechai. It will be a desert landing, but they tell us by radio that there is a place here." He pointed at the map. Wally recognized the spot because he had flown over it a hundred times. "After that, you fly over the Egyptians and make a delivery."

Wally nodded. The delivery consisted of hand-dropped bombs that were like swatting a mosquito with a matchstick. "When will the 199s be ready?" he asked.

"Soon." The five pilots in the room stiffened.

"Look, you said they were nearly assembled. What's the holdup? Those boys run out of wrenches or something? It doesn't take this long to put together a disassembled 199," Moster said. "We need them, and we need them now."

The lieutenant looked down at his papers, unsure of what to say. "Maybe tomorrow. I'll talk to Weizman. That's all I can do."

"What's the hurry?" one of the other pilots said. "The 199 is unstable. They can roll over on you at anytime because their engines are too heavy for 'em. We know their guns have a tendency to jam. And we know that they are really nothing like the German Messerschmitt in a real fight, though the Czechs say different. The plane is a coffin."

"I'd rather have a coffin that can fight back and has speed in its tail than these . . . these butterflies we're flying now," Wally said. "They're nothing but toy planes that can't keep up with camels, let alone Spitfires. Until we get some 199s or Mustangs or something like them under the seat of our pants, we'll remain rats caught in a flood, and everyone in here knows it."

Moster stood. "Tell Remez to get those planes to us today, or we're gonna come and break his office into kindling and light a fire under him."

Wally stood with the other pilots, and they all left the room. The briefing was over. Moster was the only Canadian in the bunch, while the rest of them were from places like New York and Detroit. But there was commonality. All of them had World War II flying time under their belts, and all were itching to show the Arabs what real flying was.

Wally and Goldstein split off from the others and went directly to a waiting jeep and headed for the airport, where they found their bombs and ammunition already loaded. They retrieved their hand weapons—a shotgun and .45—from the small shed at the near end of the field, climbed into their planes, did their check through, and started the engines. A few minutes later, Wally took off, then circled Ekron Airfield while he waited for Goldstein. Once they were both up, they headed south.

Potshots from Arabs on the ground hit him a couple times, but he was used to it. At this altitude a bullet didn't have much left, even if it did hit the plane. It was near ground level that things got dicey.

They were nearing Mordechai. Goldstein gave a hand signal to hit the deck. Wally followed him down, and soon they were skipping across what few treetops there were until they reached the front lines of the Palmach and buzzed over. Haganah ground forces were not engaged in battle at the moment, and some waved while others hardly gave them a cursory look, their worn-out bodies fast asleep in the dust and dirt of the Negev.

Wally followed Goldstein to the landing site. As they flew over, he could see it would be tricky at best, deadly at worst. Pulling alongside Goldstein as they made a wide turn, he radioed that he would go first. Though Goldstein was second in command, it was Wally who had the most experience in difficult conditions.

Goldstein agreed and pulled back on his stick. "I'll circle and see if I follow or send your mother a letter of condolence."

"You're too kind," Wally said. Taking one more pass over the landing area, he saw what he thought was a flat piece of ground between sparse shrubs and trees and did a tight turn to make the landing. As he pushed forward on the stick and pulled back on the throttle, the plane dipped down, and he used the flaps to float it above and then onto the ground with hardly a bump.

Suddenly his left wheel whacked something half-buried in the ground and blew out, sending him careening directly toward a large, dead tree trunk. Thrusting the throttle forward, Wally pulled back on the stick and prayed that the plane would miss the obstruction. The wheel skipped against the wood, but he was able to go airborne and gained a safe height. He was wiping sweat from his brow when Goldstein pulled up beside him and examined the damage. The obviously flat tire was still attached to the rim. Wally wouldn't be delivering his share of the ammunition.

Cursing under his breath, he radioed Goldstein. "I'll circle while you give it a try. If you make it, I'll fly over the Egyptians and drop a few bombs, then head back for Ekron. If I can land this thing and get the tire fixed, I can still deliver my load before the sun goes down."

Goldstein nodded. "Good luck." He peeled off, and Wally circled. Goldstein landed on the same line but a little to the left, missing the rock or whatever it was and coming to a halt near the troops. Wally kept circling until he saw members of the Palmach get to the plane and start unloading the ammunition, then he turned south to make his delivery.

Finding the largest congregation of Egyptians in the settlement of Nitzanim, Wally made his first bomb run. At three hundred feet, he heard the plinking of bullets against the metal of the plane and began to sweat. Lifting one of the eighteen-pound bombs, he hung it out the window with his free hand, then pushed forward on the stick while pointing the nose at a truck parked in the middle of one of the settlement's streets. He saw the troops dash for cover, dropped the bomb, then looked over his shoulder to assess the damage. The bomb hit on the front of the truck, blowing the hood and doors off and shattering the windshield. Fire erupted from the cab and caught the canvas cover, setting the entire truck on fire. He turned hard left and dipped over then behind a hill. After working his way south, he swung around and came back for a second run. As he did, he saw Goldstein coming over the rise to his right, and the two planes skipped across the landscape side by side toward the settlement. Their bombs struck two armored vehicles sitting together, bounced off, and exploded into troops running for cover. Goldstein veered left, Wally right, bullets striking both planes as they whipped over the edge of the hills and out of view. They were lining up for another run when a Spitfire came in low, its guns firing at Wally. He dove for the ground as bullets whizzed past his small plane before honing in and quickly disintegrating a part of his left wing. Banking hard, he felt the plane hesitate and gritted his teeth in hopes it would not lose power as the Spitfire flew past him and banked for another pass.

Wally flew the Piper into a canyon no wider than twice that of his wingspan, following it east until it closed and forced him above ground. Looking over his shoulder, he saw the Spitfire coming up hard behind him and turned the Piper left over a small rise, then down to within inches of the turf. There were trees ahead—the edge of the Hebron forest. He picked an opening and flew between two stands of fir so narrow that they glanced the tips of his wings. He banked hard left as bullets slammed into the rear of his plane, then heard the sound of the Spitfire as it flew past him. He saw the Spitfire's wing hit a fir, saw it careen left, and felt the heat of the explosion as it hit the ground. Fire erupted into the sky, but Wally was too busy dodging several more trees before he was finally able to look back and see the wreckage.

Sweating, he turned north and headed home. He had survived, but he wondered about Goldstein. Doing a full visual, he finally picked out the small plane flying above the hills to the east. They were both alive.

Now he had to get his wounded plane on the ground.

Glancing at his tire, he was relieved to see it still intact, though empty of air. It would hold together for the landing but after that would disintegrate in a matter of seconds. Then the plane would be very difficult or impossible to control. Time to prepare for the worst. The safety harness had been removed when the armor plating was put in, so he grabbed a short length of rope he carried for emergencies and used his free hand to wrap it around his shoulders and waist, pulling it tight. Then, holding the stick steady between his knees, he tied the rope secure. He did not intend to get thrown through the windshield if the plane came to a sudden stop after landing.

Turning the plane to the right, he set up for landing at Ekron while taking his pocketknife out, pulling up a blade and gripping it between his teeth. Taking a deep breath, he pushed the stick forward and let the plane settle toward the runway. He smoothed its decline and hovered a few feet above the grass, said a silent prayer, and set it down. As he suspected, the flat tire took the initial impact, then began flying apart. As it did, the stick jumped in his hands, but he held tight and the plane stayed straight for another hundred feet before the rubber ripped free and the rim caught in the grass and jerked him left, spinning the plane on its axis. It did a complete three-sixty before the wheel dug deep and threw it on its wing. As it dug in, Wally's rope held him secure until the plane came to a sudden halt. His head struck the metal post between windshield and side panel. He shook his head to do away with the cobwebs and looked up in time to see a Spitfire flying low over the trees, its bullets chewing up the ground in a path that led directly to the Piper's cockpit. He was a dead man. Then Goldstein's Piper flew directly across the path of the Spitfire, surprising the pilot, who jerked back on the stick to avoid a collision. The fighter hiccuped with the sudden direction change, and the pilot knew he had asked far too much too quickly. The plane faltered, then plunged onto the field with a bone-crunching thud, the prop ripping up the terrain as it skidded toward Wally's plane, less than a hundred yards away.

Wally took the pocketknife from his mouth to cut the ropes and get free but fumbled it to the floor, out of reach. He braced for impact, but at the last possible second, the Egyptian plane veered left, cleanly sheering off the Piper's tail wing before coming to a grinding halt fifty yards farther down the earthen runway.

Realizing he had survived, Wally opened his eyes to see a truck, two jeeps, and several men at a dead run converging on him and the Spitfire like ants to two cubes of sugar. It seemed like ages before he could breathe again or force his fingers from around the edge of the dash where they had left distinct indentations. One of the mechanics pulled open the door and tried to pull him free.

"The rope," Wally said, grimacing at the pain as the rope dug into his shoulders.

The mechanic apologized, saw the opened knife on the floor, retrieved it and cut the ropes, then helped Wally climb out. His legs felt a bit wobbly, and he hung on to the wrecked plane until his strength returned. Walking to the radio shack, he saw Goldstein's plane land and taxi toward the make-do hangar a hundred feet away. He shifted directions and met Goldstein as he jumped from his Piper.

"You took a big risk, Goldy," Wally said. "Thanks."

"You're welcome," Goldstein replied with a grin. "Looks like you might have a fighter to fly after all." He looked past Wally at the Spitfire.

They watched as men helped the injured Egyptian from the cockpit. The plane's prop was ruined, and from the look of the underbelly, the right wheel was ripped out of its nest, but it did have potential. "I'll take anything but another Piper."

"May the God of Israel make it so. For all of us," Goldstein said. "Come on. We could both use a drink."

"I gave it up," Wally said with slight smile. They started toward the shack.

"When did this miracle take place?"

"When that Spitfire showed up and I couldn't get out of my plane," Wally said.

Goldstein laughed, and Wally gave him his best smile, working to maintain the air of the unafraid flyboy, but it was difficult. This time, death had knocked thrice, and he had nearly answered.

As they entered the flight shack, nausea overtook him. Dashing for the door on the far side of the room, he burst through and threw up on the lawn near the outdoor toilet. Wiping his mouth dry, he spied a stand of dried grass and sat down, then lay back, closing his eyes. The door opened, but he kept his eyes shut, his stomach still growling at the sudden drop in energy it had been feeding on since his first bombing run.

"Hi."

His eyes opened immediately to find Zohar standing over him. "Hi," he replied, starting to get up.

"Stay," she said. "I saw what happened from the road. At least part of it. You are a lucky man."

"Yeah."

"You should give up being a pilot. It is too dangerous."

"Umm, got any ideas what I should do instead?"

"Infantry. They can't throw airplanes at you," she said as she sat down. She was dressed in khaki pants and shirt, men's clothing from the look of them, and used—probably American surplus. She made them look much better than they actually were.

"True, they just shoot shells at you the size of airplanes. What brings you out here?" he asked.

"I'm picking up some pilots making the run from Zatec." She paused at the sound of airplane engines in the distance. "That will be them. They have a load of rifles, machine guns, and ammunition." Another pause. "Remez wants you to go to Jerusalem, pick up Sheal'tiel and Mickey Marcus and bring them back for meetings with Ben-Gurion."

Wally nodded, his stomach still in knots from his near-death experience. Climbing back in another small, mostly defenseless plane was not an inviting thought right now. "Tell Remez I need a different plane," he joked. "This one is a bit crippled at the moment."

"It's nothing to joke about, Wally," she said with genuine concern.

"Just a way of keeping my sanity. Sorry."

She started to get up, but he reached over and took her hand. "It's great to see you."

"And you." Impulsively, she leaned over and kissed him on the cheek, the blush appearing automatically as she got up and darted away. Shocked, Wally didn't move until she had disappeared around the corner of the building. Coming to his senses, he jumped to his feet and went after her, catching up just as she was getting behind the wheel of a dusty and battered black car.

"Nice wheels. When did you learn to drive?" he asked, his hands resting on the windowsill of the passenger side.

She started the car. "I learned many things in Italy. One of them was how to handle a truck filled with refugees. I did it well enough that I never lost a passenger. After that, this old thing is a piece of cake." She smiled as she put the car in gear. "See you." She pushed on the gas and sped toward the cargo plane now parked at the far end of the runway.

He watched her until the car hit the main road. Maybe things weren't so bad after all. He passed the wreckage of his Piper while walking to the hangar. He had been lucky. Mentally he counted up his close calls. Six in Germany, one here. Rumor had it that a cat had nine lives. That meant he had two left. It wasn't comforting.

CHAPTER 11

Rhoui Aref listened as a new recruit eyed Fawzi el Kutub in disbelief. "You wish us to do what?"

Kutub's hate for Jews rivaled Rhoui's. That was why he had volunteered to work with him. It had been Kutub who blew up the *Jerusalem Post,* Ben Yehuda Street, and just yesterday, half of the Warsaw Building. The man could work death and destruction like no other with his bombs, and Rhoui's hate fed off him like a blood-sucking leech.

"The explosives are strapped to the ladder," Kutub said with a cold edge to his voice. "You, Rhoui, and the others will now carry it to the wall of the Hurva. I will go with you, keep the Jews from killing you with this." He waved a pistol in the man's face. "Once in place, we will blow the Jews to the Hinnom Valley and take their holiest synagogue." He pushed the gun under the man's nose. "If this is unacceptable to you . . ."

Rhoui watched the sweat pour down the new fighter's face as he looked death and the devil in the eye. "No . . . no . . . I . . ." he whimpered.

"I'll see it done," Rhoui said flatly. "Send this coward back to his mother." He stood to lift the ladder.

Kutub smiled evilly, pushing harder on the gun. "No, he will go now. Allah wills it."

"Ye . . . yes . . . yes . . . I will go. I . . ."

"Then pick up the front of the ladder," Kutub said. "And if

you stumble or hesitate, I will kill you and send a letter to your mother about your cowardice."

The man stepped back, then to the ladder. His arms were shaking as he picked up the ladder, sweat pouring from his face. Rhoui went to the back of the short ladder and readied himself, sticking his revolver behind his belt buckle and putting a knife between his teeth.

The Jews were near defeat but refused to surrender. Abdullah Tal, now commander of the Jordanian Army and the Irregulars fighting for the Quarter of the Jews, had ordered the Hurva taken to send a last message to Jewish leaders—surrender or be annihilated. Kutub had volunteered to see it done. Rhoui relished the opportunity. It was time the Hurva no longer violated the skyline of the Holy City.

Pushing his end of the ladder, the sweating fighter moved cautiously forward. Rhoui kept up the pressure. Death did not matter to Rhoui. He looked forward to it. Life had become misery. Martyrdom could only be better.

As they moved down the narrow street toward the square in front of the Hurva, Rhoui thought of the last few weeks of his life, his guts stirring with hatred. His father had died of a broken heart, the announcement that the world would take their land too much for him. His brother and sister, Izaat and Mary, had betrayed their people, forcing him to betray them, and his wife and children had deserted him, no longer able to understand his hatred and anger. Empty and bitter, his cold heart pushed him deeper into a lust for Jewish blood. At Etzion and the convoy going to Hadassah Hospital, he had killed Jewish men and women with his knife as easily as he would kill a chicken. He had relished burning the doctors and nurses of the Hadassah convoy alive in their buses or shooting them as they tried to escape. He had seen more gruesome dying than a hundred normal men, but nothing seemed to quench the dark, empty feelings of hate, anger, and bitterness that gripped his heart. Nothing. That was when he began looking for a martyr's death.

They reached the head of the street. The courtyard was surrounded with riflemen ready to fight into the Hurva once Kutub's bomb made them an entrance. As they left the street and became open targets for Jewish bullets, the new recruit danced with fear, pulling hard in an attempt to move the ladder faster. Rhoui stood tall, holding back, daring any sniper to shoot him. The bullets struck around his feet, whizzed past his head, and even creased one arm, but he kept walking—calm, empty, without caring. They crossed the fifty feet and set the ladder down next to the wall. The sweating recruit hunkered down, pulling up into a tight ball behind the debris of a destroyed building that had toppled into the square. He whimpered with fear while Rhoui and Kutub pushed the ladder to a better position and Kutub lit the fuse.

"Go," Kutub said. He ran back the way they had come. Rhoui pulled the new recruit from his hiding place and shoved him toward their battle lines. He made it several steps before Jewish bullets struck in a hundred places around him and he froze. Rhoui shoved him again, but he refused to go, and a bullet ended his whining. He toppled to the ground as Rhoui walked past him. A bullet struck the edge of his shoe, and he stumbled, caught himself, and continued to defy them as he crossed the open square. Always he had survived such battles. Kutub and the others in their small company thought him a good luck charm, a talisman whose very existence was Allah's sign of approval and eventual victory. He thought it a cruel joke, a curse for what he had done to Izaat and Mary.

"Allah Ahkbar!" the men yelled from their positions as Rhoui walked unhurt toward them. "God is great!" He was nearly to their battle lines when the bullet hit him in the jaw and knocked him flat on his stomach just as the bomb went off. His eyes closed as debris rained down on him, pummeling his body. His death had finally come. Allah would take him to paradise.

* * *

Naomi and Abraham were huddled behind a pile of benches with three others when the explosion blew a large hole in the wall of the Hurva Synagogue. Debris slammed against the benches and killed three men as chunks and pieces of plaster from the high ceiling fell and covered them. Coughing out the dust, Abraham ordered his remaining men to fire as the first Arab stuck his head through the hole. Naomi threw a homemade hand grenade into the breach. Other such grenades followed, and the Arabs ran for cover, only to come screaming at them a second time, depleting the defenders' grenades and bullets. Once more the Arabs retreated, but Abraham saw that only four of his men remained able to fight and knew they would be slaughtered if they stayed. Yelling for retreat, he shoved Naomi toward the main entrance, and they fled the building as dozens of Arabs once more attacked. Fifty yards outside the Hurva's walls, they set up new lines of battle and prepared to fight with what few bullets they had left. They had evacuated the civilians just moments before the blast, and Abraham thanked God for His kindness in warning them to do so, but his heart ached as he looked at the ancient building. The holiest, most ancient synagogue in all the Jewish state was in Arab hands.

* * *

An hour later, Kutub used two hundred pounds of explosives to blow the Hurva off its foundations and into a pile of rubble. Reinforcements had been sent to Abraham's position, and he, Russnak, and the few other commanders still alive were preparing for a final defense when the explosion rocked the entire Quarter. They saw the plume of smoke where the Hurva had been and knew instantly what the Arabs had done. The rumble of destruction had died away, replaced by a deadly silence. Then a wail of mourning floated through the streets, a wailing that quickly turned into a haunting, oppressive chant of Judaism's most hallowed prayer, the Shema Yisrael. Naomi felt the warm tears run down her face as she realized that this was the end. The Quarter was about to be conquered.

Russnak turned to Abraham, his shoulders slumped and his eyes filled with defeat. "Go to the rabbis. Tell them they are free to ask for a truce so that we can remove the dead and wounded."

"The Jordanians will reject it," Abraham said.

"Maybe, but it will give us time. There is still a chance of reinforcements. We must try to stop them, even if only for a few hours."

"It is over, Moshe," Naomi said. "Can't you . . ."

Abraham touched her scraped, dust-covered arm gently, and she bit her tongue. "Very well, Moshe. I'll talk to them." He went past his commander to go to the Stamboli where Rabbi Salomon and the others were already preparing the people.

"He is foolish to try and keep fighting," Naomi said, catching up.

"He knows it and does not need us to remind him," Abraham said. The man would not give up easily, but Abraham understood. He did not wish to give up either. Now they must. He felt numb clear to his toes.

Abraham and Naomi found Rabbi Salomon and the others in the basement. They had done as he asked. The people were huddled in the tunnels, their most precious belongings wrapped in bundles, ready for surrender. Naomi felt sick to see it, the memory of giving in to the Nazis haunting her. It had led to the death of millions. Would the Arabs do to these people what the Nazis had done to those of Germany, Poland, and so many other places? She hung on to Abraham's arm for support as he told the rabbis. Salomon asked the two rabbis whom Russnak had shot at to try again. They left the building with a white flag, Abraham, Naomi, and a few others behind them. They watched as the two approached the Arab front lines, afraid they might be shot on the spot. Instead, they were allowed through and disappeared over the rubble of the Street of the Jews.

It was nearly an hour before they returned. Russnak had joined the rest of them and was pacing back and forth in the street, the Quarter devoid of any real fighting. The two rabbis climbed over the rubble, and Russnak greeted them.

"It did not work. Tal will not listen to us. He wants Rabbi Salomon and a representative of the Haganah who can sign surrender documents. If you do not go in the next fifteen minutes he will assume these terms are not agreeable."

Russnak paced, delaying as long as he could, hoping for some sort of breakthrough from outside the Quarter.

"It is time," Abraham said.

Russnak sighed deeply, nodded, and assigned the three rabbis along with the Arab-speaking Shaul Tawil to go. They returned an hour later. The surrender was in place.

SEE CHAPTER NOTES

CHAPTER 12

Further meetings of surrender were held the following day. When finished, the terms dictated by the Arabs were simple: All men who could still fight were to be taken prisoner while women, children, the aged, and those seriously wounded would be sent to the New City under the watchful eye of the Red Cross and the Jordanian military. Once across the line into Jewish West Jerusalem, they would be free to go.

Naomi was in the basement of Stamboli Synagogue searching for Mithra when the news reached her. Though her heart sank, civilians screamed with joy and rushed past those of the members of the Haganah trying to protect them and into the streets, believing they were now safe. Naomi, her stomach in knots that made her entire body ache, saw Mithra sitting on a wooden chair near the back of the cellar and went to her side, then helped her to her feet.

"It is over then," Mithra said.

"Yes, we have lost the Quarter."

Sensing her young friend's despair, Mithra patted Naomi's hand gently. "Never mind, dear, never mind. As always, life goes on. Yes, yes, life goes on. Our people have lost more than one home, but we will not give up. We will win eventually. You will see."

They climbed the stairs and left the synagogue for the last time. Naomi was surprised to find Jewish citizens embracing Arabs who had apparently rushed into the Quarter to loot but were momentarily caught up in the chaos of victory and defeat, surrender and capitulation. Old-friends-turned-enemies momentarily became friends again. Could it be so easy? Could life go back to normal as fast as dust settles over the battleground?

She couldn't move, watching as Jewish shopkeepers opened their stores, offering their Arab conquerors cakes that a few hours before they had hoarded like gold, refusing to give even to hungry Haganah fighters. And they celebrated. Angry at them, amazed by it all, she was paralyzed.

Then other Arabs began pouring in, pushing their way into shops, pulling goods from the shelves, stealing, looting.

"Get out!" one yelled. "The Quarter is ours now. The city. You are finished. Get out."

Shopkeepers, confused but realizing that things were turning for the worse, stood by, unsure of what to do. They tried to close their doors. Looters shoved them aside, began beating them as Legion soldiers poured in, forcefully separating combatants, pushing the Jews one way and the looters the other.

Naomi took Mithra by the arm, "Come, we are finished here." The moment's happiness was nothing but a glitch, that was all. Just a glitch.

"Tell me what you see," Mithra said.

Naomi did.

"They will take it all, you know," Mithra said. "Our enemies always take it all when they drive us away. Always." She paused. "When will the trucks come?"

"Trucks?"

"They always send trucks. It is the way to get us to the camps, you know. Trucks and trains. They all go to the same places." There was a defeated but calm tone to her voice that sent shivers up Naomi's spine. Would they? Had the surrender all been a lie? Would the trucks come as they had in Poland? She bit her lip, fear rising in her breast. Abraham!

"Come, Mithra, we must hurry. They will take you to safety in the New City, but I must get to Abraham. I must!"

Blind Mithra hung tightly to Naomi as they scurried around and over the rubble, the Legion guards pointing the way while blocking whole streets and holding the growing Arab mob at bay. They entered the large courtyard to find the remaining men of the Haganah lined up against a far wall, Legion guards surrounding them. She spied Abraham in the back row and worked to keep panic under control while still moving Mithra toward the Red Cross ambulance standing near the gate. Frightened women, children, and the aged wept as they fled their homes and gathered here, the shock of what was really happening now visible in their pale faces and sad eyes. Their celebration of surrender and the dream of returning to something normal had quickly turned to ashes.

Quickly but carefully, Naomi helped Mithra find a place to sit and then found a Red Cross representative who spoke Hebrew, telling him of her friend's blindness. "Take good care of her," she said.

The Red Cross agent nodded in sympathy as Naomi headed across the courtyard to Abraham. Her greatest fear was that the Arabs would gather, then massacre them. Word of the Arab massacre of the doctors' convoy on the Hadassah road and the one at Kfar Etzion played across her mind, sharing room with past massacres by the Nazis she had seen. Should such a thing once again plague her, she did not want to be separated from Abraham. If death came, she would be at his side.

Stepping through the first row she grasped Abraham's hand.

"What are you doing?" Abraham asked firmly. "You cannot go, they will not allow it. Now go back to Mithra. She needs you."

"She is taken care of. I'm staying, Abraham. If we die, we die together. No arguments." She clung to him more tightly, and he gripped her hand in response, horrified by the thought of losing her. He knew he must send here away. She must survive.

But not yet. He wanted to feel her touch just a bit longer, just until the trucks came.

Naomi looked at the buildings around her. It was horribly different now—synagogues destroyed, homes in shambles, smoke rising from what little remained, the smell and sound of death, dying, and despair everywhere. Just as her life had changed in Hungary when the Nazis came, it had changed again with the coming of war to her new land. The thought made her shudder as the horror of those days washed over her again, increasing the ache inside and making this loss even more painful. They were losing that part of the Quarter her people had inhabited for millennia, and she felt the weight of it nearly crush her. Her shoulders and body visibly slumped, and Abraham grasped her arm and held her tightly to him. She felt his heart pounding in her temple and knew that, though he was strong, his heart was crushed just as hers was. They had lost it all! How could this be happening? Where was God this time? Why did He continue to desert them?

An Arab officer hurried toward them, several others at his side. She heard his words as he tried to calm their fears of massacre, but found them hard to believe. Naomi dried her eyes with the back of a dirty hand and stood as straight as her weary body would allow, her grimy, blood-stained clothes and dusty hair showing the battle-worn warrior she was. When the Arab got to them he stopped and faced her.

"No women will be taken prisoner," he said. "You must go with the civilians." He stepped away.

"I am Haganah. I will go with our men," Naomi said. "You took women prisoners at Etzion. Of course, that was after you massacred many others."

"Naomi, leave it be," Abraham said as calmly as he could. "Go where he tells you."

"I go with you," she said firmly while grasping his arm tightly.

The Arab turned back. "Etzion was a regrettable mistake. One we will not duplicate here." He lifted his chin. "We do not take women prisoners. It is against Islam."

Naomi's eyes narrowed. "You come here and butcher us with your artillery and bombs, you blow up the Hurva, a holy synagogue of our people, and you cannot take women prisoners because it is against your religion? You . . . you fool! I have shot at least a dozen of your men because they would rape and butcher me, and I will shoot you if you give me a gun!"

"No, she is lying," Abraham said.

The Arab, flushed with anger, turned to two of his men and gave an order. They stepped up and placed their barrels against Abraham's chest. The Arab commander spoke in stiff, curt words directly at Naomi. "You will go with the women, or I will kill this man. Do you understand?"

Naomi's face hardened and she turned into Abraham, trying to place herself between the rifle barrels and her husband. Abraham grabbed her by the arms. As the soldiers tensed, he gently pushed her away. She stumbled backward, the tears flowing again as two other soldiers pulled her toward the women and children.

"No," she screamed, trying to break free.

Abraham could do nothing but turn away as the command was given to march the men out of the square and off to their destination into what both of them thought might be death. Naomi watched them go, her chest convulsing in sobs as they sat her against the wall, their rifles pointed at her until they knew she would not fight them again. A wail began, and the crowd mourned as all other Jewish men capable of carrying a gun were also told to get moving, disappearing into the Arab Quarter.

Naomi lay her tired head against the wall, tears running freely down her cheeks. "Abraham," she said quietly. "My darling, Abraham."

Over the next few hours, the rest of the civilian population gathered, and just before sunset they began the march from the Old City. Naomi forced herself to her feet, her tears dried in rows of caked dust on her cheeks. With dazed eyes she looked for Mithra, finding her still in the care of the Red Cross representative.

"Come," she said to her friend. "They are taking us somewhere. It is time."

"Don't worry. They are taking you to the New City," the representative said in a comforting tone. "Everything will be all right."

Naomi nodded without really caring. As she and Mithra fell in line and walked through Zion Gate, she turned to see flames shooting from several buildings torched by the Arabs. Homes, shops, and other buildings that had existed for a hundred years were nothing but fire and ashes. She put an arm around Mithra's shoulders and faced forward, unable to watch any longer. The narrow streets were lined with Arabs screaming obscenities at them, their rage ominous and threatening. Several men thrust themselves past the guards and onto former neighbors but were pulled away and shoved back into the crowd at the point of Legion rifles. One refused and shoved a soldier back, causing him to trip and fall. The crack of the rifle sent everyone ducking with fear as the assailant toppled over, dead. The Arab mob got the message and backed away, painfully aware the Legion had firm orders to set Jewish civilians free without harm. As they drew closer to what she knew was the dividing line between armies, Naomi breathed easier. The Arab general was keeping his word, but it did not change her opinion of him, or any Arab. Watching them, knowing what they would do to innocent women and children if the Legion didn't keep them at bay, made her hate them.

Finally, they reached the battle lines that separated the New City from the Arab-held section around the Old, but she did not fully believe they were free until they passed Haganah soldiers and left the mob behind.

Finding a spot where they could sit, she eased Mithra to the ground to rest in the shade of a building, the thick cloud of smoke and flame dancing above the Old City walls where the Quarter had been. Once more her people had suffered defeat. Sitting next to Mithra, she lowered her head onto her arms, which lay across her raised knees. She wanted to pray but couldn't find the faith, the energy. Hannah, Ephraim, Abraham, all of them were wrong. God was never there, never watching, never caring. At least not for her and her people. They were on their own, and their only way to freedom would be to shed enough blood that the Arabs would refuse to send any more mobs and armies against them. They had taken the Quarter, but they would not keep it. Until her dying breath, she would fight them. Until her dying breath.

SEE CHAPTER NOTES

CHAPTER 13

Rhoui woke up with his neck and face heavily bandaged, a horrible pain coming from where his face and mouth had been. He saw the clouded form of someone standing over him and grasped at the waif with his free hand, trying to speak but unable to form the words. He tried again, nearly choking on blood that oozed into his aching throat.

The clouded form came closer, sitting on the cot next to him. "You cannot speak. You will be moved soon to a better hospital, for surgery."

He felt the needle in his arm, saw the clouds thicken, then numb his body until they reached his brain and dropped him into a black hole.

The doctor stood, shaking his head, an aide standing across the cot. "He won't live, and if he does he will wish he hadn't. There is nothing any doctor can do for a wound like that. Not among our people at least." He sighed. "That is all the morphine you are to give him. Save it for those who have a chance." He thought a moment before giving a different order. "Put him with the wounded Jews from the Quarter. They will take him with the others in the morning. Maybe Jewish doctors can save him. Or they can put him out of his misery." With that he walked away, the aide looking pitifully down at the man on the cot. The doctor was right. With a wound like this, his chances of survival lay with doctors who had more expertise than any on this side of the battle lines. Turning to two soldiers, he instructed them to take the cot to the next room of the Armenian Patriarchate where the Jewish prisoners had so recently come. His stretcher was put on the floor next to the bed of a dying woman who was being offered a cigarette by a wounded soldier. With so many packed in the room, they hardly noticed another.

The girl, ready to puff, thought better of it and shoved the cigarette weakly aside. "No, it is Shabbat," she said. The soldier, Shar Cohen, nodded. But he was not religious and smoked the cigarette himself. Who knew when another might be found?

He sat by the woman's bed as she took her last breath, then he lay on the floor and watched the red flames of the burning Quarter through a window. As he did, he thought of a line from the Torah that he had recited as a young boy. He began reciting it, over and over, softly at first, then more loudly until his bass voice drove it through every room and out into the cold night air. Others picked up the chant.

"Out of blood and fire Judea will fall. Out of blood and fire it will be reborn."

Rhoui heard the words, but only vaguely, the morphine keeping him in a deep, painless haze. He could not understand why he was hearing it. What Arab would possibly sing such a song? Had the Jews won?

He did not care. Death was coming. He could feel it in the warm tingle of the morphine. He needed only wait a while longer, only a few more minutes. He had only one regret. He had betrayed his brother and sister. He wanted to say he was sorry. But maybe, maybe he would see them. Yes, in paradise. Didn't he deserve paradise? He was dying for his people, wasn't he? Surely Allah would give him this blessing.

The darkness clawed at his mind and fear gripped his heart. No, he did not deserve it. Izaat and Mary deserved such a thing, but he . . . he had betrayed them. Anguish gripped at him as the morphine sent him reeling into a very long, churning abyss. Allah had rejected him.

* * *

Most of the Quarter's survivors were taken to Katamon, a former Arab district now controlled by the Haganah. Naomi found morbid satisfaction in the fact that the Arabs had lost valuable ground around the city and had fled this suburb overlooking the Quarter without hardly a fight. Though the loss of the Quarter left a terrible void, the taking of Katamon and its large homes helped fill it.

Because Katamon was far from the headquarters where she would work, Naomi decided to find housing in West Jerusalem where she could take care of Mithra and get back and forth easily. She had not counted on the degree of difficulty she would encounter.

The sound of fighting seemed to echo through the narrow streets as they walked away from the drop-off point into Jewish West Jerusalem. Citizens scurried about, trying to stay out of the way, their shoulders hunched as if they expected Arab artillery to find them any moment.

She learned that the battle for the Hospice of Notre Dame continued—though the Haganah occupied most of the building and its yards—that the road to Jerusalem was once again closed by the Arabs, and that the want of food and water was nearly as serious here as it had been in the Quarter. To add to Jewish misery, the Arabs, elated by their success in the Old City, were now shelling West Jerusalem at far more regular intervals in hopes of further reducing both Haganah and civilian morale. If something wasn't done soon, if supplies and reinforcements, bullets and weapons, men and medical supplies, did not arrive, the entire rest of Jewish Jerusalem, more than a hundred thousand people, would soon see the same humiliation of surrender that she had just experienced. This would surely bring an end to their state.

"Are we in the Hasidic section of the New City?" Mithra asked.

"No, that is to the north of us. Do you want to go there?"

"Most certainly not. I have never seen such . . . such stupidity. If they had fought with you and the others, we might still be in our homes."

"Don't blame them too much, Mithra," Naomi said. "They have not seen what you and I have seen. They do not understand."

"Well, now they do, or they truly are fools."

They walked four blocks before she felt they were far enough from the front to slow their pace and look for a place to live. A small market stood on the corner of the street, and she stepped inside, grateful for the smell of food and other goods that greeted her. She put her hand in her pocket and touched the money she had there. Her savings. She had shoved the entire amount in her pocket only this morning. Or was it yesterday? She could not remember, but she was grateful she had done so or, like the rest of the Old City, it would be nothing but ashes.

Asking the owner if he knew of any place they might find shelter, she received a look of disbelief that spoke volumes.

"Here? No, no, nothing. Refugees from near the frontlines take any extra space or are finding shelter in schools and synagogues. The ones from the Quarter have been taken to—"

"Katamon. Yes, I know, but I work for Israeli intelligence, and Katamon is too far away for me to take care of my friend and see to my duties."

"Possibly you could get her to Tel Aviv. Some are going through the mountains to the sea, though it is very dangerous. The Arabs watch and kill any Jew they see wandering about. Thanks to your Haganah and the massacre at Deir Yassin, Arabs want this kind of revenge," he said bitterly.

Naomi bit her tongue and, picking up a few items before paying, took Mithra's hand and left the store. She thought that by now most would understand the need to fight, but apparently there were still some who had not caught the vision. If the Arabs took his store, maybe this ignorant shopkeeper would finally decide the Haganah was worth supporting.

"I am sorry, dear, but I am really very tired. Is there someplace close by we can stay?"

"Soon," Naomi said. She desperately tried to think of a place to go, then saw the small hotel across the street. Leading Mithra, she entered the lobby but was disappointed. Several people waited at the desk and others lounged about, sleeping on every inch of space. Naomi listened to the conversation between the frustrated clerk and a small family trying to find a place to stay. He had no more rooms and certainly no more space in the lobby. Naomi led Mithra out the door, right into a small, plump woman, nearly knocking her to the ground. Naomi grabbed her with one arm and steadied her while making her apologies. "I'm sorry. I didn't see . . . We were looking for a place to stay, and they have no room so we . . . I left in too big a hurry. I am sorry."

The woman smiled. "I overheard you in the market. At first I did not . . . well . . . my apartment is very small, and there is hardly enough room for me, but . . . but if you don't mind . . . There is a couch your friend can sleep on, and I have enough blankets for a bed on the floor for you."

Naomi felt a lone tear trickle down her cheek and quickly wiped it away. She had been crying entirely too much of late. "Thank you," she said softly. "It will be more than adequate."

"Come with me then," she smiled.

Mithra gripped Naomi's hand tightly in gratitude for their good fortune. They followed the woman for another block, climbed some narrow steps, and entered an apartment on the back of a large stone building. It was small, but Naomi had never been so happy to have a door close behind her in her entire life. The woman invited them to sit down while she took their food bag and placed it on the table, then talked about various things in the apartment. Naomi saw that the woman was quite lonely and very frightened and realized that she was as grateful for their presence as Naomi and Mithra were that they were surrounded by solid walls with a roof overhead.

"I will fix your food while you wash up," said the woman with a cheery smile. "Take care with the water though. It is rationed now, and we don't have much for washing. My name is Hilda. Please, explain what happened to you."

Naomi talked as Mithra washed herself, careful to use as little water as possible. When she finished, she said, "Please, may I lie down? I am much too tired to eat." Naomi helped her get settled on the couch where she quickly fell asleep. Naomi noted the murky water, but washed off her dust coating as best she could. She could not remember the last time she'd had a real bath and longed for one, her hair particularly clumped with dust and grime. To be really clean, to wear clean clothes, would be wonderful, but right now it was only a dream.

She and Hilda finished eating and stepped onto a small patio where they could visit without waking Mithra. Naomi could hear the distant sounds of heated battle, and goose bumps crawled across her skin, forcing her to rub them out with the palm of her hands.

"My husband was killed in the rebellion of 1936. They attacked his shop and shot him," Hilda said. "Since then, I have lost another son to the Arabs. Only my daughter remains. She is at Hadassah Hospital, may heaven protect her."

"Was she in the convoy that . . ."

"No, no, she was already there, but she must stay now. The Arabs have the road cut off. The army is trying to break through but hasn't been successful yet. I haven't heard from my daughter in more than a week."

"I am sure she is fine," Naomi said.

After nearly an hour of visiting about the news of the last few days, Naomi asked Hilda if she would mind looking out for Mithra while she reported to SHAI. Hilda was quite agreeable and gave Naomi a key to the apartment in case she returned late.

"If you do not come back for a while, we will be fine except for food. I don't know what we will do for food."

Naomi picked up on the hint and gave Hilda some of her remaining money, enough for several days. Hilda was both happy and relieved. "I have never cared for a blind person. Are there any particular things she cannot do? Things that I must be careful about?"

"Show her around the apartment, let her get familiar with things, and she will be all right. She is quite a lady and very independent, living alone since losing her eyes to the Nazis."

Naomi went to the door, glancing at Mithra before leaving the apartment. She was sleeping soundly.

Her bones ached from fatigue, but Naomi knew sleep would not come until she checked with the Haganah to find out if they knew anything about the prisoners from the Quarter—where they had been taken and if they had any idea of their actual treatment. She feared for Abraham. The Arabs were notorious for breaking their word.

When she entered headquarters, she found the place in chaos but was immediately recognized by one of the secretaries and welcomed. "Is anyone from SHAI still here?" Naomi asked.

"Most of them are in Tel Aviv with central command. Our officer is over there." The secretary pointed at a man sitting at a table. He was poring over some papers. Naomi thanked the secretary and worked her way through people and tables to where he sat.

"Hello, Eleazar," she said.

He looked up with his usual scowl, then gave it up for a broad grin. "Naomi. Good to see you."

"The last time I saw you, we were both in Tel Aviv. When did you get here?" Naomi had worked with Eleazar Sukenik at SHAI's main office. She considered him the best analyst their organization had.

"Ten days ago. Sheal'tiel needed an intelligence officer and was kind enough to select me."

"Then you can tell me why we were left high and dry in the Quarter," she said.

"It wasn't for lack of trying. How would you like a job?"

"Maybe tomorrow. Right now I am just looking for answers."

He stood, retrieved a chair just evacuated by someone else, and pulled it up next to his. "Sit." He pulled out a map and proceeded to explain the Haganah's failed attempts to resupply the Quarter. When he was finished, he sat back. "The Arabs cut us off. Add to that some bad decisions, inexperience, and horrible timing, multiply it by a few egos and poor communication, and you have your answer."

Though somewhat bitter, Naomi nodded. "We'll lose if we can't do any better than this."

"We're quick learners," Eleazar said. "But our biggest problem is weaponry and training. The airlift from Zatec, Czechoslovakia, is fully on now, and we're getting more men from Cyprus all the time, but we need another month to get them ready. For now, we just have to hang on to what we can."

"If the Quarter is any indication of how well we're doing at hanging on, we can't last another week," Naomi said.

"All is not despair. We have Jaffa and Haifa under control," Eleazar said, "and we defeated the Syrians at Degania on the southern tip of the Sea of Galilee. We forced the Iraqis to retreat into territory given the Arabs by the UN, but they and the Legion of Transjordan are getting ready for another push to Haifa."

"Will they succeed?" she asked.

"I hope not. They could cut our new state in half. That could be disastrous, and frankly, preventing it was part of our problem getting to you in the Quarter. We had to send a lot of men north. Sometimes those are the choices." He faced her. "But, enough of battle plans and reasons for failure. I assume that Abraham is with the prisoners, and the real reason you've come is to find out if we know what happened to them." He gave her an encouraging smile.

"And? What do you know?"

"That they are headed for Jordan, probably the prison camp at Mafraq. They will not shoot them. The Red Cross insisted on sending people with them until they arrived at their destination. Abdullah has promised to take good care of them, and if the treatment of the prisoners from Kfar Etzion is an example, Abraham will come home twenty pounds lighter, but alive and well."

"Abraham can't afford twenty pounds. And don't forget, Abdullah was going to stay out of the fight once, then gave into his people when they wouldn't let him. He can't be trusted. No Arab can. What do we know about Mafraq? Where is it, and can we get to it?"

"Slow down, Naomi. No one is talking about going into Transjordan. Haven't you heard a thing I've said? We're having enough trouble just defending the land we've been given." He took a deep breath. "As for the camp, it is somewhere near Amman. That's all we know."

"They'll butcher them," Naomi said.

He leaned forward. "Abraham will be fine. It's you I'm not so sure about. You look like you have just crawled out of Hades. Find a bed and get some sleep. You're no good to anyone if you can't think straight."

She nodded. "Soon. How bad off are we in Jerusalem?"

"We stopped the Legion's advance. Since then, they seemed to have changed their tactics from battle to siege. They've cut off our main supply lines, shut off our freshwater pipeline, bombed or switched off power plants in their territory, and are hitting us with their artillery so regular you can tell time by it, trying to wear down our morale. Other than that, we're winning."

"You're a smart alec, Eleazar."

"So sue me. Ben-Gurion knows that the loss of Jerusalem would mean the end for us, so he will break the siege, sooner or later. Right now, like everywhere else, we're just trying to hang on until more weapons show up."

"Who are these men the UN has sent to seek a truce?" Naomi knew that since the war started on May 15, the United Nations had been calling for a truce. But no real movement had been made. The Arabs refused to listen, confident that their armies would drive the Jews into the sea in a matter of days. Since that hadn't happened, the voices calling for a cease-fire were increasing, and the UN had sent two men to try and negotiate something. Word had come into the Quarter by radio that they arrived yesterday. One more reason they were given to hold on. Apparently they hadn't accomplished their purpose. Not yet.

"A Swedish diplomat by the name of Count Folke Bernadotte and an American Ralph Bunche. They've met with our people and with some of the Arabs and presented a plan, but the Arabs dismissed it entirely. It won't go anywhere unless the Brits apply pressure to the Arabs. Abba Eban, our diplomat in New York, is trying to get the Americans to push the Brits to do just that. We'll see. One thing is sure, we're running out of everything and still can't compete with the Arabs in heavy artillery, tanks, and planes. A four-week cease-fire would give us a chance." He sat back. "The Brits will be slow to buckle to the Americans, but if we could apply some pressure of our own, give them a few deep wounds to lick, even a little thumb twisting by the Brits might work." He looked at his watch. "Maybe we can give them something to think about tonight."

"Tonight?"

"Yeah, in about an hour we're going to hit Latrun again. If we take it, we open the road to Tel Aviv. They could resupply us, and we could go on the offensive. That would make Abdullah and the others scramble before they lose the territory they've taken."

The outside door opened, and Wally Bergman came in. Their eyes met immediately, and a smile of relief crossed his face as he quickly worked his away around people and tables to get to Naomi. She stood, and the two of them embraced.

"Good to see you," he said. "When I heard that the Quarter fell, well, I was worried. After I landed, I went directly to the staging area for refugees. No one seemed to know anything about you, so I decided to come here." He had liked Naomi and Abraham from the first moment they met. That had been just after the Battle of Kastel, and at the time he had decided to stick around to fly planes for Israel.

"I am assuming that Abraham is with the prisoners," he said, his eyes showing both fear and hope.

"Yes, along with many others, some of them noncombatants."

Relief crossed his face. The news could have been much worse. "You look like you could use a cup of coffee. How about joining me?"

"Good idea," she said.

He opened the door, and they went out.

"Did you pick up Zohar at the docks in Haifa?"

"Sure, found her an apartment too. She's working for Weizman now. I saw her at the airport just a few hours ago." He opened the door to the small coffee room where a woman gave them each a small, diluted cup of warm coffee, and they sat down at the one table against the wall.

"Are you going back to Tel Aviv tonight?" Naomi asked.

"Maybe. I'm waiting for Mickey Marcus. He's directing the battle for Latrun tonight."

"Who?"

"His name is David Marcus, but around here they call him Mickey Stone. Us fellow Americans combine them just for fun.

Marcus served on Eisenhower's staff during the war with the Nazis and volunteered to serve Israel. Ben-Gurion appointed him supreme commander of the Jerusalem front thinking that a first-class commander might unify segments of the Haganah that seem to spend more time arguing with each other than fighting the enemy. This is his first battle. I hope he doesn't make a shambles of it and make all us Americans look bad." He smiled.

"Why the new name?" she asked.

"To avoid complications for Marcus in the United States. The State Department withdrew permission for any professional soldiers to fight for Israel and promised to blackball anyone who did. Marcus defied them but is trying to keep that a secret as long as he can. If you ask me, there isn't much they can do to him, being on Eisenhower's staff and all, but he chooses to be cautious. The State Department doesn't like former army personnel bucking them, and they're pretty powerful themselves."

"And guys like you?"

"I'm not professional military like Marcus. I mustered out, and so did most of the others who've come from the States to fight. But they do try to keep us from coming. If you don't believe it, just ask some of the flyboys back at Ekron. Some of them are spittin' mad at our government for the way they've been treated. Me, I was already out of the States, so I didn't get any hassles."

"Do you think Marcus can make a difference?"

"He's a leader, and he worked with Eisenhower, but he hasn't had a lot of field experience." He hesitated. "Latrun will be a tough battle to start with. It's downright foolish to try taking it again, if you ask me. Better to go around. I've flown over that place—you know, reconnaissance—and you would have to tear down that fortress stone by stone before you could root them out." He shook his head. "I was standing in the command center of the Seventh Brigade when Marcus went over the plan for the last time just a few hours ago. It is a shrewd plan. The only trouble is it calls for good timing, and I haven't seen anyone good at that in this army. Not yet."

"Timing?"

"Yeah. Everybody just seems to call their own shots, do what they want when they want. No allegiance to a central command, and until that changes, operations like this one will succeed only out of dumb luck." He leaned forward. "They had a chance to get into the Quarter, Naomi, and they blew it for just these reasons." He shook his head. "Some of these company commanders ought be shot, that's what." He sat back. "That's why we need a leader. I just hope Marcus lets them have it if they blow this again. Too many people getting killed this way, that's for sure." He looked at her carefully. "You look like somebody sucked all the blood right out of you." He stood. "Come on. It's obvious you haven't slept in weeks. I'll walk you home, wherever that is. I guess you have a place."

"Yes, I have a place."

They both stood. "They won't be finished at Latrun until after sunup. Be back here then and if there is room, I can fly you to Tel Aviv."

As they entered the command room, they found everyone gathered around the radio listening intently. The battle for Latrun had begun. She listened for a moment, then walked away, the harsh sounds of battle too much for her to bear so soon after the Quarter.

As Wally opened the door, Eleazar grabbed Naomi's arm and handed her a radio message. "This is the first good news we've had in a while. You look like you could use it." He smiled. "Will I see you tomorrow? I could use your help."

She nodded. "Yes, I'll be here."

She and Wally stepped into the street, the distant sounds of battle echoing off the dark sky. Even with a full moon, the city seemed extra dark and depressing.

"Do you have a match?" she asked.

Wally searched his shirt pocket, then his pants, and found a packet of matches. Striking one, he held it over the paper Eleazar had given her.

"Prisoners arrived safe in Mafraq. None lost. All well."

Her hand started to shake, her eyes unable to hold back the tears. Wally put his arms around her. The woman had been through a tough day.

SEE CHAPTER NOTES

CHAPTER 14

Abraham and the other captives arrived at Mafraq by truck, traveling down from Jerusalem to the Jordan River Valley, across the Allenby Bridge, and into Transjordan. They passed hundreds of soldiers in trucks, other vehicles pulling artillery pieces, and armored cars, all on their way to join the battle for the Holy City. The joyful, triumphant demeanor of the Arabs as they celebrated the capture of the Quarter, along with their ridicule of the prisoners as they passed, was humiliating but sobering for both the fighters and the Orthodox Jewish men from the Quarter, all of whom had been forced to come with them as potential combatants. Ludicrous, he thought. None of them had fought for their own homes. They were as threatening as a newborn babe.

Abraham and Russnak had both complained to the Arabs about sending these men out of the city but had received nothing but sneers for their effort. Only Russnak's demand to see the commander of the Legion's troops got any action. Even then, they were ultimately refused. To release the Orthodox men without proof they hadn't carried weapons or wouldn't in the future would be foolish, they were told by Colonel Tal, and he did not intend to be a fool.

They reached the actual prison sometime during the night to find that there were no beds, only a few blankets, and even less food. Tired to the core, Abraham had stumbled into one of the ragged tents and found a place in the dirt to sleep, waking only after the sun beat upon him mercilessly. The Kamsin was driving hot air from the southern deserts to melt even the strongest will.

Dusting himself off, he knelt and prayed, wishing that he had taken the time to retrieve his prayer shawl, Torah, and Book of Mormon from their apartment. He needed comfort. The loss of the Quarter, and especially of his parents, left him angry, hurt, and in need of solace. Then, having to leave Naomi behind, unsure of whether they would ever see one another again, had only deepened his misery.

After nearly an hour with God, he left the tent feeling better and more determined. He would find a way back, and soon. As for his parents, they were in God's hands now. They had lived good lives, and He would care for them. For now, Abraham would delay his mourning and focus on escape.

The camp was filled with hundreds of men standing around in small groups, sweat rolling through dusty rivulets down their faces. He saw the Orthodox first. They were near the western fence, gathered in straight lines with Rabbi Salomon at their head. Each wore his shawl, and each held a copy of the Torah, their bodies moving rhythmically as they read and prayed. He moved past them. He no longer wanted to pray with them. Though he tried to forgive them of their treatment of him, Naomi, and his parents, that did not mean he wished to worship with them. It only angered him, and he did not wish to be angry at them. God would not like him for it, nor would he like himself. Better to stay away from them.

Walking among the rest of the prisoners until he saw a familiar face, then another and another, he found himself with the small group of Haganah men from the Quarter who had been in his platoon. His throat parched, he asked them if there was any water.

"None yet. They say it is delivered twice a day—midmorning and midafternoon. But you don't get much, and with our arrival, there will probably be even less this first haul."

"And food?" he asked.

"It is delivered at the same time. The ones who have been here for the past ten days say it isn't fit to feed swine, but it keeps them alive."

Abraham looked around the enclosure. High, strong wire was strung between heavy posts and topped by barbed wire, making the fence look difficult but not unbeatable. It was the guards outside and along the perimeter that worried him. Their automatic weapons would be hard to get past. "Has anyone tried to escape?" he asked.

"Twice. One bunch came up with some cutters and went through the wire. The second group went under it. The first didn't get fifty feet. Two were killed, and the other three spent a week getting beatings. The second was a foursome. They got lucky. Some of the guards fell asleep. Unfortunately, they were found along the Jordan when they went for water," said Eliahu. "Only two of the four returned and haven't been seen since." He nodded toward a small, concrete building outside the wire. "They're in that place, and we're told they probably won't be coming out anytime soon."

"The trouble is getting across the desert once you're out. Heat, no water except along the Jordan, the place crawling with Arabs, and little to no cover between here and the caves and ravines on the other side of the Jordan Valley," said Benjamin.

"No sense running if you have no place to go, or at least a way to fight back if they come after you," added Eliahu.

"I suppose there is a Jewish officer in charge of communication with the guards," Abraham asked.

"The Germans could teach these Arabs a thing or two, but they have the basics down," said Benjamin, who had been in concentration camps under the Nazis. He pointed. "That's the commander's house. Our head man just went in for a conference. He'll ask for more blankets, food, and water and try to get a little news about how things are going. From what we hear,

Abdullah has ordered that we be given decent care except when we try to escape. I suppose we'll see if he is obeyed."

"Who is our man?"

"Sydney Richter. He was captured at Etzion. One of the lucky ones," answered Benjamin.

"Who else do we have?" Abraham asked Eliahu.

"Odds and ends. Men taken from captured convoys and a few from up north, but most of us are from around Jerusalem." He pointed. "See that building behind the commander's office? That's the infirmary. They say there are a dozen of our men in there. Wounded in battle, then brought here and given aid by the Jordanians. I expect a few from the Quarter will arrive today or tomorrow and be put in there," Franz said with a shrug. "Maybe all Arabs aren't out to annihilate us after all."

"Maybe, but I know for certain that if you're captured by the Irregulars or even by the Syrians or the Iraqis, they just shoot you," Eliahu added.

"It shows some humanity exists, at least in the Legion," Franz countered.

"The Legion helped butcher those at Kfar Etzion," Eliahu argued.

"The Legion has Brits as commanders, and with the exception of Etzion they have kept things under control. There were Irregulars in the Old City that would have slaughtered us if we hadn't been under Legion arrest, but they kept that from happening. Remember, one Arab took a potshot at us, and Legion soldiers killed him on the spot," said Benjamin.

"The soldier thought the guy was firing at him. He had no choice."

"You don't know that," Franz said.

"What it boils down to is they won't kill us as long as they think they might get something for us—you know a prisoner trade or something. When they don't think that's possible, they'll shoot us," Eliahu said. His words stopped the argument. With this, no one seemed to disagree.

"Then we ought to think about getting out of here, hadn't we?" Abraham said. He told them to mingle, nose around for any plans to escape, and start looking for chinks in the Arab armor. He wandered toward the gate, his eyes panning the fence, looking for dips in the ground, rusty wire, and any other weakness that might pop out at him. A guard ordered him to halt and shoved his gun through the wire, poking it at him in a menacing manner. Abraham backed away, his arms in the air while wanting to take the gun and ram it down its owner's throat.

"Abraham. Abraham Marshak." Abraham turned to see Moshe Shari coming toward him. He couldn't help but smile.

"Well, well, even ETZEL has its losses, eh?"

Moshe grinned. "The British, smartest army in the world, couldn't keep me locked up, but this ragtag bunch of wannabes gathered me up like a plucked chicken." He grinned. "Not for long though. How are you, Abraham? I haven't seen you since your wedding."

Moshe and Naomi had known each other while escaping Germany. Naomi, Aaron, and Hannah had saved his life from some stray Nazis who continued to prey on Jews trying to escape through Italy after the war. He thought highly of Naomi and had come to the wedding at considerable risk since the British were still in Jerusalem and had a price on his head. A very big price. Killing Brits did that for a man.

Naomi had told Abraham about Moshe's escape from a British prison truck headed for Acre with the help of some ETZEL friends who ambushed the convoy. Aaron had been in the same truck, and Moshe had helped him escape as well. Aaron had then abandoned Moshe and his friends and headed south back to Jerusalem.

"As well as one can do while being locked up in this chicken coop," Abraham said. "I thought you went back to the north after the wedding."

"I did, but when I heard the British had marched out of the city, I and a few friends decided it was time to go back to Jerusalem where the real fighting is. We were catching a bit of sleep in the hills just north of there when a company of Jordanians stumbled onto us. We didn't have a chance to fire a single bullet. Too bad about the Quarter. I hear the Haganah couldn't get in."

"No one could, Moshe, not even you and your ETZEL friends."

"Maybe, but we would have died trying."

"Many of the Haganah did," Abraham said. "When are you and the rest of ETZEL going to stop attacking the Haganah along with the Arabs, Moshe? It doesn't do any good to belittle Haganah efforts just to make yourself look good."

"Yeah, sorry. You're right. Besides, before getting sent here, I heard that our leaders are talking to Ben-Gurion, trying to make peace. Hey, soon, we'll all be one happy fighting family, right?" He smiled.

"For the sake of all Israel, I pray that such will be the case," Abraham said. "I am assuming you have plans for escape. When you do, I'd like to go with you."

"For the sake of our new brotherhood, you're in. We will meet tomorrow night at midnight in the tent closest to the fence at the southwest corner of the camp. In the meantime, think about how we can get to their armory. It's the building north of the hospital. I'll see you then." With that, Moshe walked briskly toward the gate where several trucks were just arriving. The entire camp seemed to gravitate in that direction, and Abraham realized the trucks were probably bringing food and water. Instead of falling in with everyone else, Abraham kept his eyes on the hospital and armory. The half dozen guards assigned the two buildings visited nonchalantly while watching the rush on the food trucks. Their arrogance was evident in their attitude and in their obvious jokes about the prisoners' rush for food.

But Abraham saw something else that garnered his attention: a window on the end of the infirmary from which anyone inside could both see and launch an attack on the armory. Slowly moving toward the food trucks, he kept his eye on the infirmary.

"You better get some food, Abraham," Benjamin said. Abraham looked down at the slop Benjamin had in a metal plate, then at the dirty water in his cup.

"Small wonder they have need of an infirmary," he said.

Franz joined them. "We should have gone down fighting in the Quarter. This will kill us just as surely as a bullet." He stared at the food with disgust even as Benjamin used his fingers to scoop up a taste of the thick porridge. His face wrinkled, and he swallowed—hard.

"Tastes like wallpaper paste. Worse even than what the Nazis used to dish out," he said. "But if we're going to get out of here, we have to eat." He scooped up a second bite. Franz sighed, then used his hard bread to eat a little. Abraham went to the trucks and was handed a plate and cup and the last scraps of bread, along with some of the slop scraped from the bottom of the large pot. The Arab dished it up with a smirk on his face.

"Nice of you to share your mother's cooking with us," Abraham quipped in Arabic. The snigger disappeared as the steel ladle swung in Abraham's direction. He ducked and stepped away, but the Arab pursued while yelling for armed guards to join him. Before Abraham could melt into the crowd, the butt of a rifle slammed him between his shoulder blades, throwing him forward. His dishes flew helter-skelter in front of him as he hit the hard ground. He tried to catch his breath as strong arms dragged him toward the gate. He wanted to fight, but the pain in his chest, lungs, and back simply didn't allow him the strength. By the time the gate was thrown open and he was pulled through, there were enough gun barrels pointed at his chest that he figured he would be a dead man if he so much as flinched. Then another rifle butt came out of nowhere and slammed into the side of his head, leaving him nothing but darkness.

* * *

Abraham awoke with a pounding headache. He touched his face. His right eye was swollen shut, and his lips were puffy and sore. There were cuts in his chin that someone had sewn shut. The beating had taken its toll. He tried to sit up, but a firm hand on his chest kept him down. A light was flipped on in the dark room, and when Abraham's eyes adjusted, he saw an Arab with a heavy moustache and dense eyebrows staring down at him.

"You are lucky to be alive. It seems you were offensive to one of the guards. His friends had a good shot at you before they were stopped by our commander."

Abraham touched his swollen lips. "I would hate to see what they would do to someone who really attacked them." He looked at the man. "And who are you?" he croaked, then cleared his throat.

"The doctor. You're in the infirmary, which is better than being in solitary confinement like some of your soldiers. It takes much longer to nurse them back to health than it does even the wounded we are sent. Would you like some water?"

Abraham nodded slightly and raised his head to sit up as the doctor reached for a glass. His ribs smarted, and his head throbbed, but he finally got his feet over the edge of the bed. Taking the tin cup, he gulped down the water, then handed it back. "If the rest of the prisoners find out you give out water in here, they'll beat each other to a pulp to get at it."

The doctor smiled. "Yes, I think you are right. But things will get better for all of you soon." He paused.

"They're sending more water?"

The doctor smiled. "No, our army is defeating yours, and soon we will have victory. Then you can go home and have all the water our government can give you."

"Or we will whip you and take as much as we want," Abraham said.

The doctor laughed. "Yes, I suppose that is an option, though a doubtful one. Our armies are much larger and better equipped than yours."

"Your propaganda won't work on me, Doctor. I've been in Jerusalem, and I know we stopped you with fewer weapons and men. Give us another month, and we'll drive you out of our country. After that, we don't much care what you do. If Abdullah wants to take control of Palestinian land, let him, but if he tries to take away what we have been given, we'll fight him to the last man."

The doctor's eyebrows raised. "You are Hasidic. Surely you do not agree with this violence, this theft of Arab lands."

"Sorry to disappoint you, but all Hasids are not as passive as you and others would like us to be. I fight with the Haganah."

"But is this not against the Hasidic way?"

"Not any more than it is against the way of Islam, which I assume you are a part of. When an enemy threatens my freedom to worship, tries to take my home and kill my family, I will fight rather than give in. Your Arab armies and Haj Amin el Husseini embody that threat. Unlike the Jews of Europe, most of us, even many who have practiced peace and nonviolence for centuries, chose to fight rather than be annihilated by your Nazi Mufti."

"The Mufti is a horrible man. Many Arabs do not support him, especially here in Transjordan. As you see, you will be treated humanely here."

"And for this I give you my gratitude, but if you beat us, can you guarantee that Haj Amin won't get the power he wants?"

He thought a moment. "No, I cannot. The Mufti is a powerful man." The doctor's anger eased a bit, and he turned to leave. "You will go back to the yard tomorrow after breakfast. Sleep in comfort while you can." As the doctor opened the door, Abraham noticed armed guards in the next room. Then the door shut and was locked.

"Breakfast. Bagels and cream cheese, I hope," Abraham said under his breath.

"More like mush and old bread, or didn't you eat today?" said one of the patients.

Abraham faced him. "I didn't get a chance, but from what I saw, it wasn't a big disappointment."

"And they try so hard," answered the patient.

Abraham could not see him clearly and didn't turn on more lights so he could, afraid that it would wake others. "What brings you to this fine establishment?" he asked.

"An attempted escape. They broke both my legs when they caught me. Said they had orders. Make me so I wouldn't try it again. The doc patched me up as good as he could. He's a good man, really, and probably the only friend we have around here, so don't push him too far, okay?"

"Okay." He stood and walked to the window. "Any lessons learned you might like to tell me about?"

"Yeah, stay put. There isn't any place to hide, and they have a bedu scout working for them who can track anything that walks." With that he turned his face to the wall, weary of talking.

Abraham walked from bed to bed. All the others were asleep, each with serious injuries. One had lost an arm, another a leg, while a third was heavily wrapped around his torso. The bandage showed blood in the right side of his chest. The good doctor had done what he could, but Abraham wondered how many of these patients could survive.

He looked around the room, getting his bearings. The window that would look out over the armory would be to his right, beyond the curtain that separated his ward from the next one. He went to the end of it and stepped around. There were more beds here, and several patients stared back at him in the halo of dim light. Other beds sat beyond his clear view, but he could see that, with one or two exceptions, the beds were empty. Those patients he could see he did not recognize. A man in a bed just outside the light asked for water, and Abraham stepped to a pitcher of water nearby and delivered it, switching on the nearest light. As he turned toward the next bed, he nearly screamed with shock. He recognized the man whose bandaged head lay on the pillow, his eyes fixed on Abraham. Abraham blinked, sure he was dreaming. He moved closer, the eyes of the patient remaining fixed on some distant object.

Reaching out, Abraham touched the man's hand to find it warm but unresponsive. He gripped it tightly and forced back the tears of shock and joy as he held tightly the hand of Aaron Schwartz.

SEE CHAPTER NOTES

CHAPTER 15

When Naomi awoke, it was quiet. A mild breeze blew through the open veranda door. She hadn't rested well, the nightmares and worry about Abraham refusing to let her fall into a deep sleep. Still tired, she wished with all her being that the peace would stay, that she would get up to find Abraham poring over his Torah on the veranda, that she was really still in the Quarter and they were living a life of love and serenity.

The first rays of the sun moved slowly across the floor, and her wish turned to ashes when the smell of fresh air turned sour by the smoke of war wafting into the room. By the time the warm rays hit the blanket on which she lay, the first shell exploded somewhere in the city, and the sounds of war in the direction of Latrun returned with a vengeance. Forcing herself to her feet, she went to the basin to wash herself and found it full of fresh water. She stared at the clear pool of liquid, longing to wash the grime from her hair, to feel clean again, but knowing this was probably the daily allotment for all three of them she resisted, dipping her hands only to rinse them, drying them on a somewhat soiled towel to her right.

"You wish to wash thoroughly, especially your hair. You should, you know. It will be quite all right," Mithra said from where she lay on the sofa. "Hilda and I do not need to wash up this morning, and if you do not take care of your hair, it will be bedding for lice."

Naomi ran her fingers through the water, hesitating. Water was so precious, and if she washed her hair this would surely be unusable for anything else. But oh, how wonderful it would feel!

Hilda came to the door between her bedroom and the living area. "Please, use it." She smiled. "I have water for drinking, and there will be more for at least a few days. By then," she shrugged, "who knows?"

Sensing Naomi's continued reluctance, Mithra got up and felt her way to Naomi's side. "Kneel down and put your head over the basin." She pushed down gently on Naomi's shoulder. Naomi went to her knees and put her head almost reverently over the pool of clear water. Mithra found the small rinsing cup, dipped it, then began pouring the water slowly over Naomi's short, curly, grimy hair, using her aged and gnarled fingers to gently move it about as the water cascaded from it into the basin. After a moment, she used the small vial of perfumed shampoo Hilda handed her and scrubbed, using her fingers to thoroughly clean Naomi's scalp. She rinsed, then washed it once more with fresh water in a pitcher. As the last of the water dripped clean from the ends of her hair into the muddy brown basin, Naomi somehow felt stronger—she could go on for at least another day. She sat back on her heels as Mithra dried her hair with a towel. As she finished, Naomi shook her curls free as Mithra sat down on the couch.

"Come, sit at my feet, and I will brush it for you," Mithra said.

They moved to the couch, and Naomi sat down between Mithra's knees, and the brushing started.

"Did I ever tell you that I had two daughters of my own? They had hair very much like yours—thick, curly, and so very soft when it was dried and brushed." She paused, the brush stopping in midair. "Do you remember having the Nazis shave your head, how humiliating it was? How degrading? It was as if they took away what made us different from animals, as if by shaving our heads they no longer had to think of us as human, as women."

"Yes, I remember," Naomi said softly.

"I think that was the day my daughters gave up living. Yes, I am sure of it. That was the day."

Naomi felt the pain in Mithra's words, and the old memories of humiliation and horror pushed up from the deep recesses of her mind. She fought them, pushed them back, as Mithra's gentle, soothing touch against her hair and scalp somehow helped blunt them. Slowly, with stroke after luxurious stroke of the brush, Naomi's hair dried, and the pain and sound of war were momentarily shelved in some distant place. She felt calm and at peace.

"There, it is done," Mithra said. "How does she look, Hilda? Did I comb it right?"

"Radiant. Wonderful, absolutely wonderful," Hilda said sincerely as she finished slicing some bread, placing it on a small plate with olives and cucumbers.

Naomi got to her feet and stepped to the small mirror above the basin. She hardly recognized the woman standing opposite her and couldn't help the smile. Though the dress was the same filthy piece of cloth, and though her skin still had a dusty hue to it, for the first time in days, she felt washed.

"Thank you," she said to both of them. "From my heart, thank you."

"Here, change into these as well," Hilda said, stretching forth a stack of khaki clothing. "They were my son's, but you are the same size as he was." Then she hesitated. "I mean, if . . . if you don't mind wearing . . . He was killed, you know. I . . ."

"I would be honored," Naomi said. She took the clothing and went in the bedroom and quickly changed. The pants were a bit large in the waist, but she simply tucked in the shirt and cinched the belt a little tighter. She had been wearing such clothing since joining the Haganah, but had left them in Tel Aviv knowing Abraham liked her best in a dress. Wearing clothes where she wasn't constantly fighting to keep her skirt in place for purposes of modesty felt good again.

She took a deep breath and walked into the living area, where Hilda glanced at her approvingly and pointed to a chair at the table. She sat next to Mithra as Hilda quickly gave a Jewish prayer over the food.

They ate, the sounds of war working their way back into their consciousness, its tension returning to their lives. As Naomi pushed her chair back, Hilda handed her a small sack of food.

"It isn't much, but . . ."

Naomi was grateful they had been led to Hilda. She shuddered to think how different their morning might have been if they hadn't. "It is plenty. Thank you. I will try to find more and bring it home when I can."

"We can do the shopping, Naomi. You will be much too busy fighting the Arabs to look for food. Besides, you may not be able to return tonight, or even soon. We will take care of ourselves, won't we, Hilda?"

Naomi noted that Hilda seemed unsettled about the prospect of shopping while the Arabs bombarded the city with their artillery and couldn't blame her. She wanted to argue with Mithra but knew she was right. By tonight, she could be fighting on the front lines or worse, and to have them depending on her for food would be foolish.

She attempted a comforting smile while handing Hilda the rest of the money in her pocket, said good-bye, and left the apartment. As she walked into the street, the bloodcurdling sound of the shelling seemed much louder. Hurrying through the streets toward work, she passed soldiers rushing about as troops were moved to different places of attack and defense. Sounds of small-arms gunfire came from no more than a block to the east, a sure sign they were still fighting for the Notre Dame near the Old City wall. But the loudest sounds of war came from the area of Ramat Rahel in the south and Latrun in the northwest. Apparently the Egyptians were trying to retake Ramat Rahel before agreeing to any truce sponsored by the United Nations, and the Haganah was still fighting for Latrun.

Entering the building, she found Eleazar sitting in the same chair he had sat in the previous day. "Did you sleep here last night?" she asked, placing her small sack on a shelf.

"You noticed." He sat back, removed his glasses, and rubbed his eyes.

"What is happening at Latrun?" she asked.

"Disaster. We have the usual poor communications and bad luck mingling with lack of experience on the part of our soldiers, most of whom haven't been in the country more than a week. Add to that no common language to take orders by, and you have what might be called a debacle. We're trying to retreat now, but we've lost a lot of lives and gained nothing while increasing Arab morale tenfold."

"Any news on the truce?"

"The Arabs continue dragging their feet. This victory will give them even more reason for recalcitrance."

The door opened, and Wally entered the room.

"Good. You're here. They want you up now. We need more information on conditions at Latrun," Eleazar said to him.

"Where are Marcus and Sheal'tiel?" Wally said with a stiff jaw.

"At the headquarters of the Seventh Brigade or maybe out trying to bring some semblance of order to the front lines. What difference does it make? Get your plane in the air."

"Fools," Wally said before taking a deep breath. "I'll need a spotter."

"Anyone want to fly with this maniac? He's headed for Latrun," Eleazar announced. There were no takers.

"I'll go," Naomi said.

"I need you here," Eleazar responded.

Wally added, "And I won't take you up. Abraham would have my skin if something happened to you."

"Neither of you have anything to say about it. I am not assigned to you at this point, Eleazar, so you can't tell me what to do, and Wally, if you're as good a flier as you say you are it will be a piece of pie, as you Americans say." She gave him her best smile. "Besides, you need a spotter, and no one else seems enamored with the idea. As for Abraham, he would not stop me. He would not even try."

"A piece of cake is the proper term." He couldn't help the smile but forced it away. "Yes, I think you're right." He sighed. Naomi, Hannah, Zohar—they were all alike, and there was no use arguing with any of them. "All right, let's go." They left the building with Eleazar mumbling under his breath.

A wreck of a car sat at the curb, and a short, pudgy civilian jumped in the driver's seat as Wally opened the rear door and signaled for Naomi to get in.

"Where did you get this? And a driver too. Have they made you a general now?"

"They should, but they haven't come to their senses yet. Actually, getting from that pasture we call an airfield up here to headquarters is always a pain. So when I ran into this kid at the hotel last night offering rides to us rich Americans, I hired him for this morning's run to the plane. You're in luck. You get to join us for a memorable ride."

Naomi was amazed the car even started but held her breath when she saw the young driver strain to peer over the steering wheel. They lurched away from the curb, sped through the gate, and turned right, barely missing half a dozen soldiers and civilians. The driver honked his horn and shook his fist at them, a dozen Arabic curses rolling off his tongue before he launched them down a side street.

"You're looking lovely this morning. Found a bathtub, did you?" Wally smiled.

"Just a wash basin." She blushed, feeling a bit guilty. A truck nearly cut them in half as they sped through an intersection. "Where did this kid learn to drive?"

"I'm not sure he has." Wally grabbed the armrest and back of the seat, while telling the kid to take it easy or he would be cleaning the lady's breakfast off his seats. The kid slowed down just long enough to make the turn, then hit the gas pedal again.

"Never mind. The quicker we get in the air, the better. It certainly couldn't be more dangerous than this."

Wally laughed. "I'm afraid it could. At least here we don't have Arabs shooting at us." They cut the last corner and raced onto the small airfield, the kid braking only a breath short of the plane. After Naomi peeled her hand off the back of the front seat, she and Wally got out and Wally handed the kid a dollar bill through the window. "Don't call us, kid. We'll let you know when we have another death wish."

The boy gave a grin, shoved the car in reverse, and sped away. Naomi circled the nose of the plane and got in the passenger seat. Wally checked with the mechanic, then did a once-over of the small Auster before climbing inside. The mechanic twisted the prop, and Wally started the engine on the first try, then taxied to a takeoff position. He adjusted the headset and pressed the antiquated microphone against his throat as he spoke, then listened.

"Roger that. I'll be over our destination in five minutes." He adjusted several dials before turning to her. "I said it before, and I'll say it again. Abraham will have my head if anything happens to you," he yelled over the roar of the engine.

"Then nothing better happen to me, flyboy." She smiled.

He shoved the throttle forward as Naomi familiarized herself with her surroundings. She had been in several Austers before, but each had been outfitted differently. This one had the usual instruments and the heavy metal plates surrounding the seats, but it also had a large machine gun positioned on the overhead wing on the pilot's side, along with bombs of various weights sitting in a crudely fashioned cradle.

"Hang on," Wally shouted.

Naomi looked out to see the plane bumping toward the granite hillside, her stomach churning as they lifted off the ground just before the plane could plant itself in the hillside. Swallowing what little breakfast she still had, she held tightly to the dashboard. Wally banked hard right and swung over the western part of the New City. Taking a deep breath, she focused on the mountain of Nebi Samwil now closing in quickly. "You were right. The ride with that kid was nothing compared to a ride with you."

Wally laughed while banking left, then sobered as the battlefield revealed itself beneath them. He adjusted his radio headset and pressed the microphone before giving details of what he was seeing. Eleazar had been right—it was a disaster.

"Get one of the big bombs ready to drop," Wally said. "Our boys are trying to retreat and a few are caught in a pocket surrounded by Arabs. We need to open a door for them. Let 'er go when I tell you."

Naomi retrieved a bomb from its cradle, shoved aside the beat-up piece of sheet metal used as a door, and waited for Wally to give the word. She noticed several new holes magically appearing along the wing as they came in low, heard the ping of bullets as they hit the sheet metal under their seats, and for the first time understood why Wally was concerned about bringing her up here.

"Drop," Wally yelled.

She dropped the bomb, replaced the door, then peered over the edge and behind them to see the bomb hit. Arabs scattered in several directions as Wally turned hard right to make another pass. "Another," he yelled.

She wiped the sweat from her forehead as she retrieved a second bomb, then a third. She could see the pocket and what Wally was trying to do. Dropping the small one, then seconds later the larger one, would have a greater effect. She told him what she thought, and he nodded.

Swooping over the battlefield as bullets riddled their plane, Wally told her when to drop the first, then the second. The bombs were on target, and as they climbed to a safer distance, Naomi could see half a dozen men of the Haganah running through the space they had created. Wally swung around and did one last run, but this time he used the machine gun to strafe the Arab section of the battlefield, then climbed high enough that bullets couldn't reach them, and circled, giving reports over the radio. Naomi felt a sting in her arm where a bullet creased her flesh and used a handkerchief to wrap it.

"There's a sack of bandages under your seat. I could use one," Wally said.

Naomi saw the blood dripping from his shirt and rolled up the sleeve to find a gash in his bicep. She retrieved the bandages and antiseptic wash and quickly disinfected and wrapped the wound.

They flew in circles for twenty minutes before Wally was told they could go home.

"That's it. It's over," he said.

She could see by the look on his face that they had lost, badly.

"Wanna do a little recon with me?" Wally asked.

"What did you have in mind?"

"Transjordan."

"The prison at Mafraq?"

"Yeah, I thought we'd fly over, give Abraham and the others a little something to know we still care. After what just happened down there, I need something to make it a better day." He grinned.

"My pleasure," she smiled. "You know that Mafraq isn't on any of the maps, and it's near Amman."

"Amman has antiaircraft. If we don't find it out on the perimeter, we come home. Understood?"

They flew across the desert area and ten minutes later were over the rift of the Jordan River Valley, the deepest rift in the earth's crust still above water. Naomi watched troop movements, counted vehicles and artillery pieces, and made notes and drawings that might come in handy for military leaders. They flew over the river itself without any opposition, the plane far too high for any rifle to reach them with accuracy. Wally banked slightly north. Another few minutes of flying brought them over the desolate hills a safe distance west of Amman. They searched for ten minutes and were about to turn for home when they flew over a narrow valley that ran east to west. Naomi saw it first.

"There." She pointed.

The high fences of a compound surrounded by guards stuck up in the valley floor, with several buildings to the east overlooking them. She quickly drew a map as they flew over.

"That's it, all right," Wally said. "Even from this distance I can see a few fellows wearing black Hasidic clothes. Last I checked, Arabs don't dress Hasidic."

"Go around, but get low, right over the camp if you can."

Wally nodded and made the turn. As he flew over the rise, he pointed to one of the small, eighteen-pound bombs he carried. "Let's give them notice, shall we? And give our men something to hope for?" He grinned.

She nodded. He banked, dipped low, sped over the terrain, and told Naomi to drop the bomb well short of the prison. He had seen these things bounce for fifty feet before exploding, and he didn't want to kill fellow Jews—just let them and their Arab captors know Israel didn't forget her own.

As the bomb exploded, they swept over the compound for a closer look at the captives. Though they were unable to pick out individuals at this height and speed, she got a clear view of the prison, its captives celebrating the new hope it gave them. In her excitement, Naomi threw her head out the open window as bullets whizzed around her head and plunked under their iron seats.

A shell exploded to their right, rocking the plane. Then another and another.

"Antiaircraft," Wally yelled, turning hard to the west and dipping over a hill. "I guess they moved at least one of them out here." He swerved left and right as the flack hit around them, stopping only when they dipped down into the valley. "That's it, Naomi. We're going home."

As the plane climbed and sped west toward Jerusalem, Naomi felt cold. Seeing the camp, knowing from experience what they could be like, gave her a chill. The note Eleazar had given her last night said that all prisoners had arrived and none had been harmed, but how long could it last, and what was to prevent them from singling out a few, making them an example as the Nazis had done? Though Abraham might have arrived alive and well, how long could he remain that way? She gnawed at her fingernails. She felt so helpless.

"He'll be all right, Naomi," Wally said, giving a comforting smile. "We'll have a truce soon. Prisoners can be exchanged. He can come home. He'll make it."

She nodded, shaking off the depressive fear. Wally was right. Abraham would come home soon. The question was, would she still be sane when he did? She had been a bundle of nerves lately, always near tears, her hands even a bit shaky. She had to calm down, get herself under control. Abraham needed to come home to a sane wife.

CHAPTER 16

Abraham was just finishing his mush and dried bread when he heard the plane and went to the window. An Auster. Definitely Israeli, but what was it doing this far away from Tel Aviv?

Several guards outside the fence took potshots as it flew over, but it was too high to be any kind of target. Abraham watched it circle, then dip earthward and disappear below the rim of the hill to the south. It was coming back, this time much lower. A moment later the plane flew over the top of the hill to the east and headed directly for the gate. Abraham watched with some amusement as it dropped a bomb on the road well short of the prison, and he watched the guards outside the gate scatter as the bomb exploded and the plane flew straight over the compound and toward Israel. They had come to let them know they hadn't been forgotten.

The exultant feeling disappeared quickly when Naomi's head flashed past him as it hung out of the window of the Auster, Arab soldiers shooting at it.

"It can't be," he mumbled as he pressed himself to the window. Surely he was mistaken. Naomi would not . . . No, she would. The woman was relentless when she set her mind to something. But how had she found him?

The men in the camp ran to the far fence, yelling after the plane in celebration. Suddenly large camouflaged guns fired at the fleeing Auster, and everyone in the camp seemed to inhale as the plane plummeted over the edge of the hill as if hit. Abraham felt his heart stop then start again as the small Auster bobbed up over the Jordan Valley and the cheering broke out again.

Feeling weak in the knees, Abraham had to sit on the edge of an empty bed until he could start breathing again. He would talk to Naomi about this when he returned. Foolish and dangerous. He frowned, but then smiled. Oh, how glad he was to see her! How glad all of them were.

"Your air force is very small," the doctor said. Abraham stood on his still wobbly legs and joined the doctor as he rebandaged Aaron's head wound.

"But full of surprises," Abraham said as he joined the doctor. "What happened to this one?" He nodded toward Aaron, whose survival he was still trying to comprehend.

"You mean, why does he seem like a child?" The doctor frowned. "He was hit in several places, but the most deadly one grazed him here, on the side of the skull. The impact seems to have caused internal bleeding, causing damage to the brain. Add to that shell shock, and you have him as you see him."

Aaron's eyes darted around the room, centering on the doctor's hand as he passed it in front of his eyes several times while unwrapping the linen bandage.

"But, he is doing better," the doctor continued, smiling at Aaron as if they were old friends. "He is an invalid, but a happy one, possibly even curable, though I do not know what memory he will retain, or what his capabilities will be." He stood. "Let me show you something. When he first came he never moved, never made eye contact with anything, just stared off into the distance as if he really were dead. Now you see he is getting better. His eyes move, he focuses on things a bit, and he seems to understand at least a portion of what is happening around him."

Abraham stood at the end of the bed. His old friend's blank stare and lack of recognition were hard to handle, and Abraham had spent most of the night holding Aaron's hand, hoping he would snap out of it. Now he understood why that hadn't happened. "How did he get here? He was fighting at Kastel."

"You know him then. An old friend?" Abraham nodded, and the doctor continued. "The bodies were being removed from the battlefield by volunteers from Ramallah where many of the dead who fought your Haganah had come from. His body was thrown in with the rest, and when they returned to the town, the doctors began their usual check of each—cleaning them up for burial and making sure there were none alive. Needless to say, they found this one still had a weak pulse and hurriedly took him to a treatment room and did what they could. When they saw that he was not an Arab they separated him from the Arabs for fear he would be murdered, then asked the commander of the Legion operating in the area what they should do with him. He was sent here by ambulance for his own safety, in hopes of his recovery and possible interrogation. I think they have forgotten about him since then, but we have not. We wish to make him well. May I ask his name?"

"Aaron. Aaron Schwartz."

"He is a German Jew. Was he in the camps?"

"His parents were killed by the Germans. He took his younger brother and fled into the hills where they survived for several years. He left Germany with my wife and others. They spent some time in Italy, then came here last year."

"This brother, does he have a name?"

"David."

The doctor sat down and held Aaron's hand. "Aaron, do you remember David?"

A sudden stop in the motion of his eyes hinted of some familiar thought.

"Ask him if he remembers Hannah and Ephraim," Abraham said.

The motion of the eyes had continued but stopped again at the sound of their names. Abraham felt his heart pound harder.

Stepping to the side of the bed he leaned over, gazing directly into Aaron's eyes. "Aaron, do you remember Mary? Do you remember Paris?" The eyes stopped moving again, but this time Aaron looked at Abraham.

"Mary. Do you remember Mary?" Abraham repeated.

Aaron's eyes stayed fixed on Abraham, and he detected a slight nod before the eyes started in motion again and the moment of brief recognition was lost.

"This Mary, who is she?" the doctor asked. "There was definite recognition. Most definite."

"His wife. She is an Arab from Jerusalem. They were married not too long ago and went to Paris for time together and for Aaron to heal from wounds received in the bombing of the *Jerusalem Post.*"

"That explains some of the other wounds. Where is she now?"

"We don't know. When Aaron returned from Paris, he went straight to Kastel, and none of us talked to him. After that, the war prevented us from making any contact. She may still be in Paris, or she may have returned to the Old City. Because of the war, it is difficult to know."

"A Jew and an Arab. Would that we could all get along so well."

"Yes," Abraham said softly. "Aaron should be sent home. Couldn't an exchange of prisoners take place? Surely we could get him to Hadassah Hospital. After that my wife could find Mary, and she . . ."

"It is out of the question right now, especially for you."

"I'm not talking about me, just him. Think of it, Doctor. You could make it happen. I know Mary could get through to him. I . . ."

"No, no, never. If I asked, they would throw me into that chaos of a prison with the rest of you. Besides, when the war is over, Abdullah has sworn to trade you for Arab prisoners. It will be safer for your friend at that time. Until then, I promise I will care for him properly. You must go back to the compound. You must go now."

He was adamant and a bit frightened, and Abraham could see it would do no good to argue. "All right, Doctor, all right. Calm down. Can I come back and see him again? I promise I won't ask you to send him home again. Just let me see if I can get him to snap out of it, all right?"

"We shall see. Now go. Go with the guards. Quickly. And speak nothing of this to others. It may get me in very deep trouble, do you understand? Especially do not talk of it to Commander Riad. He will not understand."

"I'll keep my mouth shut if you let me come back," Abraham said.

"Very well. Yes, of course you can come back. Just tell the guards, and they will contact me. I will arrange it. Now go."

Abraham left the hospital and returned to the gate where there was still some chaos from the bomb that left a two-foot crater in the middle of the road a hundred feet away. The gate was opened, and he went inside where Eliahu immediately met him and confirmed that he too had seen Naomi. "They will come for us now," he said. "Soon we will be free again."

Others chimed in, but Abraham said nothing, even though he knew they were being unrealistic. It gave them hope, and hope was necessary to survive such a place. If they escaped, it would be without any outside help.

And if they escaped, Abraham would take Aaron with him.

* * *

Rhoui knew he was awake but could not see. The pain in his face was excruciating. He wanted to cry out, but his mangled jaw wouldn't work. He heard voices, words coming from someone very close. He realized they were speaking Hebrew and stiffened. Where was he? Why did he have these bandages wrapped around his face, covering his eyes, shutting off his speech? Was he a captive? Was this some sort of blindfold? Some sort of torture by Jewish devils? He remembered the bomb, remembered being hit, remembered what he thought had been death. Was this hell then? Had the devil come for him because of what he'd done?

No, he was alive. He could feel his body and the horrible pain in his face. These he would have left behind had he died. He tried to calm himself, to listen. He knew Hebrew. He could learn where he was, but he must listen.

"Is there any chance of rebuilding it?" asked one.

"It is hard to say. Some of the bone is still intact and with recent improvements in surgical reconstruction by the Americans, there is a chance. But not here, not now. We simply haven't the equipment or the expertise, not even at Hadassah."

Rhoui knew the first man. An old friend of his father, a Jewish doctor who lived at Katamon but practiced in the Quarter. Messerman was his name. Was that where he was? Had he been taken captive in the battle? Had the Jews won? This didn't seem to fit. He vaguely remembered another doctor—an Arab one—a shot of morphine, unconsciousness. Then how did he get here, among Jews? And why were they trying to help him? He felt panic again. His hand automatically reached up to pull away the cloth from his eyes, but someone grabbed his arm and prevented him.

"You must not touch the bandages," the first voice said firmly. "The area around your eyes is badly burned, and your jaw . . . well, a bullet did very serious damage there."

Rhoui felt the energy go out of his arm, and the doctor laid it to his side. He did not care. If death came, he would welcome it. With this pain, the sooner it came the better.

"We do not know who you are and need to know so that we can contact your family. Can you write?" the same voice asked.

Rhoui hardly noticed the pencil being placed in his hand. He felt dead inside, numb.

The doctor noticed Rhoui wasn't gripping the pencil and asked again, "Young man, can you write? Your parents, your family, we can contact them. Did they live in the Quarter or were you Haganah, sent in from the outside?"

Though dead to life, Rhoui wanted to laugh. They thought he was a Jew. He, the one who had helped drive them from the Quarter, who had killed many of their people, a Jew. Feeling the pencil, then the pad being placed in his hands, he lifted them and wrote as well as he could without seeing. This should change their minds about keeping him alive.

The young doctor took the pad, and though the letters were Arabic and uneven, he read them aloud. "I am Arab." He gasped. "But this cannot be! You . . . you were found with our men when we brought them out of the Old City. If you were Arab, you would not have been in those rooms, with Jewish soldiers."

Using his fingers, Rhoui motioned for the pad again. It was thrust into his hand along with the pencil. *My name is Rhoui Aref. I and others blew up your Hurva.* He wrote it knowing his admission would convince them. Messerman would know his name, and his part in destroying the oldest Jewish synagogue in all Palestine would seal his fate. They would let him die, or they were fools.

He heard a gasp as the doctor read the note. "But how! You . . ."

"Never mind, doctor." This was the other voice, the voice of Doctor Messerman. "Hello, Rhoui. This is Doctor Messerman, an old friend of your father. Do you remember?"

Rhoui nodded as best as he could.

"Your injuries are quite serious. You are missing a portion of your lower right jaw and your eyes are partially burned. Only time will tell if you will speak again, but we feel safe in telling you that your eyes have a good chance of recovery with time.

We hope to get you to better facilities soon, but for now, all we can do is try to prevent infection and let the damage heal. Do you understand?"

Rhoui signaled for the pencil and pad. *I do not wish to be saved by Jews! I would rather die. I die for Allah and the holy war against the Jewish infidel.* When the pad and pencil were taken from his hands, he reached for his bandages and tried to rip them free. Another hand prevented it. He tried harder, tried to fight, get them off, die, anything but remain in captivity. He felt the sting of a needle in his arm and the warmth as the drug shot through his body, relaxing his muscles and making him instantly groggy. It was welcome and, he hoped, permanent.

"How could this happen?" the young doctor asked as he relaxed his grip on the unconscious patient.

"It isn't the first time, and it won't be last," Doctor Messerman said. "Both we and the Irregulars of Husseini lack uniforms, and many of us have the same physical traits. In the chaos of the battle in the Old City, he was put in the wrong place. It cannot be helped. I knew this man and his family. If his face hadn't been wrapped with bandages, I would have recognized him immediately. You know his father as well as I do. A good doctor who cared for many Jews as a part of his daily routine. Many of our people owe him their lives. The least we can do is care for his son."

"You may wish to help this man, but I do not, despite what Amos Aref may have done," the young doctor said, shaking the notes at Doctor Messerman. "The Hurva! The Quarter! Many lives have been lost to this one and those like him." He turned to one of the aides taking care of patients. "Take this one to a separate room, one with a lock and key. He is dangerous."

"I protest," Messerman said. "This boy—"

"This boy is a man and a prisoner, an Arab who does not deserve the medicines needed to keep our men alive. As soon as we can arrange it, I will see that he is taken to a place for such men. For now he will be locked up and kept sedated. You can see to his bandages and take care of him if you like, but I am in charge here, and no more morphine or other medicines are to be given to him unless I say so." He turned to the aide again. "Take him, lock him up, and bring Doctor Messerman the key." With that he turned to other patients.

"Never mind him," the aide said to Doctor Messerman. "He's got ETZEL leanings. Fanatics, all of 'em. They don't realize the Arabs will never go away—that we'll be living with them for generations and had better learn to like 'em. There is a small room near the baptistry of the church. I'll see that he goes there. Better that he is alone anyway. Once the boys in here find out he is an Arab and bombed the Hurva, well, locking him up will be for his own good."

"Yes, you're right. Thank you." As the aide and another soldier placed Rhoui on a stretcher, several ambulances pulled up in front of the convent doors and began unloading more wounded. Doctor Messerman followed others to the new patients. It was going to be a long night.

SEE CHAPTER NOTES

CHAPTER 17

After Naomi and Wally returned to Jerusalem, they sat down with Marcus, Sheal'tiel, and others and described what they had seen at Latrun. A distinct, angry mood filled the room. They had lost dozens of men, most of the armored cars, and plenty of guns while gaining nothing. All agreed something had gone wrong, but no one accepted responsibility.

"Well, Yadin and Ben-Gurion both want a full report, and I intend to give it to them. It won't take long," Mickey Marcus said. "Plan good, artillery good, armor excellent, infantry disgraceful." With that, he signaled for Wally to come along and left the building. Naomi stayed only a moment longer, the thick quiet of the commanders responsible for the failure hanging in the air, but she knew it would not last long. The blaming and bickering began before she closed the door.

Returning to Eleazar's desk she asked for work.

"Ready to quit chasing around the country, are you?" he said.

"No, and you're still not my boss. But if you need some help, I have a few hours."

"I swear, Naomi Marshak, you are the most difficult woman I have ever met."

"Do you have work or not?" She smiled slightly.

He handed her some papers, and she found a table where she could sit down to review them. By the time midnight rolled around, she had delivered her responses and was beginning to see just how far her people were from having their new state. Not only had they lost the Quarter and the battles of Latrun, but the Egyptians had overrun more Jewish settlements to the south of Tel Aviv and were poised for a final push in that direction as early as tomorrow. In the north, the Iraqis and elements of Kaukji's ALA were pushing for victory around Mount Tabor and at Acre, while the Legion of Transjordan, drunk with their success at Latrun, were already moving to take Radar Hill, which would give them even stronger control of the road to Tel Aviv and potentially force the entire Jewish portion of Jerusalem to surrender. Any one of these coming battles, if lost, could break the spirit of her people.

Naomi was exhausted. Hurrying through a report for Eleazar, she left the building to go home. As she exited, Eleazar called her back. There was a wire for her.

Naomi. Ephraim in critical condition. Surgery went badly. Tell all to pray for him. Love, Hannah.

Naomi felt her head swim and reached for the edge of the table but missed it and tumbled to the floor. Someone helped her to her feet, and she fled into the dark streets. Only one other man alive meant more to her than Ephraim Daniels, and he was in an Arab prison. She stopped, leaning against a wall, a sudden overwhelming anguish rolling over her as the tears flowed once more. The city seemed darker, more ominous than ever, explosions lighting up parts of the skyline, their impacts sounding like loud thumps, every horror nearly overpowering. If Ephraim died . . . she could not stand the thought!

She forced herself to move again. She must get home. Poor Hannah! And the children! How could they bear it if he died?

Trudging on without even caring where she was, her mind numb, she refused to think, driving the pictures of Hannah and the children out of her mind in order to keep from losing it entirely. If God did not care for such people as Hannah and Ephraim Daniels, He did not care for anyone.

Miraculously, she arrived at the apartment, stopped at the door, and dried her eyes, fighting for control. He was still alive. He would survive. He had to survive. She would have to tell Mithra. Hannah would want her to know. Using her key, she let herself in and was grateful to find Mithra and Hilda already asleep. Exhausted and overcome with emotion, she removed her khaki pants and shirt and stretched out on the blanket they had spread out for her. She only noticed the bed was softer when her arm rubbed against an unfamiliar material. Touching it, she found a thick rug underneath, and once more gave quiet thanks for Hilda.

Forcing her eyes to close, she attempted to shut off her thoughts and her worry for both Abraham and Ephraim. Her exhausted body had nearly succumbed to a restless sleep when a loud roar enveloped her and something hit her squarely in the back. The pain took her breath away, and a rush of dust and stifling air entered her lungs. Coughing and choking, she tried to get her bearings, tried to stand, when someone grabbed her arm.

"It's all right," Mithra said. "An artillery shell, that's all. It's over, we're all right. They never shoot at the same place twice. They scare more innocent people that way, the brutes!"

Naomi blinked away the last of sleep and found herself kneeling on her makeshift bed, Mithra next to her, an arm around her waist.

"Are you hurt?" Mithra asked.

Naomi felt moisture on her aching back. "Something hit me in the back."

"Let me touch," Mithra said, touching her back with her fingers. "Yes, a cut. Something must have hit you. From the feel of the wound, I'll need needle and thread." Mithra groped in the direction of the sink until she found a cloth and pressed it against Naomi's back.

"Is Hilda okay?" Naomi asked as the two of them got to their feet.

"I'm fine, fine," a faint voice said from the bedroom.

"She's under the bed again," Mithra said with some impatience. "I swear the woman must sleep under there."

"If she feels safe, why not stay under the bed?" Naomi asked as she reached for the candle she knew had been in the middle of the table.

"I suppose you're right. But if I had a feather bed to sleep on, it would take more than a few Arabs with a big gun to get me out of it."

"Yes, I'm sure it would." Naomi fumbled about the tabletop until she found the matches. Lighting the candle, she used it to see what hit her. A framed oil painting lay askance on her bed. She explained to Mithra what it was.

"Yes, well big guns will do that, I suppose. This isn't going to stop bleeding on its own. Find that needle and thread, and let me sew it shut."

They were near the veranda door, and Naomi shoved it open. There was no fire, but she could hear people clamoring west along the street below. She should probably go and help, but she was too tired, too numb. Turning back, she used the dim light to find Hilda's self-made first aid kit and searched it until she found a needle and some catgut thread.

"I suppose you have done this before," Naomi said as she handed them to Mithra.

"Of course, many times. But all of them while I still had my eyes."

Naomi stiffened, and Mithra chuckled. "I am joking, my dear. I can see with my fingers as well as you can with your eyes. Don't worry. Hilda, where is that alcohol?"

"In the cabinet above the sink," came the weak response.

"Well, come out from under there and find it for us," Mithra said impatiently.

A moment later Hilda appeared at the door, her eyes darting around the room. She went quickly to the cabinet, retrieved the alcohol, and handed it to Mithra before starting for the bedroom again.

"Stay here. You know they won't hit us again. We have survived and won't need to worry. At least for a while. Naomi must be hungry. Fix some bread and jam for her."

"Jam? Where did you get jam?" Naomi asked. The first stitch stung badly, and she grimaced and stiffened.

"Sorry, my dear," Mithra said, "but it will hurt some. Just grit your teeth or something."

"We went shopping," Hilda said with a smile. "Well, sort of shopping. Some of the apartments a few blocks away were hit last night, and when we went past them today the soldiers let us look for anything we could find. Apparently the tenants were either killed or went away. There were a lot of people, so everyone shared and came away with something. As we were coming home some woman we had never seen before tried to take it from us, but Mithra took care of her." Hilda grinned. "One swing of the walking stick I gave her, and that woman let us be. She ran away, muttering about her broken fingers."

"That's what it's coming to, eh?" Naomi said, grimacing at the poke in her skin. "Neighbor fighting against neighbor."

"Oh no, only the one. The rest were quite kind."

"That's comforting."

Hilda handed her the bread, coated with a thin layer of jam. Naomi ate it slowly, enjoying each bite but still unable to keep from feeling guilty. This was how it all started in Poland. You were nice to each other as long as you got enough to eat, but after that, things got worse and worse, until you didn't care anymore about the others, and you did anything to get what you wanted. She had been a survivor, but there had been a price—her humanity. She had struggled hard to get it back, and thanks to Hannah and the others, she had managed it for the most part.

Hannah. Poor Hannah. Naomi lost her appetite and gave the bread to Hilda. "Here, you finish this. We had food at the office, and I am quite full," she fibbed. "Ouch!"

"Sorry," Mithra said.

"Are you sure?" Hilda asked.

"Yes, I am sure."

Hilda took the bread and ate hungrily. "Now, tell us the latest news. We hear so little," she said between bites.

"There, it's done," Mithra said, dabbing at the blood with a damp rag. "Quite a nice job, if you ask me."

"Thank you," Naomi said. She turned and clutched Mithra's arm. "I am afraid I have some bad news."

"What is it, dear?" Mithra said, suddenly sobered.

She told her about Ephraim.

"Oh dear, poor Hannah. She must be in horrible condition. We should go to synagogue tomorrow and pray for her. Did the wire mention the children? Are they all right?"

"No, nothing. I wish, I wish they were here so that we could be with them. But they are so far away and . . ."

"They will be all right, Naomi. God is with them."

Mithra finished taping, and Naomi pulled down her undershirt, sliding it carefully over the bandage.

It was silent for a long time. Even Hilda, though she did not know Ephraim and Hannah, sat silent, the anguish of her two new friends touching her deeply.

"What will they do if he dies?" Naomi asked. "How can they bear it?"

"They will come home," Mithra said tenderly, "and we will help take care of them."

"Home? Here? They have no home, and if things go as badly tomorrow as they have today and yesterday and every day before that, they will never have a home in this land." She clenched her teeth.

There was another silence before Hilda spoke. "We should read from your book, Mithra. Reading from it gives me peace. Maybe it will help."

"Yes, maybe it will."

"What book?" Naomi asked.

"Hannah's book, Naomi. It is the one thing I was able to bring with me. It is there, on the table. Hilda, will you read?"

The Book of Mormon. Naomi had been given one as well, but it was smoldering in the ashes of the Quarter. She had left it in the apartment. When one struggled with the very idea of God, books about Him didn't seem all that important.

"There is a chapter I wish to hear," Mithra said. "Alma 32. Read that one, will you, Hilda?"

Drawing closer to the candle, Hilda thumbed through the book until she found the page she wanted and started reading.

Naomi couldn't listen and went out on the veranda. If there were a God, He was either dead or deaf. Either way, He wasn't interested in her, Hannah, or anyone else.

Hilda spoke louder, but Naomi let most of the words drift past her into the city. Accompanied by the thumps of artillery shells, the words seemed empty.

When Hilda finished the chapter, Mithra thanked her and received the book back.

Though her back was to them, Naomi sensed Hilda get up and start for her bedroom, then turn toward the veranda. "I'll give you another piece of bread and jam for breakfast. You will surely be hungry by then, and there is no sense letting it sit about and get stale. Good night, Naomi. Things will look better in the morning. I promise."

Naomi felt some of her hardness melt with the compassion of this woman and turned to face her. "Good night, Hilda. I am sure you're right." She forced a smile, and Hilda returned it, then went in her bedroom.

Mithra moved from the straight-backed chair to the bed-couch and lay down before pulling her blanket up to her chest. "Good night, dear."

"Good night, Mithra." Naomi wanted only to sleep. Lifting the painting from her bed, she picked up the blanket and went to the small veranda to shake it out. When she returned, Mithra was breathing heavily, sound asleep. She watched her old friend. She was so peaceful, and yet she felt just as great a concern as Naomi had and had been through even more than most survivors of the camps. Was this newfound faith the reason, or did she just have a matchless will to survive that made up the very fiber of her nature?

Spreading the blanket over her carpet mattress again, Naomi blew out the candle and lay on her side, the wound tender and sore.

Her mind could not escape Hannah, Ephraim, David, Elizabeth, and the twins. How she wanted to be there for them, but what strength would she be if she were? She had nothing to give Hannah, nothing that would ease the fear she must be feeling. If she were honest, she wanted to be there because she knew Hannah would be able to help her understand. Hannah. Always able to bring stability to the unstable and sanity to the insane. How Naomi needed her!

Closing her eyes, she tried to sleep, but the pain in her back and in her mind kept her restless. Her eyes simply would not close.

Getting up, she went to the veranda and looked across the city. The shelling had stopped, but there was a sort of wary, frightening silence instead of the peacefulness such an evening should bring. Even though the full moon spread its light over the buildings, lurking just beyond and under its soft cover was hatred, war, and death. Most of her life, evil had tried to crush her with the boots of soldiers.

She breathed deeply, trying to get control of her dark thoughts. There was still good to hope for, still the chance that Ephraim would survive, that they could all live a good life. Abraham would survive; they would have a family. She could not give up. She must take it one day, one hour, one minute at a time.

Returning to the sitting room, Naomi retrieved her bedding, carried it to the veranda and spread it out, then lay down. Maybe out here, sleep would come. She forced her eyes shut.

"Dear God," she said in desperation. "If there is a God, please be with Ephraim, Hannah, and the children, and protect Abraham. Of all Your children, they deserve Your blessing, and if You must have more sacrifice, more bodies of my people to placate Your anger against us, take me and leave them. Please, I . . . I beg You." She said it almost angrily, defiantly, but there didn't seem to be any choice. He had deserted her, deserted all of them. How could He expect her to be anything but angry? "Oh, dear God, why? Why don't You show us a sign that You still care? Why have You left us to bleed and die for so long? Have we been so horrible to You? Are our sins so great? It was not I, nor Abraham, nor Ephraim and his family who killed Your Son, if He was Your Son! None of those who are dying in this war can be blamed for it. Our hands are clean, and yet You desert us! If You still live, if You have any love for us at all, come to us now. Protect us, give us peace for once instead of a sword."

The sobs broke into her chest and though she struggled to muffle them, they escaped her throat and spread across the blue velvet of the moon's glow and echoed off the walls of the street below. A moment later, she felt strong but aged hands lift her head and shoulders as Mithra slipped under her and held her close, whispering soft words of comfort as she gently rocked Naomi's exhausted body.

"I can't do it anymore," Naomi sobbed. "I can't. It is impossible to believe in such a God, Mithra." She used her hand to gently pound the chest of her friend. "I can't! I can't! I can't!"

"You must," Mithra said softly. "He is all we have left."

Mithra said a silent prayer. *She is trying, God. She has planted her seed, even if it is tainted with anger and disappointment. Canst Thou blame her? Touch her now. Let her know Thou still carest for her. I don't expect Thee to make all the ills of the world go away. I don't even expect Thee to help us win this silly war. Just this soul, God. Just save this soul!*

They sat there for a long time before Naomi's sobs turned to crying, then to sniffles, and finally to sleep. Mithra stayed, her back against the wall, the head of dear Naomi in her lap. There was nothing more she could do.

The rest was up to God.

CHAPTER 18

"Then it is agreed. We go tomorrow night."

"Only if you're sure about this guard," Eliahu said.

"I'm sure," Moshe replied. "For fifty British pounds, this one would betray his own mother."

"But it could be a trap," Abraham offered.

"He doesn't get the money until we're in the armory. After that we can fight our way out," Franz said. "I say it is worth the chance."

All of them nodded. There were five besides Moshe and Abraham. Eliahu and Franz were from the Quarter, and the other three were Moshe's men. William was a Brit who had deserted the army for ETZEL more than a year ago. Chaim and Sha'ul ben Simon were brothers, but opposites in appearance—one dark, one light; one a joker, the other as serious-minded as any Hasid Abraham ever knew.

"How did you smuggle those pounds in here?" Sha'ul asked Moshe.

"Never you mind. Just be ready to go at midnight tomorrow." Moshe grinned.

"We'll have one more going with us," Abraham said.

"I told you, too many will get us all killed. We have to keep it small, tight, people we know we can trust to watch out for each other."

"This one won't be a problem. You know him."

Moshe looked bewildered.

"It's Aaron Schwartz. He's in the hospital."

"Aaron? But he was killed at Kastel," Moshe said.

"Is this the Schwartz they said killed Abdul Khader and practically opened the road from Tel Aviv?" Chaim asked.

"An exaggeration, but it's the same man. He deserves to go, and I won't leave without him."

"What's his condition?" Moshe asked. "If he's hobbled, he'll slow us down."

Abraham told them.

"Sorry, but it's out of the question."

"Agreed," said Chaim.

The others looked at each other, then all nodded. "He's right, Rabbi," Eliahu said. "He's better off staying. They'll free him with the exchange of prisoners."

Abraham nodded, then stood. "I won't go without him." He extended a hand to Moshe. "Good luck, and if you make it, let Naomi know about Aaron and that we're both coming home when this mess is over."

Moshe nodded. "You're sure about this?"

"I'm sure. I'll say a prayer for all of you." With that, he turned and left the tattered tent. He had his own plans to make.

CHAPTER 19

Walking slowly around the plane, Wally checked it carefully. Though it was obvious that the mechanics gleaned parts from at least three planes to piece it together, it looked solid and definitely flyable.

"Where did you say you got the parts?"

"I didn't, but now that you ask, we scavenged most of them out of a couple of Spitfires the British left behind. They were rusting over at Lydda Airport and just needed a little elbow grease and spit polish, but as you can see, we're still missing a very important piece."

"The right wheel. Yeah, I noticed."

"It was ruined in the crash. I can tell you where to find one, if you're interested. But you'll have to go after it yourself." The mechanic smiled.

"You mean the downed Spitfire in the Negev," Wally said.

"A bit dangerous, but doable if you can find a place to land. Don't you have a friend down that way or something?"

"The wheel assembly looks a bit heavy for one man, and I wouldn't know the first thing about removing it," Wally said.

"Nothing to it. Let me show you." They slipped under the propped-up Spitfire, and the mechanic explained to him how the wheel was bolted in. "This stuff for the hydraulics can be undone here and here. Just cut the tubing. I'll replace it later."

"Umm, when did they say more Messerschmitts would be coming in?"

"Another couple weeks, maybe more. If rumors are true about a truce, the fighting will be over by then. At least until the Arabs stir up enough courage to have another go at us."

"I'll give it some thought. Thanks, Hank."

As he left the hangar, Wally noticed the four new Messerschmitts warming up before takeoff. It pleased him to see them finally going into combat, but he was disappointed that he wasn't one of the pilots, especially since hearing about the critical condition of Ephraim Daniels. More than ever, he wanted to get into battle, get a little revenge. Ephraim hadn't needed to be in this spot, and if the Palestinian Arabs would have settled for what the world was willing to give them, he'd still be flying.

He caught a ride to the Hayarkon Hotel to get his orders for the day and, hopefully, see Zohar, but the entire distance, he thought about that downed Spitfire in the Negev. It could be done, and the Spitfire was a better plane than the phony Messerschmitts the Czechs were putting out. He could do a lot of damage with a fully armed Spitfire. Save a lot of lives. But using the Auster to retrieve the wheel might not be the best way. He had another idea.

As he entered the outer room of command and control, he saw Zohar busy at work to his left. "Hi," he said.

She looked up, gave him that great smile, then stood and spoke, still concentrating on papers she had in her hand. "Captain. How was your flight to Jerusalem yesterday?" she asked. "I hear you took an additional sightseeing tour."

"The word's out, huh?" He smiled. "A flyover for Naomi. No big deal."

"It is to Weizman. He wants to ground you."

"But he hasn't." Wally smiled again.

"Only because we don't have enough pilots to go around, especially with the airlift from Czechoslovakia in full swing."

"I saw the Messerschmitts take off." Wally sensed the chill and changed the subject. "What's the target?"

"To surprise the Egyptians at Isdud."

"Any word from them yet?"

"They have no radios yet. When they get on the ground, we'll know how it went. Weizman is leading them. They should do okay."

"He's the best." Zohar was concentrating more on the papers than on him. Probably just busy, Wally thought.

"Isn't Rachel Steinman in Negba, just north of Isdud?" he asked. Rachel had come out of Germany with Hannah and Zohar and had been in the Negev ever since her arrival in Palestine. Wally heard she was further south and had nearly gotten married to a soldier protecting the oil pipeline across the desert. He was killed two months ago in an ambush.

"Yes. She is in Negba. They were attacked on May 21 and repelled the Egyptians, but they expect another attack very soon. Command is trying to decide whether to pull everyone out. Why do you ask?"

"Just wondering. Hadn't heard much about her since my arrival."

Zohar gave him a side glance but decided to let it go. She handed him a paper. "That's your flight for the day. Take Marcus back to Jerusalem. You'll fly some ammo in as well. Make as many trips with more of the same as you can before sunset. They are practically out of bullets."

"What is the latest on the truce?" he asked.

"You haven't heard?"

"Nope, sorry. I don't run in the circles you do. How about dealing me in?"

"The Americans have pressured the Brits into calling for a withdrawal of all British Army personnel from the region. That will leave Transjordan without the best leaders and slow them down. Abdullah will be begging for a truce. More importantly, the Brits have agreed not to sell any more arms to the Arabs, which will make the rest of them want time to find more bullets and shells to kill us with."

"But why would the Brits agree to such a thing? It will cost them their influence here, won't it?"

"We hope so." She forced a smile. "The Americans are using postwar aid as a bludgeon. If the Brits don't agree, the Americans stop payment and the British economy suffers."

"Makes one proud to be an American. When does this all go into effect?"

"This morning. The Brits have also agreed to push the Arabs for an immediate truce. If that happens, we can catch up with arms, training, reorganization, everything."

"Best news I've heard since I got here. Well, I have to get back to work. How about a date when—"

"I'm supposed to pick up some pilots flying in from Zatec," she said, cutting him off. "You can ride to the airport with me if you like."

They left the building, climbed in her car, and were quickly on the road for the airport.

"So what else is happening?" he asked.

"The Arabs have learned about the new stance by the Brits and are trying to make inroads all over the country. The next few days will be hard, but we have to hold our ground. If we do, we'll be in good shape. If we don't, we may never get a truce. They'll force a surrender, and you and I will be looking at a flight back to Europe and the States—one way."

"Europe's a mess, and the States are so far away. Let's stay put." Wally smiled. "I asked you a question back there. How about dinner tonight?" he said with his best smile.

"I don't date men who plan on leaving Israel when the fighting is over. Sorry." She didn't smile.

"Then I'll stay. Forever if you like," he teased.

They pulled onto the field at Ekron. "I have done little but think about you for the last few days, and I've made a decision. If we continue to see one another, I know I'll fall head over heels, and I can't afford to lose my heart to someone who will just board a plane and fly away when the war is over."

"Hey," he said, putting a hand on hers. "One day at a time. It's just dinner, Zoe."

"That's my fear, Wally. It's just dinner to you—just another date like the rest of the flyboys around here. No permanency, no commitment. Just a quick fling and off you go. For me, it can never be just dinner, do you understand? Not with you." She opened the car door to get out. "The pilots are waiting inside the hangar." She stepped out and went inside. Wally sat there, a bit stunned, unsure of what he felt. Part of him wanted to chase her down, make promises, anything to keep her from walking away. But the other half was angry, hurt by the pigeonhole she had created for him. Thanks to Ephraim's influence, he was determined to keep himself a clean little Jewish boy, even if belittled for it. If she thought anything of him, she should be able to see that.

Getting out of the car, he went inside. Zohar stood with several other pilots, but he ignored them and walked to his Auster, eyeing the many patches that decorated the wings and body, wondering if it could still fly. Zoe was leaving the building as he came around the propeller. He glanced back to see her disappear through the hangar door, his pride preventing him from stopping her.

Just as well, he thought. She's right. I'm going back to the States when this is over. It's better if we don't get involved. It would only complicate our lives, and they are complicated enough as it is.

The thought gave him instant heartburn.

SEE CHAPTER NOTES

CHAPTER 20

Saad stewed over his next move. It was nearly sundown. He must do something soon.

He had nearly worked up enough courage to escape when the explosions had come and chaos broke out. A soldier was shot near him, and several bedu horsemen had appeared out of nowhere to battle the Jews. Dashing past them, he had escaped into the darkness and begun moving in the direction of the Arab lines, traveling slowly so as to prevent recapture by the Jews. A battle had broken out in front of him, and he had worked his way through the lines to find himself in the chaotic backwater of the Arab front. He had begun asking questions, describing his son and his bedu riding companions. An old soldier who had just come in for food said that he had seen such men at the mustering point a few miles farther up the road.

After two hours of much needed sleep and some bread purchased from a farmer, he had arrived at the Arab mustering point near dawn and had begun looking for Emile immediately. The place was a beehive of activity, filled with units from Iraq, the ALA, and the Arab Legion of Transjordan. There seemed to be no leadership or organization. Men sat around, some wandering off to villages to look for food since none was provided. Several units were mustered and taken toward the front. Others returned, tired, bloody, disillusioned, their blank faces impassive as Saad asked about Emile and the others. It was nearly two before a high-ranking Iraqi officer arrived and began pulling things together. All the new recruits were ordered into one area and given old rifles and ammunition. A few even got helmets, some with fresh bloodstains evident on their leather inner straps.

Saad joined the congregating troops in hopes of finding Emile, but found himself being given a weapon and instructions of where to go to be assigned a unit. Thinking that this would have to be the same path Emile would take, Saad fell in line and did as he was told and soon found himself in a farmer's field surrounded by hundreds of others. Saad watched an officer select half a dozen men much as if he were shopping for a suitable set of clothes, then lead them away, probably to replenish his unit. Another came a few minutes later, then another and another. Saad asked each about Emile, getting nothing but stern looks and angry sneers. Finally a captain of the Iraqi army told him that four men and a boy on horseback had come to the camp earlier and were sent to the front. He had pointed to where four horses were tied to a beat-up wooden fence, an old man sitting in the shade created by their bodies.

He quickly walked to the old man, who raised his rifle. "Stand back. Don't come any closer," the man said.

"Those are bedu horses. Whose are they?"

"That is none of your concern. They paid me to protect these horses, and I intend to see it done."

"Was one of them a boy?" Saad asked.

"Yes. The one who was not dressed like a bedu. The one in a green sweater," the old answered. "But don't think you can trick me and come closer. Go away."

Saad was already walking briskly back the way he had come. Emile was already on his way to the battlefield, and he would have to follow.

He hopped aboard a truck he knew was heading that way and settled down for the ride. The new recruits seemed eager to fight and sang patriotic songs while the seasoned soldiers sat apart, getting what rest they could and trying to ignore the overexuberant volunteers.

"They think they go to a wedding," said one soldier to another.

The other grumbled. "Soon they will see."

Saad felt strangely alone and spoke just to reassure himself. "Where is the front?" he asked.

The first soldier, perched against the side of the truck, responded, "From Tamra, north and east of Haifa to the southern tip of Carmel. But we go to the hot spot—the road that runs to Muhraqa and Haifa. You and your friends will be in for it."

"I . . ." Saad hesitated. "I have a son. He is fifteen, dark, curly hair, wearing a green sweater. He was sent to the front earlier. I must find him."

The soldier looked at his friend, who shrugged. "Lots of volunteers come here. They think they will be heroes, that being a martyr will give them great honor. If this was your son, he is as big a fool as the rest of them."

"But have you seen him?"

The man tossed the last remnants of a cigarette through the slats of the side rail. "He came early this morning, just as we were leaving to get food and rest. He is in the fight now."

Saad's mouth went dry. "Where . . ." He wet his lips. "Where was he?"

"On the road, where we go now," the soldier said.

They all fell silent, and as they neared the Carmel range, the new recruits stopped singing and gazed at the hills, looking for what lay ahead. They passed several trucks carrying the wounded to the rear and passed soldiers walking in the opposite direction, their feet dragging. They also passed several artillery pieces, their operators lolling about as if on vacation.

"Why don't they use them?" Saad asked.

"No shells," replied one of the soldiers with a wide face and flat nose. He nodded in the direction of a charred truck. "We're getting close now."

"The Jews have some mortars and moved a couple artillery pieces in last night. For infidels, they shoot pretty good," said the first with a wide grin.

"They have no artillery," the flat-nosed Arab said. "I told you before, it is only big mortars—Davidka's, the Jews call them. Very loud. They scare men to death." As he finished his sentence, the truck pulled into a small, deserted village where other soldiers and recruits were preparing to walk to positions along the front. An explosion hit behind them, then closer, causing everyone to duck as low as their crowded condition would allow. The eyes of the new recruits were wide with fear, the desire to sing completely gone.

The truck stopped, and a lanky, greasy-looking man with sergeant's stripes on his arm approached, ordering them out and into a nearby house. The soldier who had answered Saad's questions rolled his eyes and muttered a curse.

"That is Sergeant Hakim," he said in a low voice. "Those who know him call him Mouse. He was a common soldier like us until this morning. Then he got those stripes—who knows why—but if you have any desire to survive when we go to battle, stick with us and ignore him."

"Some say the stripes were given for speed—he runs away faster than anyone else," said another. The other soldiers snickered but all jumped to the ground and followed the new recruits into the shelter. They were given several loaves of old bread and a few oranges to feast on before going into battle.

"You!" the sergeant said.

Saad looked up to see Hakim looking at him.

"Where do you live?"

"Haifa, but I have come to find my son," Saad answered.

"Your son? Another patriot," Mouse said. "We honor such fighters who come to fight. We honor you." He turned to the other new recruits, about a dozen in all. "We honor all of you who have come to fight for your country. Your wives and your children will honor you forever."

Saad noted that the seasoned soldiers continued eating, ignoring the sergeant's poor attempt at a pep talk, while the recruits once more seemed exultant and brave, their faces glued to his as if begging for more. Saad decided Mouse was a rather small man in real stature, but he would make a good mulla or imam, an impassioned preacher of Islam who drove others to *jihad* but preferred to stay clear of the mess himself.

Saad had read a book once, given to him by a British officer. It was about World War I and very intriguing to Saad. Because he struggled a bit with the English, it took some time to finish the book, but he learned much about war from it. *All Quiet on the Western Front,* Saad remembered. In it there was a character by the name of Kantorek. The author had called him a stern, little man with a face like a shrewd mouse. He gave long lectures to his men, persuading even the least heroic to volunteer for battle, then stood back and watched them die. This Sergeant Hakim was much like Kantorek.

Saad looked at the soldiers, remembering something he learned from the book. Something about the wisest soldiers being the poor and simple people who knew the war to be a misfortune, while those who were educated and should have been able to see clearly what the consequences of such devastation could be were happy about war coming. The author had called the latter "stupid." From what Saad could see, he was right.

Sergeant Hakim turned to Saad and stepped to within inches. "We will return you to Haifa. You will see. The Jews will turn and run when they see our courage, our strength."

"I wish only to find my son," Saad replied.

The room was quiet, even the seasoned soldiers' interest piqued as their new sergeant seemed to be at a loss for a response.

"He is fifteen, has curly hair, and wore a green sweater over a white shirt," Saad said. "If you know where he is, I will retrieve him and be on my way."

Sergeant Hakim's eyes darted, a bit of sweat on his brow, probably from working himself into such a frenzy. "Ah, yes, yes, I remember him. He seemed sick, but my talk with him helped. He was ready to die a martyr when he left, ready for paradise."

"And where did he go to find this *glory?"* Saad said stiffly. His gut churned with anger at this fool, who like Kantorek, was convinced that he was acting for the best of all, costing him nothing but them everything.

"Forward, of course. Exactly where we go, though he may have been moved since. We push them back. We drive the Jews to the sea! And soon, soon we will retake Haifa, and you will have your city again!" He put a hand on Saad's shoulder. "You and your son. The heavens willing, of course."

"Yes," Saad said in disgust. He glanced at the new recruits, an impassioned look in their eyes. Like dogs needing a master, a guide, they would follow Hakim, trust him and his authority, his passion and seeming self-assurance. Only battle, only death and pain all around them, would make them see. Then they who survived would become the new soldiers. The ones who understood that Sergeant Hakim's words were empty.

"Looks like it's time, boys." The man who spoke had been standing against the wall, peering through a crack in the wooden shutters. "Some officer with more stripes than Mouse is coming."

Saad looked at the entire group—twelve soldiers, eleven recruits. The recruits stood tall and ready at one end of the room, while the soldiers sat at the other, finishing the last of their food. Though sarcastic, even defiant of leadership, they seemed resigned to fight. These were not cowards but men who had learned how to stay alive while carrying out their duty. They had learned to trust each other rather than men like Sergeant

Hakim, and they knew when to fight and when to walk away. Saad decided it was with these men he could survive long enough to find Emile. Then he would make the boy leave, even if he had to beat him.

Everyone faced the door as the officer entered. Mouse came to a traditional salute. The other soldiers stood, then straightened themselves a little. The officer ordered Mouse to take his men to the trucks where he wished to talk to them. Mouse saluted again, then commanded everyone out.

Saad fell in at the end of the line beside the soldier who had spoken to him in the truck. "Do you know this one?"

The soldier shrugged. "I have seen him. I think his name is Safa. He is a colonel. They are all the same. They stay in their tents while we bleed."

When they reached the rear of the trucks, Mouse told them to line up. Two of the soldiers were already loaded in the truck and rolled their eyes as they slipped back to the ground and stood in casual formation. The officer paced and waited for some semblance of order. Finally he spoke.

"You fight for Arab honor, for the honor of Allah."

Saad couldn't help the smile. If the Arabs did half as well with a weapon as they did with hyperbole, they would rule the world.

The officer turned to Saad and the other Palestinian Arabs. "You fight for Palestine, your homes, your wives, your children. The most honorable men of your country are already fighting for these things. Some have died. Now it is your turn to repay them and save all from the infidel Jews. Pray that Allah counts you worthy to be martyrs."

The other recruits stiffened with pride while Saad wished for a place to sit down, worn out by the weight of old arguments and overworked rhetoric. Had the Arab governments made peace instead of war, had there been less argument and more willingness to build a new Palestinian state, there would be no need for this fight. The closer he got to the tragicomedy of war, the more he wished to be free of it once and for all.

"You have weapons! Use them. If you do not know how, say so, and my men will help you. But if you do not use them, Sergeant Hakim will shoot you with my blessing. You are here to fight or to die for freedom. You are here to drive the Jews into the sea. Do your duty, and we will send you back to your villages as heroes. Turn coward, and we will send you to the grave."

"For freedom!" Mouse said exuberantly.

"For freedom!" the recruits repeated with feeling, then again, and again. By the time they were finished, the soldiers were loaded and seated, Saad beside them, the officer disappearing into one of the homes.

"My name is Khan." The soldier next to Saad smiled, showing a missing tooth. "It is because of my flat face and nose. They say my family descended from a Mongol." He pointed to the man who had answered Saad's earlier questions. "This is my friend Najib. He has saved my life many times, bless his family forever." He grinned.

"You have an old Enfield," Najib said to Saad. "Do you know how to use it?"

Saad nodded. "I owned such a rifle before the Jews confiscated all weapons after the surrender at Haifa. I used it for hunting."

Khan grinned again. "You hunt different game now. They shoot back." The soldiers around them laughed at his humor. Khan grew serious. "A slow and cumbersome single shot is no match for even the worst rifles in the hands of the Jews." Khan took the rifle, released the bolt with some difficulty, but worked it several times until it opened and closed with relative ease. "Rusty, but it will kill."

"I have no intention of killing."

"You will change your mind or you will die," Khan said, handing Saad back the rifle.

"This boy of yours," Najib said, "did he ever hunt with you, ever fire a weapon?"

"No, never, but several bedouin were with him. They may have taught him some skill." He said it to give himself hope more than anything. The thought of his son in this chaos had him on the edge of panic.

"The bedu are good with a rifle, ferocious in battle," Khan said. "I would take one of them for all these." He waved at the recruits. He grinned again. "We would kill a hundred Jews and win the battle," he grinned. "Then I would kill him to keep him from stealing everything I own."

As they neared the area of the battle, every shot, every explosion made Saad more agitated. Emile had been in this nearly all day. How could he possibly survive? He prayed even harder that Emile be protected, that he remain safe until he could find him. He looked at Najib. "You say you saw my son earlier. Is this the area?"

"Yes, but we have been pushed back since then. Contrary to what Hakim says, we are losing ground to the Jews. We are sent to be the thumb in a leaking dam."

Khan grinned again. "We have not enough thumbs for the leak in this one, but we will try."

"Why do you try? This is not your country, not your fight."

Khan and Najib looked at one another. Finally Najib answered. "We are poor men in our country. We have nothing except each other, except the army. We eat. We are honored by our families." He shrugged. "It is all we know."

Khan grinned again. "We know how to fight." He laughed. "And how to run."

Najib chuckled. "It is what gives us long life, eh, brothers?"

The others nodded with grins of their own as Najib leaned toward Saad. "Stay with us, and we will keep you alive. We are very knowledgeable on this subject."

Two other trucks pulled up behind them just as a mortar shell hit to their right, then to their left. The new recruits, all of whom were standing, plunged to the floor on top of one another, their expressions changing to fear very quickly.

Khan, the grin still on his face, leaned toward Saad. "The Jews are very close. They—" The next explosion forced the driver to jerk the wheel to his left, forcing the truck off the side of the road. Mouse, stunned by the sudden change of events, froze. The soldiers, scrambling over the prone bodies of the paralyzed recruits, jumped from the truck and ran for cover along a rock fence that surrounded a small garden of olive trees. Saad was the last of the group to dive for cover and felt the ground rock with three more explosions. Then it stopped.

"That was artillery," Najib said. "I told you they have artillery."

Khan nodded but didn't answer, his eyes glued to the truck where Mouse lay prone with the recruits, frozen with fear. For the first time, the smile left Khan's face as he scrambled to his feet. He was thick through the shoulders, short, stocky, and powerful. As he reached the truck, he lunged forward far enough that he could grab Mouse by the collar and drag him to the wall. "He is a fool and a coward, but he is Iraqi, so we save his miserable skin today." He grinned again. "Maybe tomorrow we let them shoot him."

Sergeant Hakim finally caught his breath and sat up, his back against the wall. Most of the recruits had finally found their courage and were now behind the wall as well, their eyes void of any recent feelings of invincibility.

"I will have you shot for this," Mouse hissed toward Khan.

"You will give me a medal, or I will throttle you myself," Khan said.

Mouse forced himself to his feet, brushed himself off, and straightened his uniform. "Get to your feet!" he commanded all of them. "We go to battle."

Khan leaned over to Saad. "Humiliation does wonders for a coward, don't you think?" He laughed, then got up, checked his rifle, and followed Najib toward the road. The new recruits cautiously got up. Those who had dropped their weapons to run retrieved them as Mouse gave the order to move forward in two lines. He removed his pistol from its scabbard with sweat pouring from his still-ashen face. Saad expected the Jews to raise up and shoot them all, but nothing happened, and he could not help but think they were walking into a trap. He picked up his pace and fell in next to Najib and Khan.

"They wait around this bend," Najib said as if reading Saad's mind.

Mouse, who had worked up the courage to go to the front of the group, glared at Khan as he passed in triumph. He stopped fifty yards short of the actual canyon, his pistol-toting hand in the air as a signal they should do the same. The wind blowing into their faces carried the sound of distant rifle fire. Sergeant Hakim's courage suddenly waned again as he ordered Khan, Najib, and the other soldiers to advance, the recruits to follow. It being his duty to shoot anyone who tried to run, he fell in behind them.

"Do not worry about him," Khan said. "He will not shoot you. He will be too busy running away."

Mouse, still close enough to hear, flinched, then scowled, but remained at the rear of the platoon.

They rounded the bend and came in full view of two burning trucks and a half-track, several Iraqi bodies spread around them. It was then that the seasoned soldiers suddenly burst into the trees and shrubs at the side of the road and took cover. Saad, quick to understand such signs of catastrophe, dived off the road as bullets struck around him. Three new recruits froze and were shot, four others threw their weapons down, turned tail and ran, and the rest were pulled or pushed into cover by soldiers risking their lives to save them. Saad looked back at Mouse still standing in the road, bullets striking around him, his body shaking, a horrible whining sound coming from his throat. Then a bullet found its mark. Knocked flat on his back, Mouse did not move.

Bullets flew all around them as Khan grabbed Saad and pulled him toward a large boulder where both of them huddled for safety, Saad pulling his legs in just as bullets tore into the dirt where they had been. Behind another smaller rock lay a new recruit, shaking with terror as bullets ricocheted around him. Looking up, his eyes pleaded for help, but there was nothing Saad could do. Then the recruit's body jerked and didn't move again.

"He's dead," Khan said. "The Jews are on the ridge. If we stay here, we will die also. Now you will see how we fight." He grinned. "Then you will see how we run." He pointed to a stand of thick bushes. "See the bushes? Go to them and hide. May Allah bless you to find your son." Khan raised up and fired several shots, the other soldiers following suit. Two were hit but were only wounded. They recovered quickly and scurried into the trees with the other soldiers. They were all gone before Saad could move. The bullets of the Jewish guns followed them, and for a brief moment, no gunfire came near Saad. Slithering to the bushes, he dug his way to the center like a mole. His heavy breathing crushed his chest and he bit into his knuckle to keep himself quiet, more fearful that he might have to shoot someone than he was of being shot. He could only imagine what this must be like for Emile.

Emile. It was getting dark. He must find him, but where could he look? How could he possibly find him in all this? It seemed overwhelming, impossible!

Think.

The battle seemed to be moving to his right down a ravine. Taking a deep breath, he pushed aside the bushes and peered up the road where it snaked its way through the canyon toward the west. Bodies lay in the road. He heard moaning and saw brief shadows of movement in the trees but nothing he could put a name to. Lying on his back, he listened, closing his eyes, concentrating on each sound in the trees. There it was—the sound of motors, distant but moving closer. Then, voices—Hebrew. Finally the sound of footsteps, dozens of feet shuffling along the dusty gravel, watching, ready, probably checking the bodies, looking for remnants of the enemy. Carefully turning on his belly, Saad pushed aside the limbs—men with weapons only a few feet away. Gritting his teeth, he let back the bushes and burrowed deeply into their roots, holding his breath, praying he would not be seen.

"A live one here," a voice hollered. "Arab though. A new recruit from the look of him. He won't last long. Took it in the chest."

"Three more over here," said another voice. "All dead."

"Keep moving," said a voice of authority. "I want control of the mouth of the canyon before dark."

They picked up their step. Several vehicles passed by and finally more men on foot. Saad lay absolutely motionless for what seemed like an eternity. Finally the voices faded away in the growing shadows.

He felt sick, his strength gone, pain coursing through every muscle. But there was relief as well. Drawing strength from it, he pushed himself from his hiding place and crawled into the shadow of an outcrop of stone, a still-smoldering truck just feet away. Putting his head in his shaking hands, he thanked Allah for His mercy, then forced himself to his feet. More Jews would come. He had to search for Emile while he could. He must find out if his son had died in this awful place.

Cautiously he searched, the shadows deepening. Bodies. Dozens of them. Fodder for the war machine, for the greed of men. Most of them were just boys only a few years older than Emile, some younger. Someone moaned to Saad's left, and he stumbled into the tall roadside grass to find a man lying in a small pocket of boulders, his blank eyes staring up at him. Saad turned away, afraid he would retch. He moved on, more slowly now, numbed by what he was seeing. How easily a life could be snuffed out. How easily everything could change.

He checked each body and hurried to one on his face, about the same size, build, and hair color of his son. As he knelt and gently lifted the head, he sighed in relief, then anguished for some other family who no longer had a son.

Getting to his feet, he trudged further west where the canyon widened, working his way into the trees, checking other bodies. He found many lifeless Jews here, and like their enemies, some had uniforms, some didn't. Those who didn't were thin, and Saad realized they were new recruits from the camps on Cyprus and in Europe, put into battle nearly as soon as they arrived. They too had been ill prepared for the horror of war. He prayed that Allah would receive them all.

His fear lessened a little as he neared the end of the battle area, the sounds of fighting completely gone.

Plopping down, exhausted, he laid his hands on his knees and tried to regain his strength. His respite didn't last long, interrupted by the sound of distant trucks coming up the canyon from the west. The Jews were sending reinforcements.

For a moment, Saad could not move, his energy gone. He cursed the night they had decided to leave Haifa for Beirut, cursed this war and all those who had started it.

The rumble came closer. Still he did not move, his mind turning to Rifa. She had always been a good wife, a good mother. They had wanted other children, but none had ever come. They had spoiled the boy, kept him close to them, protected him for fear they might lose him. That fear had been the biggest reason for fleeing Haifa. If they had only stayed put!

He could hear voices now. He must move. He had to find Emile. If he did not, he could not live with himself, and Rifa . . . Rifa would never look at him the same again.

Getting to his feet, Saad stumbled toward the gradual slope of the hill, then began climbing, praying Allah would lead him to his son. Approaching a slight rise that would put him out of view of the road, he realized he had left his weapon in the bushes. Turning to go back, he was shocked. In his muddled, anxious state, he had not realized how many dead there were. The sight of dozens of motionless bodies lying on the ground was grossly mesmerizing, and he could not pull his eyes away. Then he saw it. A green sweater!

Saad's heart nearly stopped. He blinked twice, then bolted down the hillside while glancing up the canyon for a sign of the Jewish convoy he knew must be close. He saw nothing and rushed into the valley, darted around a burned-out truck, and stopped short, his legs suddenly leaden, his heart thumping against his rib cage. He made himself move through the tall summer grass and low bushes. The body lay facedown alongside a small stream, the legs half submerged in muddy, stagnant water, the torso on the tall grass of the bank.

Biting his lip nearly in two, Saad knelt and gently turned over the body, knowing it was Emile. Sobs broke into his chest at the sight of the blood on his son's pullover sweater and the pale color of his skin. From his knees, he pulled the boy from the stream and into his arms, his cries of anguish muffled in Emile's neck and shoulder. He looked, touched, for some sign of life, but saw nothing.

"Emile? Please, son . . ."

The eyelids fluttered. The lips moved. Saad scrambled from under his son, laying him gently down. He felt for a pulse. Nothing. No, there it was. Carefully, he pulled off the boy's sweater, then ripped open the shirt. The wound was above the heart, a ghastly hole oozing blood, the sweater drenched with it. Saad fumbled with his own shirt, ripping most of the bottom from it, then pressing it against and into the wound. Emile stiffened and groaned again.

"Emile!" he cried in loud desperation. "Emile." Saad tapped him lightly on the cheek. "Wake up, son!"

Emile grimaced with pain, his eyes struggling to open.

"Allah be praised," said Saad. He tore more cloth from his shirt and wrapped it around the first to hold it tight against the hole in Emile's shoulder. "I'm here, son. I'll get you out of here!"

"Papa?" Emile said weakly.

"Yes, son, it is me."

"Ohh, it hurts, Papa. It hurts so bad. And . . . and . . . I . . . I am so weak. I . . ." His voice trailed off, and his head dropped slightly to the side.

"Emile! Please, you cannot leave me now." He grabbed the boy's arm and checked for a pulse, fearful it would be gone. But it was still there, still weak. He wiped his mouth with the back of his hand, sweat pouring from his forehead. Then he remembered the Jews. His ears pricked up. The sounds were close, and the shadows were deepening in the canyon as the late afternoon sun settled further in the west. He had little time. Getting to his knees, he lifted Emile until he was in a sitting position, then grabbed his upper legs and hoisted him onto his shoulder. Gritting his teeth and begging Allah for more strength, he stumbled onto the road and toward the hill. Reaching the truck, he braced himself against it for a moment, resting.

He heard the voice, but his muddled mind didn't understand the words and he turned slightly, facing the sound. A vehicle stood in the middle of the road a hundred feet away, several men around it, their rifles aimed at him. His confused mind registered only that they intended to shoot, and he shoved himself away from the truck and tried to run. The bullet caught him in the middle of his lower back and threw him forward. He tried to brace Emile's fall but failed, the white-hot pain shooting into his brain where it exploded as both he and his son hit the ground. He fought the cold that trickled up his legs, but it didn't stop.

"Not now," he said softly. "Not now that I have found my son . . ."

The voices blurred, the light dimmed, then blackness came and Saad Shawas felt nothing at all.

CHAPTER 21

It was morning, the first rays of sun coming over the hills to the east. Mary had hoped to be in Haifa this morning, but the battle Emile had run away to join prevented this. Instead, they spent the night in a small cavern that had once been an ancient tomb. Mary left their cramped quarters, walked a short distance, and gazed over the Valley of Jezreel, the sounds of summer birds a pleasant change from those of war. She found a comfortable spot, watching the sun quickly rise above the hills and its rays flow down onto the valley floor. Many wars had been fought here, many just as unnecessary as this one.

War. How she hated it and what it did to men—what it had done to her and Aaron, her brothers and their families. And now Emile and possibly Saad. Where were they, and how could they ever survive such madness?

Taking out her Book of Mormon, she turned to 2 Nephi 9 and concentrated on soothing her feelings. More than ever, she needed some peace from the horrible thoughts and despair of losing so much.

After half an hour she put the book away, said a quick prayer, and returned to the cave where she found Berak and Salim preparing for the day's journey. Neither spoke, their minds heavy with thought. They were so close to their destination and yet so far away. She slipped past them into the cavern and found Rifa putting away the few blankets they had used for sleeping, blankets Berak and his friends had been kind enough to loan them. Mary retrieved one of the blankets and folded it, then handed it to Rifa.

"Will you go directly to Jerusalem?" Rifa asked.

"I hope it is safe enough, but we shall see." She forced a smile.

"Your husband, he was a martyr of the war. It must be hard for you to go home knowing . . . knowing he won't be there." She bit her lip, her own future playing before her eyes as surely as Mary's.

Mary wanted to give Rifa the comfort she sought, but what could she say? Saad and Emile had left them, and the chance of their survival was unknown. She left the subject alone, focusing on the actual question. "Yes, it will be hard. But, I have a child coming. I am sure he will help me bear the future more easily."

"A child? You are expecting? But you do not look . . ." Rifa blushed as she looked at Mary's stomach, then busied herself, looking away.

Mary laughed lightly. "I only discovered that I am pregnant a few weeks ago."

"You do not seem to suffer with the sickness," Rifa said. "Allah's blessing. Emile gave me such trouble." She rolled her eyes, then the brief smile of memory passed and reality returned. "Saad and I can have no more children." Her shoulders seemed to sag once more.

The room was clean, and Mary doused the fire's embers with the last of the coffee. Leaving the cavern, they walked into a warm sun and the fresh smell of morning.

"Good, you are here. We're ready to leave," Berak said, handing Mary the reins to her horse.

Mounting, Mary heard the distant thunder of artillery and watched as the birds scattered on the early morning wind. Her stomach churned. Only a few more miles, she thought.

Salim spoke something to Berak before taking one of his men and disappearing up the small canyon to the west. The other bedu fighters with them stayed with Berak, taking up positions behind their small group before they went the same direction.

Moving through the ravine and over the first small knoll, they dipped down into a larger canyon where trees were plentiful. Mary topped the knoll to the sound of vehicles in the valley to the north, the location of one of the roads that ran through the Carmel range from the coast to the interior cities of Nazareth and Tiberias. Berak was avoiding the main roads and thus the war itself. The worst of the battles had forced them south yesterday, and during the evening, Berak chose to cross into Jewish-held territory, then through the Carmel range to Haifa.

The early morning air was crisp, and the shade of the trees gave them a cool cover while keeping them hidden from view as they traveled. They stopped to rest midmorning, and for the first time, Salim and his fellow bedu reappeared. They drank, ate dried meat, and discussed direction with Berak, then mounted and were gone once more. This time, Berak turned them west, then fell back to Mary and explained.

"There is a battle up ahead. We will have to be cautious." He handed her his water skin, and as she raised it to her lips and let the tepid liquid flow down her throat, she heard a sudden outbreak of gunfire. The horses pranced nervously.

"Get down and lead them into the trees," Berak said firmly to her and Rifa. "Stay put, and keep them quiet."

The sound of pounding hooves echoed in the small ravine. Mary turned to see Salim and his fellow tribesman returning fast from their forward position. Their quick discussion revealed that the battle was moving their way and they would need to stay hidden, at least for now. Everyone led their animals into a thick stand of trees, and Salim and the bedu climbed the hill and disappeared.

"Where are they going?" Mary asked Berak.

"To watch the battle from hiding. If one or the other army is driven this way, they will warn us." Berak handed over his rifle. "Do you know how to use it?"

She nodded.

"Just in case any unsavory types show up—Jew or Arab," Berak said.

Mary nodded and watched Berak follow the others out of sight.

The battle went on and seemed to get closer to their position as the minutes passed, stretching Mary's nerves to near breaking. Then the shooting died down and finally stopped. A few minutes later, Mary saw Berak come through some wild olive trees, Salim and the others with him, his face reflecting a sad smile.

"The battle is all but finished. Many have died. It was a foolish fight. The Iraqis were unorganized and used many irregulars and volunteers with no training. They are no match for an organized military." He looked at Rifa, whose face was ashen. "Our army has taken the wounded and prisoners to a holding area south of here. It is where they have taken all the prisoners who have been fighting along this front. We can go there if you like. If your son did come to fight, he might be there."

Rifa was wringing her hands, unsure and frightened. Mary put an arm around her while looking at Berak. "I will go. Rifa can wait here with—"

Rifa grabbed Mary's hand while shaking her head slowly. "No, I will go. I must," she said softly. Getting to her feet, she forced a smile. "They . . . they have to be all right. They have to."

Mary knew it would take all Rifa's strength to go. "Are you sure?"

Rifa nodded as she reached her horse. Berak helped her into the saddle while Mary and the others mounted. He then swung atop his own Arabian and reined him back toward the Jezreel Valley. Salim and the others headed east, waving a good-bye to Berak as they left.

"Where are they going?" Mary asked.

"To Allonim. It is better that they go back. They are needed by their own people more than by us, and they will not be welcome at the prisoner of war camp where we must go."

An hour later, they reached a staging area. Soldiers sat around, their faces tired and sweaty. Some loaded bodies on a truck while others placed them in a hole made for burial. *All the horrors of war are here,* Mary thought. *Death and dying, groans and anguish of the wounded.* She kept her eyes on the horse's mane, her face nearly covered with her head scarf as their horses skirted the worst of it. They approached a fenced-in area where men milled about, guarded by Jewish soldiers.

They arrived at the gate, and Berak dismounted, then helped Rifa down while Mary slid to the ground. An officer sat at a beat-up table doing paperwork and looked up when Berak stepped up. They knew each other but disposed of all but bare-minimum pleasantries. On such a day, they didn't seem appropriate. Berak told them who they were looking for.

"Their names?" the officer asked.

"Saad and Emile Shawas," Berak said.

He fingered through several pages of names. "We've registered every prisoner we have, and those names aren't here." He looked up, glancing at Rifa who was hanging desperately to Mary. "You . . uh . . . might try the hospital. After that, the burial . . ."

"Thanks, we'll do that," Berak said. They took the reins of their horses and walked toward a large tent near the road. Mary felt her heart thumping. Their chances of finding Emile and Saad alive were dwindling by the moment.

CHAPTER 22

Naomi watched as the Auster dipped into the valley and landed, then taxied to a spot fifty feet from where she stood. Wally waved hello, and she returned his greeting. Shutting down the motor, he got out of the plane, and men unloaded half the precious ammunition he brought. It was his fifth and last official trip of the day. Only a planned side trip remained.

After loading a few bombs and Naomi's rifle and bullet belt, Wally made sure the machine gun attached to his wing was loaded before they got in and took off. The sun hung low in the western sky as they turned south and flew across the hills.

He had come to the office on his first trip in, pulled her aside, and told her he was planning a trip to Negba. They needed ammo, and he needed a plane wheel. He had contacted Rachel by radio and she would be waiting with a jeep to take them to the site of the Spitfire's wreckage. Her price was the rest of the ammo he was carrying, along with a dozen Piat shells he had hidden in the back of the plane's storage compartment. Piats were hard to find.

Naomi had agreed to go along. Someone needed to tell Rachel about Ephraim, and she needed to keep busy, her mind occupied.

They flew in silence and were soon high above the southern battleground. The flight of the Messerschmitts had been considered a disaster at first. They had lost one plane, had their guns and bomb bays jam, and had nearly lost another plane on landing. But radio intercepts told them a different story.

The Egyptians hadn't known that the Israeli Air Force had acquired fighters. Thinking they had air superiority, they had been totally surprised to find four Czech Messerschmitts strafing their columns, blowing up several trucks and killing a dozen soldiers. Frightened and unsure of how to respond, the Egyptians had dug in at Isdud instead of continuing their advance. All that had seemed to go wrong with the IAF's first fighter attack had suddenly showed a silver lining. It also gave Wally a chance to get to the wreckage. Had the Egyptian advance continued, it would have been right into the hills where the downed Spitfire with a good wheel was located. The Egyptians would still come to Negba, but Wally only needed a few hours.

"Have you ever flown into Negba?" Naomi yelled above the whine of the engine.

"Yeah. You land on a field that faces the settlement. That way you can taxi right inside the gates. The plane will be safe there while we make our salvage run. Piece of cake." He grinned.

She smiled and nodded. They flew directly over the kibbutz to let them know they had arrived, then circled, dipped down, and landed. By the time they reached the kibbutz fence, the wide gates were open, and Wally taxied the Auster inside. Shutting down the motor, they climbed out to find Rachel waiting behind the wheel of a jeep, a machine gun mounted on an iron platform above her head. She was surprised but happy to see Naomi, and quickly got out of the jeep to hug them both.

Rachel stood back and looked at Naomi. "My, you have grown up. And a rabbi's wife to boot. Things have changed since we last met."

"It's been three years, Rachel, and war ages us especially quick, don't you think?" Rachel did look older. Her brown hair was sun bleached now, and there were deepening worry lines around her eyes. But then, war did that to all of them.

"I can't argue with that," Rachel said. "I'm sorry I couldn't be there for your wedding. The Arabs seem to be getting in the way of a lot of my life lately. How is your husband?"

"For your absence from the wedding, you are forgiven. As for Abraham, he is in a prison camp in Transjordan." They discussed what had happened at the Quarter and their flyover of Mafraq, then Naomi took Rachel's hand and pulled her aside. "I have news. News of Ephraim." Naomi told her about the wire from Hannah while Wally waited. He had sent another wire that morning asking for an update. The answer had been short. "Near death. Pray for a miracle." It was signed by Ephraim's mother.

It wasn't easy for any of them. It was like having a brother in critical condition and unable to be there for him. Though impatient to get to the wreck of the Spitfire, he kept his feelings hidden. Discussions about family deserved time.

Finally Rachel stood straight, took a deep breath, and walked toward him, forcing a smile. "This could get us all killed. You know that."

"It will give us a Spitfire. Believe me when I say that it's worth the risk."

"So I'm told. We contacted Weizman after you left. Though he isn't happy about you coming down here without clearance, he covets that Egyptian fighter." Rachel looked at Naomi. "You have a husband now. You stay here and wait . . ."

"I'm going, Rachel," Naomi said.

"You go if I say so, and I don't," Rachel said. "No place in the jeep anyway, and I am not about to risk you when it isn't needed."

"What about the seat next to you?" Naomi asked.

"Simon," she yelled. A short, stout man turned around, two beady eyes peeking out between a full, shaggy beard and a floppy laborer's cap. He shouldered an automatic weapon and quickly joined them, hopping in the passenger seat. "We'll see you when we get back. Make yourself at home, Naomi. You sit this one out."

"Wally, you man the machine gun. This is your idea, so you ought to be the biggest target."

"You're a mean lady, Rachel Steinman," Wally said, climbing up to the machine gun.

"This is Simon." Rachel pointed to the man next to her. "In this country, he's as good as any bedu scout, and because he has a martyr's wish, I invited him along. Just so you know, the Egyptians have decided to move east instead of north, and we're in the way. So don't be surprised if you see a couple hundred of them in your gun sights. Still want to do this?"

Wally grinned. "For God and country."

With that, Rachel released the clutch and yelled to have the gate opened, leaving Naomi fuming.

"Your sister is not happy with you," Simon said as he watched Naomi over his shoulder.

"If we get killed, she'll thank me."

"If we don't, she'll beat the livin' daylights out of you." Simon grinned.

They bounced through the gate, and Rachel shifted into high gear.

* * *

They reached the wreckage a couple hours before dark. Wally walked around the charred plane while the others kept watch. They had seen a few bedu, but only at a distance, and there had been no sign of movement by the Egyptians.

"What do you think?" Rachel asked, coming up behind him.

The plane was worse than Wally had hoped. The pilot had attempted to lower the landing gear before hitting the ground, but from the look of the plane, he had run into one of the quirks of the Spitfire. The wheels are raised and lowered by moving a lever down and out, then holding it for a short pause to pressurize the hydraulic system. Moving the lever too soon or too quickly could leave the pilot with only a partial pressurization, thus only a partial letdown of the gear, making for a catastrophic landing. Apparently this pilot had learned about this little problem the hard way. The plane had hit, and the gear took the brunt. One folded up and into the belly of the plane where it was now wedged, and the other snapped off, gouging the left wing and scattering fuel. The plane's prop had bit into rock and flipped the plane over on its back as it exploded into flames. The remains in the cockpit were a gruesome reminder of a pilot's vulnerability.

"I'll need those wrenches you arranged for, and a crowbar. Tell Simon I'll need his help as well," Wally said.

Rachel and Simon returned quickly with the tools, and Rachel kept watch while the two men worked to dislodge the surviving wheel.

"You've changed a lot since I saw you last," Wally said to her. He wiped the sweat from his forehead with the sleeve of his shirt.

"Living in Israel changes everyone. Some for better, some for worse," she answered.

"You were a fighter even in Berlin, Hannah's right-hand gal, as I recall."

"Hannah saved my life, or what was left of it at the time. After she woke me up from the walking dead, I decided no one would make me feel like that again. How is Zohar?"

"Good, strong. Headstrong that is."

"Meek little Zohar? I would love to see that change."

"She's a survivor, just like the rest of you, which is just what this new country needs, I suppose. Ironic, isn't it? It took the Nazis to make us mad enough to fight back."

Simon jerked on the bar for the fifth time, and the wheel popped free. The hydraulics still had built-up pressure and raised the wheel to a 45-degree angle outside the housing, which had protected it from the fire. "Good, that will make it easier," Simon said. They each grabbed a wrench and started unbolting the assembly.

"I heard you were about to marry, but he was killed. Sorry to hear it, Rachel. You deserve to be happy. We all do," Wally said.

She was squinting at the hill to the west. "I've learned to take the moments I can get. Nathan and I shared more than a lot of people who have come here."

"Best soldier around these parts," Simon said. "He and I served in the Jewish brigade together. A fighter, he was. Took an Arab ambush to do him in. Bloody cowards."

"You talk like you spent most of your life in Britain," Wally said, laying aside the first unscrewed nut.

"Fought with them, that's all. Picked up a little bit of the English, I suppose, but I'm Sabra. Born and raised in the Negev. I've spent more time with bedu than with Jews. The ones I knew well are still fighting with us, but lots of the others have turned colors. They either fight with Transjordan or for the Mufti." He spat on the ground as he added a nut to the one Wally had removed, then nodded toward the east. "Take those boys on the hill over there. They're looking us over, trying to decide if we can be taken. Not the friendly type, but they're not blind either. They see that machine gun on the jeep and know we'd cut 'em up before they got anything. Another minute or two, and they'll be on their way."

Wally eyed them once, then returned to his work. They disappeared by the time he finished undoing the nut he was working on.

"I'm going up the hill to get a better view," Rachel said. "Hurry up with that. We have to be out of here before dark."

"We'll need some kind of frame over this to hold it up once it's unbolted," Wally said.

"I figured we might." Simon got to his feet and retrieved several pieces of metal bar from the jeep, then positioned them over the wheel and used a single bolt to tie them together. He then hung a pulley from their center and slipped a strong wire cable into it before attaching the opposite end to the wheel assembly. Pulling the jeep closer, he attached the still-free end of the long cable to the bumper and pulled it taut. By the time he finished, Wally had all but the last two nuts removed from their bolts.

"Tell me about Rachel," Wally said as he looked up the hill where she was.

"Just like you said, she's a fighter. She and Nathan worked hard, were leaders in the kibbutz, in the whole region, and madly in love. Something died in her when he was killed, but she goes on, refusing to give up. The woman you mentioned taught her that, or so she says." He paused. "She told us some about her experience, how they escaped and all. We who have lived here all our lives can't understand what kind of trial it was for them, not even those of us who saw the camps after the war." He pulled a nut free of its bolt. He paused, watching Rachel as he took a sip from the canteen. "Since Nathan's death, she's been madder than a wet hen. Angry mad, crazy even. Like . . . like . . ."

"Like she has a death wish?"

"Blimey, he can read minds. I suppose if she lives long enough, she'll get over Nathan, but therein lies the problem. Will she live that long? The way she throws herself into battle these days, my guess is she won't, much as I'd love to be wrong."

They went back to work and soon had the wheel hanging free of the plane except for tubes and wires. Wally took the mechanic at his word and cut them free just as Rachel returned.

"Anything?" Simon asked.

"There is a good deal of dust along the road south of us. Maybe five miles. We had better get moving."

"Get in the jeep and pull forward, slowly, m'lady," Simon said. "That will allow us to lower the wheel onto the ground.

Then we'll separate the wheel unit from the armature so that we can load both in the back of the jeep."

Fifteen minutes later, they had the assembly apart and loaded. The three of them jumped into the jeep, and Rachel quickly turned them toward home, the blinding light of the sun directly in front of them, sinking into the waters of the distant Mediterranean Sea.

They ascended the rise of a hill and dipped down to the road just as a column of armored cars, jeeps, and trucks came up the valley from the south. Rachel saw them, jerked the wheel to the north, and pushed the throttle to the floor, nearly losing Wally.

"Egyptians," she yelled. Bullets dug into the soil around them, then small explosions threw rock and dirt as the enemy fired the small-caliber cannons attached to their armored cars. Wally swung the machine gun around and stood between Simon and Rachel, firing back while Simon used his own automatic weapon to do the same. Wally's bullets struck a radiator, causing a jeep to swerve. An armored car plowed into it and threw the jeep's passengers helter-skelter across the landscape as Rachel jammed their jeep into a lower gear and climbed the rise to their right, then plummeted down the far side just as Wally ran out of shells. She sped down the hillside and caught the road, then picked up the pace as they fled for Negba.

"That was close," Simon said to Rachel.

Rachel nodded while looking up at Wally, now propped against the gun platform, his hand pressed against a bloodstain in the side of his shirt. He looked at her with a disbelieving smirk. His eyes rolled into the top of his head and he fell between the two front seats, his arm flopping against the steering wheel. The jeep veered hard to the left, and Rachel fought for control as Simon moved Wally out of the way. Slamming on the brakes, she brought the jeep to a standstill just as the Egyptians came over the rise and toward them, their weapons firing. Rachel jumped to the gun, quickly fed a second belt into its chamber, and began firing while Simon pulled Wally up to his seat and slipped behind the wheel. As the bullets hit the first Egyptian jeep, it swerved directly into the path of two others, causing a series of collisions that gave them a chance to get away.

"Move it," Rachel yelled to Simon.

"Yes, countess, as you wish," Simon said. He jammed the gearshift forward and pushed on the gas, leaving the mayhem behind, Rachel emptying her weapon. When they reached the turnoff to Negba, Simon cut the corner and had them in the compound two minutes later. There were a hundred fifty fighters in the kibbutz, and at least half of them seemed to surround the jeep as it came to a stop. Wally was shaking his head free of cobwebs as Simon shut off the motor.

"Two of you, help get that man to the infirmary. The rest of you get to your positions. The Egyptians have a brigade heading this way." The crowd scattered as Naomi helped two others pull Wally from the jeep.

"How bad?" she asked him.

"Just a scratch." He forced a smile.

She looked at the blood on his shirt and knew he was lying.

"Get the wheel into the plane and be ready to go in ten minutes. No longer," Wally said. "I'll be ready in a few minutes." The two men kept going in the direction of the infirmary, but Naomi went back toward Rachel.

"What happened?" Naomi asked as the commanding officer of Negba's Haganah unit joined them.

"They'll attack first thing in the morning," he responded. "But the artillery will try to soften us up tonight. You need to get that plane out of here—and quick—or it will be nothing but pieces by morning."

Naomi nodded and asked Simon to see that the wheel was loaded and the plane turned around. Then she headed for the infirmary, Rachel right behind her. Wally was being bandaged, his face pale, etched with a good deal of pain. Naomi told him they were nearly ready.

As the final piece of tape was applied, he put his feet on the floor, and Naomi helped him into his bloodied shirt. "Can you do this?" she asked.

He nodded. "Piece of cake. I can't let anything happen to that wheel assembly or the Auster. Not after taking a bullet for it. It wouldn't be American. Let's get going."

"Your lives are more important than a wheel assembly, Wally," Rachel said. "If you don't think you can make it, you stay."

Wally was already shuffling toward the door. "Getting that Spitfire in the air will save dozens of other lives, Rachel, maybe even help you and the people here. So let's get going, shall we?" He threw open the door and was headed for the plane when Naomi caught up to him. He stumbled as a shot of pain gripped his side. She grabbed one of his arms and put it over her shoulder.

"Are you sure about this?"

"Sure. It's a ten-minute flight to Tel Aviv. We'll make it even if you have to handle the stick while I catch a wink or two." He forced a smile.

"You pass out, and I'll shoot you myself."

Rachel helped get him in the pilot's seat, then hugged Naomi. "May God go with you," she said.

"And you," Naomi answered before going around to the passenger side.

"Hey, Rachel," Wally said. "I want you to remember something. This war won't take forever, and with Ephraim's condition, Hannah and the kids will need help. You owe her. Stay alive long enough to pay the debt, you hear me?"

Rachel blinked several times but nodded. "Yes, I hear you. Good luck, Wally." She looked through the plane at Naomi. "Tell Hannah and Ephraim I will be here when they come home. And, Naomi, don't worry. Abraham will be all right. We all know you need someone to keep you in line, and I've given up trying." She smiled, then moved back from the plane.

Naomi waved as the plane's prop began to turn, the nose aimed directly at the gate.

"All right, we can do this," Wally said, beads of sweat on his forehead. "The trick is getting up to speed quickly. We'll brake until the prop is at a high rpm, then go. By the time we're fifty yards outside the gate, we should be airborne." He jiggled the stick. "Just in case I lose consciousness, this is how it works." He showed her direction, flaps, throttle, and other things she hoped not to face, then began adjusting the throttle. "Time to go." The propeller increased its revolutions, and Wally nodded at Simon who signaled to open the gate. With the engine at full power, Wally eased off the brake, and they lurched forward.

The first artillery shell hit to their left as they whizzed by several buildings, passed the gate, and flew onto the make-do runway. The plane rushed down a slight decline toward the road, lifted just before reaching it, and soared to the left. Naomi saw the artillery pieces on a distant hill and felt guilty that she was escaping while others were forced to endure the barrage that would surely come. And she worried about Rachel.

Wally's face grew whiter, and she could see that the stain of blood on his shirt was growing. "Can you make it?" she asked.

He only nodded, the last rays of the sun bouncing off clouds over the sea. His head bobbed forward. He jerked it up.

"You have to stay awake, Wally. I'll get us both killed if I have to land this thing."

He nodded, shaking his head slightly to clear his vision. Removing a canteen from behind the seat, she gave him a drink, but most of it cascaded down his shirt. Taking it, he poured the rest over his head. "Five minutes and we'll be there," he said. "Anyone can stay conscious for five minutes, can't they?" He tried to smile. The plane was bobbing left and right, up and down, and the sound of the engine wavered, faded, built to a fevered pitch, then wavered again. He handed her the headset. "Let them know we're coming, what our condition is."

She put it on, pushed the send button as she had seen him do on their flight over Latrun, and spoke. There was an immediate answer. She told them what their status was and waited for a reply.

"We copy. Can Wally land the Auster?"

"They want to know if you're okay to land us."

He nodded, even as he grimaced, water mingling with the sweat dripping from his chin.

"He says he can."

"How long before arrival?" they asked.

She relayed the question.

"Two, three minutes," Wally answered.

He pushed forward on the stick, and Naomi nearly lost her stomach, the landscape rushing at them too fast.

"Wally, ease back on the stick," she said, trying to control her panic.

"Huh? Oh, yeah." He pulled back. A moment later they were hurtling toward an open field just above what few trees there were.

"There's the airfield," she said with some relief.

The plane undulated toward the field, and she said so, stiffening again.

"I . . . I can't hold it steady enough. Too weak."

"You can do it," she said. Reactively, she slapped his face. He jerked the stick, and the plane rose, swooped left, then right, then down. He struggled to gain control, and finally the plane leveled out again.

"Sorry," she said.

Grabbing the stick with both hands, he pushed forward and eased up on the throttle. The plane drifted down. As they swooped above the ground, a crosswind pushed them left. Wally corrected too far to the right, then back, just in time for the wheels to touch down. The plane bounced, and Wally adjusted the throttle, bringing them down with a thump. Coming to a halt in the middle of the field, half a dozen people ran toward them, followed by a makeshift ambulance.

Her heart stopped assaulting her breastbone about the time Wally smiled at her. Then his head bobbed and fell her direction. She supported his head until he was pulled from the plane.

Climbing out, she saw Zohar stepping in the back of the ambulance, the doors closing behind her. Then the vehicle sped away.

"Did he get it?" She turned to face a large man wiping greasy hands on a rag.

"It's in the plane. Is anyone flying into Jerusalem tonight?"

"Nope, but you might check with the staging area this side of Hulda. I hear they're taking supplies into Jerusalem tonight over some goat track some soldiers discovered." He shrugged. "Probably just a rumor, but I can have you taken there if you like."

It wasn't hard for her to believe such an attempt would be made, and with no other options, she asked for the ride.

He whistled and another man came out of the hangar. "Give this lady a ride to Hulda."

Five minutes later, Naomi was on her way. It had been good to see Rachel. She could only hope she would see her again.

SEE CHAPTER NOTES

CHAPTER 23

They found Emile in a makeshift field hospital at the prisoner of war camp. His wound had been repaired and rebandaged, but he was unconscious, the morphine doing its work. Rifa sobbed as she stared down at him, tears of anguish for his condition and of relief that he was alive.

"Can he travel?" she asked the Jewish doctor.

"He could if he weren't a prisoner. He was fighting our soldiers on the road to Haifa. They won't let him go home just to kill more Jews."

"But . . ." Rifa looked desperately at Berak. "I . . . he won't fight again. You have my word. I will keep him out of it."

Berak glanced at the doctor, his eyes asking for mercy. The doctor nodded slightly. "Take him then. We have enough who need our medicines. Will you want the body too?"

Rifa and Mary both stopped breathing.

"What body?" Berak asked.

The doctor turned a bit red, his eyes going to the floor as he realized they didn't know about the boy's father. "I'm sorry. I thought you knew before you came in here. The boy was found with his father, at least according to the papers that were on them. Our men . . . well, they thought he was trying to run. It was getting dark, and they couldn't tell for sure. One of the new recruits from Cyprus shot him before he realized . . ."

Rifa screamed, her hands grabbing the sides of her head in shock and horror. She dropped to her knees and started rocking, lamenting in Arabic. Mary dropped to her side and once more tried to give her comfort, but Rifa would not be consoled. She shook her shoulders angrily, throwing Mary's hands aside, then lowered her head, pounding it against the ground again and again before collapsing into a motionless faint.

Berak stooped down and picked her up, carrying her from the hospital. Finding a spot of summer grass, he laid her down while sending Mary to bring the water bottle. With tears streaming from her eyes, Mary did as she was told, then knelt beside Rifa and held her hand. She knew this anguish, knew how horrible it was to have someone tell you your husband was dead. But Mary still had hope. Rifa did not.

The doctor came out of the hospital and handed Berak several pills. "It is a sedative of sorts. Give it to her when she is awake. It will help. The body is down by the common grave. I don't think they have buried him yet, but you probably ought to . . . well, you ought to check now before they do." He turned and went back inside the tent as several more wounded arrived in the back of a small truck.

Rifa groaned back to consciousness, and Mary helped her sit up, then gave her a drink and the medicine while fumbling for words.

"Where is Saad? Where is my husband? I . . . I must take him back to Haifa and bury him next to his father and mother. It is something . . . He made me promise." Rifa bit her lip, her head turned to the heavens, tears dropping from the sides of her face.

Mary knew that she would have to identify the body. Berak did not know Saad. The thought made her cringe, but she knew there was no other choice. "Berak will stay with you while I make the arrangements," Mary said. "Come, let's get you to a quieter spot. You need to lie down and rest."

"No, no, I will wait with Emile. I must be with him when he awakens. I must tell him . . . about his father. No one else." She started to get up, and Berak gave her a hand.

"Are you sure?" Mary said.

Rifa nodded forcefully and started for the tent. Berak grabbed a wooden crate and followed, motioning for Mary to wait. He would get Rifa settled and help her find Saad. Mary nodded, relieved.

Her head scarf hung around her neck, and she removed it, shaking her hair free while she waited. More vehicles with wounded men came, left their burdens, then turned back to their horrible duty. She noticed an area not far away where another large tent housed cooking facilities. Dozens of men stood in line to receive food. All of them looked spent and dirty, and yet their talk revealed a sense of muted relief—sorry that so-and-so had died but glad they were here to know of it. She listened to their conversations of lost friends, watched their faces. She understood the conflict—the guilt—that such feelings brought.

Hearing the motor of a small plane, she shaded her eyes with one hand to locate its place in the blue sky. It swung a wide bank, then dipped and landed, taxiing to a place near the tents. After shutting down its engine, the pilot got out and unloaded boxes that were immediately taken to the medical tent. A moment later, he was back in his plane and taking off. Probably for Tel Aviv or Jerusalem, possibly other places, other battles. Would it never end?

"She will be fine for a while. The doctor in charge says he'll keep an eye on her, and if she gets distraught, he will send someone for us," Berak said.

Mary was still watching the plane lift from the ground and head south. "Where would he be going?" she asked.

"Back to Tel Aviv I suppose. Pick up another load and take it somewhere else. The Jews are fighting on four fronts now, barely holding their own, but winning, just as they did here. The doctor says there is talk of a cease-fire."

She faced him. "Really? Oh, that is good news, isn't it?"

"Yes, good news. Come on, let's get this done, shall we?"

The gravesite was on the other side of the road and partially up the gentle slope of a hill that bordered the ancient ruins of Megiddo. There was long, green grass with a few early summer wildflowers scattered through it. A few goats were feeding farther up the hill. A goatherd sat on a rock playing a flute, the soft music floating down to Mary and Berak.

"It seems odd, doesn't it?" Berak said. "Here we are, burying the dead from a war that burns hot all around us, and he does what he's done since the time he stood as tall as his goats. I wonder if he knows how lucky he is."

They reached the gravesite where a dozen men were either digging graves, laying the dead to rest, or throwing dirt on them. She thought it must be a horrible duty.

"How can they stand this?" she asked Berak.

"They do it because it's their duty, because the dead soldier deserves to be buried with respect in deep earth or sent home to his family. But mostly they do it because they know tomorrow someone might have to do it for them. The thing a soldier dreads most is dying and being forgotten, left to rot, uncared for."

"How does one kill another human being and not die a little himself?"

"He doesn't, but he has to go on. When I came home from Europe nearly three years ago, I didn't know what to do with myself. For two years, I did nothing but fight and kill and try to stay alive. I had forgotten how to do anything else. It took nearly a year to relearn how to live, how to survive in a world without war. It's not easy, and there are a few who never can."

"And what happens to them?"

"They find another war or they end their lives in some way. A friend of mine drank himself to death. Another put a gun to his head. Most do what I did. They tuck the past away in a dark little corner of their mind and try to build a new life. Thankfully I had a good wife and kids who were patient and gave me the strength to go on."

"Does this rekindle memories of all those awful things that happened before?"

"Yes, they stick an ugly head up from time to time, but mostly it's under control." He looked at the young men handling the bodies. "War brings out man's primitive nature. That is the danger of it. In the name of freedom and life, he is allowed to kill other human beings. If he isn't careful, he gives in to this part of him. He becomes a brute, ready to kill as quickly as he is ready to breathe. That is the hard part to put away and keep away. My prayer for these boys is that burying the dead will remind them of how permanent it is for everyone and make them less willing to end life needlessly. One thing is sure, war will show them who they really are, good or bad, saint or brute. Some won't like what they see, but they'll know."

They stood at the foot of several bodies covered by a tarp, their feet and the tops of a few heads sticking out opposite ends. As Berak rolled the tarp slowly back, Mary covered her mouth, and sweat broke out on her forehead. She did not let her eyes dwell on one face too long, each causing her stomach to churn a little more earnestly. Saad was the third one she saw.

She went weak in the knees and moved her head up and down quickly while turning away. Berak re-covered the bodies while Mary forced the bile back into her stomach.

"Rifa will want to take him to Haifa," she said softly.

Berak nodded, took her arm, and moved her toward a group of men sitting near the road.

"These men provide a service of sorts. They'll haul anything—ammunition, guns, men, even the dead—for a price. Wherever you find war, you find those ready to make a profit from it. You can't really blame them. For most, money is hard to come by. With many of our young men off fighting, the older ones have to provide for more mouths. They do what they can."

Mary noticed several beat-up old trucks sitting nearby. None looked like they could haul anything more than a few feet before breaking down.

"Shalom," Berak said to the group. They all responded in kind as they looked up at him and Mary. They were all older men, beyond fighting age, and Mary wondered how many had lost sons or even grandsons like Emile.

Berak explained that they needed two trucks, both to go to Haifa. One would carry a wounded man, the other a dead one. The group looked at Mary, giving her the once-over.

"She is Arab," said one of the men. He was probably fifty, his hair gray and very short, with a round, fat face and scraggly beard.

"Yes, so are the ones you will carry. And there will be another woman, Rifa Shawas, wife and mother to the dead and wounded men."

"We don't haul for Arabs," said the man.

Another man stepped forward. "Did you say Shawas?"

"Yes, Saad Shawas," Berak said. "He was killed looking for his son. Rifa wants to take them both home."

"Saad Shawas was an honorable man. Both of us worked for the British for many years. He was treated badly by many—"

"We don't haul for Arabs, Ivan," the round-faced man repeated while scowling at Mary.

"We are rid of most of them now, and we don't intend to let them come back."

Berak stepped forward and grabbed the man by one ear, lifting it up until he grimaced. "My name is Berak, Benny Berak. Have you heard the name?"

The man's eyes opened wide and the fight went out of his face.

"Then buzzer off, before I have your gizzard for supper." He pushed the man, and he stumbled away toward their trucks, several others grumbling as they followed.

"He needed a good lesson," Ivan said. "It wasn't always that way, but this war has done something to him. All he can talk about is taking over the rest of the Arab homes when the time comes. Loves to loot, that one." He looked at Mary. "I'll charge you ten pounds for the boy and ten for the body of Saad Shawas. I'll include a box for Saad and bring him along shortly." He signaled to another man standing behind, who then stepped forward. He was a thin man, and from the way Ivan treated him, perhaps a bit slow minded. As Ivan instructed him on how to proceed, the brother listened carefully and nodded at the end of every sentence. "Now, do you have it?"

Another nod.

"Good," Ivan grinned and turned to Berak. "This is my brother, Dimitri. We are Russian immigrants from the time of the tsar and Lenin and his miserable revolution. Dimitri was, well, just a boy, and the revolutionaries beat him because he was a Jew. Hit him in the head with something very hard." He shrugged. "Mother and Father got us out of the country quickly, and all of us finally came here, but Dimitri has never been the same." He grinned, showing that he was missing most of his teeth. "You worry, I see it in your eyes. Do not, do not. Dimitri is a good driver and will deliver his passengers to Haifa in two hours, no more. This is my guarantee." He raised his right hand as if it was as good as a signature.

Berak glanced at Mary, who gave him a slight nod. She liked Ivan, and though she had some misgivings about his brother, the promise of delivery to Haifa in two hours made the offer irresistible. "But you will be paid half when you leave this place, half when you have us safely in Rifa's home in Haifa," Mary said.

Ivan bowed slightly. "It is agreed." Ivan pulled Dimitri toward the trucks, explaining his instructions one more time. Again Dimitri nodded at the end of each sentence.

Berak and Mary walked toward the hospital. "Ahmed tells me you will go to Jerusalem to learn more of your husband. Possibly Ivan can arrange this for you."

"Possibly. I will talk to him about it. What else did Ahmed tell you?"

"That your husband is a Jew and died at Kastel. For this alone, I honor him. The Battle of Kastel saved many people from starving in Jerusalem, and may have saved our state." He paused. "It is rare these days to see a marriage of a Jew and Arab. It is something we have in common."

Mary realized what he meant. "You are the one Ahmed spoke of—you married Kalifa."

Berak nodded. "It has been a good marriage. Ahmed says you believe your husband may still be alive. May this be so."

"Thank you. Will you go back to Allonim now?"

"No, I will see you to Haifa. There will be guards demanding papers. My name may still be of some value, and I have to make arrangements for some supplies before I return. With Farouk and his people as guests, what we have will not last long."

Mary was relieved.

Dimitri and his truck arrived at the medical tent just after Mary and Berak. The doctor and Berak quickly prepared Emile for the journey, then put him on a stretcher and into the back of the truck while Mary explained to Rifa the arrangements they had made for Saad. Berak helped Rifa into the back of the truck while Mary mounted her horse. Dimitri watched Berak mount, waiting for the signal to proceed. Berak gave it, and Dimitri grinned, put the old truck in gear, and bounced onto the road. Mary worried that she and Berak, who was leading Rifa's horse, might have trouble keeping up, but the old truck didn't have more than a horse's gentle gallop in it, and climbing through the canyon there were several occasions when she thought they would need to use the horses to pull the truck over the top.

At the summit, Dimitri pulled over long enough to add several gallons of water to the radiator. While he did, Berak led Mary to a spot where they could look over the plain and the sea beyond, Haifa in the distance along the shore. She could see ships in the docks and several waiting offshore to unload.

"Refugees," Berak said. "They come by the thousands now." He pointed to several ships at one of the docks. "Those bring weapons, medical supplies, clothing, and a hundred other things. His finger lifted and picked out several ships moving south, several miles offshore. "More going to Tel Aviv."

"And the road to Tel Aviv and Jerusalem, is it open? Can I get there from Haifa?" Mary asked.

"To Tel Aviv, yes, but even then you will need the right papers. Because you are married to a Jew, it shouldn't be difficult." He shrugged. "After that, I don't know. The old road to the Holy City is closed, but the soldiers tell me we are making a new one. It is not ready yet, and no one seems to know when it will be. Possibly, by the time you get to Tel Aviv, there will be a cease-fire and it won't matter."

Mary couldn't help the smile. A cease-fire. Possibly peace could follow. It would make it easier for her to find Aaron. But just as quickly as hope tried to rise in her breast, anxiety followed. Her path could lead to a different result. Aaron might be gone. What would she do then? She could not stay in Palestine, torn between two people, her child never sure where he belonged. Would Ephraim and Hannah help her find a new life? She refused to face that now. There was still hope, and until someone told her otherwise, she would cling to it.

They reined their horses and returned to the truck where Dimitri was just refastening the hood with wire and twine. Rifa still sat in the back, Emile's head in her lap. Both were asleep. Mary's heart ached to look at them, and she turned away. She would do what she could for them before moving on to Tel Aviv. That would have to be enough, both for her own conscience and for them.

They reached the first checkpoint outside Haifa an hour later. Berak's presence did prove invaluable, their papers being inadequate, especially those of Rifa and Emile. Only Berak's influence and position saved them from being turned back—even with Emile's condition the way it was. Instead, the soldiers gave them an escort of four men in a jeep. It gave her a bit of a chill. Was this the way it would be for her people under Jewish rule? Would they be constantly hassled because of this war? Had it turned the Jews against them that badly?

The soldiers led them through streets bustling with new arrivals, citizens and soldiers, all Jewish. She saw no Arabs, at least none she readily recognized as such. At the hospital, they were welcomed only after Berak used his influence again. Finally, after nearly an hour of argument, and Mary paying half of her remaining money for some of Emile's care, two nurses quickly put the wounded boy on a stretcher and took him inside.

"Someone should be with him constantly, and if they give you any trouble, remind them that I will be back to take care of it personally," Berak said.

Rifa, a mixture of both fright and frustration on her face, thanked Berak, then turned to Mary.

"Saad would not want you to blame yourself for letting us come back with you." She forced a smile. "I am glad to have Emile alive, glad to be home. It is what Saad would have wanted for us. Thank you for helping as you did." She hugged Mary and then went inside to be with her son.

Mary turned to Berak. "Can you do me one more favor?"

"Of course," he said.

"Take me to Saad's home."

Berak nodded, then turned to Dimitri and sent him on his way. As he drove off, they mounted and walked their horses through the busy, dusty streets.

They were deep into what used to be the Arab section before Mary realized she was seeing only Jews. Most were women, children, and old men, dressed very poorly and speaking half a dozen different languages as they milled about the streets.

Coming to a military checkpoint, Berak once more presented his papers and got them past. It was then they began seeing more Arabs.

"Will they let me out when I am ready to leave?" she asked.

"Yes, women and children can come and go freely. It is the men they search. There are still those who fight the Haganah as a sort of underground. They hide in places like this section of the city and make it difficult to catch them. Then they sneak out at night and blow up a building or attack Jews in the streets. We search for them, and we try to limit their movement, but they still exist, and we must still try to stop them." He paused. "You should not stay here long. The Haganah searches the houses and shops. They do not warn anyone. Sometimes the Arabs fight back. That leads to bloodshed. You must be very careful."

"Will it ever return to normal?"

"It will never be as it was. Haifa is Jewish now. If we let more Arabs return, we would need guards in every street. Troublemakers would attack—throw stones or yell and scream at our men—and they would react. Blood would run in the streets, and no one would be safe." He removed a handkerchief from his pocket and wiped the sweat from his brow and neck. "For years I have tried to help my Arab friends, neighbors, and countrymen understand what war would do to all of us. Once you take up arms against someone, you are no longer friends, but enemies. You cannot trust one another, so you push them away and bring in those you can trust. It is who wins that dictates the rules, and anyone who says the Arabs would do it differently is a liar. In places where they win, they run us out and tear down our houses and build new ones for their own people. It is already happening in the Old City, in Etzion, in other villages where the Arabs have victories. We are all the same. We win, we take what we want, we make the rules and carry them out. The losers don't like it, and they fight back.

That is why we remove the losers. We don't want to fight them forever. Just once."

It sounded cold and cruel but honest and accurate. And he was right—if the Arabs won, it would certainly be no better. Hate and war. In the end, they always brought hardship and death to some, usually the innocent.

The house stood on a narrow street several blocks in. The street was old and cobbled, and the horses' hooves echoed off the walls of the close-knit buildings. Mary saw several faces appear at windows, then quickly disappear.

"They are afraid," Berak said. "I cannot blame them. The soldiers at the checkpoint told me that they had to come through here a few days ago and search every home. They took all the guns they could find and hauled several young men off to prison for attacking Jews in the marketplace, killing two of them."

Mary was beginning to see why Saad, Rifa, and Emile had fled, and it deepened her remorse for bringing them back. Maybe a refugee camp was a better place, and with Saad's training, he might have found good work in the city and been able to become a citizen of Lebanon. She and Ahmed should never have agreed to let them come back.

"I know what you're thinking," Berak said. "But you saw what has happened to the homes of many Arabs already. He pointed to a house where a man dressed in the clothes of a European Hasid swept the stairs in front of a doorway. "See this man. Even here, our refugees come like a flood to find shelter, and this is not the safest place for them to be. If other houses are empty here, they will not be empty long," Berak said.

The houses stood close to one another, and several were two stories with shops on the first floor. Mary knew the name of Saad's street, but not the house number or even its description. Berak stopped near the door to a bread store where several men sat visiting. Most seemed a bit fearful of the Jew on his Arabian and were quick to answer his questions.

"Yes, yes," said one. "He lives at the other end of the street, next to the carpet shop."

Berak thanked them, and they moved on, Mary feeling the hot stare of a dozen eyes on them. She heard the suspicious voices whisper as they continued toward Saad's home.

"That's it," Berak said, nodding toward a single-story house sandwiched between the carpet shop and another house.

Mary dismounted and walked to the door. She tried the latch, and the door swung open, revealing the shocked faces of two women sitting on the bare floor of the living room. They jumped to their feet, their eyes wide. Both wore ragged dresses and spoke anxiously to one another in a language Mary did not immediately recognize. A man appeared from a back bedroom with a questioning look that turned quickly to anger. He shouted something at Mary and came at her in a threatening manner.

Berak stepped past Mary and grabbed the man's arm and pushed him back sharply, while speaking first in Hebrew, then in Yiddish, but neither seemed to have any effect. Finally he spoke in a broken language that sounded similar to that of the three refugees.

"Da, da," the man nodded anxiously.

"They are Russian. Now I wish we had Ivan or Dimitri along," Berak said. He thought a moment before speaking again. The two women and the man listened carefully, then seemed to understand and responded in hurried Russian. Berak raised his hand in a gesture to talk slower.

"They arrived yesterday and came here looking for a place. They say they were told any empty house was fair game." He listened a bit longer. "They don't like it here. Arabs came last night and threw rocks at the door and made threats. He was going to talk to the soldiers this morning about protection but is afraid, even though he has seen several other Jews in the street."

Berak spoke his rough Russian again, and they began gathering their belongings while talking excitedly to one another. "I told them I would help them find another place where they would be safe. There is a Russian community not far from here."

"How did you come by your Russian?" Mary asked.

"In World War II, my unit fought with a Russian regiment in the battle for eastern Poland." He shrugged. "I know a little French, a little German, and a little English as well. I don't brag about any of them. I'll take these people with me and see what I can do." They looked at one another, both knowing this was good-bye.

"Good luck to you," Berak said. "I wish you happiness, Mary. And if things don't turn out the way you like, well, we would welcome you at Allonim."

"Thank you, Benny." She stepped close and kissed him lightly on the cheek. He was a bit shocked by the move, and it made her laugh lightly.

"The modern Arab woman," she said. "Be safe, Benny Berak, and thank Ahmed for me. He picked a good replacement."

Berak gave a pleased nod, then instructed the Russian immigrants to follow him. When they walked into the street, a crowd of curious people gathered, visiting quietly. Seeing that the Jews were leaving, several nodded firm approval. Mary watched the Russian man swing into the saddle of her horse, a contented smile on his face, while Berak helped the two women get on the third horse. Everyone seemed pleased with the outcome of her and Berak's arrival.

Berak mounted and led the refugees down the street, turning to wave just before going left at a cross street. Mary returned it as they disappeared behind buildings at the corner. Her stomach churned as she realized she would miss his strength, his protection. She was on her own.

Turning to go inside, she saw a man nervously approaching from the other side of the street.

"Saad, Rifa . . . the boy," he said anxiously.

Mary relayed the tragic news.

"I told them they should not go," he said sadly. "Rifa and Emile will return?"

"Yes. Their furniture, do you know . . ."

He smiled, glancing over his shoulder. "The Jews started looting empty homes in the next street, so we took Saad's things into our homes and hid the pieces. I promised Saad I would take care of things for him," he said with pride. "We will bring it back to you. The authorities are treating looters differently now. They give them jail sentences, whether Jew or Arab."

"Then things are getting better," she said.

"In some ways. In others we still struggle. The electricity is still off and on, as is the water supply, but they make promises." He shrugged. "We will see."

"Food. Can it be purchased?"

"Yes, yes, this we have now. At first it was difficult to get anything because they would not let us go anywhere, and the Jews would beat us if we tried. But now the soldiers protect us more unless we make trouble. Then it is very bad again." He looked down as if debating about his next words. "You have a ring of marriage but no husband," he said.

"He is in Jerusalem. I come from Beirut and will go to Jerusalem in a few days."

He was relieved. "A hero of the revolt," he said.

She forced a smile while removing money from her pocket. "I will pay someone to bring bread, butter, cheese, and any fresh vegetables they can find, especially tomatoes and cucumbers."

"I will return shortly," he said, eyeing the British pounds. "Possibly a pound in advance?"

She gave him one and asked his name. It was Itzik. "Well, Itzik, I will give you that pound and five more if you will see to the return of the furniture and enough groceries to restock the shelves for Rifa and Emile."

"As you wish." He hesitated. "You say you were in Beirut. What is it like there?"

Mary sensed that he was wondering if it was better, if he had made the right decision by staying. "It is terrible. In many ways the Arabs are worse taskmasters than the Jews. You have your home, and soon things will get better. It will only get worse in the camps of Lebanon." Mary forced a smile, and Itzik seemed relieved as he left the porch. She felt better too.

Closing the door, Mary went from room to room. It would need a good cleaning, but there was nothing of value except the iron stove, much too heavy for either Arab friend or Jewish looter to remove. A single spout over the sink for indoor water beckoned her to wash, and she turned it on, grateful that it responded with a flow of fresh water. Putting her mouth under the faucet she took her fill, then shut it off. Seeing a large coffee can on the floor she rinsed it out and filled it, just in case the water went off. There were two small bedrooms and an indoor bathroom with a four-legged tub, another cold-water spout hanging over it. Mary knew she would have to heat her own water over the stove if she wanted a bath, and she wanted one very badly.

The knock came at the door, and she opened it to find a line of smiling neighbors carrying furniture. She let them in, and each deposited the item in the appropriate room, bowed or said welcome, then left again. Over the next hour, she was glad to see pots, pans, utensils, and other items all returned, along with linen for the beds and bath. Everything was nearly in place when Itzik delivered the groceries. As she sat them on the small table in the kitchen, she heard the sounds of lamentations in the street and rushed quickly to the door to find Ivan pulling up in his truck. Neighbors poured into the street as word quickly spread that Saad Shawas had returned.

A half dozen men pulled the plain pine box from the back of the truck and passed it over their heads to others along the street. Mary knew it would be taken to the mosque she had seen on her way in and waved for both Ivan and Itzik to join her.

They pushed through the crowd of mourners, and Mary paid Ivan for his journey, then asked them both to go to the hospital and bring Rifa back to the mosque.

"I will pay you both a pound. Saad should be buried right away, and Rifa must be here."

Both bowed and said they needed no money; it would be an honor. Itzik also said he would take his wife with him to give Rifa comfort. Mary thanked him as he left.

"Ivan, I want to go to Tel Aviv. I will pay you," she said.

"I cannot for at least a week. I have contracted to carry supplies to the troops in Galilee until then. I am sorry." He thought a moment. "A man I know, an Arab who lives in the city and also has a truck, goes south to make deliveries for the Jews. I will tell him to come and see you."

"Thank you. I want to go in three days if possible."

"I will tell him." Ivan bowed slightly and said good-bye. Then he, Itzik, and Itzik's wife climbed in the truck and left.

Mary went back inside, found pieces of wood in the space under the kitchen sink, and started a fire. After Saad's burial, Rifa would need a hot bath.

CHAPTER 24

Abraham asked the guard to get the doctor at nine o'clock. That would give him three hours before Moshe and the others went through the fence and broke into the armory. It would be enough time to ready Aaron for a plan of his own. Once out, they could join up with Moshe's group and escape into the desert.

The guard returned a half hour later and let him out of the holding area, telling two others to escort him to the doctor who was waiting at the hospital. When Abraham arrived, they went inside, the doctor locking each of the doors behind them until they reached the patient ward.

"How is he?" Abraham asked.

"He seems quite agitated. Possibly your coming will settle him down. I have a wounded man in the recovery room that I must see to. You will be locked in until I return."

Abraham nodded as the doctor left, locking the door behind him. Abraham approached Aaron's bed, pulled up a stool, and sat down. Aaron was staring straight at the ceiling, his eyes fixed.

"Hello, Aaron."

His voice got immediate attention, and Aaron's head flopped to the side, his eyes on Abraham's, then back to the ceiling.

"Mary wants to see you, Aaron."

Aaron's head came over more slowly this time, and his lips moved slightly. His eyes remained fixed on Abraham, who took his hand and squeezed it.

Abraham looked at the nearest patient. Asleep. He could not speak to Aaron of escape openly for fear others might want to join them. "We have to go there. We have to meet her. Can you walk?"

The only response was a squeeze of the hand, but that made Abraham's heart pound with hope. Standing, he pulled back Aaron's blanket. His legs were shockingly thin, but Abraham lifted them toward the side of the bed. Aaron did not respond. Abraham sat him up against propped pillows, then spoke of Mary again. Aaron's chin came up, but his eyes were still blank.

"Do you remember Paris?" Abraham asked.

Aaron's eyes fixed on Abraham's face.

"We have to get you out of bed if you want to see Mary," Abraham added.

He pushed on Aaron's legs, this time rotating the hips until the legs were over the edge of the bed. Abraham helped him stand, though he was painfully aware that Aaron knew little of what he was really doing. He led him around the room. Aaron's movements were mechanical, his head and eyes searching the room without seeing anything, but at least he could walk. Abraham kept him moving until he started to fuss, mumbling tinged with pain. He took him to a chair and let him rest. He talked to him about Mary, how they met, their wedding, how it would be to meet her again. He also talked of Ephraim, Hannah, Elizabeth, the twins, and David, saying that they were okay and eager to see Aaron again. Aaron's head stopped moving, and he seemed to listen, though his eyes continued to wander.

Once more Abraham got him to his feet. Aaron moved more energetically this time, but Abraham had the painful realization of just how very far away his friend was from being physically ready for any escape, let alone mentally capable.

After nearly two hours, he helped Aaron back to bed, sorely disappointed. Aaron could no more run from the Arabs than a horse with no legs. He sat down and took his friend's hand. Abraham couldn't look at him to say his good-bye. Then Aaron squeezed his hand. Abraham looked to see his friend looking at him, his eyes empty but troubled, his face muscles taut with anxiety. It was as if he wanted to talk, but his mind was a locked door for which he had no key. Was this what his life would be? Abraham could not bear the thought and stepped away from the bed. Going to the window, he began saying a prayer, one he had memorized years ago and used many times, most recently when praying for his father.

"O Lord, hear my prayer and let my cry come unto Thee. Hide not Thy face from me and my good friend Aaron Schwartz in the day of his distress; incline Thine ear unto me; in the day of his need, answer him speedily. I beseech thee, O Lord, Healer of all flesh, have mercy upon him and support him in Thy grace upon his bed of sickness, for he is weak in body and mind. Send relief and cure to him and to all the sick among Thy children. Soothe his pain so that his life is renewed like the eagle. Grant wisdom unto those of us who care for him that we may help cure him, so that his health may be restored speedily. Hear my prayer, prolong his life, and let him complete his years in happiness with his good wife, Mary, that they may be able to serve Thee and keep Thy statutes with a perfect heart. O Lord, give me wisdom to understand what to do for Him, how to help him . . ." He paused, taking a deep breath before going on, this time ignoring the set prayer and pouring out his heart. "O Lord, this man is a good man, but he cannot help himself. Please bless his eyes to see, his mind to understand, his ears to hear, and his heart to sense that thou lovest him." Another deep breath. "And Lord, I could use a blessing too. Watch over Naomi, touch her, and turn the bitterness I know she feels to fresh roses, that love of you may grow in her heart. Give her peace and comfort. And, help me to know what to do for Aaron. Help me to know now. Amen."

He glanced at the small clock on the table near the door. "Nearly eleven o'clock," he said softly. "They will go soon." It was then he knew what he must do. He walked back to Aaron's bed. His friend's eyes were upon him, searching his face, a smile of contentment on his lips. Slowly his hand slipped from his lap and landed next to Abraham's, then the fingers stretched as if to touch him. Abraham grasped it, leaned down, and spoke directly into Aaron's ear. "I will find a way to bring you home, my friend. I will find a way to take you to Mary."

He felt the squeeze once again, making it difficult to pull away, but he knew he must. He had to get to Moshe before they left.

* * *

Rhoui pulled the bandages from his face, but even the dim light in the room hurt his eyes. He closed them tightly, letting the pain subside, then opened them gradually, adjusting slowly. The pain returned, but dealing with it in small increments made it bearable. When he finally opened his eyes enough, he found everything out of focus. His jaw throbbed when he moved, but he gritted his teeth and forced his torso up and his legs over the edge of the bed. He could see the outlines of a small table a few steps away. Standing, he got his balance and took a step. His leg collapsed, and he fell forward. As he reached out for the edge of the table, his poor vision created a miscalculation and he fell, bumping his face against the table's edge on his way to the floor. The pain exploded in his face and pushed tears into his aching eyes. He felt someone pick him up and put him onto the bed, then there was the slight prick of a needle, and the pain subsided, the drug causing a haze in his mind, but leaving him awake.

"He'll keep trying," said the aide who had brought Rhoui to the room two days earlier. "How many times have we found him crawling for the door or writhing in pain just like this in his attempt to get free of us? He wants out. We should give him his wish and send him back to his side of the line."

Doctor Messerman put the needle on the tray, ignoring the aide's words. "Rhoui, you have to stop this. I have told you before, I will not let you leave here until your vision is better and your jaw healed enough that it won't get infected. Even then you will have to go to one of our prisons."

Rhoui moved his fingers as a signal for paper and wrote, *Let me sit up and send your slave away. I talk only to you.*

"Slave is it?" the aide said, reading over Doctor Messerman's shoulder. "The man is . . . is . . ."

"Yes, he is, but leave it alone. Go help the other patients. I will take care of this."

The aide shut the door behind him and locked it, rattling the key in the hole to let Rhoui know in a foolish sort of way who was in control of whom.

"What is it, Rhoui?" Doctor Messerman asked impatiently.

I am Arab. I hate you and your people. I know you will not fix my face or my eyes; you only make them worse with your dirty Jewish hands. I wish to go back to my people, and if you are any friend to my father you will see that I go there as quickly as you can arrange it.

Doctor Messerman read the words. They were written with such hatred. Hatred so unlike the young man he had known as he grew up, as their families celebrated family holidays together. What had happened?

"What have I done to earn such hate from you, Rhoui?"

You were born a Jew. That is enough. He lifted the pencil and handed the notebook to Doctor Messerman.

"Ahh, another Hitler, are you? Well, a Hitler come late in life, if you ask me. You had no such feelings when a boy, or even at the time you married. Your hatred of Jews seems to be born of an ill wind more than of character." He paused. "But, if you speak the truth, and you hate Jews as you say you do, if you blew up the Hurva, I would be remiss in letting you go back to your rifle and bomb. You'll stay here, locked up, whether you like it or not." He tossed the pad on Rhoui's lap.

It was a long moment before Rhoui picked it up and wrote again. *Have you heard from Mary? Do you know where she is?*

Doctor Messerman felt his heart jump. Could this be the real problem, the real reason for this overpowering desire to rush back to fight? He remembered the day Aaron came looking for word of Mary, remembered sending word to friends in the Arab zone of the battle-torn city to try and discover where she had gone. And he remembered their answer. Rhoui had betrayed his brother and sister. From it had come Izaat's imprisonment and probable death, and Mary's fear that had driven her to the convent of Souers Reparatrices.

"She is happy, Rhoui." He said it softly. Though he had no real idea of Mary's whereabouts right now, and though he knew she had lost Aaron, he knew what Rhoui needed to hear.

Rhoui wrote again. *I hated her once.*

"Yes, I know. Because of Aaron."

Yes, but . . . He hesitated with his pencil.

"But what, Rhoui?"

Rhoui thought a moment then wrote again. *But I do love her, as I loved Izaat.*

The doctor saw the jerking motion in Rhoui's chest, heard the moaning through his tightly bandaged lips, and watched the tears roll down his cheeks. Moving from the chair to the edge of the bed, he put his arms around the boy and carefully held him close, letting him cry. There was simply nothing else to do.

* * *

When Rhoui fell into an exhausted, drug-induced sleep, Doctor Messerman knocked on the door and was let out by the aide. "I am leaving for a while." He headed for the door. If he wanted to save Rhoui Aref, there was only one solution.

Walking out of the building, he hurried along the streets toward the Haganah command center, the thunder of artillery shells so commonplace now that he hardly noticed. That is, until he saw houses destroyed and burning from them or they made the earth shake under his feet. It made him stiffen with anger to see the destruction of the Holy City, but for now his mind was on the destruction of Rhoui Aref and he let the other pass. His old friend Amos would expect him to try and save the boy, and if he could find Mary, bring her here, he might do just that.

He saw the two older women going through the rubble that had once been a building and recognized one of them.

"Mithra Birkelau, what are you doing?"

Mithra looked up and faced his direction. "Doctor Messerman, is that you?"

"It is." He approached the two women, then grasped Mithra's hand. "How are you?" he asked genuinely.

"Very well under the circumstances." She felt for Hilda and pulled her over. "This is my friend Hilda. She is sharing her home with Naomi and me."

"Wonderful to meet you, Hilda. How are you getting along with this ornery old battle axe?" He smiled.

Hilda, taken aback at first by his brash statement, smiled when she realized they were dear friends. "It is difficult at times, but we make do."

"You old fool," Mithra said to the doctor. "You have never met a more gentle, easygoing woman in your entire miserable life, and you know it. I assume you are taking care of our soldiers in some horrible little hospital."

"Just a block away," he answered.

"Then you must come and see us," Mithra said. She gave him the address.

"Have you seen Naomi?" he asked. "I was just going to Haganah headquarters to look for her."

"Just this morning. What is it? Nothing horrible I hope. Not Abraham . . ."

"No, no," he said. Then he explained about Rhoui and Mary.

"Yes, I see," Mithra said thoughtfully. "She has heard nothing of Mary, I am sure of it."

"Tell her to come and see me if she does hear something, anything at all, will you?"

"Of course." Mithra smiled. They said their good-byes, and Doctor Messerman headed back to the hospital. He arrived and was immediately met by the aide taking care of Rhoui. The serious, hard look on his face told the doctor there was trouble.

"They are sending him to a prisoner of war camp. They will come for him by nightfall."

CHAPTER 25

Naomi knew Amos Chorev only because their paths had crossed in meetings between SHAI and the Haganah. He was a young, strong-willed Palmachnik with a determination that frustrated most men. But it had been that determination that had led him, David Marcus, and Vivian Herzog to explore the mountains between Jerusalem and Tel Aviv for an alternative route. After more than eight hours, they had found a way along an old goat trail and had reported their discovery to Ben-Gurion on their arrival in Tel Aviv. Plans had begun immediately to make it a road, but knowing the value of getting even a few items into the Old City, Ben-Gurion had ordered Chorev to make a return trip with them in the back of his jeep along with any others they could find. Naomi arrived at Hulda just as he was loading several jeeps with weapons and ammunition for the journey. When she learned of their plan, she immediately asked Chorev to take her along. He had balked at first but relented when Naomi had pulled rank on him.

The journey took them all night as they pushed, pulled, coerced, and begged their jeeps to climb over formidable terrain toward the Holy City. Naomi proved her worth behind the wheel of one of the jeeps, displaying a knack for maneuvering over and around seemingly impassable rocks and boulders. It seemed surreal as they worked their way parallel to the main road past Latrun and the Arab villages that they had been unable to capture only a day ago, artillery shells dropping on the New City in the mountains east of them.

When they finally pulled into the Palmach base at Kiryat Anavim, west of the city and just northeast of Kastel, they were exhausted but exultant. News of their unexpected arrival traveled quickly, and the entire unit turned out to celebrate. The goat trail could be turned into a road and the New City supplied. The only question that remained was, Could they do it before the population began to starve?

The New City was near catastrophe with its munitions supplies down to less than twenty-four hours and only enough flour for seven more days. They would need more than a few jeeps laden with bullets and rifles to survive even a half-hearted attack by the Arabs.

Naomi and Chorev left the compound and drove to the command center in the New City, where news of their feat had preceded them. Chorev went into meetings with Dov Joseph and Yitzhak Levi to discuss plans for building a road. Naomi melted into the background and found a chair at Eleazar's desk.

"You have been a busy lady since leaving here yesterday," he said with some frustration.

She forced a smile. "What's the latest news?"

Eleazar removed his glasses and rubbed his eyes. He looked more tired than she did, but the news this morning had been good enough it brought a smile. "You know about the Americans pressuring the Brits into calling for a pullout of their military personnel working for the Arabs. Well, the Brits ordered their personnel out this morning. Of course, it's hitting the Legion hardest, and Glubb Pasha is desperate to get them replaced with volunteers, but it will definitely slow them down. Better yet, we have also learned that the Brits are drying up the Arab munitions pipeline from England, and that's got the Arabs thinking about a cease-fire. They can't fight without bullets and bombs any more than we can."

"The Arabs must hate them for it," she said, grinning.

"Riots in the streets as of this morning. This could finish the Brits in this part of the world. Serve them right after the way they handled this. If they'd brought the Arabs into line years ago . . . Well, never mind. No time for a lecture on British failures, is it?" He was smiling.

Naomi's mind was racing with the news. A truce, a real truce would allow them time to regroup and reorganize. It might even lead to peace! At the very least, it would give them time to build a road over their goat trail, resupply the city, and prepare for further confrontation if the Arabs refused to make peace. There might even be an exchange of prisoners.

"When does the cease-fire start?"

"No later than ten days from now. It will get very dicey for a while, but there is a good deal of hope flying about this morning. In fact, your little trek up from Jerusalem has brought it to near euphoria."

Naomi felt the exhaustion lift from her tired bones. "What do you want me to do?"

"Get some sleep. There are cots in the room down the hall. Then I'll put you to work. Our military boys are helpless without good information."

She went down the hall and found the cots. Too tired to eat, she went to bed hungry and didn't wake up until Eleazar shook her back to consciousness. They had intercepted radio traffic in the Jordan Valley. There had been a prison break at Mafraq. Two men had been captured; four were still running for their lives.

She knew immediately that Abraham was one of them and scrambled to her feet. Eleazar followed her back to the radio room where she quickly read the intercepted transmissions, then went to the map. "The four men are here in these ruins, a mile east of Jericho, but probably trapped. We have to get them out and very quickly."

Eleazar nodded. His gut also told him that one of those men was Abraham Marshak, and he knew that if he didn't help Naomi this time, she would never forgive him for it. But then, he would never forgive himself. "All right, what do you want me to do?"

They left the room and paced the hall, a plan slowly developing. The trouble was it would take pilots and planes.

"That means Wally," Eleazar said. "Are we getting permission or . . ."

Naomi was already headed for the radio room. Eleazar followed, a bit disgruntled at the vivid picture forming in his mind, a picture of his career in Haganah intelligence being flushed down the toilet.

* * *

Wally was lying in a bed in a Tel Aviv hospital when Zohar walked in, her pace strident, her face full of anxiety, her hands full of his clothes. She sat down on the edge of his bed and told him about a radio transmittal she had received from Naomi in Jerusalem. When he heard what was at stake, he took the clothes, asked her to pull the curtain around his bed, and dressed as quickly as the stiff pain in his shoulder would allow. They left the hospital despite the doctor's warnings that the stitches might break and the wound open again, climbed into Zohar's beat-up car, and headed for the airport. He found the mechanic just finishing the repair on the Spitfire and told him to fuel it and prepare it for a test flight while Zohar rounded up Meyer Franconi, an Italian-American Jew who had come to fight for Israel. When Franconi heard Wally's plan, an evil sort of grin spread across his face. He was more than willing. They pored over a map and laid out their plan of attack, then invented a cover story for their absence. Even as slipshod as the Israeli Air Force might be at present, it was not about to let two hotshots risk two very needed planes on a rescue operation that had a fifty-fifty chance of success at best.

"The Auster won't carry six people," Franconi said.

"I'm taking the Aerovan," Wally answered.

"You're kidding." The Aerovan had just arrived from England and hadn't had a test flight. Made of wood, it had earned the nickname *Pregnant Goose* for its odd appearance. Though it had a short landing capability of three hundred meters—which made it the ideal plane for this kind of mission—it was an extremely vulnerable target.

"There aren't any other choices. We'll tell Weizman I'm taking it for a test-fly." He smiled at Zohar. "I'll leave that to you. A couple a flashes of those beautiful eyelashes, and he'll forget I've never flown an Aerovan."

She gave a reluctant nod. He ignored the concern etched in the creases around her eyes.

"Okay, my friend," Meyer said. "It's your funeral."

"Let's not put it that way, okay?" Zohar said.

Meyer grinned, and the two men hurried to the ammo room and retrieved the usual weapons. Wally tried to lift his, but the pain in his wound prevented it. Zohar picked up the shotgun, rifle, and pistol, then called for the mechanic to retrieve the other weapon Wally had selected—a thirty-caliber machine gun with a box of ammunition belts. They set out for their planes and loaded the weapons before doing their final inspections.

"Where do you want this machine gun?" the mechanic asked.

"Near the rear hatch."

The mechanic deposited the machine gun and wished Wally good luck before going back to his work.

"This is nuts, you know that," Zohar said, returning from talking to Weizman.

"They thought Roosevelt was nuts for sending us to attack Japan with bombers we'd have to fly off the very short span of an aircraft carrier. It worked. This will work too. Did you talk to Weizman?"

"Yes, you're cleared."

"He and I have one thing in common—neither of us can say no to that pretty face." He grinned.

The Aerovan's wood exterior and guppy-looking body made Zohar shake her head hopelessly. Wally saw it. "Looks are deceiving. Those engines can pump her speed up to almost two hundred miles per hour, and she can climb to four thousand meters—well out of range—in a shorter time than the Auster." He passed under the wing and examined the engine on that side, then went around the nose and examined the other.

"But you know how to fly the Auster. This you haven't flown."

"The cockpit isn't much different from the planes I have flown. Relax, Zoe. We'll be fine."

"Umm, sure you will. You look like death warmed over. You don't have to do this, Wally," she said unconvincingly.

"Yes, I do, and we both know it. My whole reason for coming here was to replace Ephraim Daniels, to try and thank him for his sacrifice in the only way this short Jewish boy knew how. Aaron is part of his family. This is what he would do. I don't have any choice." He turned to Zohar. "I lay awake last night and decided something else. Eph planned on living here, raising his family here. I've decided it wouldn't be such a bad idea."

Zohar smiled as she stepped close and put her arms around his neck. "Is that the only reason you've decided to stay?"

He grinned. "Sure, what else would there be?"

She was about to punch him in the shoulder but caught herself. "When you're . . . well, I owe you one."

"I can hardly wait."

She kissed him gently, then lay her head on his shoulder as he held her close. "Come back, Wally, or I'll hate you forever."

"With this to look forward to, it would take more than a few Arabs to keep me away." He kissed her softly on the forehead, then stepped away as Franconi walked up, clearing his throat. "I'll leave for the target ten minutes after you. That way we'll get there at the same time."

Wally nodded and got in the *Pregnant Goose*, familiarized himself with the instruments, and made sure the hydraulics for the rear loading hatch were working. Taking a deep breath and praying that he could make this work, he went through the steps and started the engines. They roared to life, and he breathed easier. Testing the flaps, he pushed forward on the throttles and the plane vibrated. He trimmed the engines before pushing the throttles forward again. The plane crept along the dry grass and dirt and onto the runway. Wally waved at Zohar and Franconi, then pushed for full throttle. The plane cruised ahead and lifted off the ground in shorter time than even the Auster. He climbed, leveled off, and familiarized himself with the stick until just before landing at Emek Hamatzleva airstrip in Jerusalem.

The plane landed smoothly and quickly, both pluses for the small runway. Wally made a mental note that this would be the plane to use between the two cities from now on.

Keeping the motors running as Naomi and another man boarded, they were ready for takeoff when they joined him. Naomi dropped into the copilot's seat and her friend in the one behind it. As the plane went airborne, Wally was introduced to Eleazar.

"Welcome aboard the *Pregnant Goose*." Wally smiled.

"An appropriate nom de guerre," Eleazar said. "Will this thing really stay in the air, or is it just an illusion?"

"They don't make them like this anymore."

"Remind me to thank them, whoever they are," Eleazar said.

"How's the wound?" Naomi asked.

"Sewn up like the hem on a baby's diaper." He smiled. It still hurt, but it didn't matter. He was fully conscious and lucid, though a bit weak. But he was quickly filling with enough excitement to make up the difference. "There is a .30-caliber machine gun back there. Set it up in front of the rear hatch. When we land, we'll take fire. I'll sweep the tail left and right. You use the gun to keep the enemy pinned down long enough for survivors to board." He paused. "I assume we still have four men to pick up."

"We don't know."

Wally nodded understanding. "We have a Spitfire joining us. I'll have the pilot take a look. We go even if there is only one alive."

There was no hesitation, and both Naomi and Eleazar went to the rear of the plane. The Aerovan soared to a thousand meters and was quickly over the Jordan Valley, Franconi's plane pulling along its left wing as Wally crossed the river and prepared to go down. The Aerovan had no radio, so Wally gave hand signals for Meyer to make his first run and identify survivors. Wally circled, watching as Meyer broke off and plummeted toward the earth, jealousy running through his bones like fire. Though the Egyptian insignia had been hand painted over with the Star of David insignia, the Jordanian soldiers would think the plane was Arab until it was too late. He took the *Pregnant Goose* down to where he could see the run and watched as the Spitfire strafed the enemy that surrounded the ruins. Two minutes later, Meyer pulled up by Wally's wing again and signaled he had seen at least three men still fighting. Wally nodded and swung in a wide circle as Meyer broke away to make his second run. The timing would need to be perfect.

* * *

Abraham saw the plane diving at their position and assumed they were dead. But when the Spitfire strafed the Arabs instead, he knew they had a chance. He looked at the last of his bullets and injected one into the single-shot rifle he held as Moshe crawled to his position.

"We have new life, my friend," he said with a grin. "Is this your wife returning for you?"

Abraham smiled. "Most likely." He spotted the second plane coming in from the north. It was a horrible-looking monster, evidently intending to land, and they needed to get to it.

"Look," he said pointing. "That's the plane we have to board. Where is the fighter?"

"There," Moshe shouted.

"It will strafe the Arabs and that ugly one will land for us. We must get to it."

Moshe nodded and crawled to the other two men, now firing their rifles at Arabs moving forward. "They know what is to happen as well," Moshe said to Eliahu. "Can you walk?"

Eliahu looked at his leg and knew he couldn't, not without help. "You must leave me," he said to Moshe. "You will never make it if you don't."

"I will carry you," Franz said. "We all go."

They heard the Spitfire coming and put an arm around Eliahu while Moshe and Abraham prepared to protect them. This time bombs fell, exploding while the fighter opened up with its machine guns. Franz shouldered Eliahu and scurried toward the far end of the ruins, Moshe and Abraham firing at any Arab that raised his head. The rescue plane landed only a short distance away, sped toward them, slowed to a near stop, then swung its tail around to reveal a hatch where two people lay at a machine gun.

Suddenly bullets zipped all around them, forcing them to take cover. The plane's tail swung left at the Egyptian position, and the machine gunfired.

"Go," Abraham yelled. All four stood and ran for the plane. This time Eliahu was between Moshe and Franz and able to move much quicker. They reached a collapsed wall and were about to climb over when heavy gunfire forced them to take cover again. The Spitfire appeared, dropping two bombs, the high-pitched sound of its racing motor near deafening as it passed over. Abraham climbed the wall and pulled Eliahu up, then lowered him to the other side. Moshe and Franz were already over and took the wounded man, scrambling for the rear of the plane, leaving their empty weapons behind. Abraham was right behind them when he felt the bullet knock his right leg out from under him. He struggled to get up, then fell back, the pain excruciating. He could do nothing but wave them on.

* * *

Naomi wiped the sweat from her face, then fed another belt into the machine gun. They were almost there. She saw Abraham come down from the wall and felt the rush as he ran toward her. She watched in horror as he went down. Reacting instinctively, she jumped from the rear door and ran after him, a revolver in her hand. The Spitfire returned as she reached Abraham, lifting him to his good foot. They were nearing the hatch when Moshe gave her a hand, the Spitfire making a final run. Hoisting Abraham up, Franz and Eliahu pulled him in, then both of them were given a hand up.

"Go," Eleazar yelled as bullets began striking the back of the plane.

Wally pushed forward on the throttles and the plane lurched forward. He could hear bullets ripping through the plywood and prayed that one wouldn't get his engines. The plane lifted, hesitated, coughed, and hit the ground. He adjusted the throttles, and she lifted again, this time for good. They headed north, then turned hard west. A moment later, the Spitfire pulled alongside.

Meyer saluted with a big grin, the cockpit cover wide open. Then he poured on the throttle and was gone. The trip for the Spitfire's new wheel had its first payoff.

Abraham held Naomi tight as the rear hatch closed, the other men celebrating, exultant, free.

"Welcome home," Naomi said.

Abraham only nodded, his lip quivering with a combination of pain, exhaustion, and gratitude for a stubborn wife. They were nearly to Jerusalem before he could finally speak.

"I left someone behind. Somehow we have to get him back, Naomi. We have to find a way."

Naomi didn't know what to say. There were still many men at Mafraq, many left behind.

"Who . . . what are you talking about, Abraham?"

"Aaron is in that prison, Naomi. Aaron is alive."

SEE CHAPTER NOTES

CHAPTER 26

The doctor threw a half dozen vials of morphine in his bag, left the medicines room, and went back to where Rhoui was still locked up and the aide waited. Using the key, they entered and the burly aide lifted the unconscious Rhoui from the bed and onto his shoulder. They started from the room and were greeted by the unhappy doctor in charge.

"Where do you think you're going?" he asked. His voice was harsh with the anger he was trying to control.

"Out of here," Doctor Messerman said.

"Put him down," the doctor said to the aide.

"Go," Doctor Messerman said kindly. The aide took a step toward the outside door, but the other doctor blocked his way.

Messerman stepped around the aide and stood toe-to-toe with the younger doctor. He had prepared for this. He jammed the needle into the man's backside and pushed the morphine from the syringe into his system. Shocked, the young doctor jerked at the pain and stiffened, then stepped back when Doctor Messerman pulled the syringe out of his flesh.

"What . . . what have you done to me?"

"Put you to sleep. Now, if I were you, I would get to a bed and lie down. You need rest anyway." He nodded to the aide, who had a grin on his face, and they left the building.

Walking the short distance to the address Mithra had given him, they climbed the stairs, and he knocked on the apartment door. By the time Hilda answered, Rhoui was beginning to nod awake, mumbling in confusion.

"What on earth?" Hilda asked.

"This man is badly wounded and needs a place to stay until I can get him to a different hospital. Can you help us?"

Hilda didn't know what to think and stood motionless, unable to speak.

"Let them in," Mithra said, moving Hilda aside with a gentle pull.

They went inside, and the aide laid Rhoui on the couch and covered him with the blanket Mithra had been using.

"This is Mary's brother?" Mithra asked.

"Yes." He told them about Rhoui's wounds. "We'll keep him sedated until I can get him home to the Old City. I owe Amos that much."

"But . . . but how can you arrange such a thing?" Hilda asked.

"I don't know, but I must try. Will you keep him here for now?"

"Is he dangerous?" Hilda asked.

Doctor Messerman looked at the aide. "Herschel and a shot of morphine now and again will keep him in line."

"Then you . . . he . . . there will be two men staying here?" Hilda asked with incredulity.

"Won't it be nice to have men in the house again?" Mithra said enthusiastically. "It is a wonderful idea, Hilda. Surely you can see we must help this poor boy."

"But where will everyone sleep? Naomi, you, I, and . . . and them. I . . ."

"It is time you shared that feather bed with me, and Naomi can sleep on the floor as always, but next to us in the bedroom."

"And I or Herschel, depending on which one is here, can sleep on the veranda if need be," said Doctor Messerman.

"It will be quite comfortable," Mithra added.

Hilda sat down in the chair, her face a bit ashen, but she was nodding ever so slightly in the affirmative.

"Good. God will make you a special place in heaven for this," Mithra said.

Rhoui moaned, and Doctor Messerman pulled the second chair to the side of the couch as the sound of a key turned in the lock. All eyes turned toward the door as it opened and revealed a tired Naomi helping a wounded Abraham keep his feet.

Realizing what it meant, Hilda passed out on the floor.

* * *

After reviving Hilda, the group of friends celebrated Abraham's return with Naomi, while Doctor Messerman cleaned and bandaged his wounds. Then the doctor took Abraham and Naomi to his small room at the monastery next to the Christian church being used as a hospital. There he left them alone.

The moment they had crawled between the blankets, an exhausted, wounded Abraham slept. Naomi lay awake, the revelation of Aaron's survival all she could think about. Dozing off just before sunrise, she awoke to find Abraham lying on his side looking at her. She turned to face him, and they embraced, holding each other tight and letting the reality of their little miracle settle in.

"How is your foot, darling?" she asked. The wound had torn away the soft tissue and part of a bone but needed no splint. The doctor had sewn it shut and bandaged it.

"I think I'll live, especially now." He kissed her on the nape of the neck.

She resisted, but it was difficult. "In case you hadn't noticed, we are in a monastery, and they are praying just on the other side of that door. Can't you hear it?"

"Then they are too busy too notice." He kissed her on the neck again.

"Stop it." She laughed lightly. "If you have that kind of energy, you can start looking for something this morning."

Suddenly she pulled away and sat up, swung her feet over the edge of the bed, and planted them on the floor. "Oh no, I forgot," she said, grabbing her trousers and pulling them on.

Abraham, shocked by her quick escape, let his head fall back to the pillow in frustration. "Dearest wife, you are a frustrating soul. What did you forget?"

"To send a wire to Hannah. Oh, how could I forget such a thing?" She buttoned her pants and put on her shirt, then jumped on the bed, leaned down, and kissed him hard, then jumped off, grabbed her shoes, and was on her way. "I'll be at central command. Join me if you can."

The next thing he heard was the door slam and the unmistakable gasp of the friars. A second later, she came back in, a bit pale. "We didn't come in that way, did we?"

Abraham grinned. "No, dearest. This is a cottage for guests and pilgrims." He pointed at the other door. "That is your way to the street." He could not help the laugh.

She gave him a dirty look and left through the proper door. He loved being married to Naomi. There was never a dull moment.

CHAPTER 27

Hannah Daniels was by her husband's bedside when the wire was delivered. Ephraim, now out of surgery, was in intensive care. He had barely missed walking through death's door, but over the last twenty-four hours, he had improved dramatically, finally opening his eyes for the briefest of moments and squeezing her hand only an hour ago.

Hannah hadn't slept in hours, so when she read the wire she thought she might be dreaming. She rubbed her eyes and read it again. She jumped to her feet with a shout of excitement. A half dozen nurses burst through the door, concern on their faces.

"What is it, my dear?" said the oldest.

"Oh, I'm sorry, I . . . He is fine, but I have to find my children. Please stay with him, won't you? I'll be back in just a few moments." She scrambled from the room, a wide grin on her face, and dashed down the hall, finding David and Beth in the waiting area, both asleep. She shook them awake, a beaming excitement on her face. David sat straight up. "Father is awake again?" he asked.

"I told you, he will be fine. But this is something else. Something wonderful." She helped Beth wake up, then handed David the wire. "Read it."

"Aaron is alive. Stop. He is—" His eyes went back to the first words as if he hadn't read them correctly. Then he looked at Hannah with searching eyes.

"Yes, it's true. It's from Naomi. Your brother is alive!"

The celebration shook the very foundations of the hospital.

Finally under control, the three of them returned to Ephraim's room where Hannah read the rest of the message more carefully. Aaron was in a prison in Transjordan. He had some physical problems from his wounds and from shock, but nothing that couldn't be resolved with good medical help, time, and the blessings of God. Her brow wrinkled with concern. How could a prison give him the required help? He needed to be in a hospital, the quicker the better.

Hannah searched the letter a third time, looking for details on how Aaron had survived and how they had found him, but there were none. For the first time since bringing Ephraim here for help, she wished she were back in Israel where she could do something, make the arrangements, get Aaron home. She felt so helpless. And then she felt guilty. With Ephraim just beginning to recover, this is where she must be.

Ripping a piece of paper from a wire tablet she was using as a journal, Hannah wrote a reply to Naomi.

Dearest Naomi,

A miracle! What wonderful news. We are so happy! Ephraim is finally out of serious danger and will recover. Unfortunately, the surgery itself was a failure, his legs still paralyzed. But with God's help, we will deal with what comes.

What can be done for Aaron? I feel so helpless being so far away. We miss you all. Please write as soon as you can with details. You have been constantly in my prayers, and I thank God you and Abraham are safe. I will plead for Aaron's quick and safe return.

Love, Hannah

Hannah had felt totally helpless after the battle for Kastel. Aaron had been thought dead, Ephraim had come back seriously wounded, and there had been absolutely nothing she could do about either. Since then, their lives had changed dramatically.

With war in Israel, they sought help for Ephraim's spinal injury by bringing him to the States as soon as he was well enough to be flown. It had been a hard, long journey, but they had finally arrived and checked him immediately into Bethesda Military Hospital in Maryland, the only hospital where recent breakthroughs had been made in surgery for injuries involving compression and serious damage to the spinal cord.

After testing, the doctors had declared Ephraim a candidate for the surgery but warned the family about complications and the chances of failure. Those dangers had become a reality.

Ephraim's naturally strong physical condition had been weakened by the anesthesia, the hours of surgery, and an infection that spread so quickly it nearly killed him. The doctors were forced to operate again, this time to drain the poison that ravaged his body. Ephraim's resistance and strength were further diminished, and he contracted pneumonia. It was a miracle he was still alive.

Hannah saw his eyes open and quickly went to his bedside and touched his hand. He looked up at her and blinked several times, then seemed to doze off a moment before he opened his eyes again. By then, David and Elizabeth were standing on the other side of the bed.

"Hi," Hannah said.

"Papa," Elizabeth said, biting her lip against the tears.

He looked over at her and David and smiled, pushing his hand toward them. Elizabeth took it, a tear dropping to the white sheets.

"Hey," Ephraim said, smiling slightly. He grimaced a little in discomfort.

"Do you need somethin', Pops? I mean, the pain . . ."

"No . . . I . . . I'm fine. Just very tired." His eyes closed again, then reopened. He rubbed the back of Hannah's hand with his thumb. "Will . . . will I walk?" he asked.

Hannah felt the sob climb up her throat, and it was all she could do to choke it down. "I'm sorry, honey, but . . . "

"Sorry? Don't be. We tried, didn't we? We knew the odds."

"Pop, uh . . ." David glanced at Hannah quizzically. "Can I, you know, tell him?"

Hannah nodded, taking the opportunity to turn a bit and wipe the tears away.

"Pop, Naomi sent us a wire. Aaron . . . Aaron is alive."

Ephraim's eyes opened wide, then a disbelieving smile crossed his dry lips. He looked at Hannah, who smiled and nodded, but couldn't speak.

He tried to raise up, then fell back, his face anguished in pain. Hannah gripped his hand and helped him get it under control, then told him what they knew.

"What do they mean he has medical problems? What's wrong? How long before they can get to him? They need to get him home, Hannah. They have to get him out of there," he said, his eyes full of concern.

"Yes, yes, I am sure they will try. Calm down, Ephraim, before you make yourself worse."

"I have to go. I have to *do* something," Ephraim said.

"There is nothing we can do. You have to get well. He'll be home by the time we get you out of here. Then we can—"

"No, you don't know that! It's war, Hannah. Like the Nazis, like . . . like what prison did to you. We—"

"Ephraim! Calm down! It isn't the same. Now, if you don't settle down, I'll have the nurse give you something." He was sweating, his body tense, and it frightened her. He wasn't well enough for this.

"Papa, take a drink of water," Elizabeth said. Picking up the cup, she lifted his head and put it to his lips. He sipped lightly. "Mother's right. You have to relax. You will only make your condition worse. Aaron will be all right, I promise."

Ephraim nodded, lying back and closing his eyes, trying to calm himself. "Have they found Mary?"

"Not that we know of," Hannah said.

There was silence. He was thinking. "You have to go, Hannah. You have to get him back."

"Don't be foolish. I can't leave you, and even if I did, which I refuse to do, I would be helpless to accomplish any such thing."

Ephraim looked at her, his dark eyes pleading. "You have to go," he said softly. "I'm here because I tried to save him. If we lose him now, it will only make this worse. Do you understand?"

Hannah's heart raced. "But I can't. You, David, Elizabeth, the twins. I—"

"You can. You have to," Ephraim said firmly. "Go to Remez, to Sheal'tiel, to Dov Joseph, to Ben-Gurion if you have to, but you have to find a way to get him out."

"I'm going with you, Mother," David said.

Hannah shook her head adamantly, "This is nonsense, I—"

"Grandmother and I can take care of Father and the twins," Elizabeth said.

Hannah's head throbbed, her eyes moving from Elizabeth to David to Ephraim. He squeezed her hand. He looked so tired, his face still pale and thinner than she had ever seen it. But his eyes were clear and pleading with her.

"You have to try, Hannah. Aaron is the same as a son to me. If . . ." He closed his eyes, his energy spent, then forced them open. "Find a way, Hannah. Find a way." His eyes closed again, and he drifted off to sleep. She smoothed his hair and rubbed his cheek with her fingers. He had come through so much. Leaving him now seemed like desertion, and yet he was in this condition because he loved Aaron. It had been that love that had sent him into battle in nothing more than a Piper Cub, a few small bombs in the seat next to him. But what could she do? How could she get him back? She felt so small, helpless.

"Mum, do you remember Sami Khalidi?" David asked.

She looked at him. "What? Yes, of course, but . . ."

"Sami knows King Abdullah, doesn't he? Remember, he talked about going to the king's palace, being honored there because of his work or something. Sami could help us, Mum."

"Sami is in East Jerusalem. The war . . ."

"But they're talking cease-fire, Mum. It was on the radio last night. The United Nations sent some guy, some count, and—"

"And you and Father know David Ben-Gurion, remember?" Elizabeth quickly added.

"Yes, I remember." They had been asked to a dinner where the new American consul was being introduced by the Brits to both the Jewish Agency and Arab dignitaries. She and Ephraim had been invited because of Ephraim's citizenship and military background. They had sat at the same table as the consul and his wife, along with the three other couples. Ben-Gurion and his wife sat next to them.

"We have to try, Mum," David said softly. "If something happened to him . . ."

Hannah felt the muscles in her stomach tighten, but her heart said David was right. She must go. Squeezing Ephraim's hand, she took a deep breath and turned to David. "I need you to stay here with Beth and your grandparents. It's too dangerous . . ."

"I'm going, Mum," David said adamantly. "Aaron is my flesh and blood, and that makes it more my duty than yours. I'm going."

"No, I'm sorry, David, but you're not. Israel is much worse than it was, and I won't put any more of our family at risk. It's enough, and you can't go." She realized her voice sounded harsh, even mean, when Beth's mouth dropped open a little. Taking a deep breath, she looked at her son, whose head hung a little. Taking his chin in her hand, she lifted it to find his eyes filled with anger and tears. "Please, David, I need you to stay here."

David's eyes softened. He had learned to love Hannah even more than he remembered loving his own mother. From the time he had first met her in Germany, he had felt safe with her.

Up until then he had been constantly afraid, even with Aaron. But with Hannah he knew everything was all right. But this time he was torn. He had grieved deeply when Aaron had been declared dead. It had been Aaron, his big brother, who had taken care of him after their parents had been killed by the Nazis. To know he was alive and then be denied the chance to try and help him was heartrending.

"Mum, I promise I won't get hurt, and I'll do exactly what you tell me, but I have to go. I have to."

Hannah looked into her son's warm, coal-black eyes and knew she couldn't say no again, even though it was against her better judgment. She ran her hand over his hair slowly, a mixture of fear and love making her ache. "All right, David," she said softly. "We'll go together."

He fell into her arms, a wide grin on his face. "It will be okay, Mum. I promise."

Hannah wasn't so sure.

* * *

Hannah could not believe their bad luck. Twice their commercial flight out of London had been cancelled—once because of bad weather over all of England and once because of mechanical problems. The delay had cost them a full day now, and another flight to Italy was not even scheduled until the plane was fixed. The Italians were the only ones flying into Israel commercially, and even then it was sporadic. If they couldn't get there, they were sunk. She was beginning to question the wisdom of leaving the States at all.

Unsure of what to do, she sat in a corner of the terminal watching for David and saying a silent prayer. There had to be a way, but if there was, only God knew it.

Where had David disappeared to? He had left for the bathroom, but it had been much too long for that. The boy's curiosity was at work again, she was sure of it. Getting to her feet, she walked across the expansive open space to the restrooms and asked the men's attendant if there was a young boy inside. He grinned, then pointed toward the door that led to the street.

"'E went that way, m'lady. Asked 'ow 'e could get a good view of the big planes, 'e did. If you turn left and walk along for a ways you'll be findin' 'im."

Retrieving their suitcase, Hannah left the terminal and turned left. She found David a few minutes later, his eyes glued to a large plane parked near the high fence. He was talking to a man who stood under one of the wings, wrench in hand, a toolbox at his feet.

David's interest in planes was not new. From the first moment David and Ephraim had met one another, David had been awed by Ephraim's ability to fly planes and had asked hundreds of questions about the planes he had flown, or seen, or even knew about.

"Did you forget something?" she asked.

His face turned red as he looked her way. "Uh, sorry, Mum. I just . . . well . . . I wanted to see . . . "

"It's all right, David, but we have to get back to town and find a place to stay for the night. It's a bit of a walk, so we should get started, don't you think?"

He nodded, turned back to the mechanic, and said thanks for the information. It was then that the mechanic answered with "Shalom." Both David and Hannah could not move, their eyes frozen to the mechanic who had the look of a little boy who had gotten caught with his hand in the cookie jar.

"The weather is very hot in Palestine this time of year," she said in Hebrew.

He took a deep breath, "Tod. Yes, it is," he responded with relief. "You are Jewish?"

Hannah nodded, her eyes blinking to keep back the tears. "We are trying to get to Palestine. My husband, Ephraim

Daniels, was a pilot for the Israeli Air Force before it was an air force and was shot down at the battle of Kastel. We had to take him to the States for surgery and . . . a son, a brother, was captured and has been found, and we have to get back to help him. He was hurt quite badly and . . ."

The mechanic dropped the wrench in the toolbox, grabbed a rag, and walked briskly to the fence while wiping the grease and oil from his hands. "I am honored to meet you. Your husband is well known by our pilots. They talk about what he did very often. Please, come to the gate, come inside." He started along the fence toward a locked gate. Pulling a key from his pocket, he unlocked the padlock, removed the chain, and let them in. After relocking everything, he led them toward a large, dilapidated hangar.

"I have been scolded for slipping with my tongue," the mechanic said. "We are not to let anyone know we are Jews." He grinned. "The Brits wouldn't like it if they knew what we're up to here. And right under their noses too."

"I am grateful you did slip," Hannah said, returning the smile. "You are an answer to prayer."

He blushed. "My boss is a guy by the name of John, at least that's the name he uses around here. His real name is Elijah, and he wants that plane I'm working on ready for a trip to Israel by tonight. If you and this lad smile just right, he might give you a ride."

Hannah gulped back the tears as they walked from the bright sun of an English summer day into the partially shaded hangar. She noticed that one section of the roof was missing, and there were a dozen large, partially boarded-up holes in the walls.

"A bit of a mess," the mechanic said. "As you know, the Germans bombed London over and over, especially airports and such. This is one of the few hangars still left standing. The others you see around here are new or heavily remodeled, but that takes money, and we don't expect to be around much longer anyway."

"Why not?" David asked.

"The Brits have been curious about us. If they look much deeper, they'll find out what we're doing and tell us to leave. Or worse, knowing the Brits."

"What are you doing?" Hannah asked.

"Buying war supplies and shipping them to Israel. With the help of a British pilot who flew with Ezer Weizman and your husband in the war with the Nazis, we got our hands on several of their fighters—"

"The Spitfire," David said. "Pops says it's one of the best."

The mechanic smiled. "Your pop should know. We tore them down in here and loaded them into planes like that one." He nodded toward the one he had been working on. "We've gathered guns and ammo, even gas masks and uniforms. You'd be surprised what war surplus money can buy, even here. But the British government is still pro-Arab, and they'll boot us out if they find out what we're doing." He blushed again. "That's why the boss won't be happy if he knows I had another slip of the tongue."

"We will try to keep that a secret," Hannah said.

There was a small office in the corner of the building. The door was open, and Hannah could hear voices speaking in English. One sounded vaguely familiar, but she could not place it. The mechanic knocked on the doorframe, then showed himself to the men inside. Telling them he had found a couple of refugees needing a ride, he ushered Hannah and David into the room. Their faces were unhappy until the tallest of the two recognized Hannah and jumped to his feet.

"Hannah! Hannah Daniels!"

"Joseph!"

They hugged each other while the others all watched with varying degrees of confusion on their faces.

"How are you?" Joseph asked her. "And Ephraim, how—" He stopped midsentence. He had heard what had happened to Ephraim, and it suddenly dawned on him it might have all ended very badly.

"He is okay, Joseph." She gave him an update while the others listened, then she turned to David. "This is Joseph Herrman. We met in Germany at the end of the war. He is the one who found your father's diary, Torah, and prayer shawl. The ones we gave you last Christmas."

David nodded. He still carried the Torah and read it regularly, and that Christmas had been the best ever.

He stretched forth his hand to shake Joseph's. "Thank you." It was all he could think to say.

"You are welcome." Joseph turned to Hannah. "This is a long way from Virginia and Ephraim's bedside. It must be important."

She told him about Aaron. "We thought we might catch a ride to Israel," she smiled hopefully.

Joseph turned to the other man in the office. "This is Elijah Bloomberg. He is responsible for this operation. What do you think, Elijah? Is there enough room for the wife and mother of two of Israel's great heroes?"

Elijah tossed aside his cigarette and stomped it out. "I knew your husband and met Aaron Schwartz when he worked for us in Paris. Yes, of course there is room. But Joseph, this will be a dangerous mission. You know we have to . . . uh . . . go south."

Joseph nodded. "We have one extra leg on our flight. It is a bit dangerous."

"Extra leg?"

"Cairo, dear Hannah. We're going to make a call on Cairo."

Hannah put an arm around David, regretting again that she had given in to him so easily.

CHAPTER 28

Mary watched the shoreline as the truck sped along the highway toward Tel Aviv. The breeze off the Mediterranean smelled fresh, and for a moment, she forgot the chaos, closed her eyes, and imagined Paris.

The day after Saad's funeral, Mary had gone to the Jewish civil authorities and asked for papers to Tel Aviv. At first she had been denied because she was Arab, but when she showed her marriage license, which effectively declared her a Jewish citizen because of her marriage to a Jew, they had let her fill out the forms and meet with the proper official. He had listened to her story, signed the papers, stamped them with an official stamp, and sent her on her way. After that, she had spent two days working with the bank for a transfer of funds to Haifa through Paris. At first it had looked impossible, but with the help of a Jewish banker who liked the challenge of taking money out of Beirut's pro-Arab banks, they had finally succeeded. A few minutes after the bank opened this morning, Mary had set up an account for Rifa and Emile that would get them by for at least the next six months, then taken the rest in British pounds and walked to the hospital where she told Rifa what she had done. Rifa had shed tears of gratitude, and Mary had left, meeting Dodi, the truck driver Ivan had recommended, at a warehouse near the south end of the city. They had met the day before and struck a deal, even though Mary felt some apprehension. The condition of this truck made Ivan and Dimitri's look inviting.

She was filled with both fear and excitement as they left Haifa. With no Ahmed, no Berak, she was on her own. Perhaps the hardest part of the trip might still be ahead as she tried once more to return to Jerusalem.

Her papers worked wonders for her at each checkpoint around Haifa, but their progress was slowed by the heavy military and civilian traffic moving north. Dust hung over everything, and the heat increased with each mile. It was nearly noon before they turned off the road, passed a village to their left, a charred truck to their right. Climbing a narrow road, they reached the Jewish kibbutz where her driver would pick up a delivery of baled sheep's wool for Tel Aviv.

Because most of the men of the kibbutz were on military maneuvers outside the community, a stern-looking woman came to the gate to clear them for entry and loading. She was obviously unhappy that the driver was Arab and questioned him thoroughly before finally allowing them entrance into the kibbutz.

She also took charge of the farm crane and the loading of the bales. Mary watched until an older man approached, pitchfork in hand. His eyes focused on the team of horses that lifted the crane's heavily loaded fork, then positioned it over the truck before lowering it.

"She is very good at such things," he said of the woman handling the team. "But she can be mean as a caged lion if she has a mind to."

Mary glanced at the man. Stocky, deeply tanned from working in the sun, his gray hair short and thick. Unsure of his purpose in speaking to her, she turned back without comment.

"I saw how she treated your driver," he continued. "He doesn't deserve it, but when you have lost a son to Arabs you thought were your friends, it isn't easy to trust them anymore."

"What happened?"

"We had an agreement with the Arabs in the village near the road. A sort of non-aggression pact. We control the well and the spring they use and they control access to the highway. It seemed like a good pact at the time. Then our armies got involved and stirred things up. Pretty soon, some of our men snuck up to the spring and shut off the flow. Before we realized what had happened, we sent a truck to Tel Aviv with a load like this one. We heard the attack and grabbed our weapons to try and help, but we were too late. The truck was on fire and the two lads in it dead. One of them was her son. We called in the Haganah. Twenty of our former Arab neighbors were killed. The rest ran off." He stuck the pitchfork into a nearby bale of wool. "For her it wasn't enough." He paused. "You know what frightens her, what frightens all of us? That men like your driver will do to us what we did to that village down there. We know how it works now. We know how much the death of a loved one makes you hate the ones who took them from you. And we know they'll want revenge just like we did, so we don't trust anyone anymore. We're too afraid." He forced a smile, picked up the pitchfork and slung it onto his shoulder. "I have lived here all my life. We have had our disagreements with our Arab neighbors, but we have always worked them out. Now I am afraid those days are gone forever."

Mary rubbed the chill from her arms as she watched him go to the haystack near a cattle pen and begin feeding the animals.

"Come," Dodi yelled from the truck. "It is loaded."

Mary took the two dozen steps to the truck and climbed in just as the woman approached carrying instructions for delivery and continued her harangue.

"If this were not already paid for, you would not get it," she said. "You Arabs can't be trusted anymore, and you better beware. This delivery is for the government clothing mill. If it does not arrive, they will throw you in prison and never let you out."

Dodi took the paper and shoved the truck in gear while continuing to hold his tongue. Mary had to bite hers as well and was relieved when they passed through the gate and were on the road again. She noticed the burned truck again when they passed it, then looked at the village more carefully. It was Jewish now. Completely Jewish.

They rode several miles in silence, both involved in their own thoughts. She dozed a bit, the heat and dust getting worse with each slow mile.

She awoke when Dodi shifted down for a road block. The soldiers took nearly an hour searching their truck and checking their papers, before finally giving them permission to move forward by way of a detour around a small village. There were several trucks unloading men, women, and children. "Jewish refugees," Dodi said stiffly. "This was an Arab village once. They say the Jews massacred more than two hundred men here. Trucked the rest of the people off to Iraqi territory to the east." He jammed the gearshift forward angrily. "Things get worse every day. Soon there will be no one left, no one willing to take this treatment."

"It is no better in Beirut," Mary said.

"Yes, yes, I understand this," he said impatiently, "and I know it is even worse in the camps in Jericho, Nablus, and Nazareth. But a man with any pride can only take so much before even those places would be better than this treatment. Look at how they treat me? I am a man of great authority in my village, second only to the family of the muhktar himself. My family has lived there for centuries. I make good marriages for my children, I am honored because I raise fine daughters who bring large dowries, and I grow rich from my herds and from the trucks I buy. Honored for my wisdom, respected for my name, I am Dodi bin Mohammed, a great man.

"And then the Jews come and everything changes. They take my trucks. My sheep are scattered and stolen. Their armies fight in my fields and ruin my olive trees, then overrun our village, and we have to leave. The muhktar takes most of them to Nablus, but some of us go to Haifa where I find a half-destroyed house no Jew wants, and we live like animals. I escape with one truck. My name is worth little in Haifa, and I have to work hard to get a few pounds to feed my family. Everything changes. The muhktar sends word that I am to come to Nablus. The tribe needs my truck, my money, my wisdom. I close my ears because I know what Nablus is like and my wife is expecting a child. How can I take her to such a place? But soon I must go or lose all honor, all respect, even among my own people. All this because of the Jews! I spit upon them and their new state."

The truck coughed and sputtered, then stopped altogether. Dodi pulled it off the side of the road with a curse, then got out and lifted the hood. A moment later, he retrieved a toolbox from the floor of the cab. Mary stepped out of the truck and watched him work until the dust of traffic encouraged a walk into a nearby harvested field of grain. When she returned, Dodi was closing the hood. "It cannot be fixed this time." He reached in his pocket, withdrew his money, peeled off several bills, and handed them to her. "I must go back to Haifa and get parts. It will take me until tomorrow morning. You can be in Tel Aviv by then." He handed her the bills. "This is what I did not earn."

Mary took the money. He was leaving. She had no choice but to either wait for his return or keep walking. Though the prospect frightened her, she felt she must keep going. He handed her the suitcase she had brought along, and she handed him back half the money. "You tried and you have a family." Dodi looked at the money, his pride making him hesitate about taking it, then he shoved it in his pocket, said good-bye, and walked north.

Mary went south, glancing back to see him catching a ride. She wondered if the truck and its large bales would still be there when he returned but shoved the thought aside. It would take a crane to move them and a better mechanic than Dodi to fix his truck.

The sun was two hours from sinking into the sea when she reached the checkpoint at Natanya. South of the roadblock, she found the traffic much lighter and the road much closer to the sea. The air was freshened by the breeze from the water, making it nearly pleasant for walking. She saw a military convoy coming her way and, like everyone else on foot, hurried off the side of the road and out of the way. As they passed in their trucks and armored cars, she noticed there were new artillery pieces in tow, and most of the men were carrying new weapons. But they had no uniforms. They were thin, pale, and tired. More refugees. She wondered how many knew what they were in for, how many could possibly survive, and yet what choice did they have? Fighting four Arab armies at once demanded their immediate involvement or they would remain refugees.

Refusing to think upon it longer, she picked up her things and walked over the rolling sand dunes to the beach. Removing her shoes, she walked into the water, wandering south while letting the cool, salty liquid soothe both her feet and her troubled mind. The more she saw that there was no real solution to the growing hatred between Jew and Arab, the more she longed to be free of it. But such escape was impossible unless one deserted the entire country. Though she had thought of it, even longed for it, those desires always left her feeling guilty. But what could she do by remaining here?

But, if she could find Aaron, if they were together, she could endure it. Oh, how she prayed he was still alive, that Hannah was wrong, that her own feelings he had somehow survived were right and not just wishful thinking!

There were a few refugees camped on the sands between the road and the sea, settling in for the night, but Mary decided to keep going, eager to reach Tel Aviv. Sitting down and cleaning the sand off her feet, she put her shoes back on. They were the one thing she still wore that had been with her in Beirut. She and Aaron had picked them out in Paris. Durable with heavy leather soles and solid construction, they served her well, and she was a bit shocked to see the small hole in the center of the leather sole.

Putting them on, she stood and straightened her dress. After getting the money from Beirut, she had gone shopping and had purchased it and a second comfortable linen dress, underclothes, a light sweater, and a head scarf. She wore the scarf around her neck, putting it over her face at checkpoints and whenever she felt it wise to keep men from looking too carefully. She now put it over her head and wrapped it around the lower portion of her face, then retrieved the sweater from her bag and slipped it on, the air cooling a bit as the sun disappeared into the sea. Returning to the road, she quickened her pace.

She noted immediately that most traffic was military and that the few civilians moving about in cars, trucks, and donkey carts or on foot were Jewish. This not only surprised Mary, but made her a bit nervous, and she removed the headscarf and stuffed it in the bag before retrieving her papers and gripping them tightly for reassurance that her Jewish marriage would continue to keep her safe.

She walked as far off the side of the road as she could and hurried her pace, hardly noticing the tent villages along the dunes between her and the beach, filled with Jewish refugees forced to flee the war zones around Ramallah and Jerusalem. After another couple of hours, she grew tired and thirsty. Seeing a small village ahead, she retrieved a British pound from her hiding place, then continued. Stopping at the first house, she knocked on the door and spoke in Hebrew, asking for water. The woman gave her the once-over, then shut the door with a "Lo, lo," Hebrew for "no, no."

"Bevakasha. Please. I will pay," Mary said.

The door opened again. "How much?"

"British pound for a metal container of water I can carry."

The door shut again, but Mary waited. A moment later, the door opened and the metal bucket with a lid was presented. Mary gave the woman the pound, a lot of money for such a container and a little water. She stayed in the shadows of the porch and drank her fill, then put the lid on the bucket and continued her journey through the village. People sat about visiting quietly, and no one seemed to give her a second thought. In the light she looked Jewish, and in the dark even more so. The smell of freshly baked bread made her feel hungry, and she looked for the source. A woman was baking with an outdoor oven in her yard. Mary walked slowly to the low fence that separated the yard from the street.

"Shalom," she said.

The woman looked up. "Shalom."

"I am traveling to Tel Aviv," Mary said in Hebrew. "I could use a loaf of your bread for the journey." She retrieved some coins from her pocket amounting to half a pound. "I am willing to pay for it."

The woman stood and took the money before moving under a lantern to count each piece. She then picked up a loaf of bread and handed it to Mary. Stepping close she spoke. "Your Hebrew is very good for an Arab, but be cautious, young one. Our soldiers—"

"Thank you," Mary said. "I will. How far to Tel Aviv?"

"Five miles, but the military has a checkpoint just three miles down the road. Do you have papers?"

"Yes. My husband is a Jew."

The woman smiled, relieved. "Ah, good, good. Then you should have no trouble. Behatzlaka. Good luck to you." She turned back to her cooking just as two small children ran past Mary and into the next yard. It seemed so normal here, and for the first time Mary relaxed a little.

She walked on, the lights of passing vehicles shining in her eyes from time to time, others honking from behind as they prepared to go around her. After another mile of feeding on the warm bread, she stuffed the remaining third in her bag. Here the dirt road turned to pavement, and over the next mile villages and houses grew in number. The night grew quiet enough that Mary could hear the soft murmur of voices, even laughter, in half a dozen languages. Twice she heard unfamiliar music and saw people dancing in the light of their fires. Probably folk dances from their past lives in faraway places. It was then she noticed there were no sounds of war, just a cool breeze and the voices of normality. Oh, how she wished it would always be just so.

She heard the group before she saw them. A band of men, laughing, joking with one another. She slipped from the road to hide in a clump of olive trees when they saw her and called out.

"Hey, daughter of Zion, come join our celebration." The slurred and coarse voice made Mary freeze.

The three men drew closer, stopping a few steps from Mary. "Ah, this is what we fight for, Peytor. The finest women. The good land." He stepped forward, his hand extended as if to touch her.

She slapped it aside. "Rega! Stop!" she said in Hebrew.

"Ahh, one with spirit," the man said. Circling to the right, his eyes scanned Mary's body. Mary knew she must make a move, and it had to be now. Forcing her fear into her stomach, she walked resolutely forward, pushing one of the other two aside as she confronted him. "My brothers will deal with you," she said firmly.

The first, now behind her, grabbed an arm and twirled her around. "Your brothers, if you have any, are off fighting the Arabs somewhere. Do you see any brothers, Peytor?"

Peytor laughed evilly, his hand reaching out. She jerked her hand free, smacking the water can against the man's head. He stumbled, and the others jumped back. Mary ran for the olive grove to her left, zigzagging through the trees, running as fast and hard as she could. The three men, angry, humiliated, and very drunk, ran after her. Mary shivered at the consequence of getting caught and regretted leaving behind the small dagger Ahmed had given her days earlier. She saw the ditch too late and fell into its muddy waters. The papers fell from her grasp, and she frantically searched for them until the voices revealed to her that she had no more time. Seeing an overhang of brush to her left, she slithered through the muddy, stagnant water and pushed herself under it. Holding her breath, she watched the dark form of one of the men jump the ditch, then the second and the third. She didn't let herself even twitch until their voices faded in the distance, then waited another five minutes before pushing herself out of the muck and returning to the spot to find her papers.

She finally spied them floating in the water a few feet farther downstream. She shook them off as best as she could, then struggled up the slippery slope of the ditch to collapse on the ground. Catching her breath, she listened for any sign of her attackers. Finally she got to her feet and walked back into the grove, then to the road. Wet and shivering, she stumbled on to the next house.

Frightened and unsure, she didn't dare knock and went up a slight hill behind the house to a small stack of cut grass used for feeding the animals. Sitting in a place that could not be seen from the road, she carefully unfolded her papers and laid them out to dry. She thought of washing them off but knew that would only smudge them worse and make them even more unreadable. She lowered her head as she realized what this might mean. Without readable papers, without others to vouch for her, the Jews would never let her pass the next checkpoint. Tears sprang to her eyes, and she wept quietly, her body shaking from both despair and the chill of the night.

Then a thought came to her. She should not wait. Her condition would be in her favor at the next checkpoint. She should go. Now. If they turned her away or held her for questioning, so be it, but her chances of success would be better now than tomorrow.

She went back to the road, this time listening to the sounds, watching the shadows and darting off to hide whenever she heard a car or person. It took her nearly two hours to reach the checkpoint, tired and frightened. She stayed in the darkness, gathering her strength, her mind racing with the possibility of rejection or even capture.

Finally, she found a spot next to a large, ancient olive tree and knelt to pray. She asked to be calm, to know what to say, and that the hearts of the guards might be softened. Getting to her feet, she held the papers up to the light of the moon. She could no longer read the signatures, nor most of the words, but the papers were dry. She folded them as neatly as she could, took a deep breath, and walked onto the road and to the checkpoint. If only Aaron were here to help her deal with this, to give her some strength. Her hand went to the Book of Mormon in her pocket. It was wet as well, but warm to the touch and gave her some comfort. God would help. He was all she had, and He would not leave her alone. Not now. Not when she had tried her best, done everything she could to follow what she knew was His will for her.

Lifting her head and taking a deep breath, Mary walked steadfastly to the truck pulled across the road. The soldiers heard her coming through the darkness and tensed, but when they saw she was a woman and alone, they dropped their weapons to their sides. She handed the nearest one her soaked papers and brushed her still damp hair to one side. He looked at both, then smiled a bit, motioning for her to stay while he went to a jeep and used a flashlight to read the papers. After glancing back at her with a shake of his head that registered disbelief, he called someone's name. Another appeared, and they talked quietly, glancing at her several times. Though anxious, she kept her shoulders squared, her eyes straight ahead. Finally, both of them, weapons in hand, came toward her.

"You are the wife of Aaron Schwartz?" the short one asked, the question in heavily accented, stuttering Hebrew. With the flashlight shining on the papers, he pointed to the few words that could be read. It was Aaron's name.

She felt relief course through her body but could muster only enough strength to nod.

"Then you are welcome here, even if the rest of your papers are ruined." He smiled and handed them to her.

Tears leaped to the corners of her eyes. "I do not understand. How do you know my husband. How . . ."

"My name is Uri. I was with him at Kastel. He saved my life. I will take you to Tel Aviv." He offered his hand, and Mary, too stunned even to speak, let herself be led to a nearby beat-up pickup truck. He saw that she was seated, then got behind the wheel, and they started for the city.

"You were there?" she finally asked.

He nodded. "We try to save Ephraim Daniels. He protects us with small Piper, helps us run away. It very dangerous to try to save him, but we go anyway. We do not leave this man behind—he saved us. We find him wounded. A man called Jack Willis carries him while we keep Arabs from shooting both. They make it to the armored car, but Jack is shot." He paused. "Another man, Judah, is also shot, and Aaron goes back. He carries him. He is shot. I go back, but . . . but he has no pulse." He pulled the jeep to the side of the road, his hands shaking a bit. "I should bring him, but I am afraid. I leave. He is dead."

Mary sensed the anguish in his voice, and she ached for both of them. She had never known what had happened, only that Aaron had died there. Now the pain hit her clear to her heels. He was gone. Aaron was really gone.

They didn't speak again, reaching the outskirts of Tel Aviv thirty minutes later. It was quiet, with few lights. He took her to a small hotel near the sea, and they went inside. She listened as he talked to the man at the desk. They knew each other, and from what she could hear, there were no vacancies. He yelled at the man in Hebrew, then took her back to the truck. "The city has many refugees, many foreigners who fight for us. It will be hard to find a bed."

They checked several more hotels but found nothing.

"Aaron had family. Are they here?"

"No, they're either in Jerusalem or the United States," she said. She still had to fight the tears, her dream suddenly washed away by the reality Uri had given her. "Can I get to Jerusalem?" Mary asked.

"It is impossible now. The road is closed by Arabs. We have a new road soon, but it is nothing. Jerusalem is no place for a woman with no husband. They are near starvation." He turned right, and they drove along the beachfront in the first light of morning, stopping in front of a single door with no markings. "My room is here. I will not need it for the next week. You can use."

Mary went to protest, but he was already out of the truck and removing her suitcase. "You must do as I say. There is no choice."

He opened the door and let her pass inside, then followed. They climbed a narrow set of stairs to the second floor, and he was unlocking the first door on the right when a woman came to the bottom of the stairs. "Uri, darling, what are you doing? You haven't used that bed in . . ." She saw Mary and was both confused and angered.

"Lenta, it is not what you think. This is wife of Aaron—"

The woman was already gone with a loud slam of a door followed by curses in the language Mary now recognized as Russian.

"Your girlfriend?" Mary asked.

He shrugged. "I will talk to her. I have very few things, but the bed is okay and the bathroom is near." He pointed across the hall. "It has a large tub with hot water sometimes." He smiled, pushing the door open and letting her enter. There was a single room with a bed and an end table. A hot plate sat on the floor near the window with several pots sitting uncleaned next to it. He gathered up a few clothes and stuffed them in a paper bag. "The sheets are clean. Lenta . . . takes care of me."

"Thank you, Uri. I will try to be out in a day or two."

"You go to the authorities, get papers fixed very soon." He tore off a piece of paper and wrote down something in Russian. "My name and unit number. Also where I'm stationed. If questions, I vouch for you." He looked at the floor. "I am sorry. I should not have left him," he said softly.

She grasped his hand and held it tightly. "Aaron would not condemn you, Uri. Risking another life to bring . . ." She bit her lip to get control. "You did the right thing."

He nodded and handed her the key before backing toward the door. "May the God of Israel be with you, Mary Schwartz," he said. The door closed, and she was left alone. Sitting down on the bed she stared out the window at the sea, numb and cold. Then the tears fell. This night she would cry herself to sleep.

CHAPTER 29

They took off just after midnight. Their flight plan indicated they were a cargo plane owned by an American company and headed for South America with tractor parts. Hannah recognized the name of the American company as the one Ephraim said Al Schwimmer had organized to buy and sell planes in the States. The pilots were both Americans, neither Jewish. Both knew Ephraim, and one had flown with him against the Germans. He had just recently come from Israel and knew Wally. While they were waiting for the time to take off, he told her and David about Wally's recent exploits in rescuing the prisoners who escaped from Mafraq prison in Transjordan. Hannah could tell that the story was already taking on mythological dimensions but realized that she was hearing how Abraham had discovered Aaron's whereabouts. It was sobering to hear a few more details.

She and David were fastened into uncomfortable seats attached to the bulkhead between the cargo bay and the cockpit, Joseph next to her. Joseph had made the trip to Israel twice and had run into both Wally and Zohar.

"Of course, these days it's hard to run into one without running into the other." He smiled. Hannah was pleased to hear it. He then told her about Wally's recent trip to visit Rachel.

Hannah remembered Joseph's feelings for Rachel. At the beginning of the Nazi horror, Joseph had fallen into the trap most Germans had. Rachel was a Jew, and as a member of Hitler's brownshirts, he had turned away from her when she needed him most. Though Joseph had never been caught up in the killing of Jews, he had fought in the Wehrmacht, returning to Berlin a broken man with many regrets. He had seen Rachel, and though they had become friends again, she would not allow the old feelings to rekindle. They had parted, Rachel going with Hannah, and Joseph staying behind where, because of his help in breaking an underground Nazi resistance ring, he moved quickly up the ladder of the American-born West German government secret service.

"Wally says she was pretty beat up by the loss of her fiancé," Joseph said. "Still tough as nails though. Still a survivor, thanks to you."

"You should see her, Joseph. When the war is over, you should tell her how you feel."

He looked away, a bit embarrassed that his feelings were still so obvious. "We'll see."

"How are we doing, Joseph? Is the new Israel still fighting for its life?"

Joseph forced a smile, but his blue eyes held no twinkle, just concern. "We need a cease-fire badly. But each time the United Nation's representative, Count Folke Bernadotte, sets a deadline, the Arabs refuse the terms, keep fighting. That's one reason we're going to visit Cairo. Send them a message they are just as vulnerable as we are."

"And if they still refuse?" The harsh, even violent rhetoric of the Arab leaders filled the American press. They continued to back themselves into a corner only a hard military thumping would force them out of.

"We will lose Jerusalem for sure, and most likely the Negev and eastern Galilee. We're running out of ammo. We still have no real air force, artillery, tanks, and a dozen other important instruments we need to beat them back. We could have a lot more of them in four weeks. Then we can handle them, even push them back." He smiled. "We have a better underground system of supply than they do." He paused. "We've had our victories, especially in the north around Haifa and Acco, but we've had some hard losses too. Civilian and military morale is down and will plummet if we lose the rest of the Holy City."

Hannah only nodded. Deep down, she hoped that a cease-fire would bring peace, but that didn't seem likely for years to come. It was a war neither side could ever end and save face—not in this generation at least. That meant David, Beth, the twins, might all have to fight an endless stream of Arab attempts to keep their foolish promises and live in an environment surrounded by an ever-thickening pool of hate that could suck them all in until both sides would simply self-destruct into one final cataclysmic war the world called Armageddon.

Seeing that David had fallen asleep, his head bobbing up and down, Hannah gently lifted it, put it against her shoulder, and experienced for the hundredth time a moment's fear of losing him to such a war. She closed her own eyes against the ache. She couldn't lose another family member.

"Will you stay in Israel now?" She asked Joseph the question in an attempt to drive away her own fearful thoughts.

"I am not Jewish, but if I can help, I will stay," he said.

Thoughts of the future occupied her while David and then Joseph slept, but finally with the steady drone of the engines and nothing but crates and boxes to look at, she closed her eyes and let herself drift off into a deep sleep. She awoke when they landed at a makeshift airfield in southern France for refueling, and she and David got out and stretched their legs. She found an outdoor latrine while David quizzed the pilots about the plane. When she returned, she couldn't find him until he yelled from a window in the cockpit, then waved. She walked and thought of Aaron, wondering what his problems might be, then of Mary and how to find her in Beirut. Surely she was still there, the war, the uncertainty, and the belief that Aaron was gone leaving her no reason to try and go back. At least not at the moment.

Since receiving Naomi's letter, Hannah had regretted sending the letter to Mary, but then she had no guarantee she had ever received it. She must locate Mary somehow. Bringing Aaron home would be incomplete if Mary were not with him.

Joseph hollered for her to come, and she quickly boarded the plane. Over the next leg of the journey, she didn't see David much as the pilot had invited him to sit in a bulkhead seat in the cockpit. She and Joseph visited about the past few years and ate cheese and bread. She was amazed at his stories about Church members in Germany and how they struggled for survival, rebuilt their lives, and tried to move on. But she was more impressed with the depth of his love and concern for both the members and the gospel itself. Joseph had changed, and it made Hannah secretly hope that Rachel would give him another chance. Rachel could be happy with this man.

It was still dark when one of the pilots began tearing apart one of the crates near the door, revealing four bombs half an average man's size and weight.

Joseph pointed out the small window on the east side of the plane. "Those lights in the distance are Tel Aviv. In another hour we'll make our delivery over Cairo, then land here in time for breakfast." He unbuttoned his seat belt and got up, stretching. "I'll send David back to you. Stay strapped in, and don't worry—they won't know what hit them." He smiled. "But it wouldn't hurt to pray, either."

A moment later, David appeared and strapped himself in next to the window. The two of them watched occasional lights pop up along the coast before Joseph reappeared and handed them each a set of headphones, pointing to a small panel of knobs and jacks where they could plug them in. Hannah wasn't sure she wanted to know what was going to happen but finally put them on and pushed the connector into a jack. The fact that she couldn't hear anything must have showed on her face because David turned a knob next to her plug and the volume came on.

There was chatter between members of the crew and those preparing the bombs, then, "Cairo Airport, this is TWA flight 716, may I have the runway lights, please? Over," the pilot spoke in Arabic.

Hannah smiled. Without radar, which the Egyptians did not have, and under cover of darkness, they had no way of knowing this was not a civilian airplane. She leaned over and looked out the window, straining to see forward but without success.

"Roger, TWA, the lights are on. Please land on runway four. Over."

"Roger," the pilot answered. The plane began a descent that quickly brought them to only a few hundred feet above ground.

"There," David said. "There are the lights!"

Hannah saw Joseph and the copilot shove the side door open while the navigator pushed the first opened crate over rollers to the door. As the plane came within two hundred feet of the ground, the pilot told them to make their delivery and the crate was shoved out of the door, two others quickly joining it. They blew up behind the plane and directly in the middle of the runway as the pilot banked hard left. The remainder of the bombs were pushed out over a row of planes parked along the edge of the field. Hannah and David watched as the bombs hit and exploded, several planes quickly destroyed.

The pilot pulled back on the column and climbed for the clouds, then turned hard to the east, then north toward the Sinai.

"Cairo Airport, this is TWA 716. Do you still want me to land on runway four?"

There was no response, but the men in the plane all celebrated with whistles, yelling, and laughter. David had a big grin on his face, and even Hannah wore a wide smile. The Egyptian army was the largest in the region and had bombed Tel Aviv and other places, killing dozens. Possibly a little dose of their own poison would make them think twice before they sent more. They were flying over the Negev when the sun came up on their right and the Egyptian fighters showed up in the clouds to their left. Men scrambled to several storage boxes, removed machine guns, and quickly had them in prepared mounts near the door just as the Egyptian fighters made their attack. Hannah watched out the window as the first fighter plummeted toward them and was startled to find that she could actually see the guns on the fighter's wings firing at them. Bullets ripped into the fuselage of their lumbering, overloaded cargo plane as the rata-tat-tat of machine guns at the doors tried to drive the Egyptians away.

A shell tore through the metal near David's head, and Hannah yelled for him to get between the two crates in front of them while unbuckling her own belt to follow. As she was about to push her small body into an even smaller space, she saw the navigator fall away from his machine gun, wounded and in anguish.

"Stay put," she told David in a tone he knew he had better obey. Crawling forward with bullets ripping the metal sides of the plane, she rolled the man over to find half his upper arm missing, blood gushing from the wound. Grabbing a light jacket that lay nearby, she ripped a bandage and quickly tied a tourniquet near the shoulder. Another strip bandaged the wound, and she pulled him away from the door before grabbing the gun's handles and aiming at an oncoming plane. She was bracing to pull the trigger when the plane exploded into pieces. Another plane, this one sporting a hand-painted Star of David on its tail wing, flew past. The Israeli Air Force had come to their rescue.

Hannah hadn't realized how close to the ground they were and stared at the hills and mountains they raced through. As she dropped the handles of the gun to recheck the man's wounds, Joseph came from his gun position with a bag of bandages and medicines, and the two of them patched him up properly.

"So much for in-and-out and no worries," he said.

"Was anyone else hurt?" Hannah asked.

"No one, but the plane lost its left engine. We'll have to stay at low altitude all the way back to Tel Aviv."

"I need to check on David," she said, getting up.

"I just saw him. He's fine and back in the cockpit."

The wounded man moaned back to consciousness, and Joseph gave him a drink of water and then morphine before telling the pilot he ought to radio for an ambulance to meet them when they landed.

The plane set down safely at Lydda Airport a half hour later. As they taxied to the northern end of the runway, Hannah and David looked out the window to see a familiar face grinning and waving at them from in front of a small building.

"Zohar," David said.

Hannah smiled. "Do you recognize the man with her?"

He shook his head. "Uh-uh."

"That's Wally Bergman, another good friend of your father."

"The pilot Joseph was talking about," David said.

The plane came to a stop, and the remaining engine was shut down. Hannah undid her safety belt and, anxious to get her feet on the ground again, reached for her bag when Joseph came out of the cockpit and told her he would see to the wounded man and then join them. David was the first off the plane and ran to Zohar, embracing her with such a lack of timidity that it shocked her.

"Is this the boy who would hardly talk when I saw him last?" Zohar said as she hugged him tightly. "And so tall. How wonderful." She laughed and cried at the same time, then saw Hannah. Letting David go, she took two steps and hugged her old friend tightly. They both cried, laughed, hugged again, and cried some more while David and Wally looked on with embarrassed appreciation.

When they wiped their tears, Hannah turned to Wally and hugged him as well, making him grimace a little as she wrapped her arms directly around his wound.

"Oh, it's good to see you again," Hannah said to both of them. "Wally, do you remember David?"

"The strong, quiet kid in Berlin. The one you were holding on your lap when you left in the back of that truck. How ya doing, sport?"

"Good. Have you heard anything about Aaron? Did they get him out?" David asked hopefully.

Wally glanced at Zohar, then forced a smile. "We're working on it, kid. We're working on it. How about some breakfast? Are you hungry?"

David was visibly disappointed, but nodded. "Yeah, we could eat, couldn't we, Mum?"

"Yes, we could."

Zohar gave Wally a signal with her head and a sharp look of the eye.

"Uh, I have to get a couple of things from the ammo shack before we go to town. How about giving me a hand, sport?"

David brightened some. "Yeah, sure," he answered, and they went off together.

"What is wrong, Zohar?" Hannah asked.

"Jerusalem is cut off. Even the airfield is closed now, the Arabs putting flak guns close enough it would be suicide to fly in. Dov Joseph sent word to Ben-Gurion that if food doesn't arrive today or tomorrow, the city will either begin starving or there will be a mass exodus to Tel Aviv. Both could give the Arabs a victory that could end all hope of our holding onto our new state."

"And Naomi and Abraham are in Jerusalem," Hannah asked.

"Thank heavens she is with SHAI and can send radio messages from time to time, but what she sends is not encouraging. David Sheal'tiel, commander of that sector, wouldn't even have the decency to give her a hearing about Aaron, so she went to Dov Joseph who talked to Sheal'tiel himself." She paused. "Dov was told to leave it alone for now, that maybe when a cease-fire or treaty was put in place, something could be done." She stopped, facing Hannah. "As you probably know, a third cease-fire date has been called for the eleventh, two days from now, but the Arabs insist they will not honor it, and we have little intelligence to believe to the contrary."

Joseph joined them in time to hear most of the conversation and spoke. "But if it did happen, something could be done, couldn't it? A prisoner exchange possibly, or—"

"There is something else," Zohar said. "SHAI received word from an agent inside Amman that following the prison break of Abraham and the others, the prisoners are being moved further east. I am afraid for Aaron, Hannah. If we don't get him home now, we may lose him."

Hannah felt her heart skip a beat. "When will they move the prisoners?" she asked.

"We don't know, but if the cease-fire doesn't take hold, Naomi thinks they will be moved in the next few days."

"Then we must get to Jerusalem," Hannah said. "This road being built, is it being traveled?"

"It is not finished and won't be for at least another week, but we did take jeeps through again this morning so that we could claim it did not come under any cease-fire restrictions, should a cease-fire come. It was very difficult even for jeeps and is still impossible for trucks, especially in the middle where the valley climbs to the heights of the Jerusalem hills then falls dramatically toward the city itself. Only men on foot can traverse that part of the road, so we will send men—hundreds of them—tonight and the next night and the next. By moonlight they will save Jerusalem from starving. It is all that is left to us."

"Then we go," Hannah said.

"And once in the city, what then?" Joseph asked.

"Then we find a way into East Jerusalem. I have to find Sami Khalidi. He is our only chance, cease-fire or not." She told them about Sami's friendship with King Abdullah and with Ephraim.

"He may turn you away, Hannah. The Arabs that used to be our friends . . ."

"We'll see. For now, get us to Jerusalem," Hannah said.

Wally and David joined them as Zohar glanced at her watch. "We have a room for each of you at the Hotel Hayarkon. If we go tonight, you must sleep and prepare for the journey. While you rest, I will make arrangements. We will eat at eight this evening, then go to the staging area near Hulda, and from there to Jerusalem."

Hannah put a protective arm around David, excitement and dread both struggling for her attention. One thing was sure, David would ask to go with them, but this time she would not give in. David would stay in Tel Aviv.

CHAPTER 30

Lenta awoke Mary with a quiet knock. From her sweetness, it was obvious Lenta and Uri had worked things out. As her way of apologizing, Lenta invited Mary for breakfast and left her a heavy terry-cloth robe, towel, and, of all the wonderful things, some bath soap.

"Take as long as you like bathing," she said. "The water is hot this morning, and after your journey, a hot bath will do you wonders."

After Lenta closed the door, Mary retrieved the second dress from her wet bag and hung it up to dry, then took a long bath before putting on the robe and going downstairs to the smell of coffee and hot bread. The food tasted wonderful, and Lenta was more than willing to answer all of Mary's questions.

Things were going badly for the Jews but worse for the Arabs, though they refused to admit it and kept on fighting.

"We know they are as desperate for ammunition as we are, but they are afraid their people will kill them if they stop. Only Abdullah is ready for a cease-fire, and he cannot do it alone, so we wait. A new deadline has been proposed by the United Nations for two days from now. There is considerable hope in Tel Aviv that it will be honored this time. If not, we could lose Jerusalem. The key is to get them food right away," Lenta told her. "They are going to do that tonight and every night if need be. I am sorry, darling, but we really must show your people that we can keep Jerusalem running. Only then will they agree to a cease-fire. Everyone is better off that way. So much needless dying, don't you think?"

Mary asked about the Arabs and Haj Amin and was told the latest news. The Arabs were determined to stick it out and, as Mary suspected, were already laying claim to parts of Palestine they controlled. Even the United Nations would not listen to any Palestinian Arab delegation with much sincerity.

"They dislike your Haj Amin intensely, and to listen to him or those he controls would only cause them grief. So they don't listen." She gave Mary a pitied look. "I am afraid the country the United Nations intended for you is going to end up in the hands of those awful Arab countries."

Tired of the same old, horrible news, Mary asked if a person could get to the Continent or possibly to the United States. Lenta went to the window and pulled the curtain aside.

"Do you see that ship? It is French—a merchant ship with room for sixty passengers. It leaves tomorrow but every space is taken." She shrugged. "Other ships will come. Other Jews will take passage. It is dangerous, and many are afraid. Even I am afraid, but I do not have any place to go, nor does Uri. If we had such a place, more of our people might be tempted, but for most of us, Israel is all we have. So we stay and fight. We don't have a choice."

Mary supposed that was one of the differences in the flood of Arab refugees and the trickle of Jewish ones. They visited about other things, then Lenta went to work at a plant she said manufactured bullets. Going back to her room, Mary dressed and brushed her hair before sitting in front of the window to read and ponder what she should do. Without Aaron, she no longer wished to stay in Palestine. She was afraid without him, for both her and their child, but where should she go? She had always thought that if this happened, she would go to the States and find Ephraim and Hannah Daniels, but the more she thought of it, the more problems she saw. Booking passage, getting permits to enter the States, then finding the Danielses once she was there seemed nearly impossible. She knew of Idaho but could not remember the city where Ephraim's parents lived. How big was this place? To how many cities would she have to go to find them? It was overwhelming.

There was Paris. There were other Arabs there—other Jews as well—but in which community would their child fit best? Could he fit in either, especially now?

Pulling out the Book of Mormon, she tried to read and clear her mind. It took nearly an hour just to concentrate well enough to get something out of the pages, but there seemed to be no messages for her, no inspiration. Bowing, she prayed for guidance, then laid her head against the back of the chair, confused and unsure. Finally she decided to get some fresh air with a walk on the beach. Maybe this would help clear her mind and give her better focus.

Leaving the room a little after three in the afternoon, Mary walked to the docks where ships were unloading military equipment, crates, lumber, and a hundred other items. There were people everywhere, a hive of bees buzzing about in a chaotic rhythm that resounded with determination and spirit. The Jews were quickly making up for lost time.

Walking along the beach, she found a place to sit away from the chaos of the city and port and watched the sun slowly move earthward toward the blue waters of the Mediterranean. No fresh ideas came to her, and she finally got to her feet and walked back toward Lenta's boarding house. It was nearly sundown when she came to a street that ran east toward the city's center and decided to turn into its dusty pavement. It was lined with a variety of shops, houses, and restaurants clamoring for people needing an evening meal, many of whom wore uniforms and spoke languages nearly as plentiful as the people. She heard talk of recent battles and what they meant, what probably lay ahead, both for the Haganah and for them as individuals, and always a cursing for intransigent Arab leaders who were pulling everyone into a quagmire no one would be able to rescue them from. Alcohol was everywhere, and the air was filled with cigarette smoke and the dust created by hundreds of feet and dozens of vehicles whose horns never ceased to honk. It was both exciting and depressing for Mary, her eyes jumping from one scene to the next while her heart realized that many of these men would die tonight. Or tomorrow. Or the next day, or the next, and that was why they celebrated now. The joy of the fearful.

She turned into a narrow side street to escape the clamor. There were fewer people here and no cars, trucks, or even bicycles. People visited quietly while sitting at tables eating their supper. She saw an empty table and decided to get something to eat. A waiter came a moment after she had sat down, and she asked for bread, lamb, and a salad. The last two were things she hadn't seen for some time and wondered if they would be available, but the waiter took her order without comment and asked if she would like something to drink.

"Possibly you have some lemonade," she said.

"I will bring it immediately." He smiled.

There was something odd here. Food was plentiful and was getting more so in Haifa. But it was not so in Jerusalem, or Nazareth, or a dozen other cities and hundreds of villages and kibbutzim only a few miles away. Here, people laughed and joked while others were fighting and dying and had nothing at all to celebrate unless they had just found a morsel of food or a taste of meat. It made her feel thankful and guilty at the same time.

The waiter returned with her glass of lemonade, a bit flushed in his face. "Excuse me, but that man over there wishes you to join him."

Mary, unsure if she heard him correctly, asked him to repeat his words, then blushed while automatically glancing toward the man sitting at a table near the wall. "Tell him that is very kind, but I am a happily married woman, and we are expecting our first child."

The waiter bowed slightly, an apologetic look on his face. Walking through the tables, he conveyed the message to the suitor, who tipped his glass in her direction in understanding. Mary looked away, her face and neck hot. She took a healthy drink of the lemonade while concentrating on a door across the street. Was this what it would be like with Aaron gone? The thought was appalling and nearly brought her to tears. Thankfully her food came quickly and she forced herself to eat, though her appetite had seemed to flee.

After she finished, the waiter returned for payment.

"What do you hear of East Jerusalem?" she asked.

"Forty thousand Arabs have left. The Jordanians control it all and will probably keep it if we ever reach a peace agreement," he responded.

She nodded, and he left with the money she had counted out. She nibbled at what remained of her food, then drank the last drops of her lemonade.

"Hello, beautiful," a man said, resting his hands on her table. He was American and a bit tipsy. "How about some company?" He was about to sit down when she shoved the single remaining chair out from under him with her foot. Already on his way down, he fell clear to the concrete in a most unmanly fashion. Two of his friends gathered him up and carried him away, while a third put the chair back in place and gave her his apologies. She nodded acceptance, waited a moment, and then hurried out, mortified and despondent at the same time. Why had she come here, especially alone? She cursed her stupidity even as she noticed a shop across the street displaying head scarves. Dodging traffic and people, she hurriedly crossed and purchased the first one on the counter. Stepping outside the store, she wrapped the scarf around her head and face and hurried toward the beach and Lenta's place.

Occupied with her own heavy thoughts and with the sound of traffic and people all around, she didn't hear the voice that yelled her name, nor did she see the boy try to reach her as she turned the corner and rushed north toward the refuge of the small room Uri had loaned her.

* * *

David pushed his way through the crowd, looking in every direction. Though he had lost sight of her for only seconds, she had disappeared. He checked the shops, then hurried to the corner and peered down the street to the north. The docks were busy, the street filled with trucks and men loading and unloading them. He looked at each person, looked for the headscarf, but did not see her. Had it been Mary?

Climbing onto the hood of a beat-up jeep to get a better view, David waited and watched another five minutes. Finally accepting that whoever it was had disappeared, he jumped off the jeep to retrace his footsteps back to the shop where he had been watching an artisan hand sew Hebrew words along the borders of a prayer shawl.

David was not happy with being left behind by the others and had snuck away from the hotel to wander the streets and satisfy his curiosity. With no one assigned to watch him but a friend of Wally's who had been called away on a mission and had turned David's care over to the desk clerk, who in turn had forgotten all about him, it had been easy.

Wandering through the streets had been exciting for David, the sights, sounds, and conversations giving him a different perspective of the war. There was a rumor that the cease-fire declared for tomorrow morning really might hold, the only catch being Jerusalem, where the Legion was so near to pushing past Jewish lines that they might delay just for that purpose.

David glanced over his shoulder again, the woman still on his mind. He had seen her reflection in the glass of the window and had immediately turned to get a better look, but she had already disappeared in the crush of people.

Was it Mary? Perhaps his mind was just playing tricks on him. Since finding out Aaron was alive, he hadn't stopped thinking about both of them. He had probably just made a mistake.

He wandered along the street in the direction of the Hayarkon Hotel. The pilots would be coming back soon, and he loved to sit nearby and hear their stories, though the language was pretty rough and the smoke thick enough to blind a person. The language had gotten a little better since Wally saw David listening and pointed it out to his friends, but it wouldn't have mattered. Planes and thoughts of someday flying excited David, and if it meant hanging from the ceiling to hear about such things, he would gladly find a way.

He saw the hotel but couldn't get his legs to carry him across the street. He stood there for a moment, the thought of the woman returning. His feet felt like concrete. Finally he pushed it aside again, but instead of going back to the hotel, he turned left into a narrow street of artisan shops, mostly those who worked with jewelry and diamonds. He looked through several store windows but kept moving, a nervousness in his gut. He turned left again and just wandered here and there, back and forth across the next street, looking into windows without really seeing anything until he found himself staring up at the French ship sitting at the far end on the north side of the dock. The woman could have been a passenger.

He stopped. No. This was foolishness. Hannah had written to Mary and told her that Aaron was dead. She wouldn't come to Tel Aviv just to catch a ship. She would catch one in Beirut.

But he couldn't turn around, the large steel hull and majestic superstructure drawing him through the bustle of people and trucks to where he could look directly up at its main deck and loading plank.

He looked along the railing to see a number of individuals casually watching the organized chaos below them. None were women. Could she be inside, below deck, ready to leave?

He noticed several finely dressed people scrambling around workers, equipment, ropes, and general untidiness to reach a seaman dressed in a white uniform at the foot of the loading plank. He greeted them, checked a list he had attached to a clipboard, then called to sailors to take their luggage and help them aboard. When the man was between people, David interrupted him to ask about Mary.

"What is her full name?" the seaman asked.

"Mary Aref, I mean Mary Schwartz." He described her. The seaman checked his roster then shook his head, stating he would remember such a woman.

David nodded his thanks, feeling foolish. Shoving his hands into his pockets, he returned the way he had come without really noticing much of what was going on around him.

"Hey, kid, watch where you're going," a workman said.

"Sorry," David replied.

"You shouldn't be out here," said another firmly. "Go on now, get to the street and out of the way before you get hurt."

David nodded and hurried on his way, dodging left and right to keep from being a nuisance. He had to duck under a long, thin crate carried between two workmen, and as he did, he nearly tripped but caught himself. He was then thumped from behind by another workman and knocked over the edge and into the water. He spluttered back to the surface to look up at a dozen grinning faces all having a good laugh at his expense.

"Eh, lad," one said. "Needing a bath, are we?" He tossed a long rope. "Grab hold and we'll hoist you up."

David did as he was told and soon found himself being hoisted the twenty feet to the top, water running off his wet clothes.

"Do you have a place close by?" the worker asked.

"The Hayarkon," David answered. He wasn't really cold and rather refreshed and said so.

The workman slapped him on the back and pushed him slightly toward the street. "Be off with you then. Cool air will come with sundown."

David sloshed to the street where he sat down and took off his shoes, pouring out the water. Removing his socks, he wrung them out before shoving them inside his shoes. He was about to get up when he noticed a door fly open and a woman run toward him.

"David!"

A big grin spread across his face as he realized it was Mary. Running at him with her arms open, she wrapped them around him and picked him up, circling round and round. His face turned a bright red with joy as he held her tight, then with embarrassment as he realized people were watching, smiles of curiosity on every face.

Putting him down, she stood back. "It is you. I do not believe it! And you are very wet." She laughed. "I saw you fall into the water but didn't recognize you until you sat down here." She hugged him again. "I cannot believe it!"

"I saw you come out of a shop, but I couldn't find you and was about to give up—"

She gave him another hug. "Oh, I'm so glad you didn't. But . . . but what are you doing here? I thought Hannah and Ephraim . . ."

He grinned from ear to ear. "Mum and I came back. We've come to get Aaron." He threw his arms around her waist. "And now we can get you too."

Mary felt weak in the knees and had to sit down on the post David had been sitting on. "What?" she asked softly.

David took her hand with one of his. "Naomi and Abraham found out he survived, Mary. Our Aaron is alive."

Mary felt her head swim, her vision blur, and her head throb. Completely breathless, she teetered left, and David had to steady her. No, she hadn't heard him right. It couldn't be! Uri . . . Uri had told her . . . The blackness burst into her head, and she fell forward onto David's shoulder in a dead faint.

Young but strong, David steadied her while crying for a hand. A woman pushed through the crowd and helped him, then ordered a brawny-looking seaman standing in the circle of curious onlookers to pick her up and follow.

David held him back, and Lenta gently took his arm. "I am Lenta. Mary lives at my house across the street. Don't you think we should get her inside?"

David nodded, and the seaman hoisted Mary into his arms and carried her across the street, David hanging tightly to one hand. He did not intend to let her out of his sight again.

SEE CHAPTER NOTES

CHAPTER 31

Mary awoke with a cold cloth on her forehead and only dim light from the window outlining the image of someone standing over her. She sat bolt upright, her hand ripping the cloth away.

"David!"

Two hands embraced her shoulders to calm her. "He is here," Lenta said.

David stepped forward, and Mary took his hands and held them tightly. "I was afraid you were nothing but a dream." She smiled.

David grinned. "You are beautiful as ever."

"Hannah. Where is she, and what did you mean that Aaron was found?"

"She is going to Jerusalem," he answered. He told Mary what had happened, then about Aaron. "He is not well, Mary. Mum said he was hurt bad, but they are trying to get him out of the prison in Transjordan. She had to go to Jerusalem to try and see Sami Khalidi in East Jerusalem and . . ."

"Sami! But I know Sami. He is a dear friend of my father! Yes! He would be the right one!" Mary got to her feet and quickly put on her shoes. "I must go to Jerusalem as well."

"I'm going with you," David said.

Mary turned to him. "Your mum would not let you go. I can't either. Stay here with Lenta. She will take care of you or see that you get back to your hotel."

"No," he said. "I won't let you out of my sight ever again! I go, or I will not tell you where they are and how they will get to Jerusalem. You will never find them without me." His face was firm as granite, his mind made up. Mary didn't know what to do.

"Uri. I will find him. He will protect you both," Lenta said.

"There is no time. Mum and the others leave very soon," David said.

"They go with those who resupply the city," Mary said.

David turned pale, an angry look in his eyes.

She took hold of his arms. "David, you can come with me to the staging area. We will find Hannah, but she is your mother now, and she must decide, okay?"

David nodded lightly.

"If we can't find her, you must come back with Lenta."

He stiffened.

"David, Aaron would never forgive me if I endangered you. Do you understand? You must stay with Lenta," she said firmly.

"He would never forgive me if I let something happen to you, if we lost you again."

His concern touched her heart, and she embraced him again. "Come on, let's find Hannah. After that, we'll decide." She looked at Lenta. "How far is it to the staging area?"

"Miles, but we'll find a way. Let me get a shawl while you pack. We'll have to stop and get the boy's things as well."

Mary was already off the bed and gathering her few pieces of clothing, her papers, and her books, her head swimming with a sudden overwhelming fear she might lose Aaron again. How sick was he? How would they treat him in such a place? Would they ever free him? So many questions, so many fears.

They met Lenta at the bottom of the stairs and left the building. At the Hayarkon, Mary found the desk clerk ready to give David a thrashing, but she quickly resolved the problem, and they went upstairs to his room. He grabbed dry clothes and quickly changed in the bathroom, grabbed a jacket and a small sack of apples, and they were on their way again. When in the street, they headed east, then north, finally catching the main road to Jerusalem as darkness replaced daylight.

Lenta said the staging area was at Kfar Bilu, an old British Army camp five miles' distance from Tel Aviv. They must find a ride. Lenta saw a truck rumbling toward them and walked to the middle of the road, extending her arms, forcing it to stop.

"Get off the road," the driver hollered angrily.

"Just as soon as you say you will give us a ride to Kfar Bilu," Lenta yelled back. "We wish to help haul food to Jerusalem."

"It is work for men, not women and boys," he said, jamming the vehicle in gear.

Lenta walked directly toward the truck, then to his side. There was no door and she stepped onto the sideboard and grabbed him by his shirt. "You will take us, or I will beat the bloody guts out of you," she said.

"All right, all right," he whined.

Mary and David were already sliding into the passenger seat, and they were on their way.

The truck's heavy load took a toll on its speed, and they crawled into the staging area at nearly eleven. By the light of a half-moon, the camp seemed surreal as hundreds of men and women moved about with hardly a sound. Some were lined up, large sacks hanging from some sort of rack strapped to their backs, while others were already reboarding buses taking them into the hills. Dozens of women were at tables where lanterns cast an eerie light over sacks of rice, flour, sugar, chocolate, and other items. They filled small, cloth sacks full of each, sealed them, and shoved them into larger bags that were then attached to more racks and finally over the men's backs.

"So many," David said. "How can we find Mum in all this?"

Mary thanked the driver and got out of the truck with David. Lenta thanked him more personally by planting a heavy kiss on his lips before joining them. He drove to an unloading area with a smile on his face while his three passengers began moving through the crowd, searching and calling for Hannah. In the dim light, Mary thought she saw Hannah a dozen times, only to be disappointed when she got close enough to see more than blurred shapes. They searched every section, building, nook, and cranny of the camp but found no Hannah.

"They were as eager as you to get to the city. They must have gone with the first group," Lenta said.

"Then that is where I go," Mary said. She thanked Lenta for her help. "Tell Uri about Aaron. He will want to know."

Lenta nodded. "The night it happened, he cried like a baby and has not gotten over it since. Please, bring your man back. Only seeing him with his own eyes will give Uri peace again." Mary nodded, then turned to David. She wanted to tell him he had to go back, but the words would not come. Finally giving in to her heart, she told him to stay close, kissed Lenta on the cheek, and thanked her one more time before she and David got in a short line where Mary picked up a rack, then went to have it loaded, David at her side.

"You are a woman. You cannot do this, neither can the boy," said a man strapping on the sacks. "It is very hard, very dangerous."

"We're going. You can either strap on a load to take advantage of a strong back, or we will walk it on our own. But we intend to be in Jerusalem tonight."

The man frowned, then sighed. "You are fools." He lifted the sack, set it on the rack, and tied it down. Mary felt the load and widened her stance to carry it. It would not be easy, but it could be done. "I will not give the boy such a load. He can help you and others."

David shook his head. "I will take something."

The man reached under some bags next to him and retrieved a canvas container with "U.S. Army" written on it. It had a heavy strap for carrying. "Bullets. They are needed as much as food."

David flung it over his shoulder, then helped Mary adjust her load more equally, only to remove the whole thing when they boarded the bus. A moment later, they were on their way to the mountains.

Lenta watched the bus pull away while praying for them, the sound of distant artillery thumping away at the night. Flashes of light skipped across the hills between her and Jerusalem, a sign that the city still suffered at the hands of the Arabs. She wrapped her shawl tighter around her shoulders. One thing was sure—it was not a good night for travel to the Holy City. Only God could help them now.

* * *

The ride was relatively quiet, all of them nervous about what lay ahead. Most of those onboard were older men dressed in the short sleeves of a humid Tel Aviv summer. Called away from their work, home, or synagogue to make this march, they made it possible for younger men to get on with the fighting. Mary thought of the men where she had eaten. Such men should be on this journey, drunk or not.

She figured she had seen more of the war in the last week than anyone aboard had since November, but she also admired their willingness to take on this task though they were frightened. Each pack carried into Jerusalem would keep a hundred people alive one more day.

The bus went through Hulda, then east toward Latrun, the deserted British camp the Arabs still held and used to keep the Jerusalem/Tel Aviv Road closed. Mary knew that nearby was Kastel, where Aaron had fought and was supposed to have died. She rubbed the goose bumps on her arms and bowed her head, thanking God for giving them one more chance. Then she prayed even harder that this new hope would not disappear as quickly as it had come.

The bus turned east along a narrow, winding dirt road she knew went to Arab villages along the rim of the hills. The windows were open, and the cool mountain breezes scented with lavender brushed through her hair. She relaxed a little as the bus jerked and bumped over the rough road. She had been so hurried to find Hannah that she hadn't had much time to think, and now that she could, it made her a little uneasy, especially for David. He was just a boy, and though strong and very determined, these traits would not keep an Arab bullet from putting an end to his short life. As if to accentuate the point, an explosion ripped into the side of the hill fifty feet to their left, then another and another.

"Mortar attack," someone yelled. Everyone dropped to the floor next to and on top of one another, and Mary and David were no exception. She heard rock projectiles hit against the bus and felt the sharp sting of glass when one broke the window above them. She pulled David as close as she could to protect him while feeling terrified for the both of them.

Then they dropped into a valley, and the shelling stopped. Slowly everyone got to their feet. The distinct smells of sweat and urine permeated the close confines of the bus, and Mary was very grateful when they pulled into a battered village where other buses were unloading or patiently waiting the return of men already on their way up the mountain.

"The Haganah controls the ground on both sides of the road, but do not wander," the bus driver said. "Snipers watch and wait for just such lunacy." He got out and everyone picked up their racks and followed.

A man appeared out of the darkness and gave them instructions to strap on their racks and then get into a single line.

"Grab hold of the shirttail of the person in front of you so you don't wander off the trail. It is difficult enough where we have begun work. You will only make things harder for yourselves if you do not stay in line." He saw Mary, her head scarf now in place, and hesitated, then spoke. "If you fall behind, we will leave you."

She nodded, beads of sweat already breaking out on her forehead, even though the mountain air was quite cool.

"The same for you, boy. Do you understand?"

"Yes, sir. We will make it."

The man went to the front and led out. Their group fell silent as they got in line behind one another. In the dim light of the half-moon, Mary could see many more men forming a snake-like procession up the mountain. There were hundreds.

They climbed, their feet slipping again and again on the soft soil and rocks of the steep hill, making Mary's muscles burn. After the first half hour, sweat soaked her hair and dress, and she grunted, panted, and gritted her teeth against the desire to stop.

She tried to forget the pain but couldn't, tried to ignore it but it just got worse. Finally she closed her eyes, pictured Aaron—his face, his smile, his arms around her—and kept moving.

They finally rested at a spot where bulldozers and hundreds more men pushed and shoveled away the mountain in their attempt to make a switchback that climbed the heights she and the others were struggling to conquer. Boulders the size of large buildings were being pushed to the side, dirt leveled, shoved, and packed into place a few feet at a time, but slowly the mountain was being made into a road.

They started again, passing men laying pipeline. She knew that Jerusalem's water supply lay in Arab-held territory. This was the Jewish answer—pipe it from Tel Aviv. For the first time, she realized the magnitude of the undertaking and the determination that lay behind it. The Burma Road would change the direction of the war. How could the Arabs even think to conquer such a people?

Another half hour and the path turned downward, the muffled sound of machinery disappearing as they breached what seemed to be the top of the mountain. For the smallest of seconds, she let herself entertain the thought that it was over, but then she looked up and saw the nearly vertical precipice in front of them. The worst was just ahead. Her body nearly gave out at the thought.

"Remove your packs, take a rest, then we go."

Mary fell to her knees, gasping for air. She rubbed her dry mouth with the back of her hand and slowly undid the scarf and let it hang loosely around her neck so that the breeze could cool her overheated neck and face. Too weak to even lift her chin from her chest, she wondered if she could go on, then realized someone was lifting her face, putting something against her lips. She felt tepid water wet her lips and chin and reactively grabbed the cup and was about to drink it all when she realized it was David giving her the water.

She forced herself to take only a little and extended it him.

"All of it. There is more," David said. It was a lie. Seeing Mary's condition, a man had given him his last half cup. There was no more. David licked his lips, aching for a drink of his own but knowing Mary needed it more. The load each carried had already driven half a dozen men to a dead stop and more would follow.

"I will carry it now," he said.

She shook her head adamantly. "No, I can do it," she said hoarsely.

David was already getting into the straps. "For another mile, you will carry the ammunition. Then we will see."

Mary nodded and picked up the ammo pack.

"Time to go," said their leader. They all pushed themselves to their feet and fell back into line. David grimaced against the load, felt his knees buckle a bit but stiffened them. One foot, then the other, he told himself. One foot and then the other.

They climbed. This time it was much steeper and more dangerous. After only a hundred yards, David understood why Mary was so tired. His lungs and legs ached, and sweat poured from him in rivulets. Then a man just above them stumbled, sending rocks and dirt flying into them. He gritted his teeth and held on while Mary braced the backpack from behind as best as she could.

They moved again. Another hundred feet, inch by horrible inch. Then a man fell, tumbled past them and rolled clear to the ravine, no one able to muster the strength to stop him. Two men slipped to one side, too tired, too beaten to go on. Mary helped one man remove his rack, then began strapping it on her back.

"Can you handle that one clear to the top?" Mary asked.

He nodded that he could. "But you are already exhausted," he said softly.

"A hundred people will eat tomorrow if we get it there, David. A hundred."

David only nodded, then started off again, struggling upward. Stronger men passed them, weaker ones stepped aside and let them by. Neither of them thought it could get any steeper, but it did, and each was forced to get foot and finger holds on rocks to inch their way upward. *How could they ever make a road through this?* Mary thought.

She felt her toehold slip and grabbed for a root to save her. Then there was gunfire, the pinging of bullets off of rocks. The Arabs had found them. She felt something hit her in the side, felt her strength go, and knew she had been hit. "Oh, Aaron," she moaned. Then the strength went out of her grip and she fell backward, tumbling down the hill. Pummeled by the rocks until she came to a stop fifty feet below, she stared up at the stars, her body numb, her eyes blinking as they began to blur. She heard voices shouting her name, familiar though muffled voices that she could neither answer nor recognize. She just lay there, feeling a cold chill creep up her legs. Shadows flitted about above her, and she knew she was being put on a stretcher. But she felt so far away from it all. Then a warm hand gripped hers and a face came into view.

"Mary," the voice said.

Mary smiled. "David."

"Don't leave me, Mary. Don't . . ."

His voice trailed off, then went away entirely. She didn't want to leave, but the air smelled so fresh and clean and the stars looked extra bright as they gathered into one great light that made her feel warm all over. It seemed like someone was there, someone reaching out to her, urging her to come. It was such a good feeling, such a feeling of love and peace, and she extended her hand to take his. Then there was nothing.

CHAPTER 32

Hannah, Zohar, David, and Wally were greeted at the door of the hospital at Bevingrad by Doctor Messerman, Mithra, and Hilda. Hannah hugged each of them, then turned to the doctor. "Is he ready?" she asked.

The doctor nodded, "Yes, and surprisingly eager, but he still hasn't committed. He must see—"

"Yes, I know." She, Zohar, David, and Wally sat down on the hard, wood bench near the door, unperturbed by the wait. After all, they had worked hard and waited many days for this moment. A few more minutes would not be difficult.

Mithra leaned forward from her own bench and took Hannah's hand. "It is nearly over, dear one," Mithra said. "Did you receive the wire from Ephraim's mother?"

"Yes, Ephraim is fine. The doctors say the news has improved his morale one hundred percent." Hannah squeezed her friend's hand. They had spent most nights together since Hannah's return to Jerusalem, Mithra and Hilda sharing Hilda's small apartment with her and David while they made the arrangements.

Though a shock to many, including their small group, the cease-fire had started as arranged by Bernadotte, the Arabs finally seeing they needed time. Its coming had opened the doors necessary for Hannah to make contact with Sami Khalidi, who drove to Amman to meet with King Abdullah and make their plea. Sami's influence had been critical, but the king had only agreed to meet with them, if they could get to him. A place and time had been arranged, and Sami had returned with the good news.

Two nights later Abraham, Hannah, Wally, Joseph, and Naomi had flown into Negba where they had a reunion with Rachel before driving the backroads of the desert to the spring of Ein Gedi. Climbing down the narrow trail to the ancient spring where David hid from Saul, they waited for nightfall before meeting camel drivers who took them to the ancient ruins of Qumran where they waited for long hours, wondering if the king would show.

After four hours of excruciating doubt, the cars of Abdullah appeared, Sami Khalidi with him. After the usual niceties and presentation of a gift to the king, as was Arab custom when one sought a favor from such a man, they discussed their wishes. After hearing them and knowing he would be treated well in the Arab world for his part, he agreed. Hannah had nearly knocked him over with a sudden hug, which made the short, squat king grin from ear to ear.

"I will miss you, dear friend," Hannah said to Mithra.

"And I, you," Mithra patted her hand.

Mithra, strong Mithra. Always there when needed, always wise, and always determined to think only the best.

Hannah put her arm around David. It had been a rough time for him. After Mary had been shot, then brought to Jerusalem on a stretcher, he had been alone and unsure of what to do. Hannah had cut her hand in their climb and had ignored the wound, wrapping it in bandages, but it had begun to bleed worse, and Zohar had insisted she get some stitches. It was a shock to walk into the field hospital and find David huddled on the floor, tears of fright and concern washing dirt from his cheeks. Falling into Hannah's arms, he had poured out his story, then led them to where Mary was lying. Just out of surgery, she was pale but out of danger. It had been a night of mixed emotions for all of them.

The door to the small hospital opened, and Mary, still in a wheelchair, appeared, Abraham pushing her through while Naomi held the door. Though pale and weak, there was a glow of happy expectation radiating from her face, and she extended her hand to Hannah as she came close.

"Are you up to this?" Hannah asked with genuine concern.

Mary nodded with a smile. "It would take much more than a little bullet and a bout with infection to keep me away." She glanced at the door. "Is Rhoui in there?"

Hannah nodded. "Waiting. Do you want anyone with you?"

"No, thank you. I should do this alone," Mary said.

Naomi opened the door, and Abraham pushed the wheelchair inside, then left Mary facing Rhoui where he sat on the edge of the bed, his lower face still heavily wrapped in bandages, his eyes on her. She had been told about his injuries and knew he still could not speak, though his eyesight was quickly returning to normal. She saw the old, welcoming glint in them and gave him a pleasant smile in return.

"Hello, Rhoui."

He nodded a response, then picked up a pad and pen. *It is good to see you, but you look very pale.*

"I am all right, especially today. And you?" she responded.

He quickly wrote more. *I am very good today as well.*

She knew he was lying. Doctor Messerman had come to her room that morning to prepare her for her visit. Rhoui's jaw had an abscess infection, and it was causing him a good deal of pain and could be very bad for him.

"I know you are in pain without the morphine. I am grateful you are willing to suffer this way so that Aaron and I—"

He put up a hand to stop her, then quickly wrote. *No, no. It is I who am grateful.* He lifted his pencil a moment before writing again. *For weeks I have hated myself for what I did to you and Izaat. My mind, my heart, rot inside me, and until now,* he hesitated, *I did not wish to live. Now maybe something good can come from my miserable life.*

She saw the pain in his face, saw it in the writing, and knew it was not from his wound.

Wheeling her chair close to him, she took his hand and looked into his eyes. "I love you, Rhoui. No matter what this horrible war has done to us, I still love you. I will always love you."

Tears sprang to his eyes, and he got to his knees before her, holding her hands tightly. She stroked his head, then lay it in her lap, tears dropping off her cheeks onto his bandages, the grief for the wounds to his heart too much for her. After long moments, he leaned away and wiped his eyes, then sat on the bed again and took his pad and pen in hand.

Have you heard from Margaretha and the children?

His wife and family. "Yes, I saw them in Beirut. They are well. Her father is taking good care of them. They wait for you, Rhoui. Do you hear me? They want you to come when you can."

His eyes filled with sadness, his hand going to his jaw, then to his pen. He had removed the bandages yesterday and looked at his grotesque face. He was nothing more than a monster in appearance. *They will never see me like this. Never.*

She reached up and touched his face gently. "Don't you understand that they love you? Can't you see that this will not make any difference?"

He pushed her away gently, shaking his head adamantly before quickly writing, *It is time to go.*

Mary pulled some papers from her dress pocket and handed them to him. "Hannah had these made at my request. They are legal and binding. The first gives Father's house to you and Margaretha. The second gives you complete access to your share of the money Father left us. It is in the bank in Beirut, but you can have it sent here by using these papers. I sent similar papers to Izaat's family."

He stared at them, his eyes showing confusion, then understanding. This was her gift to him, but he could not take it. He scanned the papers, found the blanks he was looking for and put in the proper names and finally his signature on them before handing them back to her. She saw that he had signed everything over to Margaretha.

"But . . ."

He pressed his fingers against her lips, then wrote. *It is my wish, just in case something happens. Do it for me?*

She nodded, refolded the papers, and put them in her pocket as Rhoui got to his feet. Pulling a black-and-white-checked *kaffiyeh* from where it was hanging on a hook, he put it on and covered the lower portion of his face and bandages before getting behind the wheelchair and pushing it to the door, knocking on it.

Hannah opened the door, and Rhoui pushed Mary toward the exit. Everyone else stood and followed. When in the street, Abraham picked Mary up from the chair and put her in the backseat of the car while the others loaded into different vehicles. Rhoui slid in beside Mary while Hannah went around the car and got in beside her as well. Abraham drove and Naomi rode in the front with him, David between them.

Mary put her arm through Rhoui's, and they both watched out the window at the bustling city, its supplies replenished and its people filled with renewed hope.

For Mary it was good to be here again, and yet there was so much that had changed. It no longer felt like her home, like Jerusalem. It was now a divided city with hate on both sides of a barbed-wire partition that now separated them into warring nations. She noted that many of the streets had been cleared of debris, though everyone was aware that the truce was going nowhere toward peace and could end any moment. As stark evidence that such was the case, the long barrels of the Legion's artillery stood on the Mount of Olives, vivid against the blue skyline, while newly placed Jewish artillery jutted up along the line of hills to the west. If she and Aaron stayed in Israel, they would not live in Jerusalem.

The cavalcade reached Mandelbaum House in ten minutes. Abraham parked in the middle of the narrow, beat-up road, then got out and checked with the military officials who had agreed to help.

Mary fidgeted, nervous and excited and a bit dizzy all at once. Though it had been more than a month since he last saw Aaron, Abraham had told her early in her recovery about her husband's condition. Had he worsened? Would he even recognize her? What if coming home was traumatic? What if it sent him deeper into this . . . this state of shock or repression or whatever it was? She worried and feared for him, and she prayed every night and every morning that she would have the strength to help him.

An ambulance pulled up on the other side of the no-man's-land that now existed between East and West Jerusalem. A man got out of the front seat and delivered some papers to a Jordanian soldier. Abraham came to the window, and Mary rolled it down.

"Time to go," he said, trying to control his smile. It had been hard to get to this point, but it had finally come, and his old friend was about to come home.

As Hannah, David, and Naomi got out of the car, Mary turned to Rhoui. "Are you ready?" She smiled, searching his eyes.

He nodded. *Leave this land, Mary. Leave this hate and bloodshed and never come back. Find a place to be happy.*

She hugged him tightly, then slid to the edge of the seat, where Abraham put her in the wheelchair. With Hannah and David at their side, Rhoui pushed Mary over the rough dirt and cobblestone to where soldiers were opening the heavy gates of the Jewish barrier.

Rhoui glanced over his shoulder at Dr. Messerman and the others, giving the doctor a slight nod of thanks before pushing

Mary's chair through the open gate. Mary put up a hand and touched his.

"Stop," she said. "Please, I must get to my feet."

"Are you sure?" Naomi said.

Mary nodded. "Yes, yes, I am fine. I will not have him see me like this."

Rhoui and Abraham helped her stand, then each kept a strong arm under hers while David and Naomi held tightly to Hannah's hands, and they all continued their walk.

Weak but determined, Mary hung tightly to both men, her eyes riveted on the other gate. She saw three men come around the back of the ambulance and recognized Aaron immediately as the one in the middle. He was walking. She wanted to run to him but knew she couldn't, electing instead to simply push herself a little faster.

"There he is, Mum," David said. He also wanted to bolt, but Hannah held him back. There were soldiers along the fence, all armed, all watching them as they crossed the divide between fences of barbed wire. One wrong move might bring a tragedy none of them could bear.

As both sides drew closer to the middle, Abraham could see that his friend held his head straight, and his eyes did not wander from side to side as they had just a month earlier. His heart pumped as he realized what a difference that month had made. "He looks much better than before," he said to Mary.

"He looks wonderful," Mary responded. With only a dozen steps left between them, she released her hold on Rhoui and walked quickly to Aaron, wrapping her arms around his waist. Aaron stumbled back, and his Arab escorts had to keep him from falling.

"He's still not completely well. His mind is slow to understand. Give him a minute. Talk to him," one of the Arabs said.

Mary looked up at Aaron's face. He seemed frightened, unsure. His head bobbed slightly, and his eyes filled with fear.

"Aaron," she whispered, firmly grabbing both sides of his face with her hands and making him look at her. "Darling, it's me, Mary. I love you. Can you hear me? I love you!"

Aaron's eyes focused, the fear turning to recognition as he searched Mary's concerned face. She kissed him lightly, calming him, rubbing her hands softly against his cheeks. "It's me." She took his arm and turned toward Hannah. "And here are Hannah and David, come to take us both home."

"M . . . Mary?" Tears trickled from the corners of his eyes, and Mary threw her arms around him again. This time he lifted his own and placed them around her in a tender embrace while Hannah and David joined them both, tears running down their faces.

Rhoui's eyes smiled, then filled with tears. He nodded his satisfaction as his sister wept with joy, then began the short walk to his homeland.

"Rhoui," Mary said, wiping her eyes while looking at her brother.

He turned back.

Ignoring her pain, Mary caught up to him and removed her Book of Mormon. "Go with God, Rhoui. There is peace in these pages. I hope you will find it."

He nodded, taking the book. She hugged him and kissed both cheeks, then let him go, turning back to take Aaron's hand as they started back to West Jerusalem. She cried, then closed her eyes and thanked God for keeping them both alive and bringing them together again.

Aaron put his arm around her shoulder and pulled her close. "Ephraim. I must . . . see Ephraim."

After thanking Sami Khalidi with a tearful hug, Hannah caught up and put an arm around Aaron's waist. "You will see him soon, Aaron. Very soon."

"You have worked miracles, Doctor," Abraham said, extending a hand of gratitude.

The doctor shook it while wiping away a tear. "After you spent that night with him, he changed. He was suddenly eating anything I would feed him, and he fussed until he could get up and walk, but he never spoke until this morning when I helped him dress and told him he would see Mary today."

"What did he say?" Abraham asked.

"'Thank you.' That's all, just thank you." He and Sami Khalidi started for the Arab fence, then he turned around. "Tell them to be happy. It will be nice to remember that something good came out of this horrible mess."

Abraham promised he would, then quickly caught up with his friends and walked through the gate to Jewish Jerusalem.

After everyone had a chance to hug Aaron, they got in the car and started back to Tel Aviv. Mary was in the center, Aaron's arm around her shoulders and her head resting on his chest. He seemed contented. David was kneeling in the front seat, facing backward, his eyes on his big brother. "I'm glad you're back," he said softly.

Aaron smiled, his eyes fixed on David's, then a hand came up and he touched the side of David's face. "Me too," he said.

Hannah lifted her head to heaven and said another heartfelt thank-you. They had come through so much, and yet with God's help, they had somehow survived.

They passed out of the city and down the newly paved switchbacks of the Burma Road. There was still much of sorrow and anguish ahead for her country, her people, and she felt sad for it. They would return, by the millions, but they would return in sorrow and hardship. Maybe someday that would change, but not now. Probably not in ten years or fifty. It would take more than David Ben-Gurion and a new Israel to return the Jews. It would take their Messiah.

She closed her eyes. For now she would count her blessings, foremost of which was the comfort she had received during all this. She thought back to those days in Germany when Ephraim had taught her about God and given her hope, then about that day she and Beth and David were baptized in the Jordan. She knew from that moment that whatever happened, God would never desert her again.

Today she knew that more than ever.

AUTHOR'S NOTE

The cease-fire of July 11, 1948, did not hold, and peace did not come to Israel and Palestine until 1949.

> Dr. Ralph Bunche on the island of Rhodes negotiated armistice agreements between Israel and Egypt, Lebanon, Jordan and Syria early in 1949. Those agreements put a formal end to the hostilities. They did not end the war, and the Arab states resolutely continued to proclaim their intention of one day terminating the existence of a state they would neither accept nor recognize.
>
> What the Israelis would call their War of Independence thus came officially to an end. (Collins and Lapierre, 561)

And thus this series ends. Thank you for reading. I hope you have come to learn at least a small portion of what has caused so much unrest in the land of Palestine/Israel. However, the story is far from complete, and though I will not include the telling of it in this series, I hope to give you more pieces of the puzzle in future books.

CHAPTER NOTES

CHAPTER ONE

> From August 1946 to December 1947 the 51,700 immigrants who arrived illegally off the shores of Palestine—on thirty-five ships—were taken to Cyprus, put in camps, surrounded by barbed wire, and guarded by armed British soldiers. Many of the soldiers disliked the task assigned them; they were from the same army, and wearing the same British uniform, that had liberated so many DPs from Bergen-Belsen a year and a half earlier (Gilbert, 136).

When partition was passed by UNSCOP, it "contained a recommendation that a Free Port for Jewish immigration should be opened—in Haifa—on 1 February 1948. At last the Holocaust survivors would be able to go to Palestine" (Gilbert, 151). Unfortunately, the British did not follow the recommendation, and refugees from Cyprus could not leave the island until after the declaration of the State of Israel on May 14, 1948.

Zohar was aboard the *Pan York,* which had seven thousand passengers. It was stopped at sea, boarded, then sent to Cyprus where they disembarked along with seven thousand passengers of the *Pan Crescent,* a sister ship also captured. Military training for the "prisoners" on Cyprus began on March 20. Jewish leaders knew they would need every able-bodied man they could prepare for the war that lay ahead. Mock rifles and grenades made of wood were the principal weapons, and the Hebrew language was taught as a part of the training, but the short time and number of people who could be trained did not allow for effectiveness.

"The British opened the detention camps in Cyprus on May 15 [the day after the State of Israel was declared by Ben-Gurion]. Several hundred new arrivals in Palestine who had been trained by the Haganah while in the camps were hurried to the battlefield" (Gilbert, 191). More refugees arrived from Cyprus in the days following, and immigrants able and willing to fight were "integrated into the existing, battle-tested units" (Gilbert, 209). The last of the Cyprus refugees arrived in Israel in February 1948. They had been held up by the still intransigent British until January of that year. From the beginning, British decisions were made with their own interests in mind. Reluctant "nursing kings and queens" at best, they acted their part only after feeling pressure from the United States and others forced them to fully act the part.

CHAPTER TWO

There were multiple causes of mass exodus.

> The spiral of violence precipitated mass flight by the Arab middle and upper classes from the big towns, especially Haifa, Jaffa and Jerusalem, and their satellite rural communities. It also prompted the piecemeal, but almost complete, evacuation of the Arab rural population from what was to be the heartland

> of the Jewish State—the Coastal Plain between Tel Aviv and Hadera—and a small-scale, partial evacuation of other rural areas hit by hostilities . . . , namely the Jezreel and Jordan valleys.
>
> The Arab evacuees from the towns and villages left largely because of the Jewish—Haganah, [ETZEL] or [LEHI]—attacks or fear of impending attack, and from a sense of vulnerability to such attack. The feeling that the Arabs were weak and the Jews very strong was widespread and there was a steadily increasing erosion of the Arabs' confidence in Arab military power. Most of the evacuees, especially the prosperous urban families, never thought in terms of permanent refugeedom and exile; they contemplated an absence from Palestine or its combat zones similar to that of 1936–9, lasting only until the hostilities were over and, they hoped, the Yishuv vanquished. They expected the intervention, and possibly victory, of the Arab states. (Morris, *Birth of the Palestinian Refugee Problem,* 59–60)

Between November 1947 and the end of March 1948, neither the Yishuv nor the Arabs had a policy of removing the Arabs from Palestine, though on occasion they had to move them because of military considerations that put them at danger. However, during the period of this book (April to June), the Jewish position began to change. Pacification of the Arab villages in the area of the New State and particularly in the areas of battle

> meant either the surrender of the villages or their depopulation and destruction. The essence of the plan was the clearing of hostile and potentially hostile forces out of the interior . . . of the Jewish state. . . .
>
> The Haganah wanted to preclude the renewed use of such villages as anti-Yishuv bases. . . .

However during April–June relatively few Haganah commanders faced the dilemma of whether or not to carry out the expulsion. . . . The Arab townspeople and villagers usually fled from their homes before or during battle; the Haganah commanders had rarely to decide about, or issue, expulsion orders (though they usually prevented inhabitants who had initially fled from returning home after the dust of battle had settled). (Morris, *Birth of the Palestinian Refugee Problem,* 62–63)

By late January, the AHC was itself worried by the phenomenon [of large numbers of refugees leaving the country], according to British military intelligence. Those who had left, the British reported, had been ordered by the Mufti to return to their homes "and if they refuse, their homes will be occupied by other (foreign) Arabs sent to reinforce (Arab defenses in) the areas." . . . The Mufti had apparently been especially concerned about the flight from Palestine of army-aged males. (Morris, *Birth of the Palestinian Refugee Problem,* 58)

On 10–11 May, the AHC called on officials, doctors and engineers who had left the country to return and on 14–15 May, repeating the call, warned that officials who did not return would lose their "moral right to hold these administrative jobs in the future." Arab governments began to bar entry to the refugees—as happened, for example, on the Lebanese border in the middle of May. By the end of May, with the Arab armies fully committed, the Arab states and the AHC put pressure on the refugee communities encamped along Palestine's frontiers to go home. . . .

However, the sudden pan-Arab concern . . . came too late and perhaps was not expressed forcefully enough. . . . The Arab states proved powerless to neutralize its momentum. (Morris, *Birth of the Palestinian Refugee Problem,* 69–70)

The exodus continued and grew throughout the war, and even though the Arab Higher Committee under Haj Amin threatened, belittled, bribed, and coerced, most refugees did not return during 1948–49. After that time, the Jewish policy, born of frustration and fear of a "fifth column," or underground movement inside their new country, along with the tremendous numbers of Jewish refugees out of Arab countries, the interment camps on Cyprus, and from Europe, refused to let the Arabs return. It would be a policy that would haunt the new Jewish state until the present day.

Upon instructions from their governments, the Arab consuls in Palestine stopped issuing visas freely and co-operated with the AHC by scrutinizing the growing demand for entry permits into their countries. These endeavours, however, only raised the prices of the visas and the level of bribes paid to consulate clerks and AHC officials. . . .

Reflecting ALA defeats, the mass flight of Palestinians snowballed in April–May, amplifying frenzy in the Arab countries. An uncontrollable flow of escapees crossed the borders, compelling the authorities to address their accommodation and provide them with basic needs. (Gelber, 257)

Public opinion in the Arab world condemned the exodus and held hard feelings towards the escapees. Newspapers in Beirut suggested dispatching them back to Palestine. Young men, they asserted, should enlist in the ALA and fight. (Gelber, 256)

Demanding that they either go back to Palestine or move to the interior, Lebanon's government forbade the escapees to stay in the country's southern district. . . . They

> feared that penniless deserters might indulge in espionage; consequently, the authorities pushed the Palestinians to Saida and beyond. (Gelber, 258)

In the battle for the Litani Bridge, "a company of Israeli soldiers crossed the Lebanese border and marched over rough, hilly terrain seven miles into Lebanon, where they blew up a road bridge over the River Litani. This seriously impeded the ability of the Lebanese to send armoured vehicles and troop transports southward" (Gilbert, 192).

CHAPTER FOUR

Tel Aviv was first bombed on September 9, 1939, by the Italians. They killed 107 Jews, and world war came to Palestine. In our story, the first to bomb Tel Aviv were the Egyptians. That attack was on the day Ben-Gurion declared the Jewish state. There were no deaths in that raid, but a good deal of damage was done. Apparently there was another attack on the May 18, and 42 people were killed, and most of the Israeli Air Force planes, all of them small Austers and Pipers, were damaged or destroyed. As Gilbert says, "In any other air force those planes would have been written off, but there was no choice. They were painstakingly restored . . . and flew again." Gilbert goes on to quote Barrard in saying that "the role of these little planes, the Austers, Pipers, Fairchilds, 'in the first crucial weeks before the Czechoslovakian airlift brought Messerschmitts' . . . tends 'to be overlooked. But they were vital in checking the better equipped enemy's rapid advances'" (189–90). It is this bombing that is referred to herein, though I have, for the sake of the story, moved it to a later date. Once the Messerschmitts and other planes arrived, the Egyptians no longer ventured into Israeli airspace, and the IAF went on the offensive, bombing most Arab capitals and controlling the skies over the battlefield. The story of the development and bravery of the volunteer pilots from around the world can be studied more carefully in a number of books on the subject, including *The Secret Battle for Israel* by Colonel Benjamin Kagan.

The Messerschmitts sent to Israel were actually not the vaunted and very effective ME-109 used by the Germans in World War II but the Avia S-199 made by the Czechs. Though the 199 looked like its German predecessor, the Czechs could not get the German motors. Instead they put a heavier, less-powerful one in the 199. This inadequacy made the plane "hard to fly, and posed a serious maintenance challenge. They exacted many casualties among the pilots that flew them," but they did much in staving off the enemy advance.

CHAPTER FIVE

Most Hasidic Jews were never in favor of the Zionist efforts to gain a state. Even during the final battles for the Quarter, they continued to blame the Haganah and not the Arabs for their condition. They based their assessment on past riots against the Quarter by the Arab population and how peace always followed. They considered this no different, and they thought, had not the Haganah and their leaders escalated warfare in the Quarter by their presence, they were sure they could have worked out their differences with the larger Arab community around them. As our story showed in book 2, the Arabs had changed by 1948. Under Haj Amin and Abdul Khader Husseini, the Quarter became a prime target.

The massacre at the Etzion Bloc is well documented. To some degree it and the massacre of a convoy of doctors, nurses, and patients on their way to Hadassah Hospital were both responses to the Jewish massacre of Arab villagers at Deir Yassin at the time of the Battle of Kastel. Such events were perpetrated on both sides and led to great panic of both the Arab and Jewish populations. Arab radio tried to use Deir Yassin as a rallying cry for war but only succeeded in frightening their own civilians and adding to the mass exodus from Arab villages and cities into neighboring Arab countries, thus adding to the disastrous refugee problem that has existed ever since.

The Arab massacre of Jewish civilians caused a good deal of fear as well, but the Haganah was able to control the populace and keep them in place because of two factors. The Jews knew that if they fled, the Arabs would literally drive them into the sea and they would lose their chance for a state and the freedom and safety they hoped it would provide.

It should be noted that over the years, both Jews and Arabs have researched and documented atrocities perpetrated by both sides. Besides Deir Yassin, massacres by the Haganah or other Jewish military organizations include those at Ilabun, Majd al Kurum, Arab al Mawasi, Jish, and Safsaf. More allegations have recently arisen concerning the massacre of more than 250 Arabs at Tantura on the western coast of Israel just north of Tel Aviv.

CHAPTER SIX

It is a misunderstanding that the bedouin are only desert wanderers and lived in the south of Israel. More than forty thousand bedu could be counted in northern Israel, most living in villages in the area of Galilee and the coastal plain. The war brought many changes to their people, and many fled the area—"the Arab Balauna on 31 December 1947, the Arab Abu Razk on 31 January 1948, the Arab an Nuseirat on 3 February and the Arab Shudkhi on 11 February. Most of these bedouins evacuated because of fear of Jewish attack. The Arab an Nuseirat fled after an actual Haganah attack and the Arab Shudkhi after an attack on their encampment by the [ETZEL]" (Morris, *Birth of the Palestinian Refugee Problem,* 53). Many other tribes evacuated in the months that followed. Yosef Weitz of the Jewish National Fund's Lands Department, who was largely responsible for land acquisition and the establishment of new settlements, privately and then openly promoted the removal of the bedu and other Arabs from the new Jewish state. He

> realised that the circumstances were ripe for the "Judaization" of tracts of land bought and owned by Jewish institutions . . . on which Arab tenant farmer communities continued to squat. Under the British, the Yishuv had generally been unable to remove these inhabitants from the land, despite offering generous compensatory payments. Indeed, on occasion, Arab tenant-farmers accepted Jewish compensation and then reneged on their promises to decamp. (Morris, *Birth of the Palestinian Refugee Problem,* 55)

Weitz noted that some of the bedu were moving on their own and stated, "It is possible that now is the time to implement our original plan: To transfer them there" (in Morris, *Birth of the Palestinian Refugee Problem,* 55). Though there were some Jewish settlements that welcomed the bedu to stay, general policy was to remove them and, as it was in the large cities, once the Arabs started to leave, the Jews began to see both a need and an advantage to "aiding their removal."

There were exceptions. *The Scout,* by Steven Plaut, is one source of such an exception. In a chapter called "The Butcher," Plaut talks of Fawzi al Kaukji who persecuted those who did not support the revolt against the British and the Jews. Plaut states, "From 1936 until 1939, Palestine was torn by the Great Arab

Revolt, a set of pogroms and riots directed against the Jews and the British. Al Kaukji commanded the Arab militias of the Galilee" (32) and persecuted any who were on friendly terms with the Jews. He talks of two bedouin youths instructed to drive some cattle to the Jews when "suddenly a squad of the Butcher's militiamen materialized" (33). One of the boys, twelve years old, was caught and taken to a prison operated by Kaukji's men. There he was "beaten, interrogated, and accused of being a spy, of helping the infidel Jews. It was treason to bring food to the Haganah fighters" (33). Because of such treatment in the rebellion, Kaukji did not find all bedu ready to fight for him against the Jews when he returned as commander of the ALA in 1948.

Those who continued to have good relations with the Jews were rare, but there existed a very strong exception that rankled the Arabs and other bedu. This good relationship was especially true of the Saadiya tribe and Kibbutz Allonim in the Galilee (36). Some of the bedu held jobs on the kibbutz, and the two groups helped and protected one another. "When the War . . . broke out in 1948, there was fighting in the vicinity of the Saadiya Quarter. The Saadiya had decided they wanted nothing to do with al-Kaukji's barbarians and refused to join them in their war against the Jews. The Butcher [al Kaukji] regarded the Saadiya as traitors." One of the Saadiya, Salim Saadi, was confronted in his camp by al Kaukji's men, then locked in prison, beaten, and interrogated. He escaped with the help of a guard who was married to a bedouin. He knew he was in danger of recapture, so he went to Kibbutz Allonim, "where he was greeted warmly by his Jewish friends." Palut goes on to tell the scout's story of trying to get back to his family who were being kept inside al Kaukji territory, but he was not able to get all of them back until after the Haganah drove Kaukji out of the area.

Another tribe that did not honor the Arab war were the al Heib, who were targeted by the militiamen of al Kaukji.

> Sheik Abu Yusuf had leased some land to the Jews on which they built a kibbutz in the Galilee, and as a result, the Butcher's men issued a contract on his life.
>
> Even before Israeli Independence was formally announced, Sheikh Abu Yusuf approached the military commanders of the Jewish brigades. The sheikh proposed a bond of blood. (45)

As the Jews expanded their operations, the al Heib bedouin fought and acted as scouts. "These were the first fighters in what developed into a long tradition of bedouin serving in the military forces of the new Jewish state" (46).

"When the Syrian Army invaded the newly declared state of Israel, it targeted the al-Heib tribe of bedouin with particular ferocity. After all, these bedouin were fighting alongside the infidel Jews. The Syrians sent infantry and armor to attack the bedouin, and even dropped 50 kilogram bombs on them from planes" (53).

Jews and Arabs had lived in Haifa in relative peace for decades,

> but relations deteriorated during the first months of the war, with the two sides exchanging shots along the border between the two communities and planting bombs in each other's neighborhoods. The Haganah's onslaught, in line with Plan D, came on April 21; Arab disorganization and isolation, and a general feeling of weakness and of Jewish superiority, aggressiveness, and self-confidence, determined the outcome in just twenty-four hours. (Morris, *Righteous Victims,* 211)

Over the next week, "Arab resistance gradually evaporated, and civilian morale broke, most of the population fleeing. Repeated pleas by Arab leaders for reinforcements from outside the city went unanswered," and "a number of prominent Arab military leaders left Haifa just before or during the battle, ostensibly to seek aid" (Morris, *Righteous Victims,* 211). They never returned. Civil leaders had already deserted the city.

"Arab efforts on April 22 to obtain a truce were turned down by the Haganah, which demanded what amounted to unconditional surrender. The Arab leaders, preferring not to surrender, announced that they and their community intended to evacuate the town, despite a plea by the Jewish mayor that they stay. During the following week, all but three or four thousand of the Arabs left, and the town came completely under Jewish control" (Morris, *Righteous Victims,* 211).

CHAPTER EIGHT

The Quarter had been under attack intermittently since March, but with the combination of Haganah and British protection they had not suffered extensively.

> On May 15 hundreds of Arab irregulars attacked. During May 16–18 the Haganah made several attempts to reinforce and resupply the Quarter and establish a permanent corridor to West Jerusalem through Zion Gate, but they proved unable to keep the passage open after the Legion entered the Old City. For 10 days the Legionnaires, commanded by Abdullah Tal, battled the defenders, house by house, gradually compressing the Jewish area. (Morris, *Righteous Victims,* 225)

Moshe Russnak is a real character. A soft-spoken Jew from Czechoslovakia who had been sent to command the Quarter just prior to British withdrawal, he was determined to keep the Quarter out of Arab hands. Coupled with the endless promises of reinforcements, which would never come, he held on longer than he probably should have and until the rabbis and his own men helped him see that surrender or massacre were their only options. Even then, it was not an easy decision. Russnak knew that if they surrendered to the Palestinian Irregulars of Haj Amin el Husseini, they would surely be massacred. It was even difficult to trust the Arab Legion. Therefore, negotiations for surrender were slow, and Russnak held out as long as he could, continually hopeful that the central command would finally keep their promise.

CHAPTER NINE

The Hashomer, or Watchmen, was organized during Ottoman rule and, according to David Ben-Gurion,

> its principal task was the defense of *lives and property* in the Jewish villages against Arab *thieves and marauders*. This task was carried out by trained watchmen, organized on a national basis, and subject to strict discipline. They were trained to use rifles and were expert horsemen. They taught their Arab neighbors to respect Jewish courage and strength, and at the same time developed friendly relations with them, insofar as possible.
>
> After the First World War, Hashomer was disbanded and the Haganah established. Its task was the *defense of Jewish settlements* against Arab attacks, not by individuals but by bands incited and organized by a *central Arab political body.* In the early years of the [British] Mandate, the British recognized, in part, that the Jews had a right to defend themselves. But the Haganah was not a legal body and did not depend on the Mandatory Government for anything. . . .

> As Arab terror increased in intensity, the Haganah steadily developed into a more centralized body, with a National Command responsible for the coordination of defense needs on a countrywide basis. . . .
>
> The first fully mobilized units were established during the period of the riots [by Arabs] before the Second World War. They were called the Field Forces. In 1941 a special striking force was established. This group, the Palmach, trained in the settlements and supported itself by doing agricultural work there. (Ben-Gurion, 61–62, italics in original)

CHAPTER ELEVEN

Fawzi el Kutub should not to be confused with Fawzi el Kaukji, leader of the Arab Liberation Army who fought in the north where the fictional character Mary is. Kutub was an actual person and the man responsible for the destruction of the Hurva. He was first introduced in book 2 as the man who blew up the *Jerusalem Post* building and nearly killed Aaron Schwartz in his hotel across the street. As Collins and Lapierre state of this infamous bomber's destruction of the Hurva, "Using the last explosives left in his Turkish bath, Kutub had wreaked his final revenge on the neighbors against whom he had waged his life-time's crusade. The skyline of Jerusalem had lost one of its great monuments. He had reduced what was left of the city's most precious synagogue to ruins" (496).

Of the surrender, we learn that

> a few minutes past nine o'clock Friday, May 28, the tele-phone rang in Major Abdullah Tell's [Tal in Arabic] head-quarters at Rawdah School. It was Captain Moussa. "Two

> rabbis," he said, "are coming out of the quarter with a white flag."
>
> Walking into Moussa's headquarters in the Armenian School of the Holy Translators, Tell found himself face to face with the first Jews he had ever met: the seventy-year-old Rabbi Reuven Hazan and the eighty-three-year-old Rabbi Zeev Mintzberg. . . .
>
> The situation was indeed hopeless. The Legion was six yards away from the synagogue in which the residents huddled [all civilians had been moved to the Stamboli Synagogue]; the hospital was out of virtually every form of medicine. His men had ammunition for no more than another half hour. After that, seventeen hundred people would be at the mercy of the Arabs. (Collins and Lapierre, 496–97)

During the time between the rabbis' asking for a truce and the final surrender, Tal had "invited the Red Cross's Otto Lehner and the United Nations' Pablo de Azcarate to witness the proceedings" (Collins and Lapierre, 497). Their involvement would ultimately add much needed incentive for the Arabs to keep their promise to give safe passage to the civilians and treat the combatants with humanity.

CHAPTER TWELVE

> From a street corner near Zion Gate, the man who had led so many destructive forays against their quarter watched the last Jewish refugees leave. All his life Fawzi el Kutub had been used to seeing Jews in the streets of his native Old Jerusalem. Suddenly he understood that he was seeing them there for the last time. Their pathetic parade

was the final triumph of the strange and vicious career he had begun twelve years earlier, only a few yards from the doorway in which he now stood, hurling a homemade hand grenade at a Jewish bus. . . .

As night fell, only the quarter's 153 wounded remained in the Old City, crowded in their wretched hospital, waiting for the inspection by a team of doctors to determine which of them would be returned to the New City and which would go to prison camp. Soon the fires raging in the looted quarter began to creep up on their sanctuary. Persuaded that the hour of their massacre had come, the wounded saw a company of Legionnaires march into the building. They had come, however, to carry their injured enemies to the safety of the nearby Armenian Patriarchate. (Collins and Lapierre, 500)

CHAPTER THIRTEEN

The young woman who would not smoke on the sabbath was Esther Cailingold. She left a note under her pillow addressed to her parents. It read:

Dear Mummy and Daddy,

I am writing to beg you that whatever may have happened to me, you will make the effort to take it in the spirit I want. We had a difficult fight. I have tasted hell but it has been worthwhile because I am convinced the end will see a Jewish state and all our longings. I have lived my life fully, and very sweet it has been to be here in our land . . . I hope one day soon you will all come and enjoy the fruits of that for which we are fighting. Be happy and remember me only in happiness.

Shalom.

Esther

Shar Cohen was also a real character and was at Esther's bedside as depicted here. The chant revived many that night who might never have survived. The next day, the severely wounded were taken to the New City. The rest followed the other prisoners to Mafraq prison camp in Transjordan. Eight hundred prisoners were interred there, most of whom came from Kfar Etzion and the Old City. These stories are more fully told in Collins and Lapierre (501–2).

David Ben-Gurion felt it very important to unify the military of the whole area of Jerusalem under one top-notch leader. "His choice fell on a graduate of West Point, Colonel David Marcus, who had served on Eisenhower's staff in Europe . . . and had volunteered for service with the Haganah at the start of hostilities" (Gilbert, 205). The appointment was made on May 28, and he was given the rank of colonel and the name of Mickey Stone to hide his identity. Under Stone's command, the second Israeli attack on Latrun would take place.

Count Folke Bernadotte was to represent the United Nations in bringing peace to Palestine. Once in the area, he developed a plan of his own which he thought would be more acceptable, especially to the Arabs who had rejected the plan Bernadotte and Bunche had brought from the UN—a plan developed by the United States and Britain that was better for them than for Palestine and rejected by both sides.

Bernadotte's arrival gave many hope of a peaceful solution, but that didn't last long. The count wanted to give the Negev to the Arabs and the Galilee to the Jews.

> Jerusalem would come under Arab Transjordanian rule, with its Jewish inhabitants granted urban autonomy. Given Jerusalem's substantial Jewish majority, this was a serious blow to Jewish hopes of control of at least the Jewish sections of the city. When Bernadotte's proposals were rejected by both Israel and the Arabs (who did not want the Jews to have any

> autonomy at all), a negotiated political solution was ruled out, and a renewal of hostilities became inevitable. (Gilbert, 210)

Bernadotte was assassinated in Jerusalem in September 1948 at the order of leaders of LEHI or the Stern Gang. The man who pulled the trigger was caught and "claimed that the deed was done because Bernadotte had proposed an Arab administration for Jerusalem" (Gilbert, 228).

"Bernadotte's murder was forcefully denounced by the Israeli government. Ben-Gurion ordered, 'Arrest all Stern Gang leaders. Surround all Stern Gang bases. Confiscate all arms. Kill any who resist.' The killing of Bernadotte marked an end to whatever tolerance of Jewish underground activities" still existed (Gilbert, 228). Ben-Gurion had earlier used force to rein in ETZEL in June. This gave him opportunity to do the same to LEHI. The armed forces were now a single organization known as the IDF, or Zahal in its Hebrew acronym.

CHAPTER FOURTEEN

From most accounts, this is a pretty accurate description of the treatment of the prisoners in Mafraq prison, though it may not be even close to the actual prison itself. Abdullah of Transjordan wanted peace as quickly as possible but was pulled deeper and deeper into the war by the overall Arab fervor and poorly calculated rhetoric. He did want Jerusalem, and because it was considered fair game—it had not been given to either Arab or Jew but was designated an International City—he tried his best to acquire the whole of it. But most of the territory he fought for had been designated Palestinian by the UN Partition. He saw himself as their advocate and wanted to be their king. He worked it well enough that he received most of the West

Bank when the fighting was over. Unfortunately, Haj Amin and Abdullah hated one another, and it was under the orders of Haj Amin that Abdullah was later assassinated. The action did Haj Amin no good but did prove to what lengths he would go to punish those who opposed him, Jewish or Arab.

CHAPTER SIXTEEN

Ishmael is

> the eldest son of Abraham by Hagar. . . . He is the immediate patriarch of the North Arabians just as Isaac . . . is of the Jews.
>
> The Koran does not name the son who was to be sacrificed by Abraham, but it does say that for his obedience Abraham was rewarded, and it is understood by most Muslim commentators that the reward . . . was a second son: Isaac, born to Abraham and [Sarah] in their great old age. This and other arguments, have generally meant that in Islam, Ishmael is considered to be the son Abraham was about to sacrifice, although great commentators who hold the opinion that it was Isaac can also be found. (Glassé, 193)

As the sacrifice does not take place until after Hagar and Ishmael are cast out, it takes a good deal of creative manipulation to make the sacrificial son Ishmael. A part of this manipulation is to blame the Jews for changing the Bible in order to steal Ishmael's birthright as the favored son, this despite the fact that the Koran says that the Pentateuch or Books of Moses, which includes the story of Abraham and Isaac, are divinely revealed. Of course, the Gospels also create a problem for Muslims as they are also said to be divinely inspired by the Koran. As Glassé says, "the Gospel poses particular difficulties in Islam. . . . The Christian Gospel clashes with Islamic understanding of doctrines on several points, most importantly regarding the nature of Jesus" (Glassé, 72). Muslim interpreters have also changed a portion of the New Testament to give credence to the Prophet Muhammad. In John 16:7, Jesus promises to send the Comforter. The Greek word for Comforter is *Paraclete*. Muslim interpreters changed it to *Paracleitos* or "Praised One," which is the meaning in Arabic of the name of Muhammad and its cognate Ahmad, also used for the prophet.

> The Gospel would then echo the words of the Koran. . . . Muslims believe that the New Testament as used by Christians is incorrect and has, somehow, been falsified. Because the Koran affirms Christianity as a Divinely revealed religion, Muslims expect Christianity to be exactly like the Divine revelation that is Islam. . . . In practice, however, the religions do not, and cannot coincide. . . . Not finding exoteric Islam in Christianity, and finding rather a doctrine of Jesus which contradicts the basis of Islam as salvation through the recognition of God as Absolute, Muslims readily came to the conclusion, now established as dogma, that Christianity has somehow been altered. (Glassé, 72–73)

Thus we see the reason for the orthodox Muslim view of both Judaism and Christianity and why both of these faiths must be put in subjection to Islam by *jihad* or holy war in the view of fanatics within Muhammad's religion. We also see why there has been a steady decline in Christian numbers in Palestinian-held territory since Muslims have gained control of political, economic, and religious institutions in Arab-held territory in the Holy Land. Under Islam, Christians are considered *dhimmi,* a tolerated, but second-class who are afforded protection by Islam. Dhimmitude is integral to Islam; it is a "'protection pact' which suspended the [Muslim] conquerors' initial right to kill or enslave [Jews and Christians], provided they submitted themselves to pay the tribute" (Ye'or, 41).

Christianity under Islam has often had a good deal of difficulty.

> Over the centuries, political Islam has not been too kind to the native Christian communities living under its rule. Anecdotes of tolerance aside, the systematic treatment of Christians . . . is abusive and discriminatory by any standard. . . . Under Islam, . . . the targeted *dhimmi* community and each individual in it are made to live in a state of perpetual humiliation in the eyes of the ruling community. (Malik, 9)

The best examples in the century are what has happened in the civil war in Lebanon and what is happening in many Arab nations, including Iran, Egypt, Saudi Arabia, and Arab Palestine. In Iran, for example, the printing of Christian literature is illegal, converts from Islam are liable to be killed, and most evangelical churches must function underground. Christians are not allowed to testify in an Islamic Court when a Muslim is involved, and they are discriminated against in employment (Ye'or, 225).

In Israel too, Muslim fundamentalists seek to assert dominance over Christian Arabs. Attacks against and condemnation of Christians are often heard in mosques, in sermons, and in publications of the Muslim Movement. The events of Easter 1999 in Nazareth in which violence broke out between Christians and Arabs is an example (Ye'or, 194).

CHAPTER NINETEEN

The attack on Isdud, though only mentioned here, was the first real attack by assault planes during the war. Though it was relatively ineffective in the damage it did, the Egyptians were so shocked at the show of fighters that they dug in, changing things dramatically in the south. Eddie Cohen, a volunteer from South Africa, flew one of the 199s. Ezer Weizman, the most experienced Jewish pilot in Israel and commander of the volunteers, saw Cohen's plane plunge downward, dipping lower and lower until it crashed. Cohen's first mission would be his last, and as Weizman says, "Our attack had been successful . . . according to the notions then current. However, our triumph was mingled with despondency. The mission had ended with the loss of a fellow pilot as well as one-quarter of the air force's combat planes" (Gilbert, 200).

CHAPTER TWENTY-TWO

Negba was a real settlement and integral to the protection of Tel Aviv to the north. Founded by pioneers from Poland in the summer of 1939, it was first attacked by the Egyptians on May 23. There were 145 defenders fighting against some 2,000 Egyptian soldiers. "After nine days of continuous bombardment, during one of which 6,000 shells fell on the settlement, the Egyptians launched a tank and infantry assault . . . The defenders possessed a single PIAT anti-tank weapon." By the time it was over, the Egyptians "had lost six tanks, two Bren carriers and 100 killed and wounded. They had also lost a Spitfire, brought down by one of Negba's machine-gunners. The Jews lost eight men killed and twelve wounded" (Gilbert, 194–95). It is this downed Spitfire that Wally needs to get to in our story.

Negba was attacked again on July 12 after the first truce. It lasted seven hours, and the Egyptians reached as far as the inner fence, but by nightfall they had failed to penetrate the settlement itself and retreated, leaving a tank and several Bren gun carriers behind (Gilbert, 219). Negba would never be captured by the Arabs.

CHAPTER TWENTY-FIVE

The Haganah tried to open the Jerusalem/Tel Aviv Road by attacking the main Arab stronghold at Latrun. They were unsuccessful—twice up to the point of our story. Ben-Gurion told them to attack a third time, but Mickey Marcus and Yigal Allon talked him out of it. An alternative route had been discovered by chance by two Israeli soldiers trying to get to Tel Aviv on leave, they told him. Much of the story as told here is taken from Collins and Lapierre (509–19). The new road became the lifeline to Jerusalem nearly overnight. Known at first as Route Seven, it was soon renamed the Burma Road after the World War II route. There was one portion of the road that was almost impassable by vehicles and very dangerous, though the first jeeps did manage it, simply by going far out of the way. Vivian Herzog reports the following about how to get past this point once they started building the road:

> I suggested that we put hundreds of porters at the bluff to take supplies from trucks, which could approach through the orchard. Porters would then carry supplies to the valley below, where trucks from Jerusalem would be waiting to take the supplies to the city. . . .
>
> At night, against the background of Jordanian shelling, the scene was almost unreal: hundreds of porters silently carrying food and supplies down the hill to waiting trucks and jeeps and even mules. (Gilbert, 207–8).

Of course, getting supplies up to the bluff could not be done at first either. Porters were used here as well.

During the truce, the road was much improved, and Jerusalem would not go hungry again.

CHAPTER THIRTY

> The UN Security Council on May 20 appointed Count Folke Bernadotte, a Swede who had helped rescue Jews during World War II, as special mediator for Palestine, empowered to seek a quick end to the fighting and a comprehensive, lasting settlement of the conflict. He got nowhere on the latter. As to a cease-fire, first one side and then the other balked, each interested in making as many gains as possible on the ground. But the weeks of the Arab invasion were intense and exhausting for both sides, and eventually Bernadotte's efforts were crowned with success. (Morris, *Righteous Victims,* 235)

The Arabs, realizing the British had deserted them and quickly running out of ammunition, were further convinced as the Jews took ground in every area and bombed both Cairo, Egypt, and Amman, Jordan. The last few days before the cease-fire went into effect were disastrous for the Arabs and convinced even die-hard Arab leaders they must regroup.

> With the arrival from abroad of immigrants, volunteers, and returning Palestinian Jews, and more efficient mobilization procedures at home, the manpower pool almost doubled between May 15 and July 9, the number under arms rising from around thirty-five thousand to sixty-five thousand. Several thousand of the recruits—

perhaps as many as four thousand—were veterans of the Allied armies (British, American, Canadian, Czech) of World War II who came to help the Israelis win the war. They included specialists, such as sailors, doctors, and logistics and communications experts; most of the IAF's pilots during the war were such volunteers, many of them non-Jews. (Morris, *Righteous Victims,* 236)

SELECTED BIBLIOGRAPHY

Ben-Gurion, David. *Israel: A Personal History.* New York: Funk & Wagnall, 1971.

Collins, Larry, and Dominique Lapierre. *O Jerusalem!* New York: Simon and Schuster, 1988.

Gelber, Yoav. *Palestine 1948: War, Escape and the Emergence of the Palestinian Refugee Problem.* Portland: Sussex Academic Press, 2001.

Gilbert, Martin. *Israel: A History.* New York: William Morrow, 1998.

Glassé, Cyril. *The Concise Encyclopedia of Islam.* New York: HarperCollins, 1991.

Malik, Habib. "Christmas in the Land Called Holy." *First Things: A Journal of Religion and Public Life* Jan. 1999: 11–12.

Morris, Benny. *The Birth of the Palestinian Refugee Problem, 1947.* Cambridge: Cambridge University Press, 1987.

———. *Righteous Victims: A History of the Zionist-Arab Conflict, 1881–1999.* New York: Vintage Books, 2001.

Plaut, Steven E. *The Scout.* Hewlett, NY: Gefen, 2002.

Ye'or, Bat. *Islam and Dhimmitude: Where Civilizations Collide.* Lancaster, England: Gazelle Book Services, 2002.